Louise Clarkson Whitelock

The Shadow of John Wallace

A novel

Louise Clarkson Whitelock

The Shadow of John Wallace
A novel

ISBN/EAN: 9783337000301

Printed in Europe, USA, Canada, Australia, Japan

Cover: Foto ©Andreas Hilbeck / pixelio.de

More available books at **www.hansebooks.com**

The Shadow

of

John Wallace

A Novel

By L. CLARKSON

New York
White, Stokes, & Allen
1884

THE KEYNOTE.

—————————————" *I raise a ghost*——
Because——————————*man makes not man ;*
Yet by a special gift, an art of arts,
More insight and more outsight and much more
Will to use both of these than boast my mates,
I can detach from me, commission forth
Half of my soul; which in its pilgrimage
O'er old unwandered wasteways of the world,
May chance upon some fragment of a whole,
Rag of flesh, scrap of bone in dim disuse,
Smoking flax that fed fire once ; prompt therein
I enter, spark-like, put old powers to play,
Push lines out to the limit, lead forth the last
(By a moonrise through a ruin of a crypt)
What shall be mistily seen, murmuringly heard,
Mistakenly felt."

From Robert Browning's
THE RING AND THE BOOK.

PRELUDE.

Comprising a letter from "Artist-haven" written to a well-known journal early in the summer of 1879, *describing an obscure hamlet by the sea.——Signed Leslie Bracebridge.*

A wail from Mount-Desert, crying that it is no longer a wilderness, has doubtless found its echo in many another remote region where one goes to be a recluse, and finds the primeval soltitudes already over-crowded with the world's people. But there re-mains at least one happy hunting-ground which the Philistines of fashion have not yet overwhelmed.

Somewhere on the eastern end of Long Island, is a little settlement to which I shall presently give a name. It was supposed to have been discovered in the summer of 1878 by *The New York Tile Club*, and is consequently but one year old to the knowledge of the artistic world. That it was two hundred years old before *The New York Tile Club* began to be, has added somewhat to the artistic world's interest in its existence.

It is a quaint and lovely town of one long street ; a grassy avenue so broad, that over its green ex-panse meandered two or three unpremeditated road-ways, worn at different periods to suit—so at least it seems to the eye of the peregrinating stranger—the

varying convenience of the inhabitants. On either
side is a walk bordered by huge elms and sycamores
and horse-chestnuts ; and these same great trees
shelter the picturesque little houses that stand, in their
uncalculating simplicity, close upon the road. They
are two centuries and more old, some of these shingle
cottages, whose roofs take so steep a slant, and whose
color is so delicious a gray, that it is no wonder the
artists have settled down upon the place and claimed
it for their own. So, for the present, I shall call this
little hamlet " Artist-haven."

The flat country is full of a subtle interest. On
one hand are the farms and grass-lands by which the
simple folk live : upon the other, shut out by flats
and low hills of sand, forever rolls the sea.

There is a mellow haziness in the atmosphere, a
harmony in form and color, a wonderful prevailing
" tone," which makes the pensive painter fancy himself once more among the sea-walls and dunes of
Holland ; while the happy colorist, who wanders inland among the ancient farmlands and comes back
with sketches of gray wall flecked with the soft light
and shade that filter greenly through willow trees, de-
clares the landscape to be a piece taken out of the
heart of Brittany.

The Holland man has the best of it, when at
twilight he stands gazing upon one of the antiquated
windmills that still lift their uneasy arms in grim
silhouette against the melancholy sky. But he of the
French school has his themes thrust upon him, when
into the simplicity of the uncrowded landscape comes

a leisurely group of dun-colored cows ; or when a clumsy hay-wagon, piled high with its luscious, ochre-tinted load, crosses his point of view. Then they two shake hands and gasp, each from his different outlook : " What exquisite harmonies ! " " What marvellous grays ! "

A party of artists have taken up their abode in the old academy,—(the first place of learning in New York State, it claims to be,) where they hold innocent revels. There is a saying, somewhere, that " Providence provides for poets and painters, as He provides for the birds of the air." That may be true ; but the poets and painters have, therefore, to be satisfied with very much such food and lodging as is vouchsafed to the birds. It may be true that, after all, it is but a small penalty to pay for the luxury of taking no thought for the morrow !

The artists and their harmonies, however, are not all of this blessed Arcadia. One sees, now and then, faces that belong neither to the natives nor the artists. They appear upon the beach, then vanish back into the village and are lost in its hotel-less shelter.

Did it never strike you, dear reader, that sometimes even the very best people may tire of going to a few prescribed places, and may rejoice to hide themselves from their oppressively inquiring friends, who seek their names in that book of life—the Hotel Register ? (We might digress here to demand who " the very best people " are ? whether they must be superlatively good, or great ? wise or wealthy ? But as Thackeray himself has stumbled upon that very inquiry, and failed to solve the problem to his satisfaction, we may leave the qualification to stand at the indisputable " best.") If you were down, here in this quaint town by the sea, you might meet a handful of such, who have left their formalities and convention-alitics behind them, and stolen hither in the footsteps of the artists, to bask upon that serene plane forbidden to American society—a natural life.

If, in the course of time, all the world and his wife should come down upon the peace of the place, to the artists be the blame. But as yet, they have *not* all come : and so precaution steps in and warns me to throw a friendly veil over the mystic name of this charming village whose atmosphere is still untainted by those belligerents of style, who wrestle each year with the discomfort of summer resorts. . . . .

If we look back half a hundred years or more, even then the little island settlement wears an untroubled and time-forgotten aspect. From end to end its long avenue is as tranquil as though no echoes of the nineteenth century turmoil had yet reached its fair green highway. The old Town Pond still lies far up in the bed of " the street " and the geese and ducks are paddling about in happy unconcern of the passer-by. For now and then the foot of a stranger is led hither by some freak of fancy. But, as yet, Artist-haven has no existence on the map of the fashionable world. Or if it has appeared, a tiny speck upon very domestic copies of the social chart, the finger of the ordinary place-hunter passes it over unnoticed.

Entering the village from the south, two busy wind-mills fling their arms about as if to say, " Here, at least, steam is despised." Beside the restless shad-

ows of these veteran mills, lies the venerable south-
end cemetery, where the villagers have laid their
dead for many generations beneath quaint inscrip-
tions and rude sculpture.

Then comes a mile or more of rural street, with its
straggling farmhouses, some fashioned with a dignified, aristocratic air ; but for the most part framed in
shingle, with Puritan severity. Their doors open
confidingly upon the deeply shaded sidewalk ; while
their long acres stretch away behind them to meet
the flat, untenanted, but readily arable sands of the
interior.

At the north end of the hamlet stands another
time-mellowed windmill, with a still more ancient
burying-ground beneath its long gray shadows. These
little cities of the dead are situated in the broad bed
of the public road, where " two ways meet," after a
time-honored custom ; and the wagon-tracks clear the
low fences to right and to left. The sojourners, passing over the decaying steps of either stile to examine
the blunt-edged dates carved upon those leaning and
moss-covered slabs, may well linger over the suggestions called up by those dim figures. They are
well-nigh obliterated by a crust of gentle lichens
which one may brush carefully away and, after some
puzzling manage to read the time-worn dates of
nearly two hundred years.

Hanging upon these records are many quaint stories
which portray the stern virtues of dead-and-gone Puritan settlers. For, be it known, Artist-haven is not
without its bit of historical pride, and can even show
some few points of revolutionary interest, besides gos-

sip told of the traditional forefathers. There is a tiny, semi-dilapidated structure midway of the single street which was the village Inn more than a hundred years ago, beneath whose long slanting eaves Lord Percy, and young Lord Erskine, and hapless Major Andrè congregated sometimes, with a handful of companions, when the close of the war had left a few British ships in the harbor near Gardiner's Island. It is gray, and weatherbeaten, and vine-covered to-day, and occupied by the gentlest of gentle-folks— a sister and brother whose heads have slowly whitened among their garden-flowers, in lovely innocence of the new world beyond their sheltered village.

There are other memorable buildings in the village, but, somehow, in Artist-haven, the fancy always wanders back to the occupants of the old graveyards. Moreover,—if there should ever be a story written of Artist-haven,—and if it should chance to terminate in the South End Cemetery—what odds? It would not be the first history which has reached a terminus in the grave.

The environment is blown over just now by the winds of a damp and characteristically chilly evening. A lively sound startles the air, just as it did upon equally chilly and misty evenings in the past. Swinging around the corner of the old graveyard comes the great rattling stage. As if in defiance of the peaceful sleepers, the solemn references to the last trump upon yon leaning headstones, the driver raises to his lips, an ancient bugle upon which he blows thrilling blasts. The shabby coach topples from side to side, and its clumsy wheels groan beneath the weight of the huge body. What a clatter it all makes, and how the peaceful echoes start up affrighted, and die away trembling! The man on the box blows another trumpet blast, cracks his long whip, and the machine goes rumbling up the street. No wonder the fancy is carried back half a hundred years!" . . . .

N. B. It may be inferred from several vague allusions made in the foregoing letter, that Mr. Leslie Bracebridge had nursed some chimerical notion of writing a story of Rest-Hampton, over which he threw the friendly veil of " Artist-haven." If so, we crave pardon for taking the pen from his hand to trace for him the history and mystery of the little village.

The Author.

BOOK I.

THE MAN.

" A story I could body forth so well
By making speak, myself kept out of view,
The very man as he was wont to do,
And leaving you to say the rest for him.
Since though I might be proud to see the dim
Abysmal Past divide its hateful surge
Letting of all men this one man emerge
Because it pleased me ! Yet, that moment past,
I should delight in watching first to last
His progress as you watch it, not a whit
More in the secret than yourselves who sit
Fresh chapleted to listen."

ROBERT BROWNING.

CHAPTER I.

THE ARRIVAL.

" A pretty piece of narrative enough,
Which scarce ought so to drop out, one would think,
From the more curious annals of our kind."

THE RING AND THE BOOK.

IT was on such a raw and misty evening, in April 1840 when the sea-fog was rolling hard upon the little island town that lay on the hither side of its primitive peace, untroubled by the few strangers who came and went, that there arrived in Rest-Hampton—a gentleman. Had there been any doubt about his claim to that title, the reflected respectability cast upon him by a most gentlemanly valet, would have decided the question in his favor. But there could be no doubt. Tall, sparely though vigorously made, with clear cut features and a noble poise of head, the stranger's appearance was the embodiment of the gentleman.

He stepped with a certain dignified alacrity from the belated stage which had brought him at so late an hour from Sag Harbor, at the door of the only "Hotel" the place boasted—a small, pitched-roof affair scarcely big enough to be called an Inn, but dignified by the larger name in the minds of the by no means humble villagers.

And how, indeed, were they to compare their "Hotel" with those enormous piles of architecture elsewhere which no man in Rest-Hampton had ever beheld?

As the stranger stepped from the rickety travelling engine, the manner of the valet betokened great solicitude, as for a personage of high degree, or for an invalid. It could not be the latter: for when John Wallace crossed the shaded sidewalk and passed under the low-roofed "stoop," it was with the firm and elastic step of perfect health. The care of the man was then bestowed upon the luggage, while the master stood, unwelcomed, on the threshold.

"I wonder where to gracious Ham Daggett's up to? He's always gadding when he's wanted. But 'tisn't often that smart wife o' hisen's missin' when there's anything likely to be goin' on. Look there, Betsey! he's got a arrival," this and more from the neighbor opposite.

Mr Wallace glanced about him.

"Can you tell me," he asked, in a clear, well modulated voice, "where I may find Mr. Joshua Castlewood?"

The person addressed was a rough-looking man with smudges of his trade-suggesting black upon face and hands, who had lounged up to take part in the arrival of the stage. It was the one event that broke the monotony of the days at Rest-Hampton for the village folks; but the old-world repose was still upon them, and the innkeeper had not yet stirred forth to look for anything so improbable as a guest. No doubt his forefathers had taken the attacks of the Indians, and later the visitation of the British troops with much the same solidity.

" Well, I reckon I kin," replies Ben Adams, after eyeing the new comer for a few seconds,—

" Be you come up to see him ? " he adds, taking a pipe from his mouth to ask the question and then returning it. His glance had fallen upon a letter in the gentleman's hand and then wandered off to the valet busy with trunks and portmanteaux.

" Yes, I should be obliged if you would direct me to his house."

The tone had the same even and beautiful modulation which would have struck pleasantly upon a more sensitive ear than Ben Adams'.

" It's queer, now, he didn't send over for you to the Harbor," Ben grunts, shifting his weight from one foot to the other.

There is no reply ; the stranger half turns as if to quit the doorway ; the valet looks up from his occupation over the luggage. Seeing his master pausing as if in uncertainty, he comes hastily forward. But Mr. Adams gets in one more question, with his pipe in his teeth,—

" Be you a kin of hisen ? "

" Mr. Castlewood is not a relative." replied the stranger, with a slight shade of coldness in his voice, which might, but for his unfailing politeness, have been silent. He took a step forward and joined the man who carried his valises.

" I say, do you know where Mr. Castlewood lives about here ? " demands that person abruptly of the stage-driver.

The man grinned,—

" I reckon you be a stranger hereabout, mister,

or you'd know the way up to Squire Castlewood's."
The remark is flung at the older gentleman, who
answers quietly, although the coldness is distinctly
audible in his exquisite voice this time,—

"Yes, I have not been in Rest-Hampton before."

The valet drops his valises with a scowl at the two
lubbers. Then he turns to his master :

"If you will come this way, sir, I think we must
find some one to show us. These people seem to be
either vastly ignorant or horridly impertinent."

John Wallace turned his aristocratic face towards
Ben Adams. He evidently felt no personal offense,
but took the mode of his replies as the way of a blockhead.

"If you will be kind enough to explain what direction we take, I will not trouble you any further."

It was spoken in a decided way that had the air of a
command, while uttered in the tone of a request,
Moreover he crossed Ben's smutty palm with a
bright silver piece. Then he turned simply and left
the vine-shadowed doorway. Evidently, he was accustomed to walking before.

"O no trouble to me, stranger, I ain't got nothing
to do—I'll jest go along with—with your friend
here."

In spite of Ben Adams' unconsciousness of class
distinctions, something in the new comer's manner
distanced the rude countryman and caused him to
change the latter part of his sentence and his intention at the same time.

Mr. Wallace bowed with a gentle "I thank you,"
and walking towards the direction indicated by Adams,

that person fell behind with the valet. His curiosity, which possibly had but little to do with the personal appearance of its object, and would have been equally bestowed upon any new arrival, did not long remain quiescent.

" Who be your chum, yonder ? "

Now it happened that the circumspect Andrews was furious at the incivility which had been shown Mr. Wallace, and his faultless balance nearly deserted him at this new indignity. However, he smothered his wrath and replied shortly,—

" That is my master."

" Be you his servant ? " cries honest Ben, aghast : " Lord ! I thought you was a pair o' town chaps."

If Andrews felt a sense of exultation, he repressed it in his own bosom. He walked on in silence, keeping his careful eye upon the figure in front. It was the figure of a student, with bent head and hands— such smooth white hands !—folded behind, betokening a habit of revery.

" A preacher ? "

Ben Adams was growing laconic under the pressure of Andrews' silent wrath.

" No," responded that individual, adding under his breath. " I'm dashed if it's any of *your* business."

" Well, in the Lord's name, who be he ? "

" A gentleman."

Ben stared.

" Well neow—really—so's every one, I reckon ; " and he tried to laugh at the very poor joke.

(Silence.) Andrews thought otherwise.

" Lookee here, mister !" cried the blacksmith angrily,

"You know how to answer a civil question, I
s'pose."

"What do you want to know, then?" demanded
the injured valet, wisely concluding not to quarrel
with his brawny inquisitor.

"What's the name o' yon chap,"

Andrews winced :

"Mr. Wallace."

"Got no first name, eh?"

"John Wallace."

"Umph! From New York, mebbe?"

"London."

"Lord!" ejaculated Ben Adams again : "I never
see a Englishman afore, leastways except a old sea-
dog now and then lyin' at Sag Harbor.   Be you a
Englishman, too?"

Andrews may have heard the foreign imputation
that Yankees are the most inveterate questioners upon
God's earth; but his habit being to reserve his
thoughts, he merely responded,—

"Yes," adding, "which way do we take?"

For the watchful eye had followed its master to
what appeared to be a branch road, but was in reality
only one of several straggling wagon-tracks travers-
ing the grassy street.

"Oh, don't you bother," replied Mr. Adams : "no
one can't get out o' this here street yet a while, we've
only got two cross-roads and they're at each end o' the
town.—I say!" elevating his voice to a shout—"Mister Wallis!"

The gentleman addressed did not lift his head, but
kept on at the same even pace.

It was Andrews' turn to stare, which he did, seizing mechanically the other's arm as if in trepidation. "Be your man deaf?" queries Adams, nothing abashed.

"No—no. For God's sake stop."

But Ben was not easily overawed,—

"Hollo, there! Mister Wallis!" he shouted, still louder; and this time John Wallace paused, raised his head, and slowly turned a somewhat puzzled and exceedingly puzzling face upon the two men.

"Hold your dash'd tongue, can't you," mutters Andrews, beginning to hasten forward : "What sort of a way is that to speak to a gentleman ? "

"Oh, I ain't pestered about your furrin ways o' speakin'," growled Ben; "one gen'lman's as good as another here," and he let his companion go on a few paces.

"I beg your pardon, sir," said Andrews, deeply humiliated, and catching up with the hesitating figure : "That low-bred fellow would have your name from me, and now he shouts it after you in the street. —— The valet's mortification was supreme.

"My name? oh, yes," with a faint smile, "It's all one, Andrews. The town will soon have it by heart."

"But the blockhead was ill-mannered about you and asked nasty questions—and that!" Andrews was too incensed to hold his peace.

"Never mind, Andrews," said the gentle voice. "We must not quarrel with our new friends; we are to live among them, you know."

Andrews groaned.

"Do you think they are all like that, sir ? "

" Please God—no," murmured the elder man, a blank, set look crossing his white face. Then he brightened up with a visible effort, as though he were struggling to come from under some cloud : the valet watched him keenly with an expression that was almost anguish.

" This is a quiet place, think you, Andrews ? "

The man started as if from a dream.

" A most quiet place my L——— Mr. Wallace."

John Wallace let his searching gaze, that had wandered off into space, fall for an instant upon the valet's flushing face.

" Be careful, Andrews," he said in a low tone.

" Yes, sir. I shall be careful, sir. That clown flustered me. It won't happen again, I assure you, sir. It is the third place to the right——Mr. Wallace."

There was a singular pause that preceded the name. Perhaps it was homage ; perhaps it was the unspoken gratitude of a trusted servant who is treated by a much revered master as his confidant. Perhaps it was sympathy with some mute thought that lay in the gentle scholar's eyes. Whatever it was, the two men recognized its significance : and after exchanging another look—a grave puzzle still in one face, a deep and peculiarly apologetic deference in the other—Mr. Wallace resumed his former attitude and gait, while Andrews again fell behind with Ben Adams.

That person who was good-natured enough when not over full of liquor, as was too often the case, having ceased to nurse his wrath, began again :

" Be you come to bide with old Joshuay Castlewood ? "

Andrews was too oppressed to be angry.

" Perhaps."

" I'd a thought he'd druv over in his waggin an' saved your mister a joltin' by the stage. He do'ent look over strong."

No reply. Andrews had still in his face, a commonplace visage otherwise, which we need not describe, the same look he had raised to meet the perplexity of John Wallace. A mother might look so upon a child whom she cannot save from sorrow. She, too, can only sorrow. It was as though he and that other were treading together a new path of life; the surprise and doubt was upon them both, but most upon that other, since Andrews himself had, by his calling, only to follow in moods not his own.

Ben Adams could not be expected to penetrate into this maze. He cast lowering looks at his silent companion, who presently roused himself and began to speak, hoping thereby to forestall any probably pending question.

" This is a quiet sort of town, isn't it ? "

" Depends on what you mean by quiet," grunts Ben, ready to defend his native place from a possible slur.

" Oh, I mean no offense. A pleasant kind of quiet, you know."

" Well, as to that," said literal Ben, "folks may differ. Now I should like the place a sight quieter. We've heaps o' comin' an' goin' here 'bout harvest times, with the new reapin' hands, and the buyers, and the heavy teams that hauls the stuff to Sag Harbor fur shippin'."

"Fine farm lands?" Andrews tried to fill a gap.

"Well rather. You take a look at our hay and you won't see purtier anywheres on the Island. Be your mister a lookin' fur a farm?"

"No—no," cried Andrews, inwardly cursing the man's pertinacity of interrogation. "Is not that white house in the trees Mr. Castlewood's?"

Ben nodded, and again Andrews hastened his steps until he was side by side with the thoughtful figure.

"Mr. Wallace," he said, so gently that the start with which the person addressed came out of his revery was scarcely perceptible, "this is the house. Shall I knock?"

He laid his hand upon the ponderous brass knocker, a lion's head with a ring in the mouth.

John Wallace acquiesced and stood waiting with his form erect and the strangely absent look banished from his face, which gained thereby in beauty and strength.

He became conscious for the first time of his surroundings, though they were obscured enough by the late hour and the mist : and the aspect of the house at which he waited gave him evident surprise and pleasure. It was a great old farmhouse, or more properly speaking, mansion, with gables, and porticoes, and oriel windows, and a certain air of comfort and good breeding.

A stranger who was acutely sensitive to impressions must instinctively have felt that only true refinement and a quaint old-fashioned culture could greet him from such a portal.

A young girl who was passing through the well-lit hall singing gaily, paused and opened the huge door.

"Oh, I thought it was Tom!" she murmured blushing and drew back on seeing strangers.

"May I ask if Mr. Joshua Castlewood is at home?" says Mr. Wallace, lifting his hat and exposing to the maiden's wondering eyes a more nobly though delicately modeled head than she had ever beheld in her brief, village bound life.

"Yes sir," she stammered, "If you will come in I'll fetch him."

The stranger bowed his thanks and entered, leaving Andrews outside with the officious Ben, disappointed of his desire to follow. (The account which poor Andrews subsequently gave of how he was bedeviled would be graphic if detailed.)

"Please to walk in and sit down, sir:" and the girl designated, with a pretty gesture, a large and airy parlor full of quaint but rich furniture, and rare though old-fashioned ornaments. It was before the days when old style bric-a-brac had become the rage, remember, dear reader. These choice "antiques" were inherited and made use of in the natural order of things; and not in that aristocratic old home beneath the horse-chestnuts was there ever any incongruity or any modern affectation.

"If you will hand your father this, Miss Castlewood," with a swift warm smile, "I think that he will see me."

It was by one of those rare touches of discrimination which are sometime, vouchsafed to mortals, that the stranger's glance penetrated into this household

and read the daughtership of the flushing maiden.
There have been people,—wise physicians and scien-
tists, who have named this power clairvoyance.

The pretty face vanished and left John Wallace
standing fair and firm as the marble image of a man.
Many shadows flickered in the lights of his peculiarly
transparent eyes. Perhaps that was their wont ; for
with it all he preserved a noble tranquility as beautiful as unusual.

CHAPTER II.

———————" *Thus far take the truth,*
The untempered gold, the fact untampered with,
The mere ring-metal ere the ring be made !
And what has hitherto come of it ? . . . .
———————*Was this truth of force ?*
Able to take its own part as truth should ?
Sufficient, self-sustaining ? Why, if so,—
Yonder's a fire, into it goes my book,
And who shall say me nay, and what the loss ?
You know the tale already."

From THE RING AND THE BOOK.

THE stranger's eyes brightened pleasantly as they met the approaching form of a small but courtly-looking gentleman. He was of that old-school type so nearly banished from our rapid, if not altogether progressive, civilization. When we meet one such, we wonder vaguely why he has abandoned the small-clothes and three-cornered hat that would have so well become him.

The two men bowed and exchanged names. Mr. Castlewood held in his hand the letter which his visitor had given the pretty daughter of the house. After the commonplaces of greeting, Mr. Wallace observed,—

" I presume the Rev. B—— H—— is not unknown to you, Mr. Castlewood ? "

" Certainly not," replied the old-school gentleman, with his obsolete bow, glancing dubiously, however, at the letter. It was so brief that it can be transcribed,—

NEW YORK CITY, *April* 1, 1840.

To
    JOSHUA CASTLEWOOD, ESQ.,
        Rest-Hampton, Long Island.

DEAR SIR,—I take the liberty of introducing to your courtesy, Mr. John Wallace, of London, who wishes to make his home in your town. What he desires in America is to find a place where he can live in the utmost retirement. If you could take him into your family for the present, I think you would not regret it. He is able to pay for whatever he wishes, and would, I am sure, be no trouble to any one. I believe him to be in every sense of the word a perfect gentleman. And yet I scarcely know why I have undertaken to plead his cause with yourself, both he and you being personal strangers to me. I presume that his superiority has impressed itself upon me. Hoping that I do not calculate too far upon your well-known hospitality,

I remain very truly yours,
B—— H——, D.D.

Jushua Castlewood paused an instant to glance again at the letter and then held out his hand.

" I am glad to meet you, Mr. Wallace," he said heartily, with another three-cornered hat bow. The two men, who were much of the same age, were far from alike in appearance, the country squire being ruddy, with twinkling blue eyes and a shrewd mouth. They shook hands somewhat formally, and drawing chairs together, fell to talking as strangers must who are thrust upon each other through a letter of intro-duction.

Any one watching keenly the sensitive face of the new-comer, might have seen the look of relief which passed over it at this reception. It was as though, through some mysterious mischance, he had known what it was to hunger to be taken by the hand.

"Have you been long in our part of the world, Mr. Wallace?"

"Only a fortnight. New York is a fine city, Squire Castlewood."

"Yes, it's a busy place, I'm told. I don't go about much myself. They say it's not unlike London."

John Wallace gave gracious assent, and a pause followed, broken by the Squire:—

"May I ask if you have any special reason for coming to live in our town?"

The stranger seemed to search mutely for some motive or object before he replied:

"I have no reason—excepting that it is the only place which has been suggested to me."

Squire Castlewood looked surprised, and the other added:

"The clergyman who addressed that letter to you referred me to the village as a quiet one, and to your-self as a gentleman of well-known benevolence. I hope that I have not intruded myself upon your no-tice, Mr. Castlewood."

The visitor's dignity was apparent even to the good

squire, who did not trouble himself about nice distinctions. He made a faint movement as if to rise;
but his host detained him.

"Oh dear no—not at all! I beg of you not to be
disturbed. But pardon my curiosity, Mr. Wallace, if
I ask another question. You are a churchman, I suppose?"

"I am."

"And you went to the Rev. B.——H.——as a clergyman of the Episcopal Church——"

"I met him," answered John Wallace, "on the
steamer as I came over to the States."

"Ah, I see, and you had letters to him? or an introduction, possibly?"

"Neither: we met as strangers."

The guest rose this time, with a grave sort of
majesty although he held himself with a gentle courtesy very winning to see.

Squire Castlewood rose too, eyeing him keenly:

"I suppose you know the contents of this letter?"

"I have not read it" answered John Wallace. "I
fancied there could be nothing personal to myself
since the Rev. B.——H.——had no means of knowing
me. I took it to be a friendly communication to yourself, Mr. Castlewood."

"I have never seen the Rev. B.——H——"

"Indeed!"

The delicate hauteur that was creeping over Mr.
Wallace's face gave place for an instant to surprise,
he then made a motion to leave.

"Will you just look at it?"

The squire held out the letter, Mr. Wallace took it,

a singular light trembling in his eyes while he read.

Then he looked the other full in face.

"All that I can say," smiling gravely as he returned the letter, "is that our mutual acquaintance is gifted with keen perceptions, and is not afraid to judge a character intuitively."

"Am I to suppose, Mr. Wallace, that you saw but little of him on ship-board?"

"Very little. Only when entering the New York Harbor."

The squire stood irresolute. Plainly this gentleman was not going to smooth by any polite subterfuge, the way to his better reception. There was a chill in his manner which fully met the chill that had overspread the squire's blunt cordiality.

He stood with his hand upon the door, and bowing, said with perfect politeness:

"I apologize for the invitation which the Rev. B.—— H.——gives me in that letter to take up my abode with you Mr. Castlewood, I had no idea he was so strongly recommending me to your mercy. I wish you good-day."

Was it the finished speech of a man of the world who had perfectly mastered every art of suggestion and modulation? Or was it the genuine outcome of a pure and undesigning mind, such as only belongs to that highest and rarest of all types of gentleman— a polished Christian? Who could tell? For an instant Squire Castlewood had hesitated; but at that courteous "good-day" he started forward:

"Stop, Mr. Wallace, I entreat you. I am very glad to take you, not so much for our friend's evidently just appraisement, as for the estimate which I find myself setting upon you—if you'll excuse the scrutiny which one is forced to give a stranger," and he held out a second time a cordial hand to the visitor.

" At least," said Mr. Wallace, grasping it firmly in his white palm, " we need make no great mystery of my almost self-introduction. That is the way," with one of his rare smiles—" that our countrymen must needs ask you people for a welcome. If I had brought a letter from Her Majesty the Queen, it could not have made any link between us, you know."

Squire Castlewood still studied his guest's face, holding his hand meanwhile with a fascinated forgetfulness. This certainly was a strange man who deported himself with such pride, and yet answered with such humility. And wherein lay the majesty of his bearing ? John Wallace was smiling into his eyes, as though he too read the unusualness of the acquaintance.

" I hope, Mr. Castlewood, that I may so far trouble you as to ask to be directed to some hotel in the place ? you will give me your guaranty ?"

What was that peculiar smile ? Did he mock the honest squire ? or did this stately John Wallace actually feel pleasure in the other's ingenuousness ?

Joshua Castlewood could not for the life of him tell ; but a curious spell was upon him to keep hold of the stranger. It was as though the soul of Jonathan went out to the soul of David. Whatever the fascination, it prevailed ; he spoke out abruptly :—

" Mr. Wallace, we've never had an inmate in our family circle. It seems a strange thing for any one to have suggested it to me. But, do you know, I like it, and besides, the hotel—— "

He paused with a short laugh, the idea of this majestic personage crowded into the little inn was ridiculous.

"You would have to dine and room with your servant, most likely," and they both smiled.

A look of conscious power shone in John Wallace's face. He knew that this kind-hearted squire would not resist him.

"Am I then at home?" he asked pleasantly.

"Well," said the other, "I like the notion. I should only be puzzling myself about a whim if I tried to unravel any reason other than a chance which caused the Rev. B——H——to address his letter to me. But I'm glad he did it, sir, glad he did it, I believe I like you, myself: and the novelty of a 'mysterious guest' may not be unwelcome to my wife. If you will wait a moment, I'll go and speak to her."

When his host had gone, John Wallace relapsed into his meditative mood; but his lips were pressed together with a sad suppression that fell upon them at the latter part of the squire's speech.

"Mystery—mystery," he thought, but did not speak, —not being one of those who utter their meditations *sotto voce*—" why should that word have greeted me on landing upon this desert region, and where I am to abide so long as I shall be in the flesh."

He sighed heavily, and then the cloud was thrown off as by a powerful effort of the will. Looking about him with an active though composed assurance, he took note of the large pleasant windows with their tiny panes and the moonlight streaming in, for the sea-mist had given way to a brighter aspect. The cheerful light from the open fire fell upon the rich old Turkey carpet, the claw-foot tables, the high-backed chairs, and tall corner cabinets tipped with brass, lingering upon them with a friendly glow. But most of all it penetrated his heart until it warmed responsively towards 'the sequestered world without, and the comfort within.

"At least," he mused—that being his favorite method of beginning a sentence, as though all things uttered were but the desultory fragments of unspoken thoughts—"I myself belie the word. It is not to be wondered at that this good squire calls me 'mysterious' since I have alighted upon his threshold as from some unknown sphere. But my daily life shall be clear and open before him,—and if I am a reticent man and not given to questioning—nor to being questioned—why, what mystery is there in that, save that the past and the forgotten are always mysterious."

He got up and stood looking out into the chec-quered moonlit quiet of the orchard—one of those fragrant and beautiful old orchards that one sees no where so tenderly kept to this day as in the little Village of Peace where John Wallace found himself a sojourner. There was not a trace of leafage upon the trees ; but still there was in the air a pensive joyous-ness that means Spring. Long afterwards, that peace-ful outlook lingered in the wanderer's mind as a promise of rest.

When Squire Castlewood returned, there came with him a demure little woman in a mouse-colored gown, with a mousey step, who gave a quick and rather prudish look towards the tall figure by the window. The figure came forward with grave courtesy, and received the mention of his name with so courtly a grace that it seemed at once to take the place of a personal recommendation.

"Joshua tells me that thee wishes to make thy home with us."

The Quaker speech fell consolingly upon the traveler's ear, like an unconscious recognition of him-self as already one of the family.

"Wife is a Friend, and is disposed to cultivate good will towards all men, hey mother?" spoke the Squire in his hearty way. "She has got to my thinking, a hankering after the outside world and is therefore about to bid you welcome——as a hostage for some new interest in life"—he finished with a chuckle.

"I thank you, madam," said the guest, with his princely manner and his humble words, which never-theless were in unquestionable harmony.

"I cannot deny the right of strangers to break bread with us," said Mrs. Castlewood, looking with veiled approbation upon the new comer. "If thee will tarry with us for the present, we will try to make thee at home. Is not thy servant without? I will bid him fetch thy luggage."

When the door was opened, Andrews stood revealed, his face still flushed from his wrangling with Ben Adams, who had gone grumbling away having failed to elicit satisfaction from what he subsequently termed that "'tarnation airy chap."

And so it was all settled : and John Wallace began then and there the thirty years which he spent in

peace and— shall we say happiness ?—under the hospitable roof of Squire Castlewood—the " big man " of
Rest-Hampton, who answered for county magnate
counsellor and judge, for the simple folk.

CHAPTER III.

A DOUBT SETTLED. ʼ

" This self-possession to the uttermost
How does it differ in aught save degree
From the Terrible patience of God."
THE RING AND THE BOOK.

THERE are groups of life-stories which come to us as a symphony, full of concealed melody, which is repressed in the simple and bright *Allegro* of common experience, the deep, full *Larghetto* of some high, masterful passion; the gravely rolling *Andante* of placid years, or the mournful minor strains of those sadder movements which come to every human lot.

Now and then the melody gushes forth in a happy union of sympathies, but oftener, all is broken and fragmentary as the lives jangle one upon another or are attuned only in brief bursts of harmony.

The symphony which is written in the pages of this book takes its name from him who is its moving motive; but there are mingled, here and there, the fitful themes of many other and less marked destinies.

Moreover to every creature that exists, even those who are flattened out between the pages of a romance, must be given the privilege of an opinion, and the opportunity to express it.   *   *   *   *

" Martha, what do you think of our Mr. Wallace by

this time?" queried the squire, somewhere about the second week after the stranger's arrival. For, in spite of his wife's narrow experience of the world, the chivalrous gentleman invariably appealed to her for the solution of any little social problem which came in his way.

Perhaps it is scarcely fair to represent Mrs. Castlewood as "wise in her own conceits;" and yet she possessed largely that very self-assurance which in worldly people runs to vanity, but in pious souls takes the form of extreme reliance upon scriptural maxims and precepts. It was partly this, and partly her Quaker bringing up, which made the staunch Calvanists of Rest-Hampton look upon her somewhat askance.

"I think him a godly man, Joshua," she answered, without hesitation. Indeed she was always prompt in her decisions, having a firm conviction that her judgment was supernaturally guided.

"It is the spirit of truth which directs my counsel," she was wont to say ; and took no account, openly, of the frequent mistakes which—being human, she made. Her husband also overlooked the misjudgments, and had, or let her believe that he had—the profoundest faith in her wisdom. "Always let on to a woman that you think her right," was his chivalrous and would-be-worldly wise policy.

This time, Squire Castlewood took the initiative :

"Don't you think it rather remarkable, my dear, that he should have come in so mysterious a manner, without something more like—like a pledge, you know, of his being a gentleman ? "

" He is a man, Joshua, who carries that in his face
and manner," promptly replied the oracle.

" Oh ! I know all that, my dear ; but, you see, it isn't
precisely the way of the world to go about unintro-
duced—without a guarantee of some sort."

" A God-fearing man has no concern to follow the
way of the world."

The good squire, dubious for once in the face of
his wife's argument, ventured to expostulate :

" But Martha, even God-fearing men don't wander
about like the disciples of old, asking food and lodging from strangers—in these days, do they ? "

" They ought to," responded Mrs. Castlewood feeling the weakness of her side and shifting to a broader
basis. " It is scriptural."

" Yes—it's scriptural, admitted the other, "and so
it is scriptural to sell all one's goods and give to the
poor, and a heap of other things nobody thinks about
doing."

" Because the world is falling away from grace,
Joshua, shall we misjudge a man when he is merely
acting as the disciples did."

" But, my love ! " cried the squire astounded, " Mr.
Wallace did not come among us as a disciple,—that
is in any other way than his sudden appearance—nor
even as a preacher. As far as I can judge, he is a
man of the world—unmistakably a man of the world."

" He may have been in the world but never of it "
proclaimed Martha Castlewood, unconscious that she
was but adding another testimony to the silent acceptance with which all people met this man's peculiar
fascination.

"How do you know, my dear?" It was the squire's one helpless resource when his wife grew obstinate as she always did whenever she had "taken a stand."

"I know because my eyes are open to see the things of the Spirit." Poor little Martha! good, true soul! with thy contracted and untried views of the world thou hast never seen, how far short of sufficiency wouldst thou find thy unfounded assurance to cope with the duplicity of men and women in that actual world where the surface and the finish are ever paramount!

But the reply served as usual to silence the safer common-sense of the squire. "There's no getting back of the Spirit—what ever that may be," he was wont to say, relapsing into the contentment of a finished argument. For to tell the truth, he was not disputatious, and was oftenest glad to escape a discussion. So he readily gave up that thread of the discourse and turned to a new proposition.

"Don't you see how he evades all questions in reference to his past life, his home, his occupation, his parentage, everything in fact "—with a despairing sweep of the hand—" which is in any way personal—in any way personal."

"I see, Joshua," replied his wife, with an access of primness, " that thee has overstept the bounds of propriety in asking our guest many questions which do not appear seemly or in good taste. John Wallace has a perfect right to preserve his family history if he chooses."

"Lord, Martha!" cried the squire, half perplexed

half amused; "suppose the man is some impostor
who has settled down upon us! Just suppose it!"

"I thought thee had fancied him greatly when thee
first saw him, and came up to me, speaking of his desire to remain with us." Mrs. Castlewood always experienced an influx of dignity at any suggestion of
temper on the part of her husband. Indeed it was
her way to receive icily any tendency to warmth of
comment which fell upon her ears. "Violence is a
self-indulgence," she often said.

"Why, so I did fancy him, confound it!" ejaculated the perplexed squire, "and so I do! But a man
must protect himself! This mania for retirement is
so half suspicious. I hope," he continued lugubriously, "that we sha'n't be placed in any awkward position. Suppose he has run away from his own country
for some crime or other!"

Mrs. Castlewood rose in the climax of her virtuous
self-possession.

"Joshua, I must say that thy suspicions are most
unaccountable. Suppose I had looked upon thee as a
possible criminal when thee came over a stranger
from the Island!"

"The folks in that Quaker community treated me as
if I was one, sure enough," muttered the injured gentleman. But the feminine side of the argument, having
carried the battle over into the enemy's camp,
left the room in that sweet spirit of silence which is
often worn to cover alike a triumph or a discomfiture.

"Hang it! it *is* a mystery though!" grumbled the
squire, beginning to walk, man-fashion, up and down
the large low-ceiled room, nursing his doubt of John

Wallace; when looking from the window he beheld the person in question, walking vigorously along beneath the great overshadowing elms. Andrews was beside him, both in animated talk. The two were just returning from an exploring expedition down the beach. For, in spite of his somewhat sedentary and introspective life, it must not be supposed that Mr. Wallace was a physically indolent or phlegmatic man. He had a singularly athletic though slender frame, which gave him the air of continual activity. When at rest, his physique was full of strong repose, such as one sees in the marble images of Greek divinities; but in motion, he had more the fire and impetus of action which belonged to the heroes and athletes of ancient days. His unbearded classic face and whiteness of tint rather increased the resemblance, and brought into marked prominence the half Greek, half Roman outline of his feature.

"Ah, Mr. Castlewood! I wish you had joined me in my tramp. This is a lovely bit of country, and a quaint, almost old-world civilization." He entered the room with the ease of one quite at home; and that he would have carried that same fine air into the palace of a king or the hut of a peasant, did not detract from its pleasantness. It reassured the puzzled master of the house, who invariably felt all questions—they were too vague to be called doubts—vanish before the genial unconcern of his lodger's manner.

"What have you found to-day to pay up for the rain and mud?" he asked cordially.

"I have found a most interesting little town some

five or six miles below here—Amagansette, you call
it, I believe. Is it not charmingly situated in that
wide curve of the shore?"

"Yes—it's a pretty village; not so aristocratic as
ours, maybe, but a fine place."

"It has," mused Mr. Wallace, after a pause, his
gaze wandering out of the window, and into nowhere,
after his spirit,—"a look of home about it."

"Do you mean that it looks like your home?"
queried the other, catching at an opportunity.

"I mean this," replied the guest, seeming to pleasantly accept and reply to the question as he understood it : "that it has an undefinable aspect of being dear to the people who live in it. It looks sheltered, and breathes content, even in this nasty weather,
and upon the edge of a gray and joyless sea."

"Ah—yes—so it does, so it does!" responded
Joshua Castlewood, wondering if he had been parried,
or simply misunderstood. And so it always went. Mr.
Wallace never left a question unanswered. His
courtesy endured all things. Indeed, he replied with
apparent willingness to every suggestion thrown in
the way of his notice. But there was always this
peculiarity: that they whose curiosity led them to
ask prying or even interested questions, never discovered aught that they would know from the answer.
There was always an evanescent reserve, a remoteness
of generalization in the turn he gave to the conversation whenever it bordered upon a personality.

At this present juncture, the good squire merely
rubbed his head, and eyed the handsome figure, cogita-
ting: "I wonder what manner of man you are, any
way."

Then it occurred to him in one of those sudden disclosures that come even to unimaginative people in perplexity, that here was a way out of the doubt. He would take this man's identity by the hand and say: " Let me know you. I will be your confidant," and without second thought he broke the apprehensive silence that had fallen like a pall upon the other, because of a strange clairvoyance by which he seemed to read the unspoken thoughts about him.

" Mr. Wallace—you are a stranger to me—to us all. We like you, and are interested in you, but you puzzle us. Now, I don't ask you to go on the housetop and tell the village your business. All I want is that you should give me personally some rights in your acquaintance."

The firm white face was a shade graver, more resolute. Clearly, this was not a man to be questioned. The squire's shaft had missed its aim.

" I cannot perceive that there are any rights which I withhold from you Mr. Castlewood. There may be privileges of intimacy which I have possibly been slow to consider "——

" It isn't that I want to be a familiar friend," hotly interrupted the squire, his native pride rising,—" only that I should have liked more respect shown to my good faith—my good faith, sir."

John Wallace's gaze again wandered out into space, and again came back bringing the fugitive spirit captive. In the long perspective of somewhere, perchance, he saw once more a lonely and homeless shadow that was himself.

" When I first came to you," he said slowly, " you

offered to accept me upon your own estimate of me. Have I done anything to shake your confidence, Squire Castlewood?"

"No—oh, no!" cried the other, beginning to back out of his assumed position, as he saw with real consternation the trouble in the face of his guest.—"On my honor, Mr. Wallace, I like you better every day. I admire you—I respect you. Only—don't you see how it is?—we have never got one step beyond that first acquaintance. I can't grasp your—your personality, I may say. All that I know of you is surface—surface."

"What do you wish to know?" The look that met the squire's honest gaze was as full of integrity as his own.

"Your life—your standing—your reasons for coming here—the 'retirement'—the mystery—all of it."

For another instant the two men gazed at each other. The word "mystery" had struck somewhere near John Wallace's heart. Then he spoke:

"I am a reticent man, Squire Castlewood, but I have no story that would interest you. An honest man's life is his own—as his soul is his own—to give account of to his God. I decline to discuss mine with any human being. If this seems to you disingenuous; or a breach of candor; or a cause for ambiguity, I can only withdraw myself from your hospitality, since it must perforce be but tolerant."

Never was mien more grandly tranquil; never had words seemed more to come from a superior disdain of inquisition. Squire Castlewood looked and beheld that the man before him was right; he knew, there-

fore, that he was wrong.   A great self-condemnation
swelled up from his singleness of heart, and he hastened
to acknowledge his error.

" Mr. Wallace—if I beg your pardon, I can scarcely
hope you will grant it.   I don't know what came over
me that I should have so trespassed upon your prero-
gatives. I seemed to have forgot that while I owe you
unquestioned liberty, you owe me nothing in the way
of confidence, nothing !   I've made a great mistake "——

" Say no more about it, my dear sir," interrupted Mr. Wallace, his voice as gentle now as a
woman's, and his whole aspect changed to one of
graciousness and magnanimity : " We all make blunders
in our dealings with our fellowmen, who may have
wounds just where we take hold of them.   Suppose
we forget that you and I ever came to a place of
denial."

" Forget it, I beg you," cried the humble squire :
" and be sure, Mr. John Wallace, that I shall not only
remember this rebuke in leaving your motives and
actions uncriticised ; but in my own innermost mind
never again will I question your past, or present, or
future."

And Joshua Castlewood, keeping his word as only
Puritan stock can, from that day forward never once,
in his most secret consciousness, admitted that there
was anything equivocal about his lodger.   From then
until their two lives had run out, side by side, there
grew and strengthened between the mild, city-bred
scholar and the hearty country gentleman, a beautiful

friendship such as only an unintentional offence perfectly forgiven can create between unlike natures.

But "what manner of man" Mr. Wallace might be,
there were others than the Castlewoods to discuss.
The new resident was stitched into the neighborhood
quiltings, and knitted into family socks, and sewed
into half the garments of Rest-Hampton and its envir-
ons. From Hardscrabble, and from Amagansette ; from
"Sag" and from Jericho ; even from Montauk, the
natives came forth to look upon the *rara avis* of the community ; a fine English gentleman who was a scholar,
and who was rich. And this was their testimony ;
that he was a harmless man, who might have been
a lovable man—to his own.

As the years rolled on, however, he took none of
all who watched him into his great heart. He hunted
up the poor and the wretched, giving to them his
time, his patience, his means. It was his one thought,
or rather, the one thought to which he gave outward
and unguarded expression. To give, was his only
utterance ; and it burst forth like the unconscious
melody of a song whose words were in an unknown
tongue ; but whose sweetness was apparent to all.

Annie Castlewood alone came near to comprehending the words of the song.

What "new interest in life" the squire's wife found,
was not from the outside world, or any echo of it
which came through her guest's voice. It was from
the contact with a nature finer, broader, and, withal,
wiser than any it had been her fortune to encounter.
It was from that refreshing study which a wakeful
understanding must ever give to unaccustomed per-

sonalties within reach. As time slipped away, there never once occurred, even to her inquisitive mind, the suspicion of a mystery. So evenly did the gentle scholar live his life ; so rare was his refinement and so just his estimate of men ; so full his knowledge, and so deep his perception ; above all, so wide were his charities, that the only consciousness which came to the household, and the village that knew and loved him, was a sense of the harmony of his character and the beauty of his daily living.

CHAPTER IV.

THE CASTLEWOODS' GUEST.

————————*" See it for yourselves,*
This man's act, changeable because alive !
Action now shrouds, now shows the informing thought."
From THE RING AND THE BOOK.

JOHN WALLACE was a student ; but it appeared that he did not follow any one class of subjects. He read much Gospel and some Law. He kept abreast with the new theories of the day, such as comparative philology, the development of the species, and many other thoughts just dawning upon the intelligence of science lovers. He was of luxurious breeding, since he knew no more than an infant how to wait upon himself, and depended upon the constant Andrews for every common service.

"That man," Dame Martha would ejaculate with a sigh, "knows not enough of taking care of himself to pull back from the fire if it scorches him !"

Such helplessness was a heretofore unheard of phase of life to the sturdy and self-reliant inhabitants of a hard-working village, which had seen few changes since its pioneer days. Self-indulgence was a weakness which the Pilgrim fathers had not brought with them over the unknown ocean.

It was his breeding, not his habits, however, that

had been luxurious, since he ate, and drank, and slept sparingly, and was never idle for a moment. Each day, through rain or snow, or cold or heat, he walked for miles over the flats of dreary sand by the lonesome and desolate sea ; or among the dismal marshes that skirted the dunes ; or inland among the farmlands, taking but little notice of the goodly crops and the well-filled granaries. He made friends everywhere, but these friendships took no hold upon him : consequently he was rarely accompanied by any one in his long tramps. What thoughts filled the breast of the solitary man,—solitary even in the presence of his faithful valet, or of any other human creature—who shall guess ?

After a few months, when he had thoroughly familiarized himself with his surroundings, he fell into the habit of a daily pilgrimage to and from Three-Mile-Harbor—a lonely spot where vessels of any kind were seldom seen. It might have been merely habit, or preference, or restlessness. If John Wallace had a superstition that, one day, a ship would come to him there, it never appeared.

Andrews failed not to bear him company to this deserted Harbor. What long talks the two men held together, only the valet knew. If Mr. Wallace had a confidant on this side of the troubled sea, it was Henry Andrews. It may be that he preserved towards this one friend who had come with him out of the unmentioned yesterday, the same impenetrable reticence as was his habit towards all whom he met. Of this, Andrews never spoke. It was like master, like man with regard to his rigid silence on whatever touched the personal affairs of Mr. Wallace. For the rest, Andrews loved him as his own soul, bestowing upon him that purest of hero-worship,—the sort that looks for no recompense excepting the permission to serve and to revere.

For a while the newcomer was, as we have hinted, the lion of Rest-Hampton. The country-folks called upon him, after the manner of friendly interchange known only in rural places ; for the fame of his sus- pected learning had gone far and wide, and it was also rumored that he was of a noble family and lived away from his heritage because of some difficulty in decid- ing the heir-ship.——A very pretty story, and quite romantic to speculate upon ! though what gave rise to it could not well be determined, since it was possibly the offhand suggestion of some gossip whose imagina- tion was more daring than that of her neighbors.

What they saw who came to look at the lion, rarely disappointed the innocent people, to whom a man of the world was indeed a prodigy. He certainly looked a prince to their admiring eyes. What they heard was less edifying. There were no jovial stories of old world cheer; no marvellous anecdotes of life in strange places ; no talk of court or of crown.

He even seemed shy of answering their blunt queries about London and its attractions, or Paris and its temptations ; and soon all mention of other scenes dropped from their limited range of topics ; indeed John Wallace spoke but little to the coming and going ele- ments of his new surroundings. When he did talk, it was of haying and planting ; of sowing and reaping ; of the price of crops and the value of cattle. Those of the

population who were refined and cultivated, such as
the family who had given him their hospitality,
respected him as a man still more refined and cultivated than themselves.   The middle-class revered
him as a benevolent Christian gentleman, and the
embodiment of all dignity and wisdom.   The lower-
class, that largest proportion of every community—
adored him as their protector and benefactor : a half
celestial being whose only likeness to mortal folks
was in the cut and material of his trousers and waist-
coats ; and even they were better and finer than anything of which Rest-Hampton wot.

After a while, however, he began to take a place
among them.   He was in their world if not of it.   He
gave freely to all of their little schemes for self-im-
provement, and for moral benefit.   By and by, from a
never apparent source, newer and larger schemes began to evolve out of the old stupid routine of ineffi-
cient means : and the little township grew in importance in its own eyes and those of its neighbors.
Modifications and improvements began to be manifest here and there, and a general air of waking up
became apparent among the younger generation.
The fathers were not greatly impressed by this pending evolution ; but the sons hailed it as an omen of
some future opening, not yet made plain.   Old stay-
at-home traditions were somehow shaken ! and here
and there a lad left his plough and his scythe, to go
forth into some remote city a-seeking his fortune.
And John Wallace's purse was always open.   It is
true that there were those who grumbled.   They did
not want new notions, and liked the old ways best.

They preferred to tell the same threadbare jokes their fathers had told, over the same blazing firesides ; but nevertheless, they let their boys go out to see a bit of the world.

No one thought of blaming Mr. Wallace personally. It seemed all in the natural and unavoidable order of circumstance. But, strange to relate, the new revolt began in Squire Castlewood's own family—at the very heart of his affections. Over his daughter there came a change, and his two boys turned their faces world-ward, after a few years. At first, the waking-up was scarcely perceptible, so long and soundly had the village slept. Even after the strange power of John Wallace's life had passed away, the little hamlet seemed still so primitive a place to the denizens of the great Beyond, that its peace was hailed as a discovery, we have seen, by the artists in 1878.

And so the influence of this man was, after all, but a slow-working and possibly much exaggerated element in the history of Rest-Hampton. But what of the family among whom he had come so unawares ? In the pretty springtime of this story's commencement, when the heart of that family beat quietly in the routine of its forefathers, the old farmhouse of The Homestead glowed in the early sunshine, seeming to embody in its cheerful exterior the contentment within. There was something stately about it, which caused strangers to stop and inquire who lived there. The high portico with its white pillars, the wide portal with its great door nearly always hospitably open gave it an air of repose most inviting to the beholder.

And yet only those who passed over the friendly
threshold knew the real luxury of comfort which the
old house offered to all visitors, rich and poor alike.
For the handful of well-to-do families, known as " our
set," to the gentlefolks of Rest-Hampton, was very
limited ; and humbler friends came and went and
were made welcome with the easy cordiality of village
life. There was something richer and truer than the
style—"the mode"—of city life in the quaint old-
school *noblesse* of these country gentry, who could
mildly encourage intercourse, without permitting
familiarity, from the hewers of wood and drawers of
water that make the background—"the shade and
the real,—" of every civilization. It was too small a
community for the narrow etiquette of Gentility and
Obscurity. They came together upon the democratic
terms of the New World. But the aristocrats held
unbroken the traditions of their Old England : and
never was nobility more respected by commonalty,
than the gentlefolks of Rest-Hampton were respected
by the villagers.

As for the Castlewoods,—their thoroughbred accustomedness to refinement felt itself in no way
abashed by the courtly manner and patrician aspect
of their new inmate. There was a simplicity about
him which fell in easily with their unaffected ways.
That heaviness of atmosphere which often hangs
about the advent of a stranger into the home-circle
did not settle upon the homestead. The first meal
is usually the test of probable restraints ; and upon
this occasion the family conversation went on as
naturally as ever, only turning aside now and then to

take cognizance of the newcomer. Squire Castlewood spread himself comfortably to relate his favorite
anecdotes, of which he soon found an answering
fund in his guest. The Quaker wife began to bring
forward certain themes and theories which she had
long ceased to harp upon, since their vagueness met
with but an opaque non-comprehension from her
matter-of-fact husband, and a frown from the somewhat hard and narrow village mentors.

There were many new things of which she had
" heard tell " vaguely, and she wanted to inform herself
about them. For the Friend is usually both intelligent
and inquisitive, and when once let loose from the bonds
of the Society is apt to go wool-gathering after many
doctrines. John Wallace could answer all of these
questionings, she thought. Doubtless he had studied
them out : at least, he could discuss them learnedly
with her.

As for the strapping boys, they pronounced Mr.
Wallace " a brick," at once ; and fell easily into the en
chanting subterfuge of escaping their tasks under the
pretence of " studying mathametics " with their new
friend—who, good man, allowed himself to become absorbed in difficult problems while his play pupils caught
flies behind his back, or spun tops and pitched marbles
under his very nose.

Even Annie, the maiden whose smiling face had
first greeted him at the door, soon began to accept
Mr. Wallace as " one of themselves." Perhaps this
somewhat unexpected ease with a stranger was a reflection from the demeanor of the mother, who never, in
her life before had felt so " at home " with any crea-

ture outside of her own family. There was to her a charm of discovery about this new acquaintance, which was a perpetual inspiration to freedom of discourse: and, as we have suspected, Dame Martha's wisdom presided, Quaker-fashion over the family, with the counsel of authority, none the less marked that it was the rule of love.

CHAPTER V.

" Not one flower of all he said and did
Might seem to flit unnoticed, fade unknown,
But dropped a seed has grown a balsam tree
Whereof the blossoming perfumes the place."

THE RING AND THE BOOK.

THERE never was a life-story that had not some other life-story woven into it, like a silken thread running through a pattern of wool.

When the pleasant shadow of John Wallace passed under the roof-tree of The Homestead, the squire's only daughter, Annie, was a baby in experience and still a child in years.

Her days among the pastoral scenes of village life had brought her only a fair education, a little knowledge of sewing and psalm-singing, an aptness for housewifery—such good things, in sooth, as were deemed needful in that day and generation, to the people of the village.

Strange to say, it was not the Quaker training of her mother, but the Puritan prejudices of her father's house, which made her rearing a limited though most careful one. These old-school gentry had not risen above the traditions of the town's-people who looked suspiciously upon what they called " forwardness " in a girl. Annie had fallen under the secret condemnation of the deacons more than once, for her revolt in the matter of reading and opinion ; for she had an ever-increasing love for such books as she could find in the scantily supplied farmhouse libraries. With it, she possessed an inexplicable appreciation for all things beautiful and new. The mentors had rarely approached the household on the subject of " Nancy's notions," for the mother was by no means a subscriber to their ways of thinking. The little Quaker woman attended the village church, since it was all that offered ; but having been cast out by her marriage from the narrowness of her childhood's faith, she was loth to find herself confronted by an equally stern and repellant form of belief. Her acceptance of the mentors was tolerance ; but she possessed in a large degree that woman's weapon, policy, with which she led not only her honest spouse, but also a considerable portion of the village community, blindfold.

So it happened that Annie was left to herself, to think out her own fancies, which ran riot in a world beyond the narrow vicinity of a couple of rural townships.

Is there not a half pathos in this girl of high capabilities and wide desires being thus buried in the obscurity of one little settlement, destined, it then seemed, never to wake up to the roll-call of nineteenth century civilization ?

It cut her off from those episodes which young women of the world call " Experiences." It barred from her eager eyes even a distant glimpse of that en-

chanted land of social successes, over which she had
brooded in many a romantic tale. Even the footsteps
of a coming lover—a real lover, with wonderful eyes
and a thrilling voice, such as the novels pictured—
was a remote possibility, only to be dreamed of and
wistfully forgone.

Ah! when in that mysterious realm of unknown
lovers does not the fancy of a young girl revel? And
so, was it strange that in the home-nest, surrounded by
the only earth and sea and sky she had ever known,
Annie Castlewood was often possessed of a homesick
longing she could neither define nor dispel? a yearning
for another earth, another sea, another sky, which would
bring to her empty little heart a story such as came to
the happy heroines of her books and her fancies. The
modicum of sense and wit which was sufficient to amuse
and satisfy the village girls of her acquaintance left her
with a restless consciousness of something better, she
knew not of. And even among the few old aristocratic
families of the vicinity, she felt a want of originality and
of live interests, which brought her a sense of dissatisfaction. What was vastly enjoyed by these companions was often a weariness to her; and although
her fresh spirit kept her happy and gay in the midst
of the merest mediocrities of pleasuring, still the
young creature had a rare intelligence above her as-
sociates and, indeed, above her age. Her father patted
her cheek, and called her a " sentimental Miss ; " her
friends wondered at her " airs " while they relished
her society, as being more piquant than their own.
More than that, the Castlewoods were of fine stock,
and stood high from end to end of the long Island.

But the mother looked askance ; comprehending her vague yearnings, and—after the manner of her bringing up—held her peace. She too had known indefinite longings which had made her look away from her native village and spring out at the invitation of the rich squire, then frowned on portentously by the members of that society secretly irksome to her spirit.

Her sons, like their father, she could manage, working upon them with her cautious influence : her daughter evaded her, with what had been her own impulse to be free of conventional restraints. And she saw in some trepidation, the eagerness with which Annie, then but sixteen years old, welcomed the advent of an outsider into the somewhat humdrum life at The Homestead.

Was it not the reflex of her own eagerness in welcoming the stranger who had come a courting twenty years before ?

But John Wallace had not come a courting :

The mother, having a good substratum of Yankee shrewdness, comprehended the difference, and the danger. . . .

It was, for a time, all a story to Annie. Her young soul was not yet awake, and the stranger came to her this wise in a dream,—

" John Wallace is a real gentleman. He is an Englishman of high birth—perhaps of title, since he wears a seal ring upon which is a mysterious crest.

" He is a scholar ; for he reads books—in every tongue upon earth"—little Annie thought.

" He wears the finest of linen and cambric, and has

a servant to wait upon him, who has far better manners than Mary Harding's lover, or even"—here Annie colored—" than Tom himself."

(Tom Hatherton was Annie's sometimes lover, whom she encouraged or abused according to her whim ; but who was gradually falling away in her eyes from any approach to her ideal standard, since Mr. Wallace had over-topped it unwittingly, and built it up higher and higher to sustain his ever increasing perfections.)

Gradually there crept into her heart a more definite consciousness of the simplicity of her existence, the obscurity of her surroundings, in that world-forgotten hamlet by the sea. The want of experience, the absence of originality in her friends became more and more apparent to her. She began to question about the enticing complexities of a more world-wise sphere; and Annie grew—not discontented but sobered and quieted. Her little bursts of song through the house were quenched, " because Mr. Wallace might hear them and know she had never been taught to sing." Her gushes of frank opinion gave place to half-studied remarks, when he was present. She was natural and sweet still, upon the surface: but at her heart if there be what is sentimentally called "a heart," at that tender age,—was an ever increasing disturbance that at times amounted to trepidation in the presence of her divinity.

As for Mr. Wallace, he had liked the fresh young voice and girlish enthusiasm. Sitting in his study, day by day he learned to look for them when they grew less frequent ; and finally, as he took notice of this budding girl, he found that she was not a mere clod as were many of those he saw—indeed the woman of the great world is oftenest little more!—and that Annie Castlewood possessed a soul. Then he began to take an interest in her little plans and her thoughts; for he had that interest in very young girls which men of fifty are apt to possess. The only way in which this fatherly interest thought to manifest itself, was in her studies.

One morning at breakfast he turned to Mrs. Castlewood,—

"May I interest your daughter, madam, in some of the studies which I used to love? with your permission, I think we might read a little French or German together."

The color sped vividly to Annie's delicate face, and lit her soft eyes with a flash like tears,—

"Oh, Mr. Wallace! *would* you?" was all she could ejaculate; but she said it with her whole being on her lips. It was a sequel to her story; an exquisitely romantic climax of which she had never even dreamed.

"Mother, *may* I?" she cried, getting up and going around to her mother's chair with a burning eagerness in her face, and the pretty emphasis she invariably used. Martha Castlewood looked up, surprised. Annie never had any confidential talks with her mother:—how many daughters have? How many mothers know the tritest secrets of those creatures they have brought into the fitful fever of life? She was therefore ignorant that the beautiful web her little "Lady of Shalott" had woven, was warp and woof, a romance about this strange knight, this stately John Wallace, around whose feet she herself had more than once cast the shuttle of her faded fancy.

She thought her charge safely shut in that tower called home, within range of her all-protecting eye. But alas! the little lady had looked towards Camelot! —Long and intently she had looked, not with a woman's passion, as yet, but with a maiden's inspiration of quest.

She did not mean to love her Launcelot. To so bring him down to her own level had not entered her bedazzled brain ; but already she worshipped him. Ah! little Annie! where is the boat to bear thee to Camelot—to the death of thy maiden fancies and of thy sweet unborn hopes ?

At a glance, Annie saw that her timid illusion stood in danger of being surprised from her, and took refuge in innocent stratagem,—

"May I study French, mother? I do *so* long to know French."

The little Quaker woman paused. It was opening the door to the things of the world which had always been unknown temptations to herself, and about which she had heard untold warnings in her youth. Having suffered too much restriction to value its wisdom, however, she was not very narrow in her principles. She prided herself, indeed, upon being a law unto herself, and if this man from the world, who was, withal, a Christian gentleman, chose to fancy her daughter, well——

If Mrs. Castlewood had read the story of Abelard and Héloise, perchance she might have held out against the questionable relationship of master and

pupil which has so often found a surprised termination
in a tangle of tender emotions.   But, having outlived
the period of her own romance, she had come to think,
as older people will, that after all sentiments are but
fleeting things, and can harm nobody.   So she consented.   Annie stood flushed with the coming triumph
of some vague achievement of which as yet she only
saw the glitter.   Her hero had crossed her horizon
but a few months before, and yet already his silhouette loomed up giant-like and overshadowed all the
realities of her life.

"O Mr. Wallace !" she cried, "when may I begin ? "

"To-day if you wish," he answered, smiling brightly
in the infection of her enthusiasm.   Then to Mrs.
Castlewood.

"May we bring our books into your sewing-room
every morning for an hour or two, Mrs. Castlewood ? "

Annie's flutter experienced a faint chill.   The
mysterious study, lined with books great and small,
which had come in boxes from out of her hero's past,
had formed a charming background to the picture
which flashed before her at the unexpected proposition.
But John Wallace had the unfailing *savoir faire* which
comes alone from a knowledge of the world.   The
story of Abelard and Héloise was not unknown to
him ; and he had no wish to reproduce among modern
commonplaces, the pretty pathos of that tale so lovely
in its mediaeval setting.   Apparently he was not a
man to cause or care for the sentimental in woman.
Indeed, at this time and always during those years at

Rest-Hampton, he seemed to have but little capacity to receive the magnetism of the other sex.

It might have been that a woman who would touch his life must be made of finer stuff and rarer moods than any creature whom Rest-Hampton could afford. It might have been that some woman had once wrought such a spell upon his high, strong nature, that ever after he was blind and dumb to all feminine attraction. Whatever was the cause, as a result, he was isolated beyond the infatuation of woman's charms, and he knew it. He knew also that early maidenhood, with its budding sensibilities is over-susceptible in the matter of masculine influence, and seeing the sudden illuminating of little sixteen-year-old Annie Castlewood's eyes, he was aware that he must withdraw his best self from an easy conquest.

Had Annie been a woman, he might have kept his natural course, and taken little pains to avert a possible evil. But this man's honor was of that tender and beautiful texture which caused it to reach out and protect all innocent things, not only from outward harm, but from any disenchantment that might befall their own imaginations. Only a few months had passed since his advent into Squire Castlewood's family, and already he found himself the self-appointed champion of a sweet and simple-minded girl against herself.

Gradually his manner took that form of all others the most prone to disenchant an impressionable mind, —the fatherly. He watched his words that they never touched upon the ideal ; he was mindful of his voice, beautiful in spite of the matter-of-fact tone, that it never took a too personal sound ; he took note of his movements, that no gesture might mislead his little charge into presupposing a sentimental attitude. In fact, he banished from their relationship all significance so as never to cause a self-conscious thought, and thus became truly a help and a benefit to the hungry-hearted girl, where he might otherwise have proved a hindrance and a snare.

That he could control the power of his wonderful gaze was a victory worthy of his pure endeavor, since his eyes were of that " dark yet mild intensity," which, says a great writer, " seemed to express a special interest in every one on whom he fixed them."

This "large-eyed gravity, innocent of any intention" is a quality which is possessed by few men ; and with it goes invariably the power to dominate their fellow beings. But John Wallace's was a mellowed nature. He had depths of memories to draw upon which gave a rich generousness to his impulses: and not for worlds would he have found Annie Castlewood's inexperience entangled with his conscious fascination. He had learned, no doubt, through lessons taught in that world beyond the gates of Rest-Hampton, the measure of his "makedom and fairness," but the sharpness of those lessons had quenched forever all desire to make himself a necessity to the human creatures about him. These more subtle points, however, were lost upon the villagers in genera'.

All that came to pass from the new bond of intimacy between him and his young *protegé*, was that it saved Annie from falling in love—deeply, romantically, desperately in love.

Gradually the demi-god descended from the pinnacle where she had placed him, and came to be her watchful friend, her patient instructor, her trusted adviser. From a dreamland, beset with many risks to the unsophisticated heart of a woman-child, they passed out into the open country of a wise and safe intercourse. And Annie was uplifted, mentally and spiritually into a region above her own, while she was strengthened for the realities of her daily life.

In all the after years of her life, the girl never forgot the ripening influence of her wise friend's sympathy, the restful self-reliance which grew out of his comprehension of her character, as it broadened and beautified beneath his moulding.

This friendship became also a chief resource to the being who suddenly found himself buried in a—to him —social grave : and perhaps it helped the grave scholar to hear whatsoever things he had to endure, through many hours of tedious lack-interest in his narrow surroundings, the prison house of a master-soul.

Sometimes, when he bent his penetrating gaze upon her, as if by his superior will-power he would compel her understanding to grasp and retain the more difficult themes to which French and German soon led the way,—Annie would sit spellbound, drinking in not so much the man's speech as his magnetism, and through it a whole world of unspoken possibilities.

Then he would look at her curiously for a moment, abruptly call her back to the question in hand, a far-away trouble in his own eyes at the resurrection, possibly, of some ghost of past fancies that Annie's newly awakening imagination called up.

Often he thought—but never said to her,—

" Child, you are dear to me as a revelation of my lost youth and hope."

Or—" Annie, you are my one link to bind me to my old interest in all things fresh and new."

Or—" But for you, innocent child-heart, there would not be a ray of sunshine upon my lonely track, where I must forever wander in renunciation of what might have been my happiness."

Surely John Wallace was not learning to love the little country-girl he had lifted with so paternal a pity out of the stagnation of her unfulfilled dreams ? If he were, he taught himself at once that her untroubled life was not for him. If, by degrees, his heart began to yearn over her sweet and trusting face, no one ever knew. It was put, with all things else, behind the delicate mask of his habitual reticence, Annie Castlewood, like all the rest of the world, was kept on the outside.

It is to be feared that, by the side of this supreme intelligence, Annie's quondam lover Tom Hatherton will figure as a somewhat coarse-grained personage. To her own fastidiousness, which was growing acute, he seemed indeed blunt in his perceptions and stupid in his expressions.

Any approaches to love-making on his part, formerly viewed askance with a shy dubiousness, suddenly grew so distaseful to her, that it was not a difficult matter to evade their recurrence.

While Mr. Wallace's intentions were keen-edged,

gently opening to himself as with a wedge her innermost reflections, Tom's comprehension had seemed
latterly rather like the blunt end of the same instrument. And yet—who can tell which of those two
men was of pure stuff and which of base! There
was the ring of the true metal in Tom Hatherton.
All Rest-Hampton could vouch for it! As for Mr.
Wallace—well, he was very fine, and very benevolent
—and all that. But as to his devoting himself, at his
time of life—to the Squire's Nancy!—

Rest-Hampton wondered how the mother could
allow it. Was he not, after all, a stranger, and made
of different material from themselves?—A foreigner,
too! Something that Rest-Hampton questioned, in
spite of his fascination.

Whether he was good gold, or only fine brass,
Deacon Potts strongly doubted. Certain it was, he
said, the stranger was not of their faith. He never
attended their meetings, and took no part in their
Sabbath school. He went to the village church, it is
true : but, the Deacon averred, he sat abstracted and
aloof as though he heard nothing of the long discourses,
even the village choir, with Nancy Castlewood's voice
leading the treble, did not appear to impress him.
Clearly his heart was not in any of it. In the eyes
of Rest-Hampton, this was where John Wallace failed
and came short ; and he began unconsciously to bring
upon himself the antagonism of Deacon Potts and his
disciples.

CHAPTER VI.

A PHANTOM.

———" Now begins
The tenebrific passage of the tale :
How hold a light display the cavern's gorge?
How, in this phase of the affair, show truth ?"

From THE RING AND THE BOOK.

IT was a gentle afternoon in the first part of September. That tender luminousness, which haunts
the early autumn in moist climates, was veiling the
land and the sea in a transparent loveliness difficult
to be imagined by those who dwell in a less humid
atmosphere. It is this soft and translucent vaporous-
ness which makes the purple and gold of Italy so far
transcend the clear blue and green and white of
Switzerland.

It lingers about the beholder like the caress of
nature in her most sympathetic mood ; while the crisp
brightness of outline makes the beauty of drier locali-
ties stand remote from the observer, with but little
appeal to his affections. With all his sensitiveness
of temperament, John Wallace was not a sympathetic
lover of nature. Facts and not aspects made up the
interest of his life, dreamer though he was. Places
were but little to him : otherwise, how could he have
endured his thirty years in an alien land ?

I doubt if the mildness of the landscape around him,

contrasting and yet harmonizing with the restlessness
of the sea, ever occurred to him as constituting a
part of his satisfaction in life. Neither in speaking
nor in writing was he likely to refer to those mute
attractions from the outer creation which enter so
largely into the thoughts of nature's worshippers. The
greater and more vivid portion of his existence had
probably been spent among crowded scenes of intellectual and social activity ; and he had never felt a
need of affiliation with the infinite as expressed in the
animal and vegetable worlds. His natural surroundings, like his mental confines of the little sea-side
village, were but a blank—a "biding": and the
characteristics of the place were but little reflected in
his fancy. Its people, its peculiarities, its progress,
became a study to him ; with these he could in a manner identify himself.

But on this September afternoon, he felt creep
over his senses a recognition of the charm of Earth
and sea and sky. The amber haze descended upon
him and wrapped him in a spell of delight almost child-
like in its unconsciousness. He dismissed Andrews
and began walking alone upon the widespread sands,
watching the waves chase each other inland, and even
stooping now and then to pick up a shell or a shining
pebble. These he examined with a charming relish,
singular to behold in one who so seldom relaxed from
his introspective habit of mind. Thoughts and reminiscences of his early youth swept over him and there
came into his face the care-free look of a boy.

Meanwhile, some distance back from the beach,
hovering about the nearest dunes, was a figure in a

gray robe, that seemed to appear and disappear, to flit and to follow the figure of John Wallace. Any one seeing it 'for the first time might have mistaken it for a wraith—so ghostly were its movements. But any one that had seen a strange lady whose arrival had aroused the passing curiosity of the little hotel, might have recognized this gray shape as the same.

During the few days since her stay at Mr. Daggett's, she had come and gone at her will, speaking so little that the good man had several times pronounced her to the secrecy of his wife's bosom " a harmless innocent."

" She don't know no one hereabout," he commented, " and she don't come for no purpose, that I can make out."

" Maybe she wants to get up a school of some sort," suggested Mrs. Daggett, shrewdly.

" Well, why don't she begin then ? I ain't heerd of her as applyin' to nobody yet for their children."

" She's likely to pay her board, I reckon: and nothink else don't matter, as I can see," was the practical help-meet's rejoinder.

The only people about whom she had asked any question were the Castlewoods ; and she had selected for her inquiry a person who appeared to her as she had appeared to Mr. Daggett—' a harmless innocent." It was none other than old Uncle Seth himself—the village postmaster—whom she had accosted, and whose gossiping propensities were well known to the natives. Still, nothing had come of her inquiries beyond a few repetitions of them at the " post-office," as Uncle Seth thumbed over the mail.

"Squire Castlewood seems to catch all the strangers a'go'en," commented Uncle Seth.

" Oh, as for that," cried the innkeeper scornfully, " it ain't much of a catch for the squire, if the lady pays her board here, and don't do nought but philander about the street, an ask questions about the family up to The Homestead. Now that there Mr. Wallace *was* a good fish to hook ! "

" Well I reckon *we're* likely to make as good a haul from him as if he'd put up to your place, Ham Daggett," said Uncle Seth with a wily smile ; for Mr. Wallace had paid him liberally for looking after his mail. This mail was the marvel of all the idlers at the little stuffy shop of all work, where at one counter was designated in staggering capitals on the broadside of an old board, POST OFFICE. Such piles of letters and papers and pamphlets as came to Mr. Wallace swelled the sides of the hitherto attenuated mail bag : while there went forth in return, enough leretts to make Uncle Seth open his eyes in amazement and wonder " to gracious " what a body could find to write that would cover so many sheets of paper.

" And all to one chap, tew ! " he was wont to exclaim, for, sure enough, the envelopes were all alike, for they bore the same address in the same rapid literary hand :

To Mr. Roderic Clarkson Banker,
    Lothbury,
        London, E. C.,
           England.

When the female stranger had arrived, the old cronies had put their heads together over each mail that came and went, to find some food for gossip in any letter that had to do with Mrs. Williams, as Ham Daggett announced her name to be. But they looked in vain. She never appeared at the post office, nor did her name pass under Uncle Seth's snuffy thumb. Truly the strangers who came to Rest-Hampton gave these old gentlemen a deal of trouble. It is well there was no system of postal-cards in vogue, to make their burden of inspection intolerable.

To leave the gossip of these interesting fossils, with whom the village was replete, and follow the footsteps of " The Lady " in question, brings us back to the beach. After she had left the straggling houses behind, her quick walk became almost a flight. As she approached the sea, the flight grew uncertain and stealthy in its progress. Very likely she feared tramps or stragglers, for she looked furtively around. Upon perceiving the tall figure of a man upon the beach, she quickly hid herself behind the dunes.

Now this figure was only Mr. Wallace, amusing himself with the waves and the pebbles ; but it seemed to inspire her with some sort of terror. As often as she peered forth, which she frequently did, so often she shrank back as if to conceal herself from possible discovery.

An hour or two had passed since the habitually serious scholar had thrown off the burden of years and cares to conceive himself once more—a youth. The shadow had lifted from his spirit. Any one watching him casually would have called him light-hearted. As he wandered towards the dunes, stooping now and then to pick up a shell, white like a lily-petal, or pink like a roseleaf, he suddenly seemed to return to a consciousness of his entity. He passed his hand over his forehead with a weary sigh, turning his head slowly from side to side, as one looking for he knows not what.

A cloud settled upon his face ; and his eyes were fixed restlessly upon the dunes. He seemed like a person slowly rousing to the suspicion that he is under an evil spell, or in whom some miserable memories of the spot had surged up.

" If I had any belief in the supernatural," he muttered to himself, " I should say that my spirit is at this moment visited—haunted—by another spirit."

And he stood gazing into vacancy like one in a trance. Presently he roused himself and shook off the hallucination :—

" As if," he thought, with a faint smile,—" It were possible for all the miles of space between us to be traversed by an influence—or an infatuation ! "

He turned himself resolutely around, and began, solitary and thoughtful, his homeward walk.

As for the gray figure lurking among the sand-hills,—when John Wallace had stopped and changed countenance, lifting his hand to his head in bewilderment,—she had fallen into a panic, leaning forward in her hiding-place with parted lips and suspended breath, watching him with an animal intensity, that doubtless made itself felt in the mind of the unconscious object.

" Can it be," she whispered, with fierce exultation,

"that he feels my presence?—That my magnetism has even now a power over him?"

She covered her eyes with her hands as if to shut out the dangerous fire of their gaze, the blood bounding through her frame with frightful vehemence. Presently she found herself again watching the melancholy figure as a snake is said to transfix its prey.

"What did I risk it for, if not to see him- —to have him see me?" she muttered. "Oh! if I only dared to follow him—to speak to him!"

It seemed for an instant that Mr. Wallace would walk toward the dunes and discover her, so keen was his look in that direction. The possibility struck such terror to the woman that she cowered and shrank, and covered her face and turned her back upon the spell she had wrought. Then it was that the figure on the beach drew itself up majestically, as if asserting its superiority over a fanciful illusion. The next moment, as we have seen, John Wallace had turned away, and was walking towards the village. Then the woman breathed freely once more, her eyes still glittering with a baleful exultation. Furtively, like some escaped convict who believes that he is pursued, she peered out and finally stole forth. She stood, half hid by a jetting sand-bank, and watched the unwitting man. She felt that she had narrowly escaped detection, but her trepidation was momentarily swallowed up in the evil triumph that she had perceptibly dominated this creature by a secret but undeniable power. The power had acted like a flash of some electric current which she could neither explain nor command.

If there are those who will call John Wallace weak, in that he was overwhelmed unawares by the force of an unseen will, let them look closely into the psychological facts of mind acting upon mind. There may, however, be two opinions about the probability of a nameless magnetic sympathy having the directness of force to cover any considerable space. Possibly—to advocate the negative side of the question—John Wallace was not overwhelmed by the influence itself, but by a sudden resurrection of would-be forgotten things conjured up by a subtle, and to him unaccounted-for, reminder of a woman's existence in his past life. It was the rush, then, of painful reminiscences which made him pause, and press his hand to his head, rather than any spiritual cognizance of an unseen proximity.

It will be perceived, nevertheless, that Mr. Wallace possessed some singularly sensitive mental force which both acted upon others, as in the case of Annie Castlewood, and was susceptible of being acted upon, as we have seen in the present instance. That he did not more directly resist the influence, was because he was unaware of it.

So ungovernable was this woman's mental excitement, that she was wholly unaware of the going out again of the same violent force. All at once John Wallace turned sharply, looked back, and even retraced a few steps. The suddenness of the movement caused the watcher to catch her breath and rendered her, for the space of a second, wholly unable to dart out of the range of his vision.

A cold sweat broke over his brow, and he stood ir-

resolute. Any other man would have acknowledged
to himself that he had seen a phantom ; for the amber
haze had melted into the violet mists of evening,
which rendered objects far from distinct.

He remained transfixed for a palpitating moment,
and then went calmly on his way, without again looking back.

" I should be a weak fool," he said within himself,
" to think of it again."

And, there being no taint of superstition in his
blood, which had doubtless been book-cultured for
generations, he did, in fact, let the circumstance slip
from his mind. He never again, however, on the
beach or off, had in his face that beautiful look of
youth. It was gone. Something had killed it. Or,
more likely, it had long since departed, and the surprise of that lovely September afternoon had only
called up a fleeting likeness in its image.

And what became of the creature whose passionate
insistence had conjured so fatal a spell? She hung
about the dunes for an hour, in momentary fear of the
return of him she nevertheless sought. Even as
she called up the look of his clear and penetrating
eyes, with an inward fire in them which she probably
knew well, she trembled and clasped her hands over
her heart. Truly, she was in abject terror of John
Wallace. And he, during the next few days, felt, it
must be confessed, an unaccountably keen prescience
of some disturbing force at hand.

Probably if he had believed in all those soothsay-
ing phenomena of the mind, the contemplation of
which gave Mrs. Castlewood such singular pleasure,

he might have made an excellent clairvoyant, or even a so-called medium—in expert hands. For his sensitive organism was easily played upon and responded with painful acuteness to every influence. Had he been disposed to play the impostor, he might readily have claimed gifts of divination, or a foreknowledge of events. Equally, he might have been made a dupe of by those precious individuals who call themselves mind-readers, thereby filching money from the ignorant and the superstitious, had not his force of character and principle been greater than his force of temperament. The fact was, that a grey figure passed and repassed the squire's peaceful house with untiring persistence. There were nights when, unknown to any living creature, she paid stolen visits beneath the casements of those windows where Mr. Wallace, restless and sleepless, burned his midnight lamp in uneasy thought or disturbed study.

Once he fancied he heard a sound of some creature sobbing near the house. He opened his window and gazed forth into the night. All was as still as the grave, save the eternal rushing of the sea upon the shore, and the sighing of the wind through the great sheltering-trees.

" Sometimes I am weary to death of yonder moaning and restless ocean," he murmured to his own thoughts. "Sometimes I long to be land-locked by those far away hills of purple heather "——

He sighed heavily, and then paused, listening. A sigh seemed to answer him which was more human than the wailing of the wind in the distant elm-trees. Then he closed the casement and soon after lay down upon his solitary bed, wakeful and beset by a strange phantasmagoria within.

Probably that is the only time when Squire Castle-wood's house can be said to have been haunted.

Certain it was, that such a restlessness had come over the spirit of the lonely man, as to cause him to take a brief journey. This was not in any sense a retreat, for no suspicion of the truth crossed his mind. He went forth driven, as he thought, by the unquiet of his own heart ; and the shadow went with him.

CHAPTER VII.

A NEW ACQUAINTANCE.

" I want your word now ; what do you say to this ?
And what did God say and the devil say ?—

THE RING AND THE BOOK.

MR. WALLACE was going down to New York, to be
absent for a week—" on business," he said ; though
what the "business" might be, none could have told,
since a more profound ignorance than his of business matters could not well be imagined.

It was the first time he had quitted the neighborhood of Rest-Hampton since his arrival eighteen
months before. His portmanteau was made ready,
and he started on his drive to Sag Harbor to take the
boat, not in the old rumbling stage by which he had
come, but behind a pair of the squire's best horses.
Andrews was in transports at the prospect of a change ;
and the family stood at the door to bid them God-
speed.

"Bring us something first-rate when you come
back !" called the graceless boys, and with a flourish of the whip and a profusion of farewells, he was
whirled away.

There was a lady in a gray dress passing by on the
other side of the wide green lane, or was it only the

phantom of a lady in grey? At least no one noticed her.

Annie burst into tears:

"My dear," said the mother reprovingly; for she looked upon crying as an indulgence.

"I feel as if something *dreadful* were going to happen; as though he would *never* come back," sobbed the girl.

No sooner had Mr. Wallace fairly gone, than Annie Castlewood had a caller—a rare event within the village precincts. It was a tall and majestic lady, who had superb eyes and an unquestionably high-toned mien; who wore a dress of some rich gray fabric made in a stylish mode.

There was nothing more significant than "Mrs. Williams" on her card; but Annie fell deeply in love with her royal appearance and her gracious manner. Moreover, there was something a little odd or foreign in her intonation—or was it only an unusual perfection of pronunciation?—which delighted the girl's unsophisticated ear.

Mrs. Williams had come to see if Miss Castlewood did not wish to take lessons on the piano-forte: she was anxious she said, to form a music class in Rest-Hampton. Annie had no instrument, so the idea was out of the question. She was dazzled by it however, and eagerly said she would beg her father for the long promised piano "when he went to New York," a thing he had always meant to do.

"Has he not just gone?" questioned the lady.

"Oh, no!" and Annie's blue eyes opened wonderingly.

" I thought I had seen a gentleman with a portmanteau start from here as I came up the street."

" *That* was Mr. Wallace," and foolish Annie felt the scarcely dried tears spring to her eyes. She could not understand why she was so sad about Mr. Wallace's absence ; or why she would have minded if he never returned ; but——

Suddenly the young girl became conscious that her visitor was looking with unpleasant keenness into her face, and she recovered herself instantly with some pride.

" Mr. Wallace is your foreign friend of whom I have heard, I presume," she said sweetly, adding : " Has he left you permanently ? "

" Oh, no," answered Annie ; " he will be back this week."

Still the lady's questions annoyed her, and she said with less warmth :

" Will you not allow me to fetch my mother ! She will be glad to see you."

But the visitor had found out what she came to know and she arose saying with *empressement,*—

" No, my dear—I will not trouble Mrs. Castlewood. I am sorry about the piano. But at least I am glad to have met you. You will come to see me sometimes ? "

A most engaging smile beamed upon the unsophisticated maiden, who was quite enchanted with the lady's beauty and grace ; and she promised readily.

The next day Mrs. Williams returned. A new subterfuge to gain some intimacy with the family at the Homestead had struck her.

"Forgive me, my dear child, for coming after you again.   But, after I reached the hotel, I was haunted by your sweet face—you will forgive my saying it,— and I tried to think of some expedient that would bring you to me. I am very lonely, my dear, a widow and childless—I had a little daughter once who died. Don't you think you can care a little about me?" She paused gently, and Annie blushed, hold- ing her head down like the little country girl she was.

"It occurred to me," continued the lady, who had not let go of her hand, but kept stroking the pretty fingers with her own gloved ones—"that you might like to come and let me teach you how to draw and paint in water-colors. I have done a great deal of such work in my life, and found it a real pleasure. Would you like it?"

Annie assented eagerly, and Mrs. Williams went on :

"I have a pleasant little sitting-room at the—the hotel, and you could come to me every morning for an hour.   She smiled with winning sweetness, and Annie found herself gazing into the great dark eyes, en- tranced.

"I will speak to my mother, if you will excuse me," she said, running out of the room and springing up the stairs.   While she was absent, the visitor made a keen and rapid scrutiny of the apartment ; into every crack and corner she peered, but found nothing of what she sought.

"Pshaw," she muttered fiercely ; "there is no trace of him here. That pink-and-white-faced chick has the range of his apartments no doubt,—I will get it all out of her, though !—Great God," she cried, making a passionate gesture with her hands, which were locked nervously together ; "I would give ten—twenty —years of my life to spend one hour there, wherever his presence has been."

Annie returned with her mother, who met the stranger rather chillingly, and was not disposed to lend her sanction to the plan. She considered that her daughter was too easily led away by an impulse.

But Annie warmed towards the notion, and urged her long-standing desire to study painting and drawing.

"What are thy terms ? " asked the little Yankee woman with characteristic watchfulness of being taken in.

Mrs. Williams had evidently not considered that phase of the matter ; but hers was a well-schooled face that showed no surprise. She mentioned a very modest sum, and it was finally arranged that Annie should go each morning to the little village hotel.

"I should prefer that thee came here to instruct my daughter," Mrs. Castlewood argued.

"I would, gladly, madam ; but I am unable to walk any distance," the lady hastened to explain, and the other consented, reluctantly.

Annie soon became charmed with her pursuit, and found her instructor both talented and fascinating. She told the village maiden many things which delighted her and seemed not unlike the romantic climaxes of a novel, while in reality they were—or professed to be—pages from the handsome widow's own experience. Annie wondered how one person could possibly be the heroine of so many romantic situations. Moreover, she gave a good deal of information, unbeknown to herself, which the dark-eyed lady desired to obtain.

Usually, Annie had little to say about Mr. Wallace to any one ; but this charming new friend had such a frank way of claiming confidence in return for professions of ingenuousness, that the conversation generally tended upon the perfections of the one wholly interesting person whom the girl knew. With her innocent face bent over her drawing, Annie Castlewood never saw the sinister looks of hatred, or some other passion, dart from the black eyes, always drooped when she lifted her head to meet them.

Mrs. Williams made a great pet of her pupil ; and finally begged her sentimentally to wear, for her sake, a little ring which she drew with some difficulty from her own finger and placed upon Annie's.

It was a tiny serpent, coiled several times about the finger, encrusted with diamonds, and having emeralds for eyes.

That night Mr. Wallace returned.

The next morning, Annie did not carry her books as usual to the sitting-room ; and when he looked up from his writing to ask after her, the mother told him briefly the story of Mrs. Williams and the drawing lessons.

He listened politely, and then returned, without comment, to his occupations. It is a part of " the irony of fate," that we can listen calmly to something the purport of which will presently go as a dagger to our heart.

When Annie came in, flushed from the pleasure of her lesson and from the exercise of her walk, she was told that Mr. Wallace had asked for her.

"Mother, may I go up and knock at his study-door?" she asked, and gained the rare permission. Martha Castlewood was not sorry to encourage the intimacy between her lodger and daughter, but she was judicious.

Annie's timid knock was answered in the kind friendly voice she loved so well.—

"Come in Nancy."

He looked at her almost affectionately, and placed a chair for her near his own.

"And now tell me about your drawing and painting.

"Oh, I have only *just* begun," she answered blushing, and beginning to look through her drawing-book for the little sketch she was at work upon. Her naïve emphasis always amused her friend.

"It isn't *only* the lessons," she added. "O Mr. Wallace! the lady who teaches me is *so* beautiful and *so* noble!"

"How do you know that she is noble?" he was smiling indulgently upon her sweet impulsiveness.

"Oh! I *know* it! The way she carries her head, and turns her neck! why, she is like a princess."

"Have you ever seen a princess, Annie?" Mr. Wallace was laughing heartily.

"Of course not," said Annie, something abashed, "but I know how a princess *ought* to look. She should be tall, and stately, and imperious. She should have a grand air, and a majestic walk like "——

"Like the heroine in a three-volume novel, eh?"

"I *was* going to say 'like Mrs. Williams,' Annie answered, smiling merrily, and looking up with unconscious coquetry in her eyes; "but the name struck me as a *little* out of keeping."

"It is not very impressive, that is true; but majestic people cannot always have magnificent names, any more than the daughters of her majesty Queen Victoria are likely to resemble your traditional princess. Doubtless Mrs. William's husband is a painfully practical and commonplace individual."

"She hasn't any husband, she is a widow."

"Ah, indeed! That is immensely interesting. To be romantic a woman must always be a widow, both young and beautiful."

"Now you are making fun of her," Annie said, trying to look offended.

And so the banter, with which Mr. Wallace delighted to indulge himself, at the expense of the pretty and innocent young girls who came in his way, ran on, until Annie drew her finger from the book where she had placed it to mark her drawing.

Then he leaned forward with a look she did not see,—

"My child, what have you there?"

There was nothing remarkable in the tone or manner, and Annie did not perceive how ashy pale he grew; but at that instant, John Wallace's heart had ceased to beat for an instant.

Annie began to chatter about her friend, her gentleness and goodness, and the friendship she had proffered in the pledge of the ring. Mr. Wallace paused long enough for her to pass over the ring, and dilate upon the lady's charming accent. Then he spoke quietly.

"Would your mother wish you to accept a ring from a stranger, Annie?"

That was all he said.

Annie colored. Her mother had not seen the ring. Somehow, she often felt beforehand her mother's disapproval of certain things, and this intimacy did not altogether recommend itself to her from the maternal standpoint. There was nothing hypocritical about the young girl; but she simply delayed her confidences.

"I never thought of it being a *gift*," she stammered. "It is only a token of regard, don't you see? I do not mean to keep it. I shall only *wear* it."

"If I were you, I should not wear it."

Annie looked distressed,—

"What shall I say! How shall I return it without seeming to thrust her friendship back upon her!"

Mr. Wallace could not suggest that the friendship was a pretense.

"Suppose," said he, rising, "you say to Mrs. Williams that *Mr. Wallace asked you to return it.*"

Annie wondered. She could not see her companion's face, and she was too much pre-occupied to notice any peculiarity in his manner. But that her hero should condescend to express an opinion about her new friend's action was something unparalleled.

"How much longer will you take these lessons;" he inquired, after he had asked her to describe the lady's appearance, listening attentively meanwhile.

"I do not know, sir. I *thought* you would be pleased that I should learn all I can"——

Annie paused : she felt aggrieved. Also, she was disappointed ; for there is nothing so delightful to the soul of a very young girl as the friendship of an older woman who is beautiful and fascinating, especially if that friendship is delicately perfumed with fine flattery.

" Well—well " said the other gently, seeing her crestfallen look ; "go on with your painting. Only I should not wear the ring if I were in your place."

When the young girl had gone, and for an hour or two after, the lonely man paced his rooms—astounded, appalled, at the thoughts which threatened him. Not many nights before, the woman who had wellnigh bewitched him upon the beach, had spent the hours just so, pacing like some wild creature, the narrow limits of her rooms. The difference was, that her step was stealthy and leopard-like, so that the unconscious sleeper beneath heard not a sound of that sinister rustle, while Mr. Wallace's tread was slow and measured and steady. Then she had made her resolve.

" Could it be possible ? " he muttered over and over. Had the ghost of his past dared to pursue him ? was the figure in gray that flitted across his disturbed imagination on the sea shore a reality? Had she planned to tempt him anew, or did she come to contaminate the pure creature who believed in him ? —to destroy Annie Castlewood's peace and innocence? was the child to be doomed because her life touched his ? But what had induced his tormentor to flaunt that trinket—his own once gift—before his eyes ?

Doubtless she dared not seek him out; but it was a challenge that said to him,—" Come, face me."

At least he would accept. John Wallace was not a coward.

" I shall confront her. She shall not escape me," he said with stern lips : "only first the child must return that ring."

All that day and the next, Mr. Wallace kept the house. The thought of meeting face to face a phantom, gave him a feeling of suffocation. But the idea of being pursued, dogged, hounded in secret, was worse.

The next morning Annie had gone again to her painting. An unpleasant consciousness was upon her, however, and the lesson was not very brilliant. Mrs. Williams twitted her lovingly upon being *distraite*. Finally, when she could postpone her departure no longer, she offered the ring to its owner, having held it for some minutes in her hand.

" What," said that lady reproachfully ; " you are tired of my attachment so soon ? "

" Oh *no*," cried Annie distressed ; " but "—she hesitated : " Mr. Wallace *asked* me to return it to you."

She was really startled at the lightning flash which darted from her friend's brilliant eyes. Mrs. Williams at that moment perceived that she was checkmated ; moreover, she had a suspicion that she was also betrayed. Still, she controlled herself instantly, being well-used to dissimulation, and said calmly,—

" And who is this Mr. Wallace ? "

" He is an English gentleman who lives with us,"

said Annie. "I thought you knew?" she added, questioningly.

"Is he a relative?" still the sinister fire gleamed beneath the lady's eyelids. She looked not unlike an enraged wild beast, that is beautiful in spite of its subtle fury. "You know all about him, I suppose," she added sneeringly.

"No, he came to us a stranger, I think."

"That is curious. I wonder," mused the lady as if to herself, "if he can be an impostor—or a criminal——"

"Mrs. Williams!" cried Annie starting forward with her face ablaze, "you must *not* say such a thing as that: Mr. Wallace is a *friend*—of my father's."

"And yours? Is it not so, Mignon?"

There was something so insinuating in the speech that Annie drew back uncomfortable:

"Yes—of *mine*, also," she replied simply.

"You are a wonderful child, Annie," the lady murmured after watching her stealthily for a few seconds:

"You ought to be very proud of the friendship of such a man. Do you not know that he is a great intellectual light—a person of high degree——"

Annie was looking in undisguised amazement, and the lady stopt abruptly.

"You know him then, Mrs. Williams?"

"Only by what you have told me," she answered calmly, changing, for some reason, her tactics: "He is a Scotchman, I think you said?"

"An Englishman," corrected Annie.

"Ah?—the name is quite Scotch; you know that."

If all these suggestions were intended to convey

doubts to Annie Castlewood's mind, they were entirely unheeded. Her trust in Mr. Wallace could not be shaken. Moreover, Mrs. William's manner perplexed her. She seemed to scintillate with a dangerous fire that made her appearance nervous and her laugh hysterical.

Annie turned to leave.

"Good-by," she said, looking wistfully at the handsome and imperious face, which was more dazzling than usual with its suppressed passion. She was oppressed with a thought that the new interest she had found was closing against her. And to the proscribed circle of village life, a new interest was a boon.

That afternoon, Mr. Wallace and Andrews resumed their accustomed walk.

He was gravitating towards a, to him, tremendous climax or *denouément :* and the calmness of the Rest-Hampton routine smiled in his face with that mock interest which only nature and the unconsciousness of friends can oppose to the violence of our own concealed emotions.

All that came of the impression which Mrs. Williams made upon Annie Castlewood was that the girl asked suddenly one day,—

"Aren't you an Englishman, Mr. Wallace?" and he had answered simply,—

"No I am Scotch-born."

She had wondered all day at Mrs. William's perception, but, somehow, she never told it. Unconsciously, she, too, was learning reticence.

CHAPTER VIII.

IN A GRAVEYARD.

" It is a thorny question and a tale
Hard to believe, but not impossible
Here has a blot surprised the social blank,—
Whether through favor, feebleness, or fault
No matter—leprosy has touched our robe."

THE RING AND THE BOOK.

TRUTH is sometimes like fiction, in that a life often pauses in its smooth career, coming into sudden collision with an object or a person totally unlooked for and not to be accounted for in the ordinary run of events.

Walking dreamily along the pleasant highway, that evening towards. dusk, Mr. Wallace raised his head without an apparent cause ;—unless those inexplicable impulses called attractions may be named as reasons for action. His eyes did not rove absently, as is usually the way with a person in motion who looks up without a motive. Clearly, whatever influence had called outward his introspective gaze, the softness of the landscape had nothing to do with it.

He was walking towards the south burying-ground, and straight as an arrow to its mark his glance shot on ahead, and fastened for an instant upon a scarcely discernible shape at the far end of the street.

It was a tall, slender figure that seemed to flit rapidly along with a certain indefiniteness of purpose ; for it had crossed several times from one side of the road to the other, like a startled creature who was in doubt of the way. It was making one of those sudden changes of direction when the scholar's glance marked its outline. Perhaps there was a backward glance in response ; for the figure hesitated a moment, and then seemed to plunge into the hollow from which the hillside graveyard sloped gently up.

"Andrews," said Mr. Wallace, turning calmly to his companion, who was absorbed in speculating about a flock of birds, "you may return. I shall finish my walk alone."

After taking a few steps forward he paused by the roadside, looking off towards the unseen but never-forgotten sea. It may be that, in spite of his grand and silent mien, he was endeavoring to collect his faculties for a strange encounter.

"Lord bless him," muttered Andrews to himself, catching a last glimpse of him still standing there, as he crossed to have a chat with Ben Adams, leaning idly over his fence, the day's work at the forge being over.

"Your pard's a mighty queer chap," volunteers that direct individual, indicating with his smudgy thumb, the thoughtful figure in the distance.

"D'ye think so ? Perhaps he is, if 'mighty queer' means too good for this world," says Andrews.

"Heow be he better'n most ?" grunts Ben, his mind not capable of nice distinctions.

"Any fool but you could see how he's better than

the people around here," cries the valet who is invariably riled by the blacksmith's obtuseness.

"Wall, now—what wages do he pay?" Ben's head is on one side in an aggravating way.

"Dash your impudence," mutters Andrews *sotto voce*.

He would have liked well enough to parade before the lubber's eyes what he knew would have appeared to him an enormous compensation; but it bordered too closely upon his master's own affairs to be safe in Ben's dubious keeping.

"He pays me more than you ever got your fist around," says he, then dropping suddenly to Ben's level, —"I say, though, who is that spirited-looking woman that's come to the hotel? She's powerful handsome, but lonesome, like."

Ben shook his head. His curiosity was of that dull description which needs to be actively appealed to by a present demand, and like his other mental efforts, never went out of its way for a job. Just here, Uncle Seth came ambling up, and joined in the blindman's holiday palaver.

"Here's 'un what knows," remarked Ben, taking his pipe from between his teeth and grinning, " he kin tell a sight more 'bout folks an they ever knowed theirselves."

"What's to pay, now, gentlemen?" asks the sprightly octogenarian. He wore queer old breeches and a long-tailed coat "all buttoned down before." Moreover, he wore the old-school manner with his ancient apparel, both of which he cultivated with great assiduity.

" I was asking," begins Andrews with an air of patronage which he could not help bestowing upon the fossils of the village——"who that tall female may be that's turned up lately at Daggett's."

" That ? "—Uncle Seth produced with a flourish his grandfather's snuff-box, and took a friendly pinch, which he did not appear to relish, but practised to be in keeping with his conception of a fine old-style gentleman.

"That is *another* mysterious stranger, Mr. Andrews."

The emphasis was so marked, and the significance of his nod at Andrews was so obvious, that the valet reddened visibly, but made a pretence of unconsciousness. Ben roared. It will be seen that Andrews' path had a thorn now and then.

" Dash them both," he thought, but only said :

"Mysterious, is she ? All strangers are mysterious in this dead-and-gone-to-seed place, I should fancy. You must get precious tired of the old ways, you see."

Ben glared, but left the defence of his people in the hands of Uncle Seth's wisdom, which spoke,—

" No—I'm not tired of 'em. The folks at Rest-Hampton is considerable of a study. There's a great deal in human nature, Mr. Andrews, besides mysteries."

He cocks one eye at the discomfited valet, who is on his guard by this time.

" What brings 'em here, any way ? " grunts Ben uncompromisingly. " Nobody don't want 'em."

" Who ? strangers ?—oh, ask Mr. Andrews, he may

know," and Uncle Seth gives Ben a sly wink, which
it is needless to say, is lost on that individual.

" They're no account, only to upset our ways," he
continues, for he has been drinking, and is therefore
very cross.

" What a lumbering idiot you are, Adams," cries
Andrews contemptuously. " If you had half a notion
about improvement and that, you'd see that Mr. Wallace has done more to help this dead-and-rotten town
up a bit, than all your old dunderhead villagers put
together. Your ways, indeed ! " with terrible scorn.
" I'd like to know what ways you've got, except to
stand still and let the world get ahead of you."

Ben took his pipe slowly from his mouth, and spat
with great deliberation in dangerous proximity to Andrews' dapper boots, which made that person skip to
one side with his favorite " dash you " under his
breath.

" That's just what we don't want—'improvin'.' "

" No, no, Mr. Ben," puts in the elderly oracle, who
feels that his opinion is law in the village, and of
weight even with persons of the surly smith's type ;
" Let us be just, Mr. Ben. I admit that this Mr.
Wallace has imparted many ideas which have been of
advantage to our society "——

" Can he tell me a better way to shoe a horse or
draw on a tire ? " interrupts Ben angrily, " what I
want is to be let alone ; " and a blow from his sledge-
hammer fist makes the rickety fence totter.

" There is no use talking to such a dashed, whiskey-
soaked old grampus," mutters Andrews, going off in
a rage, being joined by the wise man of the village.

"Don't mind Benjamin, Mr. Andrews," says the fossil condescendingly, " he is a person of very limited intelleck. Now *I* like the addition of strangers to our more select circles "—for Uncle Seth belonged to an ancient family, (quite extinct excepting himself and several dozens of gravestones), and was admitted with the freedom of country tolerance, into the houses of what Rest-Hampton called the best society.

" I consider," he proceeds,—snuff-box in hand for its effect,—" that the presence of so fine a scholard man among us is a genuine benefit ; and I hope," eyeing his companion sidewise, " that he is going to remain up to the squire's ultimously ? "

The rising inflexion at the end of this sentence was lost upon Mr. Andrews, who returned to the original topic of discussion.

" But the other stranger, Mr. Seth—the lady. Come now, a mysterious lady ought to interest a gay bachelor, like yourself." Andrews looked prodigiously knowing, and the old fogy smirked in a way that nearly made the other explode with suppressed laughter.

" O don't, now, Mr. Andrews ! My time for encouraging the ladies is over. I used to fancy them, once. There was Betsey Price, now, Josiah Hatherton's wife as is—she and I took a great shine to each other. But Lud, sir, the girls always snapped so quick, I had to hold back—and Hatherton got ahead of me someway. But it's just as well," pursued the old gentleman airily. " Marriage is a vexin' state, Mr. Andrews. A woman now, has no respeck for ancient customs, and always wants a man to change the style of his neckcloth." This was said to attract the valet's attention to that superannuated article of attire. He felt called upon to compliment the wearer on its good form, which led to such a dissertation upon the sanctity and inviolability of obsolete fashions, that they had reached the door of the little post-office before he had more than half got through. In parting, Uncle Seth dropped his voice to a sepulchral whisper,—

"These garments, Mr. Andrews, is the secret of my influence in this community. They impart to my appearance the venerableness and dignity that I desire to cultiwate. This coat was my grandfather's, likewise, these breeches. In the eyes of my fellow citizens, Mr. Andrews, I represent my grandfather, who was a great scholard."

By this time, Andrews, who felt himself considerably bored with the history of a man who aped his grandfather, nodded a good-day, and disappeared in search of livelier companionship at the little Inn. His time hung rather heavily on his hands, and it was a constant source of regret that his master had no expensive luxuries such as horses, and hunting gear for him to take pride in.

"What a pity that he doesn't hunt," he mused. "Though what there is to find in this God-forsaken place I couldn't say—unless it is the natives!"

Andrews, it will be seen, felt somewhat belligerent towards the place and people about him. He mused on :

"Or if he would race, for instance—only it would have to be with plough horses and meeting-house hacks. Oh, dear!" he groaned, "if people here only knew enough to have a bit of running now and then, one might stand the rest. Fine horses, too, those of Squire Castlewood's. And the Ley's and the Cruddle's! To think of their dawdling along at that churchyard gait! It's as bad as a funeral to see them. Dash'd, but I wish I had a couple of thorough-breds!" and Andrews sighed heavily over his pot of ale.

But what has become of Mr. Wallace, whom we left pausing meditatively by the green roadway?

The shadows of evening are gathering about him as he stands with his noble head bared to the peace-fully falling twilight, and the gathering dew. Then— Andrews and the old postman having strolled up the street, and Ben Adams lounged back to the shadow of his doorway,—he covers his head and walks steadily forward. He has the suddenly aroused look of a man alert for a purpose. Presently he reaches the South-end burying-ground, and passes over the stile and among the crumbling old tombstones. He does not halt to mark the soft gloom of the spot, but with a keen glance sweeps the enclosure, and then comes, with a few rapid steps, face to face with the gray shape that starts up, stretches out a trembling arm, and then shrinks back.

The power which this woman seemed to have held over his unconsciousness utterly forsakes her, when confronted with the man himself.

The two figures face one another with a long, chill, unrelenting gaze, like two Fates who have crossed each others' paths. Not a vestige of his accustomed gentleness is in John Wallace's face or voice when he speaks, which he does in a hard, dry tone :

" Why did you follow me ? "

" I was driven to do it," answered the other Fate, in a voice of forced coldness that matched his own.

" What do you expect to gain ? "

" Nothing—only to be near you."

" It was to be rid of you that I have given up my home, my position, my kindred, my fortune."

The other bowed her head upon her hands and moaned, rocking to and fro.

" I ask again, what do you expect to come of this pursuit ? "

" Nothing—nothing "—moaned the shape.

" Then go back to where you came from. . Go back and hide in your unhappy bosom that you ever tracked me here."   He stood with his long arm out-stretched, and his thin hand pointing towards the sea, an awful embodiment of the unrelenting destiny that was to overwhelm that other destiny.   She raised her head, and once more confronted him.

" I——cannot ! It has been a slow death ever since —I seem—to have died and been buried—and this is my unlaid ghost that has followed you."

Her voice was choked and terrified, his was stern and calm :

" Go back to your grave, then.   Did you think you could tempt me—even if you came from the dead ? "

She moaned again, and wrung her hands,—

" I do not wish to tempt you : only to see you."

" You shall not see me.   I will escape from you. Unless you give up this pursuit, we shall be wanderers over the earth—you seeking, I evading; I, a phantom, you, a shadow. It is decreed."

"Oh," she moaned, twisting her fingers together in anguish, "you are hard still. Cold and hard—the same."

"The same," he echoed drearily.

"Are you still a maniac!" she cried, a sharp terror vibrating in her unearthly voice: "Is the same madness still upon you, that you cast out happiness—and me? What harm that I have done or could do is deserving of an eternal retribution like this?"

"Sin."

Only one word; but it had a long muffled reverberation, that seemed to arise from the deserted graves at their feet and mock them. She covered her face again and swayed like one in bodily torment.

"I never sinned!" broke from the shuddering lips, "Was it a sin to love—to long "—

"It was a sin."

If a sound from the darkening heavens had smote upon her, levelling her to the earth, the figure could not have cowered to the ground in greater terror of him who stood and accused her.

"What must I do?" she wailed, stretching her arms upward, and casting her terrified gaze upon his face, its sternness fixed upon her like a marble mask. All else seemed to fade and melt into obscurity but that one cold, white face: "what must I do?"

"Go—and repent."

The woman sprang to her feet. A new passion seemed to sweep over her terror and her abasement.

"Who are *you*," she cried, "that you dare stand

there like an avenging angel!—were you never human? had you no weakness."

"I have been tempted," came more gently from the white set lips, "but I was kept from falling. And yet I must shrive my soul from the memory of what has been. Not for myself, it is for you that I must repent! I have not sinned, excepting that the accursed tie which binds us has made me a beholder of your sin. I could not betray you, and so my life is one long penance!——It is I—I—who must forever make atonement for the secrets of your life, woman! I have renounced all—all. I must shrive my soul."

Something gurgled in the throat of the man, and a faint red stain came upon his lips, and even tinged the front of his garments. He caught hold of a tall slab, as though he felt dizzy, and needed support.

The cadence of that broken sentence had been in his own natural voice, its pathos making still lovelier its mellow tone. It seemed to smite anew the broken chords of the woman's heart; for she flung herself towards him, clasping his arm with her passionate hands and sobbing,—

"Be merciful to me, Love! Don't drive me away! I will never speak to you or seem to see you! Only let me be near you "——

His grasp was like steel, as he unfastened her hands and tore himself from her embrace.

"My God!" burst from him, with an echo of the terror that had possessed her.—"After all my expiation, has it come to this?"

She hung upon his accents, uncertain if he were tempted, or if he scorned her.

" Are you mad ? " he panted. " Do you think I could live, and breathe the same air with you ? "

He seemed to totter, and fell rather than sat upon one of the neighboring horizontal slabs, pressing his hands to his head. The movement struck upon that pity never wholly crushed in a woman's nature, however distorted and torn.

"Oh," she moaned, "do *you* suffer—you ? And you are not hard ? You *feel?* "

She fell upon her knees, and began stroking the relaxed hands and the drawn face, over which she could detect a deadly pallor, even at that late hour.

John Wallace struggled to his feet and cast her off ; but not in anger ; for he stood gazing at her with an infinite answering pity. They were no longer two Fates, but two palpitating human beings who had somehow fatally ruined each other's lives. Their aspect, at this moment, was so startlingly similar, that any one who saw would have named them brother and sister.

" Yes, I, too, suffer. Can the past be undone or forgotten ? When I cease to suffer, I shall have expiated. I shall be lying asleep among these mossy stones— unless you drive me forth to be an exile, even from this lonely corner of the world."

" Not here "—she sobbed, though her eyes were tearless, " not here ! not forever ! Some time you will return ? "

" Never. This is my home,—unless, I repeat, you stay here to drive me again into the homeless world."

" No—oh, no ! Only say you do not hate me ; and I will go back—go back."

" When will you go ? "

" To-morrow."

" Will you swear to me never to trouble me again! Never to seek for me ? Never to follow me with a thought ? "

" I swear," she articulated, while for her the tombstones, the earth, the sky, seemed slowly to revolve about her head.

" Then, I do not hate you, I "——he broke off—and stood regarding her with a fixed intensity, which she returned with passionate fervor. It had grown so dark that they felt rather than saw, each other's looks.

" One thing more," she implored, creeping nearer to him, and groping to reach his hand, or his arm,—anything in that slowly reeling world :—" You must write to me. I cannot keep my oath unless you write to me."

" Then I will write."

A silence followed. The world was beginning to reel faster, and only the woman's will kept her conscious. Suddenly she started forward with a smothered cry : for the other figure seemed to turn away as though in that look he had taken his last farewell.

" Oh ! you are *not* going that way ! You will say good-by to me ! "

He paused, but did not come towards her. In the darkness, and with the earth reeling about her, she could not find him with her groping hands.

" Good-by."

" Nothing more—nothing tenderer ? Oh love ! "

She flung out her arms with a supplicating gesture. Her utterance was agonized pleading. She stumbled over the graves, for he seemed to recede from her.

"No" he answered solemnly: "nothing tenderer :" and his voice came to her as from a great distance.

He receded more and more from her straining gaze that sought to penetrate the uncertain gloaming, and to steady the reeling earth.

"Love," she called again, "Love—O Love!" Her voice was only a whisper ; but she did not know it. She was staggering about like a besotted creature ; but she did not know it.

All she knew was that he had gone. Had he vanished into the mist? Had he sunk into the ground? or had the darkness only covered him from her gaze? Then the rocking of the elements about her grew palpable. She fell prone upon a dew-drenched mound, and lay for hours in the deepening night—a crushed and dishevelled creature.

At first she moaned, and moaned.

"Not that way! Come back—for an instant, if only to tell me that you live—that you forgive me "— Then the sentences trailed off into incoherent fragments and moans. The rocking of the earth, the reeling of the sky, had obliterated, at last, her struggling consciousness.

Once a warm breath upon her cheek, and a tender touch partly roused her; she faintly articulated— "Come back—speak to me—once more!" And all fell into silence again.

The hours passed as serenely as though no creature lay in that deserted spot, save only the long-ago dead amid their dust.

Something rubbed her cheek again, and she started up, shivering with cold, startled to find herself lying in a flood of moonlight, bathed in dew.

It was a gentle ewe that had roused her, one of the denizens of the place, and she threw her arms around its woolly neck, sobbing upon its patient face.

She got up, shaking as with an ague, and hurried as best her cramped limbs would carry her, back to the little hotel.

It was barely half past ten o'clock, and the door was still open. She slipped unseen to her room, and when she had somewhat composed her wild aspect, she summoned her landlady, and said in answer to her curious look,—

" I find I must return to New York at once, Mrs. Daggett. Will you see that the early stage stops for me !" and she shut her door upon the glib remarks on the woman's tongue, who tossed her head outside, and grumbled at so sharp a warning.

" Folks needn't be so snappish," she muttered ; "and as for waitin' till the middle of the night to tell a body they're goin'—I've got my opinion of such manners !"

The next morning, when Annie Castlewood came slowly in for her lesson, she received with several chapters of comment from Mrs. Daggett, a little note faintly scented and daintily written.

Mrs. Williams was called home very suddenly. She was sorry, indeed, not to see her little friend again, and would not forget her, etc.

Annie walked thoughtfully away, in the midst, it must be confessed, of Mrs. Daggett's tirade, thereby increasing greatly that good woman's wrath against "airy folks of all sorts."

She met Mr. Wallace on the threshold.

"Mrs Williams had gone home," she said, and passed into the house.

Of the scene in the graveyard ; of the fact of a link between the soon-forgotten " Lady " and John Wallace, no creature, save himself, ever guessed. For to Rest-Hampton, there was in him still *no mystery*. They had not seen his shadow.

CHAPTER IX.

ANNIE AND HER LOVER.

" He is ordained to call and I to come."
——THE RING AND THE BOOK.

As the tenor upon the operatic stage must needs, for harmony, play love to the soprano, so should the hero of a novel take the part of lover to the heroine. But fate would have it that the village maiden's hero was not her lover. The history of John Wallace is a tale which had passed its mid-day climax before Time had written the first word of the romance of Annie Castlewood. Life is not always heedful of harmony.

  * * * * * *

Tom Hatherton, Rest-Hampton said, was in every respect a most estimable fellow. If his late appearance upon the scene puts him in a somewhat unimpressive light, it is because he is necessarily placed in contrast with Annie Castlewood's vague and impossible ideals.

There is nothing, perhaps, more at variance with the over-fine sentiments of a visionary young girl, than the matter-of-fact sense of an unimaginative young man, especially if he be country born and bred. For, in spite of its town-meetings and its air of organization, the atmosphere of Rest-Hampton was that of the country. Life there was almost pastoral, and under the touch of a transcendental novelist might have been converted into an idyl.

But the purpose of this rather psychological study being merely to set forth the outward workings of a never-fathomed character—that the reader may join hands with those who loved but never quite comprehended, John Wallace——it moves like a quiet brook through the pleasant fields, and old orchards, beside the low roofs of the village.

If, here and there, it reflects a face beside that of him for whom we trace it, let it be remembered that he did not live apart as a misanthrope or a recluse, but that he was warm of heart and dwelt—after a fashion, at least—among his fellows, whose images must, therefore, blend sometimes with his own, upon the surface of the story. If, often, the way seem remote, or the murmuring of the brook to grow tiresome, listen awhile, dear reader, and you will hear again, above its inarticulations, the voice of that good and pure man, who stood before the world and—so far as the world could judge—knew no guile.

Those who went down that human current, keeping peace with the lovely and lofty character of the stranger, were seldom puzzled with his intrinsic qualities. It remained for those who never saw him to question his motives, to suspect his integrity. Only Annie Castlewood was given to analytics, in the fresh and feeble fashion of one who has never been taught in books or in society to say "I doubt." And the mother, in a dry, dull way, wondered sometimes over the hieroglyphics which she saw impressed upon the man's life, and would have secretly deciphered them, never thinking to evolve a plausible fiction out of the barrenness of her knowledge of John Wallace, but merely to read his riddle.

     *   *   *   *   *   *

Three years have gone since the advent of the stranger in Squire Castlewood's family, and Annie is no longer a child, save to him. She has developed into one of those "highly cultivated, intelligent, and refined women" of whom, says Mrs. Stowe, "New England possesses a great many." She was thoughtful and conscientious, kind and charitable ; delicate in her feelings, but honest in her opinions. Moreover, she was beautiful, with a beauty difficult to sketch.

The strong yet delicate outlines of Mr. Wallace's face come out sharply, like a profile in a cameo. Squire Castlewood is not a difficult subject, with his old-school manners and his jovial face. The little Quaker woman's appearance could be described by a kindly touch or two. But Annie's was one of those characters called by a modern writer "irridescent" : and this luminous quality was reflected in the varying expressions of her brow and lips, and the changeful color of her eyes. These latter were of a calm and serene blue, as to actual tint ; but that described them no more than the word "straight" suggested the outline of her nose.

The dark yet delicate brows took what might hyperbolically be called a straight curve across the most expressive of foreheads ; and her mouth had that exquisite sensitiveness which made you forget to complain that the red line of lips was scarcely full enough for beauty. Her tint was like a pink pearl ; you only knew it had any color when you compared it with dead white complexions. For the rest, she was of medium height and extreme slimness ; but moved always with the peculiar springing motions which belong to a few gifted creatures, and which entirely preclude any notion of stiffness or bonyness.

To return to Tom Hatherton,—since this chapter must needs do penance in descriptions—he was as I have said, a fine fellow. You would have loved him for a certain openness of countenance and frank boyishness of manner, which may not be of interest in that artless animal, the boy, but have their fascination in a man,—suggesting a certain bloom and freshness of life that go with good health and good will and youth.

The village maidens thought Tom a splendid creature, and admired the direct gaze of his merry eyes far more than they fancied Mr. Wallace's dreamy and middle-aged intensity. Indeed, if the two came up for contrast at all, which happened sometimes, when the squire's Nancy and her chances were under discussion, Tom came out with flying colors as a youth of good prospects and taking appearance ; while the other—well there were those, (silly young things of course), who called the grave scholar a pedagogue and a prig. That there could be any question of preference between the two, seemed ridiculous : if, indeed, either of them really wanted Nancy Castlewood. There was much doubt about that. There always is a doubt about the intention of gentlemen towards

other ladies in the minds of young women, however
certain they may wish their own opportunities to
appear.

Tom's relationship towards Annie had grown of
late to justify the scepticism bestowed upon it. The
old intimacy which he had given with a very honest
purpose and she had accepted tacitly as the only
thing in her way, fell away—first to a fitful friendship, then to a merely unsatisfactory acquaintance.

Tom had had stormy fits of remonstrance at times,
which did little to make the tie pleasanter ; for Annie
hotly resented any allusion to Mr. Wallace as the disturbing cause of their slackening friendship ; or, in
fact, as the possible cause, however remote, of any
event in her probable outlook.

"It is only that I have *out-grown* him," she said
apologetically to herself ; but there were seasons in
which she regretted dimly that she was losing her
boyish lover, and not replacing his affection with anything definite. Still, it offended her for Tom to speak
his mind, which he had seldom done lately.

At last the time came when it appeared to the
honest fellow that he must talk plainly. Perhaps
this determination was precipitated by the echoes of
gossip which rang in his ears. They seldom reached
the hearing of Annie herself, who lived on the outside of the village chatter.

"Look here, Nancy," he cried, blustering into the
old-fashioned sitting-room at the Homestead, with his
usual breeziness. " What's all this talk I hear about
you and Mr. Wallace ? "

" Indeed *I* cannot tell you," Annie replied with

dignity ; and her face did not change color as it might have done in the first few months of her hero-worshipping.

" Oh, you can't, can't you ! " Mr. Tom ejaculated, getting excited in a minute ; " well, I can ! They say you are flirting with him."

" Do they ? "

" And what's more they say he makes love to you on the sly."

" Then they *lie !* " and Annie's eyes blazed upon her mistaken swain.   To vilify John Wallace was not the way to win her favor.

Tom whistled.   Annie rarely used strong expressions such as were common with the villagers, having " dropped all hearty talk   when she   took to being a scholar," Tom had grumbled in great umbrage at the change in his sweetheart's habits after the appearance of the new planet in her sky.   He was, therefore, somewhat mollified upon succeeding in arousing her to an old-fashioned expression of disapproval.

" They say," he went on less fiercely, " that he reads heathen love songs to you by the hour."

Annie laughed in spite of herself.

" Poor Goethe !—a heathen ; Oh my townsmen ! " she cried softly.

" Well," demanded the other, " doesn't he ? Didn't Deacon Potts come in and catch him at it, only the other evening ? "

" And if he does—what is that to Deacon Potts— or to *you* ? "

Tom winced ; but he was bent upon a disclosure,—

"Just answer if he doesn't, Nancy."

"He *happens* to be reading German poetry to me just now—Goethe and Heine—and reads it until I think I am listening to one of Beethoven's Sonatas."

"Oh, you do!" such expressions gave annoyance to Tom's material soul at the best of times.

"Yes," Annie went on, her enthusiasm rising not towards her hearer but her theme; "and his *voice* is a rapture, only so hushed, so tender."

"The devil it is!" and Tom jumped up angrily, knocking over his chair; "I should like to know what right he's got to a tender voice. What does he mean by it? Does he mean business? Or is he fooling, as I've heard city chaps are fond of doing when they get hold of a country lass—especially when they're old enough to be her grandfather!"

Annie's color burned uncomfortably, but she saw it was best to explain matters:

"You should not be so violent, Tom," she said drily. "The tender voice is not for *me*. It is for the poetry; and besides, whatever it means, or whatever he means, it is not for *you* to question. *I* am mistress of my own situations."

Tom was aghast. A final rupture seemed pending.

"Great Heavens! Annie," he cried penitently, "don't talk in that hard, cold way. Don't let that man come between us—any longer."

"*He* has not come between us, Tom; it is your *hatred* of him that has come between us."

"I believe it is," cried the honest fellow, a sensation rising in his throat which would have caused a great burst of tears not many years before: "Oh,

Annie; I believe I am jealous of him, and that it is he and not I, who is worthy of you."

"There is no question of his worthiness," said Annie, gently stifling an unborn sigh in the depths of her heart. "It is I—we—who are not worthy of him. I often think of the old Bible phrase; '*whose shoe-latchets I am not worthy to unlace!*' Mr. Wallace has no thought of us and our ways, Tom. I think he sees us somehow as figures moving through a play upon the stage, and a poor enough comedy, too."

"Why do you think such things about him, Nancy, as if he were a god ?"

"Because I see his life, and it is without fault."

"But surely he's not better than your own good, kind father."

"He is of a higher and rarer type, Tom, than any creature here."

"Tell me what you mean," said Tom humbly, "what does he do ?"

Annie smiled,—

"It is not so much what he *does*. There is nothing awful or mysterious about that. Besides his long walks, and his visits among the poor, and his teaching the fishermen at Three-Mile-Harbor, and the sailors once a week at Sag Harbor——"

"And reading to you Annie," interpolates Tom, reproachfully.

"Yes—and teaching *me*," said Annie quietly, "who am as far still from his standard as those poor ignorant fishermen ; besides the thousand and one things you all see him do, and the heaps upon heaps of letters he writes, he sits and ponders a great deal, as though he weighed problems in his mind which he could not quite solve."

"What's wonderful or useful in that?" asked Mr. Tom, not impressed.

Annie went on, not noticing the interruption,—

"He reads much in old books whose tongues are unknown to me—*Sanskrit*, I take them to be, but most of all, he writes letters."

"Who does he write to, in Heaven's name?" cried Tom appalled.

"I do not know?"

"Why don't you look?"

Annie's cheeks flushed,—

"Do you mean why do I not look at the *addresses?*"

"Of course. What else could I mean?"

"I have seen some of them lying on his table when I go into his study to dust of a morning. I have never read the directions in full, for I think he prefers having his affairs to himself. But the name on them seemed to be Mr. Roderic Clarkson."

"And does he get as many as he writes?"

Tom was growing interested in the practical workings of such an eccentricity.

"I *think* he does. They come every mail, but always in large outer envelopes addressed in the same handwriting, as if they were forwarded from some one point. And yet," added Annie thoughtfully, "they seem to be the only threads that hold him to a past world that would else slip from his grasp."

"How did you make it all out, Nancy?" queried Tom, not without admiration.

" It *came* to me—from living near him, and seeing
things as they happen."

" Don't he talk about what he's studying over ? "

" Never. He speaks sometimes of the books he
reads ; but only when his suggestions seem likely to
benefit some one."

" Don't he ever tell you of the people that write to
him ? "

" Never a word. He burns the letters in his fire
as soon as he has read them."

" A waste of stationery, I should say. But don't he
speak of his home, or his folks ? "

" He has never mentioned them."

" Kind of aggravating, ain't it ? "

Tom's crude comment jarred visibly upon Annie's
sensitive nerves, which were growing more susceptible
every day. An observer,—who did not count for much
the higher culture of the soul, and the finer possibilities which accompany such culture,—might have
said that John Wallace's wisdom was unfitting his
young *protégé* for her daily life in a work-a-day and
never very sympathetic community.

" I say though, Nancy ; you're a heap changed,"
broke in Mr. Tom upon her revery, after having contemplated her sidewise with a lugubriously wistful
expression.

"Am I ?" dreamily.

" Yes you are less like yourself, and more like your
Mr. Wallace, every day."

" *Like Mr. Wallace !* " Annie was roused from her
dream and sat staring incredulously at Tom.

The girl looked at that moment too winning not to

attract admiration. She sat with her hands lying
loosely, one upon the other, palms upward, in her lap.
Her head, with its smooth bands of golden brown
hair, finished with a heavy coil low upon the neck,
was a little to one side with that bird-like aspect a
modern writer describes as " half posed for rest, half
poised for flight."   Her soft eyes, too, had looks like
birds flying to the light.   It was her favorite attitude,
and very likely the one in which she sat and caught
eagerly at the rare thoughts of her instructor on many
a pleasant summer morning and long winter evening
in the pretty sewing-room of the Homestead.   The
mother came and went in summer, through the always
open door that led into the song-filled orchard.   And
in the winter nights, when the wind swept about the
farmhouse and the sound of the sea was heavy upon
the sands, the two students were often wrapped in
that oblivion of all else only known to boon spirits in
intercourse—whether of the intellect, or of the affections—which prevented their even hearing the somewhat dull prosing of the elder people, or the conten-
tions of the boys.

She sat so now, distractingly pretty and unconscious, gazing upon Tom :

" How do you *mean* that I am like Mr. Wallace ? "
she questioned slowly, having a dim idea that whatsoever this unimaginative intelligence perceived must
have an existence.

" I don't say how I mean, or that I mean anything
particular.   I'm not one of the fellows that's always
meaning something."   Tom was affronted at Annie's
sparkling look.

" Do you think I *talk* like him ? " Annie asked, keenly interested in the pursuit of her theory.

" Well, yes, I don't know but I do," Mr. Tom assented, vernacularly. "You use big words, and always seem to be having something on your mind besides what a body's saying to you." Tom's tone had a personal grievance in it.

Annie laughed merrily.

"If that is all, it's a very faint resemblance," she said.

" Oh," persisted Tom, not liking his remarks to be taken too lightly, "that's not all. You walk about in a moony sort of way, and—I declare to you, Nancy, *you actually look like him.* And I'm not the first to say so ! so there ! "

" I ? "

Annie started up and stood on tiptoe, facing the quaint old mirror that extended its two or three feet of height along the mantel-shelf. Apparently, the face she was comparing with her own eager one was not difficult to conjure up. One might have supposed it to be delineated upon the glass, to have heard her accurate description of it.

"Straight brow ; straight nose ; wonderful dark eyes ; complexion clear and pale ; mouth large and firm ; jaw square but delicate—mine is not at all like *that*," she said disappointed.

" Oh don't now," cried Tom impatiently, " I didn't say it was the color of your eyes, or the shape of your nose. It's the way you look."

Annie relapsed into her old attitude, and pondered with a lovely light in her eyes. Could it be that she had so absorbed what was granted her of this lofty nature that she—plain Annie Castlewood—had caught something of its aspect ? something of that ineffable charm which shone from the face she knew so well ?

"But," thought Annie reprovingly: "even if it *were* so, and Tom sees something he mistakes for a likeness, it is only a reflection after all : the original is a power."

Tom Hatherton, it seemed, was not the only villager who had noticed, or fancied, the resemblance between the squire's Nancy and his boarder. It might be, they tattled among themselves, that this Mr. Wallace, whose business nobody seemed to know was some kin to the mother, (who being a stranger to the place was frequently suspected of having mysterious kin, either creditable or otherwise according to the provocation of the moment). Suppose he should turn out to be an uncle, or a rich cousin, come in disguise, to study the ways of his folks before he revealed himself ! Of course if he were, he meant to make Nancy his heiress, since it was with her he took such pains.

And even if he were not any kin, mightn't he take a notion to leave his money to Nancy anyway ?—who knows !

Tom had kept these things in his heart, having picked them up among the confidences of the neighbors' daughters ; but neither Squire Castlewood nor his family was made a party to the country gossip. Indeed, they had never been very intimate in the village, occupying as they did, the doubtful ground of being " better than most."

"Well," said Tom, almost roughly, "you seem to be mighty glad."

"I *should* be glad, if I thought it might ever be possible," sighed Annie.

"I wouldn't," remarked Tom, still harshly. "It's bad enough, as it is, and makes you hold yourself a sight above a common-place fellow like me."

Poor Tom! he had so good a heart! and this time he spoke the truth in so discriminating a way.

"I don't *hold* myself above you, Tom."

(But Annie added to herself. "I am upheld.")

"O yes, you do, Nancy! You used to be right smart pleased when I came and fancied you. Now, it's a bother for you to talk to me—I see it is."

"No, *indeed*, it is not," she cried earnestly, her childish affection for the lad stirring in her warm and—thanks to John Wallace's wisdom—unspoiled heart. Indeed, I like you as much as ever, Tom, only—I'm *so* preoccupied."

"What about, Nancy?"

"Why, my studies, and my reading, and my music. Mr. Wallace is helping me with the science of harmony."

"What are you going to do with the science of harmony," queried Mr. Tom with pardonable contempt.

"I am going to study the theory of music. Father says he will buy me a piano, soon. Oh Tom!" Annie cried, her sweet face flushing joyously, "why are you not *glad* with me, if you want my friendship, for this great benefit that has befallen my lot?"

Tom Hatherton looked at her curiously.

"What benefit, Nancy?"

"Do you not see that the greatest good which could have come to me, is that I have been able to open up my life and to take some part in the wide culture outside of this poor little village?"

"No—I don't," responded Mr. Tom decidedly, "not when it makes you talk that way about the only place you've ever known, or are likely to know."

"It has made me enjoy even this place, which before was a grave to me," said Annie hastily.

"If you mean that you were discontented before your Mr. Wallace came and put notions into your head, all I've got to say is that you didn't talk about it."

"I did not *know how*," she answered, after a pause. "Myself was a sealed book. I was sad without knowing why. It is Mr. Wallace who has opened my eyes and my heart to a great world without and within. He has taught me first to perceive, and then to express. It is a revelation—a gift."

"And what I want to know is," cried Tom desperately, "what you mean to do with all of this wisdom and experience? Can your father buy you something to practise it on? like the piano, for instance? What's to come after?"

It was a supernatural gleam of perception on Tom's part, and showed a dormant shrewdness which only wanted waking into activity.

"There will be nothing more to come," Annie said, half sadly, "except that I can study on, and improve"——

Her sentence trailed off into a pause.

"It sounds rather like all work and no play, don't it,

Nancy?" Tom spoke drily, his opportunity was not lost upon him.

" Perhaps it does, but there is at least, no limit to it." Then she added, trying to regain her late enthusiasm. " I can acquire continually, I can broaden and expand."

" Then what? "

The girl met her questioner's eyes with a half impatient look.

" What nonsense, Tom! As if one could always look into the future and say what comes *next !* As if one *wanted* to !"

" Nancy," said Tom, seeming somehow to have suddenly developed into a superior creature who had the advantage of her,—" Nancy, do you believe that you will always be satisfied to live as you are living now, with nothing but books, and ambition and what you call expanding? "

Annie Castlewood sat mute, confronted for the first time during many months, with a future in which the heart and its affections had no part.

Tom crossed the room, and sat down beside her, gaining every instant in that indescribable advanage.

" Do you, Nancy? Tell me true? "

" I have not thought about *that* for a long while, Tom. I've been absorbed," stammered poor Annie.

" How old are you? " he asked abruptly.

" Why *you* know, I am nineteen," replied the girl, surprised.

" Suppose you should live to be ninety—you might you know—do you think improvement, and progress,

and all the rest of it, would satisfy you for seventy
years ? "

Annie looked appalled, and Tom noted another point
gained.

" Why, no, of *course* it wouldn't ! " she said emphat-
ically.

" What are you going to do when you get old ? "

" I hope," said Annie rallying, "to see something
of the world.   I shall not live here all my days."

" Is your father going to buy New York for you ? "

Tom was growing magnificent, and Nancy smiled
through her doubts.

" He may take me to see New York some day," she
ventured.

" And then bring you back to Rest-Hampton. What
good would that do ?   You're already unfitted enough
for living here.—No—no, Nancy, you can't look forward to *that* sort of thing either, to bring you satisfaction."

Annie was silent.

" Is it a good thing for a girl, dear, to be made dis-
satisfied with the things about her, and unfitted to be
an honest country lass, unless there is some one to
make an honest great lady of her ? "

" Yes," cried Annie, struggling hard against the
convictions so forced upon her : " it *is* a good thing for
any person to be elevated intellectually above the dis-
advantages of birth and surroundings, and taught that
there *are* things in the world besides baking and sewing, and keeping a house ! "

" But a woman, Annie, I mean a woman."

" Yes," she said with an attempt at bravado : " I

mean a woman also. I have no patience with the
notions of our people here that book-learning
is not safe for a woman. Would *you* have er ignorant ?"

" I would have her live, as God meant every woman
should live—with a man who loves her."

There was another silence in which Tom still
gazed, and Annie still faltered—their two hearts, so
long separated by diverse ways of thinking and living,
beating in unison at last over the same solemn
thought.

"Annie, do you believe that Mr. Wallace ever
intends to love you ! "

" Oh no—*never*!"

"Do you love Mr. Wallace ?"

" No, Tom—of *course* I don't ; you should not ask
me such a question ! "

" Then it's not your heart that is absorbed in these
fine notions of yours ? "

" I think not."

" But you want to see the world, Nancy ? you are
sure of that ? Would you be willing to leave—Mr.
Wallace ? "

" Yes, I would be willing," after a painful pause.

"Do you recollect what you called him, last
week ? "

" No," said Annie, wondering.

" You called him your Inspiration. Would you
be happy to leave that behind ? "

" Yes, I could be happy ; for I should always
have with me the *things* which Mr. Wallace has in
spired."

"Then, Annie, I am going to make a place for you in the world."

"Oh Tom!" began the girl deprecatingly ; but he stopped her :

"Don't speak yet, Nancy. Don't be hasty. When I came here, I had no idea of saying what I have. I had meant to go and make the place for you first. But it has all come about so that I couldn't keep silence. You'll think well of it?"

His voice shook a little; but he had the masterful look still. When a man dares to ask an unwon woman to marry him, he at least possesses courage.

"How *can* I think of it, Tom," she asked despairingly. "We have been estranged—we have ceased to be in sympathy——"

"Don't say any more, Nancy. Jealousy in my own heart has made war between us. The want of sympathy is only on top. Don't drive me away this time, dear. For, as God is in Heaven, I will never come back and ask you again, if you do."

Annie sat staring helplessly at her lover's agitated face. He did not need to tell her that he loved her. His life had proved it. But she—what could she say? Surely, she had no love in her heart for Tom Hatherton. But the vision of him going away and never coming back !—*that* appealed to her with a humiliating sense of her own dependence upon his only half noted devotion.

"What *shall* I do?" she cried, feeling herself in a dire strait.

"I don't believe you can send me away—for nothing, Nancy."

"No," she said, "I cannot; but why can't we live on as we have been doing?"

"Because," cried the young man hotly, "I am not willing to be nothing more than a dog, to come and go, and get noticed or not just as it suits you! And because, Annie," softening, "I love you dearly and need your presence to make me happy."

"What can you do, in a great city, Tom?" she asked evading the question, temporarily.

"I can make my way as other men have done," he answered determinedly; "But Annie—you have not promised me anything. Suppose, when I come back, things will have changed."

"How changed?"

"Suppose Mr. Wallace should make up his mind to marry you, what then?"

"You need not question about that!" said the girl firmly. "It could *never* happen."

Tom looked at her and read her thoughts; for his own sincerity of purpose made her face very transparent to him.

"I see," he said sadly, "that there would be no chance for me,—if such a thing *could* happen."

Annie did not speak. She too felt the truth of the statement.

"As it is sure never to occur, please don't let us talk about it," she said finally.

Tom Hatherton looked reproachfully at the troubled face of his companion. It was but a poor love-making that he could do, with such a wide spiritual distance between them. At that moment he would not have dared to approach her with any of those tender caresses which help so wonderfully in a wooing. Still, he loved the girl and was bent upon winning at least a partial consent.

He rose up and stood close beside her, looking down upon her with a patient seriousness.

"Will you at least give me your promise, Nancy, that you'll listen to no man until I come back to claim you to be my wife?"

Annie pondered. There was no man "*but* Tom," it was not likely that another strange being would come down like a god upon the village. So she answered gravely:

"I will wait. That is, Tom, until I myself let you know to the contrary, you may believe that I am waiting."

It was a poor response to his whole-hearted desire. Tom felt more sobered than triumphant.

"Did you know that I am going to New York this afternoon, Nancy?"

"No!—*are* you?" She looked up quickly with a sense of relief which Tom could not but see.

"Yes—good-by, little woman."

He stooped and kissed her gently.

"You are a good scholar, Nancy. Won't you write to me?"

"Yes, Tom—sometimes."

CHAPTER X.

" Here are the voices presently shall sound
In due succession. First the world's outcry,
Around the rush and ripple of any fact
Fallen stonewise, plumb on the smooth face of things
The world's guess, as it crowds the bank o' the pool
At what were figure and substance, by their splash :
Then, by vibrations in the general mind
At depth of deep already out of reach."

THE RING AND THE BOOK.

IT will be seen that, as yet, the girl was not quite
spoiled ; for, having turned aside but a few moments
from her ambitions and from beholding John Wallace's
face, Annie Castlewood had pledged her boundless
fancies and her unwon desires to honest, unimaginative Tom Hatherton. Truly hers was, after all, but a
woman's heart, and she, like the weakest of her sex,
was most appealed to through that part of her nature
which craves the support and protection of the sterner
nature that, sooner or later, seeks her.

More than all, the accustomedness of years had
been at work: and when it came to the test, the
newer and keener motives failed. Still, it was likely
to prove a dangerous experiment. The girl was incapable of ennui, since it presupposes satiety. But
she was an easy prey to that vague form of dissatisfaction which knows not for what it hungers.

Certainly, she had never hungered for Tom.

When he left her, the new purpose that had sprung up in his life lending as he went a manliness to his gait, and a dignity to his figure, Annie was dazed and bewildered.

Her gaze wandered first up and down the quiet street to the front, and then from the side windows far into the green and sheltered depths of the orchard. She was thinking—or was it only dreaming? picturing in a fantastic medley, her early childhood with its joyous content, her girlhood with its uneventful and almost hopeless calm, until the coming of John Wallace. There, the whole scene was altered. Life for three years, had been vivid in interest, intense in aim. All this was *real:* but the future confronted her like a dense mist in which all things were vague. Even "the place in the world" Tom had talked of making, seemed unsubstantial and remote.

She thought of the old farm-house without her, going on with its monotonous succession of domestic comforts and cares. What would Mr. Wallace say? Would he miss her from the placidly ordered routine of his retirement? It smote Annie's heart with an acute pain that she was forced to answer herself in the negative.

And Tom; did she care anything about Tom Hatherton? She was not sure that there existed for him a spark of feeling in her breast beyond that accustomedness of years.

" However, I have *promised* him nothing—excepting to wait," she sighed from the depths of her bewildered dream. And looking up, she met the kind and searching gaze of Mr. Wallace.

" Child, why did you do it ? "

" I—oh, I do not know!" she stammered, not surprised that he should read her new secret, since it always seemed to her Mr. Wallace knew all things by a certain miraculous discernment of his own.

" Do you love that young man, Annie ? "

Annie shook her head dubiously,—

" I do not know *that* either, Mr. Wallace." and her birdlike glance flew straight to his with a troubled flutter.

" Then why did you promise to marry him ?"

" I did not promise *that*," she protested.

" I met him in the lane, just now, and he burst upon me with the news that he had got a promise from you."

" Yes :—a promise to *wait.*"

Annie said it drearily, already, at the first sound of her hero's voice, the prospect seemed to grow dull, and the thing for which she was to wait, poor. A sense of disenchantment, when some project is first held up to the critical gaze of another, is no new thing in the history of small events.

" What will you wait for ?"

" For Tom to make his fortune."

"*Here ?*"—the tone betrayed more amazement than Mr. Wallace often permitted himself to bestow upon the ways of the village.

" No, he will go to New York,—and make a place for me in the world," finished Annie, quoting unconsciously her lover's own words.

" And that is what you wish for, Annie? To be in the world."

" I have *always* wished for it—even more than now ; I used to crave it. Oh, Mr. Wallace !" cried the girl, her sweet eyes shining with unshed tears, " life is *so* narrow in this place ! Before *you* came, there was nothing but to eat and sleep ; to wake and work ; and then to eat and sleep again. You have broadened and beautified my life ; but all that I can feel or do is in spite of the place. There are no helps from without —only hindrances. There must be something better than this ! "

" Something more varied—yes. But the world is not a good place, nor a kind place, nor a restful place. You are happier here, child."

Annie looked blank. Mr. Wallace was using, in different words, the same argument *against* Tom, that Tom himself had used to further his cause.

Her companion saw that she misunderstood him,—

" I mean to ask you, Annie, if you love Tom enough to satisfy all the possible demands of your developing nature ? "

She shook her head. Somehow, she could not answer lightly those penetrating eyes.

" Are you not happy as you are, child ? " searching her with that " mild intensity innocent of any inten- tion." He probed her also with the tones of his voice, not so much like music, for it was without marked cadence, as like the voice of a poet speaking a rapt monody.

Annie's being was thrilled with a nameless emotion, far echoes of which she had felt stirring in her bosom when first she saw this man and worshipped him. One of John Wallace's peculiarities, we have said, was his marvelous intuition. It was swift, keen, unerring, like a woman's ; only unlike hers, it was speechless. Looking, he beheld in Annie's eyes, something, at which there came over his face and his demeanor that fine thin veil of coldness which is but the silent withdrawal of the spirit.

The young girl felt it ; for her sympathy with this singularly sensitive nature had made more acute her own sensibilities. Mutely she accepted the withdrawal as an uncomprehended rebuke for an uncomprehended blunder of her own. So in dealing, however tenderly with fine, high-strung natures, we are all apt to prick our spiritual fingers. It was one of the penalties which Joshua Castlewood's "sentimental" little daughter had to pay for her privileged relationship towards the honored guest.

Often, some look met hers, that seemed to come from out the depths of Mr. Wallace's heart, and to show her a still sunny region, not made quite desolate by its untold memories. But if such a look drew from her transparent eyes either surprise or pleased response it would vanish like one of his own rare smiles, which was so swift, one only knew it had been, by the still gravity that followed. So Annie would be conscious, only after the look had vanished, that something had come and gone which it would have been sweet to keep.

This man's tact, however, was no less than his insight : his sensitive responsiveness never failed. And so, when he knew just now, by the voiceless power of the spirit which telleth all things to him whose inner ears are open, that he had chilled poor Annie, he

gently resumed the fatherly affection which had led
him to take her hand as he said : " Annie, you are
much to me."

He held it still, and caressed kindly the pretty rosy
fingers.   Then he went back to the momentous
question, but without the momentous look or purport.

" When I ask if you are not happy, Annie, I do not
mean in any transcendental sense ; this is not a world of
ideals.   Happiness is, after all, a thing of temperament,
a condition of the mind and body, rather than a result
of circumstances.   You are sound and well, and have
plenty of hope,"—smiling, " you ought to be radiant."

" I *am* happy," said Annie, answering his smile,
" when I live one day at a time, and allow myself to
think of nothing but my studies, and the beautiful
things *you* teach me.'

" And at other times ? " he questioned her with his
kind looks.

"Then—I am restless—I long "—Annie paused,
even to this man, high-priest in her temple of fancy,
she could not reveal the secret yearnings of her
woman's nature.

" It is the old story," mused the other, more to himself than to his companion " the restless dreams, the
nameless aspirations of the heart ; and you think it is
your ambition, child, that is crying to be fed ! "

Annie was disturbed.

" Why " cried some consciousness within her, " does
he *trouble* the waters of my soul, when he cannot
lead me to be healed ? "

After a silence, Mr. Wallace rose abruptly,—

" Perhaps I am wrong, Annie. Experience after all

only teaches us of our own ways, not those of another. All must pass through vales of tears to learn the true relations of things. I have been trying to lay the old burden of my knowledge of the world upon young shoulders. Go, live for yourself, child, you may find the happiness that somehow I have missed."

He walked from the room; but Annie sat and wept.

The waters were indeed troubled, and John Wallace had not proved an angel of healing.

After a while she got up, and went slowly to her mother's presence. She felt doubtful about her approval. The demure little woman was quick to see the traces of tears, but it was not a way of hers to remark upon the emotions of her children. Above all, she never encouraged weeping.

" They must learn to be self-contained," she said,—"Sympathy undermines self-control. The craving for commiseration is a weakness, a selfishness." So she had been taught in her own youth.

" Mother," said Annie abruptly, in a lifeless tone that showed she spoke from a sense of duty and not from impulse: "I have come to talk to you about something; Tom Hatherton is going to New York to make his fortune."

" Indeed, I trust he may be successful. Has thee seen him lately?"

" He has just left. And mother, I have promised to *wait* for him."

"'To wait for him?'" echoed Mrs. Castlewood, startled out of her poise: " And what does thee mean by that!"

"To marry him, I suppose."

"To marry him:" the echo annoyed Annie, but she made no response.

Her mother began to sew again vigorously, with a nervous twitching of the fingers. She had always managed her husband and the boys—without their knowing it. The girl seemed to see through everything, and had never been easily managed. She sewed on as though nothing had interrupted the flow of her spool-cotton.

"What do you say about it?" asked Annie, at last, watching intently the rapid movements of the needle.

"Is it not rather late for thee to ask me?"

"Not at all, mother. I have only promised—to wait."

"Which means that thee has encouraged Thomas."

"I have *listened* to him—yes."

"I did think, Annie, that thee would have looked higher——"

Mrs. Castlewood did not lift her eyes from her work. She felt awkward about betraying to her daughter her secret hopes and ambitions.

"Who *is* there to look to, mother, in this dead-and-buried place?"

Again Mrs. Castlewood went on sewing before she answered cautiously,—

"It has been made clear to me, Annie, that John Wallace——"

But Annie would hear no more.

"Mother," she cried, with a sudden flash of anger in her cheeks and eyes, "*never* couple Mr. Wallace's name with mine. You might as well plan to have me wed the Angel Gabriel!"

Mrs. Castlewood was shocked :

" If thee is going to blaspheme, Annie, we had better drop the subject. I suppose, if Thomas Hathcrton suits thee, it is no great concern to thy father and myself."

" He *doesn't* suit me," almost screamed poor Annie, with a hysterical burst of tears ; " only there is no one else, and I *must* get out of this grave."

" If thee would control thy impetuous ways, we might confer to some purpose in this matter."

Mrs. Castlewood's wounded dignity was immense, and she sat prim and cold until Annie's sobs had subsided. To tell the truth, the coldness was the surface training of her life. In her heart, the mother was bitterly disappointed. She had had ambitions in her youth which lifted her somewhat from the obscure surroundings of the little Quaker settlement in Rhode Island. But her married life had soon closed about her, and she had accepted John Wallace as a late re. compense, who was to atone to her, in still further elevating her child, for her own only half-satisfied aspirations.

When Annie grew quiet, she began cautiously :

" Is it possible that thee is proposing to marry a man whom thee admits does not suit thee."

" It is what nine-tenths of women do," said Annie obstinately ; " one *must* marry somebody."

(A sentiment, dear reader which nearly every girl is brought up to have and to hold ; but which few will utter. The rack could not extort from some single women that they desire marriage.)

"It is ᵃ godless thing to contemplate," said the

elder lady, genuinely shocked at her daughter's sentiments : " there can no happiness come out of it."

" *Everybody* is prophesying against my happiness,"
moaned poor Annie deeply aggrieved.

" Everybody ?—who knows of this thing ? "

" Mr. Wallace."

" Then it is too late !   Thee has made the mistake
of thy life ! " cried the mother, with suppressed
anger.

" Did you suppose I would hide it from him ? "

" Thee might at least have consulted thy parents
first."

" Tom told Mr. Wallace, himself."

" Doubtless.   He wished to prevent the undoing
of this piece of folly.   Has thee seen thy father? "

" No—I will go and fetch him," said Annie starting
up, glad to escape from her mother's presence.

" Every thing is beclouded.   Every thing points to
misery," she cried to herself as she passed out of
doors : " why cannot things come easily and pleasantly
to me ?   This ought to be a time of congratulations and
proud joy.   Oh dear, what *have* I done that I should
be so miserable ? "

As no one was near, Annie asked the wind.   If the
wind could have answered, it would have said :

" Poor child ! thou hast pledged thy hand where
thou hast never given thy heart.   Thou art asking for happiness to come out of a sham—a mockery."

She ran through the orchard to search for the kind
father who, if he did not quite understand her girlish
fancies, had still so tender a heart for them.

At last she found him, in the garden, examining his prospect for early potatoes.

"Oh, father!" she cried, and flung herself upon his breast ; Oh, father ! "

The good Squire was much astonished at this demonstration in his staid and wise daughter, who because of her self-command he often called his "little Puritan," telling her she resembled her pretty grandmother Prue, whose portrait in demure dress and cap was greatly prized by the Castlewoods.

" Hoity—toity ! what now ? " he exclaimed. " Is the pony dead ? or have the boys drowned some kittens ? "

" No–o—father ! but Tom wants me to w–w–ait for him to c–come and *ma–marry* me."

" Hey ! what ! Bless my soul ! Tom Hatherton wants to marry you ? "

" Yes—and I do–on't believe I w–want to ? "

Annie's grief was excessive.

" You don't, 'hey ; well you needn't, you know, Nancy."

" Oh—but, I've *pro–o–mised.*"

" Well now, don't cry my lass, Tom's a fine fellow and will make a capital husband. But bless my soul ! this is all very sudden, isn't it ? very sudden."

" *Awfully* sud–sudden," sobbed Annie burying her face deeper in his bosom.

" Well there, lassie, cheer up a bit ! You won't have to marry him suddenly, you know. Bless me ! you're a sight too young these many years.

" Ye–es—father ! "

" And he's a first-rate fellow. He'll make a fine farmer yet ; see if he don't."

" No," cried Annie shaking her head and weeping :
" he is going to New Yo-ork—to make—his fortune."

" The devil he is ! " cried the dear old Squire, almost
upsetting Annie in the suddenness of the surprise—
" Oh—so, so ! And that's the reason you're breaking
your little heart ? "

" N-not altogether."

" And what does Mr. Tom propose to do with
you ? "

" I'm to—wait—until he comes ba-ack," wept
Annie.

" With the fortune ? In about six weeks, I suppose ? " and the Squire laughed uproariously, glad to
have hit upon a comical side to the question.

His hilarity did not grate upon Annie's nerves as
her mother's poignant criticism and apparent want
of sympathy had done. It was a contagious sort of
mirth, and she began to smile through her tears.

" That's right, Lassie," cried the father, who never
could bear the distress of any woman, least of all his
petted daughter's ; " There's nothing to break your
heart about. But hold on ! It isn't your heart at all—
It's Tom's, you know." And the kind old gentleman
laughed as heartily as before, giving Annie a sly
squeeze under the ribs to indicate where Tom's organ
was kept.

" What do you think of it, Father," Annie asked,
almost merry again. It was *such* a comfort to have
some one take it naturally : not ominously as Mr.
Wallace had done, nor mournfully, like her mother.
After all, the sunshine might break through the
cloud.

" I think it couldn't be better, Nancy ; it couldn't
be better. I always said Tom would come out and
do something to scare us all. His father is such a
trump ! And you will make a first rate little farmer's
wife——ah, no! I forgot—a first rate little fortune's
wife ; " and the great guffaws broke out afresh.

" Now you are making fun of me, father," cried
Annie, making believe to be hurt, but nestling close
to him meanwhile.

" Not a bit of it, my dear ; you're all right, and so
is Tom Hatherton. It's the fortune ! " The squire
had to prop himself against a tree-trunk to enjoy his
laugh. Whether this mirthfulness was altogether unalloyed, may be questioned.

" But Father," said Annie, rubbing her soft cheek
against his whiskers, "people *do* make fortunes in
New York, don't they ? "

" Of course they do, my dear ! No doubt about it !
And then you see, the other Governor and I can help
him out handsomely on it."

His eyes twinkled comically, and they began stroll-
ing towards the house :

" Come Lass," he said presently ; " we'll go and
scare mother a bit."

Annie hung back.

" Mother knows," she said, briefly : "You go and
talk it over with her, father dear." And giving him
a kiss which he returned with a hearty embrace, she
vanished to her own upper chamber, and to who
knows what despondence and humiliation.

For she was certainly likely to commit that rash
act from which her own conscience recoiled no less

than all her preconceived notions of sentiment and bliss,—she had promised to hold herself subject to a man for whom, in searching her uttermost heart, she found no passion.

And we?—what shall we say of Annie and her acquiescence to Tom Hatherton's wooing? Doubtless, we are disappointed, and disposed to view the matter somewhat after the manner of Martha Castlewood.

Perhaps there is nothing more unfair in this world of misconceptions,—intentional, and unintentional,—than the quiet assurance with which we each and all judge our neighbors' actions. We have only the results of their reasoning, to be sure, and cannot take into account the motives which have influenced them, or the amount of pressure that has been brought to bear upon them. But that is no matter. They do an unexpected thing; or they leave undone an expected one, and we forthwith pursue them with over criticisms, more or less scathing—not according to the merits of the case, but our own mood, or the state of our own digestion.

These criticisms do not follow their actions afar off, with a respectful sense of everybody's right to his own conduct; but we—(not thou or I dear reader, but friends on the other side of the street, whom let us call "we," for courtesy)—dog their heels with our comments, and hound them up and down with our opinions.

And so we must needs make up our minds about the propriety of Annie Castlewood's acceptance of her lover. Only do, in pity's name, let us take into consideration the circumstances of her life. Let us sit down calmly and ponder upon the dead level of monotony to which destiny had doomed her. Let us reflect upon the forever unsatisfied impulses of a nature which ardently craved those changes and chances that make up the sum of most lives.

Moreover, recollect the influence over her of a man whose wide experience had tried all things. His campanionship had opened to her the door unto much upon which he himself had turned his back.

Then, as Annie said ; there was *no one else !*

After all, dear Reader,—in whose eyes I somehow seem to feel it necessary to vindicate Annie Castlewood from possible censure——the child was not selling her soul for gold, or for position, or for spite. She was doing no violence to any prejudice ; she was not even strangling another passion which has been withheld from this quiet story. She was merely taking the best that her life was likely to offer her, thereby fulfilling in a most natural way that inexorable law of " the commonplace," which is a perpetual mockery upon the romance of youth and the belated aspirations of middle life. It is a law which over-rides all prejudices, and tramples down all passions, compassing itself in the very lives of those who scorn and deny it.

CHAPTER XI.

A BRIEF CALM.

> ———" *What if he gained thus much,*
> *Wrung out this sweet drop from the bitter Past,*
> *Bore off this rosebud from the prickly brake*
> *To justify such torn clothes and scratched hands ;*
> *And, after all, brought something back from Rome.*"
>
> THE RING AND THE BOOK.

PERCHANCE the meager supply of heroines—a little Quaker woman, a young country girl, a phantom,—may strike the critic as a strange paucity of very cheap material. And yet it was characteristic of a man like John Wallace—if there was ever such another man,—whose spirit dwelt apart from other spirits as a recluse, that he should live for thirty years in the little Island town, and yet make no woman his heroine.

Indeed it may be seen that this story has throughout but a slim corps of *dramatis personæ* ; and that even those few actors play but a subordinate role. The hero looms up and overshadows with his majestic presence any part left to less important players, however simple he may wish his life to appear, and however profoundly he would bury the secret locked in his bosom. We cannot in any event fancy him sitting unobserved at a side-scene, watching with interest the actions of any inhabitant of Rest-Hampton. Still less can we imagine ourselves, the self-constituted audience for the time-being, permitting him so to sit forgotten, while we become absorbed in the convergence of events which have no bearing upon our ultimate decision regarding him.

Wherever a creature of this peculiar stamp may abide, he unconsciously becomes a centre about whom all approximating figures revolve, like—shall we ignore the old metaphor of a planet and its satellites and say—the puppets at a country show?

Only Annie Castlewood was no puppet. One could tell pretty well how the little Quaker woman would move upon her narrow and self-absorbed base; it is not difficult to divine by what strings the good Squire could be worked; Tom Hatherton, too, was not a person of deep designs and unaccountable proceedings. There are others who come upon the stage with but a clumsy mental mechanism to approach their ends. But Annie's was a complex nature. You could not calculate beforehand how a mind of such varied moods was to be affected by even the ordinary wire-pulling of village life.

Brought into contact with the overcharged forces of John Wallace's character; her whole being became the medium for currents of attraction and repulsion which swayed her quite involuntarily to herself, and with a sense of some dissatisfaction to her friends. She did not pretend to understand herself; still less did she undertake to comprehend Mr Wallace, whose inner life was remote from her experience as the smouldering crater of Mount Vesuvius. Indeed, he affected her oftentimes—this man of calm demeanor and lovely silence,—as one is affected by the lull of a half extinct volcano beneath a peaceful sky. The force of those upheavals, the law of those fires which preceding the calm, are as uncomprehended by us as though they had never belched forth their fury and obliterated the summer peace. * * * * * * *

Tom Hatherton, who has gained something in effect by being withdrawn from contrast with Annie's hero, has been for several months in New York; and life has gone on undisturbed at Rest-Hampton. The small pebble of the lad's departure had made, at first, a great ripple on its tranquil waters, Many were the frowning looks flung upon "the Squire's lass" by the village belles, who had each thought her own charms might prevail against her as a final choice. For Supervisor Hatherton was well-to-do; and Tom was regarded as a fine match in those parts.

By some unlucky combination of circumstances it often happens that there are but few marriageable young men in a small village, while the maidens——well, *all* maidens are marriageable!

A great story of sudden wooing and hasty departure was told and retold. There were new predictions set afloat; that Tom would come to no good in the great wicked city; or that if he got the fortune, he might never come back to fetch Nancy Castlewood; or that if he came back at all, she would still be "fooling her fancies away" upon Mr. Wallace.

Annie went calmly on her way. studying a little less perhaps, (for since her talk with Tom she had let go her vital hold upon self-culture as a hobby.) but working now and then among what the whole village called

" Mr. Wallace's poor folks." If we could follow her up and down these by-ways, the study of a crude and honest and self-supporting race might form a strong background to throw out the more delicate pencillings of our plot. "Amphibious" has been applied to the sturdy villagers ; and justly, since they farm and fish, toiling on the land or on the sea, as the necessity calls.

There came from time to time somewhat labored epistles from the absent lad. Like most country-bred youths, he had no great liking for such a sedentary occupation as letter-writing : "I would rather break a colt than write a letter, any time," he wrote. In fact, in his hand, a pen was nearly as clumsy as a plough, and its guidance was quite as warm work.

Every time he forwarded one of these performances, he had "struck a new thing which was bound to come to something." Each new "something" covered the ignominious slip-up of the last. Poor Tom! his was a record that many an untried youth has kept since !

Finally, after many mischances, he wrote—in a hand now considerably modified, by contact with new demands, that he had "found something certain this time, and it was all settled."

But after another six months, even Tom began to despond, and just when the poor fellow was ready to throw up his manly endeavor—for he declined to accept aid from his "folks,"—he did actually happen upon "a sure thing." If this story had not its sails set in another direction, it would be both pleasant and pathetic to follow the brave lad in the uncertain steering through his sometimes stormy and sometimes becalmed voyage of discovering for himself the difficult haven of a " fortune."

There were usual wanderings, blunderings and disappointments ; there were some impositions, too, from which he suffered. Once he was swindled out of his last dollar and left upon the mercy of picking up jobwork for a month. It was the next thing to being a day-laborer. Still, the young fellow had plenty of pluck, plenty of grit, and kept up his courage manfully. He was not above day-laborer's hire, if the worst came. Only Annie must not know. It might distress her to follow his struggles towards self-support. For, strange to say, Tom's jealousy about his sweetheart had all vanished. He was such a trusting fellow, that it was not possible for him to conceive of infidelity. He actually believed that she loved him.

Annie had promised. That was enough. She was his, and he would have trusted her unhesitatingly to the ends of the earth.

But there came a time when something very like despair took hold of Tom Hatherton, struggling alone against the overwhelming tides of the vast selfish, money-making city.

He had spent a mentally starved—perhaps a physically hungry, who knows ?—week, in dogging faint hopes and poor chances from end to end of the utmost limit his opportunities had offered him.

When Saturday night came around again, he shrank back to his comfortless lodging (for which he had owed his needy landlady many a week ; and it nearly killed him to know that she was needy)—the picture of hopeless misery, the shadow of his buoyant self.

He stood by his dirty window, looking over the dark
roofs into the faintly-lit street, wondering as many
another shipwrecked man has done, if ever the fates
would again turn friendly faces upon him.

" If I had a pistol, " he muttered," I believe I would
shoot myself and be done with it——God forgive
me ! "

And John Wallace, sitting apart in far-away little
Rest-Hampton, had so withdrawn from the turmoil of
life that the ears of his spirit were open in some
mysterious fashion to that bitter cry.

He had been reflecting much of late upon Tom's
courageous endeavors to make a home for Annie
Castlewood ; and his possible hard luck was not unsuspected. The young man was proving himself worthy
even of his little favorite. Besides, who was he that he
had dared choose for the girl ? She and her lover were
untried. Their desires were innocent. Their hearts
were fresh. They had hope still by the hand. He had
only memory. How then was he fit to choose ?

Gradually, the picture of a united destiny for these
two young creatures began to shape itself before his
gentle fancy. Then he grew solicitous for Tom. In
his wisdom he read between the boy's brave lines, and
saw an undercurrent of disappointment and humiliation.

" Perhaps," he said to himself, " if I go to him, I
can be of use. The lad may be in actual want. I am
an unknown man "——he paused with a strange sad
smile flickering across his face—" but money is a
power, and I may be able to buy with bank-notes
what I could not command with influence."

And so,—after the wretched empty Sunday had dragged itself away, and Tom had gone back again and again restlessly to the thought of the pistol until he coveted one more than food all that dinnerless day, on Monday morning, before the sun had fairly crept above the dingy roofs, that other stood before him, a very angel of light.

"I thought I would come down and bring you Annie's love to cheer you up," was all that he said.

But by some inward perception, Tom understood. Moreover he never forgot the relief of that instant, when he felt at last his relaxing fingers, that had let go one by one the straws of hope, clasped in a strong and saving hand.

Mr. Wallace was not omnipotent ; but he had lived in the business world once, and he knew the back-doors to its favor. He spent freely, and considered wisely ; and at last the young man was carried within the notice of one or two merchants who (even in great wicked New York towards which remote little Rest-Hampton looked in such horror and dread) could value an uncontaminated mind and a genuine purpose. They wanted integrity rather than ability, and soon Mr. Thomas Hatherton had a little branch office for a well-known firm, in the center of a crowded business locality. It seemed to him,—what wonder ?—the very center of the world from which all purpose gravitated.

Then, at long last, he wrote Annie proudly in a fairly business-like hand, that he had "set up for himself," and was beginning to make his way in the world.

" I shall soon come to fetch you, now, Nancy," he added, his hand almost trembling with happiness.

Was Annie glad? She tried to believe so ; for she had a loyal heart, that never once, since that first tumultuous day, had permitted her to question the policy of the promise she had made.

As a result, there settled gradually upon her unquiet soul, a sweet peace :—or was it only a lull ?

She had said to herself in the beginning,—

" I must steadfastly turn my heart away from ideals. I must stand up and take my future in my two hands and say 'for this alone, I live ?' If once I should sink into the depths of repining, I am lost."

And so she had passed safely over the shoals, having set her mind upon the haven. She wandered about like one in a pleasant dream. Under the deep shade of the familiar trees, among the pleasant grasses and friendly field-flowers, she came and went. If there was no dazzling radiance of new-born love upon her path, at least there were no defined shadows. Her daily life, as it pictured itself to her own fancy, was all in quiet, restful tones that seemed to promise a future undisturbed by violent lights or shades.

CHAPTER XII.

JOHN WALLACE'S RELIGION.

" But I, most privileged to see a saint
Of old when such walked earth with crown and palm,
If I call " saint" what saints call something else—
The Saints must bear with me,"
THE RING AND THE BOOK.

MR. WALLACE'S trip to New York was one of the " flittings " he made of which no one knew the purport. Annie, in her new-found serenity, was as unconscious of it as she was of her lover's day of peril.

The older man's consciousness seemed untouched by any changes of her mood. So it was ordained. For what had the child been to him? A sunbeam that had crossed his solitary shadowland. A singing bird that had fluttered in upon his cage and tasted of the food the inexorable gods had provided for him. A stray blossom that had fallen upon his breast and been plucked away, like all else, from his great need. A cloud—it may have been—across the vision of his snow-white soul.

His days went on, and it seemed as though he knew no loss. His mind was busied with a plan that was to work good in the island community. His reveries, that had been but broken and intangible reflections,

began to take form and adapt themselves to the necessities about him. Whether he had come to transfer
to the little village of his adoption his real interests;
or whether he had felt painfully in the unmitigated
Puritan settlement, the need of his own church, he now
began to contemplate the building of a chapel where
he might participate once more in that Service dear to
every English churchman's heart. The people of the
town were dissenters, to his way of thinking, and the
rigid outline of their inflexible faith was to him an
austere and forbidding form of worship. He was a
liberal man, and attended regularly the " preaching "
in the place, giving largely to its support. But, like
Martha Castlewood, he was not " at home " among
the Presbyterians. Many were the talks which these
two persons of diametrically opposite bringing-up held
on the subject of creeds, and schisms, and dogmas ; and
the narrow mind of the woman grew and expanded
beneath his broadening influence. It was to Annie,
however, that he first intimated his intention of building a church.

One afternoon,—a mild and peaceful day in the late
summer—he came upon her as she sat beneath an old
riven tree in the orchard, over which a climbing rose
made splendid riot. She had been reading Tom's
last letter, and held it meditatively in her hand.
" Nancy," it said. " I am coming for you—soon."
Tom was certainly improving, she admitted. But this
man who slowly approached her, with his courtly mien
and his saintly face—how different he was ! how in-
comparable !

" Annie," he said, seating himself on the fallen

trunk beside her, "have you ever thought of other modes of worship than your own?"

The question would have been abrupt to one less in harmony with Mr. Wallace's thought. Annie, as we have said, was never surprised. It at no time occurred to her that her friend was "peculiar;"—that indefinable and often meaningless stigma which has injured many an original thinker.

"Do you mean the heathen, who worship idols?" she asked naively.

Mr. Wallace laughed pleasantly.

"No;—only the differences of creed—or rather of creed-form,—which divide the Protestant church into a score or so of sects. You did not suppose the whole christian world lay in Presbyterianism, did you?"

"I believe," said Annie, smiling, "that I have never thought much about it. There is no other sect here, you know."

"This is certainly a staunch community of loyal Puritans," Mr. Wallace remarked.

"Tell me about the others, please."

And resting her elbow upon her knee, and her chin upon her palm, Annie was composed for listening.

"You must ply me with questions. I don't want to begin at the Reformation with 'Once upon a time there was a golden epoch when sectarianism was unknown!' For, in fact, that was not a golden time at all, but full of turmoil and controversy."

"What shall I ask?" The girl hesitated; for the tangled sophistries of scientific and all other sorts of infidelity, were unknown to her

"Tell me the names of a lot of sects," Annie pur-

sued. " I know several to start with :—the Presbyterian, of course ; and the Methodist church at Bridge-
Hampton; of my mother's sect, I have some faint
notion ; and there are the Roman Catholics at Sag
Harbor."

" And what will you do with England ? " asked her
companion, amused at the girl's limited category.——

" Oh ! the Church of England, *of course !* How
could I be so stupid ? Tell me about it, Mr. Wallace.
It was—or no !" she broke off perplexed : "Is not
the Presbyterian church the Church of Scotland ? "
She colored as she referred to the difference of nationality, which still was to her a memorable piece of information.

" Yes—it is so called ; but what were you going to
ask ? "

" If the Church of England was not *your* church."

" Yes, it *is* my church," with a scarcely perceptible
emphasis on the indicative present. "I am not a
bigoted Scotchman. I love the Anglican Church, and
have never been inside of one of those noble Protestant cathedrals, without the great glad thought going
up as an impulse from my heart. " *Lord, I love the
habitation of thy house.*"

" How you must have missed it !" cried Annie,
watching sympathizingly the lighting up of his sensitive eyes.

" I do miss it," he answered simply, again unconsciously correcting her mood and tense : " It is the
greatest of my deprivations."

Annie looked earnestly at the masterful face, shadowed with its forever unspoken grief : and a pang

smote her heart that, while she had been with this man, living upon his generous out-giving nature, she had thought so little about the sorrow or trouble which had driven him from his own. It did not, for the moment, occur to her that John Wallace had so willed it that she should forget to question. It seemed selfishness that had kept her brooding over her own trivial affairs. So she spoke out impulsively,—

"Ah, Mr. Wallace! How *could* you leave your church, your home—all of it—to come here?"

Instantly there was revulsion. Annie was frightened at her own boldness. Never had she seen so inscrutable a look upon the face that had showed her many emotions.

After a brief pause, he said gently,—

"That is a question, my dear child, which would be most difficult to answer. There are many reasons which cause a man to uproot his existence and transplant it in stranger places than this."

"Oh—I know! I did not mean to question you, sir. I only meant to—to—sympathize with you!" cried the girl, in real consternation.

"I understood you perfectly," he answered, smiling reassuringly upon her.

She hastened to revert to the former subject.

"I have never heard the service of your church. Oh, Mr. Wallace! it is dreadful never to have been more than a dozen miles from this little town!"

"How unrelenting you are, Nancy, to this pretty little Village of Peace." (It was John Wallace who first called it "the village of peace," let us hope that he found peace there!)

" Where did you get the revolt that is in you against the simplicity and sanctity of your birth-place."

" From my mother, I think," she answered briefly : " but please tell me what they do in your church ?   Or what they believe, rather."

" They do many things in a devout spirit : they believe much, with their hearts."

" They wear gowns ; and have candles and altars, like the Catholics, don't they ?"   Annie felt her way vaguely back to what she had read of English Churches.

" They do many of those things, which belong to the symbolic side of worship, and which I should be sorry to forego.   They make the service of God at once the most humbling and exalting act of the human soul.   They make religion not only necessary, but beautiful.   Listen, Annie,"—

He drew from an inner pocket an exquisite little book, bound in ivory mounted with gold, upon which was carved and inlaid the crest of the seal ring.   Inside, there were brilliant and delicate decorations and illuminations upon its parchment pages which made the tiny volume resemble an old missal.

" How *lovely !* " cried Annie taking it in her hand ; " Can you buy books like that, Mr. Wallace ?"

" Not often : I had it illuminated myself,   It is done on vellum, and copied from the style of missal-painting of the thirteenth or fourteenth century."

" Do you always carry it ?"

" Always.   I am much attached to it.   I should like it buried with me, Annie."

He did not look at her ; but at that moment the

young girl felt that she had received a sacred commission.

" And what is the crest upon it ? "

" That,"—the scholar paused—" is one of the things
which mean nothing, in America."

He was turning over the leaves, slowly, and presently
read in that wonderful voice which none ever forgot
who heard it :

*"Almighty and most merciful Father; we have erred, and
strayed from Thy ways like lost sheep. We have followed too
much the devices and desires of our own hearts. We have offended against Thy holy laws. We have left undone those things
which we ought to have done : and we have done those things
which we ought not to have done. And there is no health in
us."* . . .

" Oh ! " cried Annie, enchanted, although perhaps
with the majestic voice as much as with the majestic
words ; " how beautiful it is ! Somehow I hear chanting, but the sounds are not like human voices."

" The chanting of the church is from two choirs of
young boys, with voices like angels, who call back and
forth to each other in strange old-world music, the
words of the Psalms. It is called singing anti-
phonally."

Then Mr. Wallace read on, turning the pages at
random :

*" Remember not, Lord, our offenses, nor the offenses of our
forefathers : neither take Thou vengeance of our sins : spare us,
good Lord, spare Thy people, whom Thou hast redeemed with
Thy precious blood, and be not angry with us forever."*

Then shall the people respond and cry with one
voice.

" Spare us, Good Lord !"

" I can see," said Annie, her face becoming suffused with a sudden glow, " a great, dim-lighted edifice, so large and so dim that you cannot distinguish from one end to the other.   It twinkles all above with hundreds of lights, like stars : and below a vast assembly of people are waiting on their knees in breathless silence. Upon an elevated platform, about which is a dividing rail, there stands a minister of God, clothed in white, in whose face is a great light ; he lifts up his hands —I cannot hear what he says—and the whole multitude of human beings is bowed down, as if swept over by a great wave of prayer :—Oh, Mr. Wallace ! " cried the girl excitedly, with a strange terrified look—" it is *you* that I see ! "

Had John Wallace raised his hands ? or was it only in her vivid imagination that she saw his figure elevated before the silently prostrate throng, his exquisite head bowed also, and the celestial light in his face ?

She gazed at him breathlessly.   No—he was not clothed in white : his hands were not raised.   Only in his face was the great light.

" Have you ever been in a Cathedral, child," he asked looking curiously at her.

" No," said Annie, " never before.   Did you not describe it to me—once ? " she was looking puzzled and still somewhat terrified, with a clairvoyant gleam scintillating in her eyes.

" It was before me very clearly when you spoke," he quietly remarked.   " Very likely the picture carried its impression to your brain.   Such things will happen."

Then John Wallace read on, through the all-covering supplications of the grand old Litany, in the same hushed tone that would have been tremulous, but for its masterful steadying.

" *Son of God, we beseech Thee to hear us !*

"*O Lamb of God who takest away the sins of the world !*

" *Grant us Thy peace !—Have mercy upon us !* "

After a pause, in which Annie sat with wet eyes, he read the passionate praises of the *Te Deum Laudamus.*

"It is like voices crying in the wilderness," she said.

" Yes ; *Vox clamantis in deserto parate viam Domini ;* it is the Bible set to music, from first to last.   There are no theories of men in this little book, Annie.   All of its dogmas are pure, unadulterated gospel." And the impressive voice took up, farther along, the wonderful thread of devotion that has swayed men and women since Christ's kingdom was :

" *O be joyful in the Lord, all ye lands : serve the Lord with gladness, and come before His presence with a song. . . . For the Lord is gracious, His mercy is everlasting ; and His truth endureth from generation to generation.*"

"We all have the same creed, thank God !" said John Wallace devoutly.   "Christians never differ there."

"And what comes—afterwards ? " Annie asked, still enraptured with the new revelation she was receiving.

" Afterwards ?—while the Ten Commandments are

uttered there is from some unseen place the low
monotone, or progressive harmony of a distant organ
—you have never heard an organ, child. Some day,
when you go to New York, you will hear one. And
in response to each one of those commands so simple
to repeat, so difficult to keep, the people break forth
into a low chant, upon their knees : '*Lord have mercy
upon us, and incline our hearts to keep this law.*' Is
not that the soul of worship ? "

Annie bowed her head. She could not speak for
tears.

John Wallace read on and on. Presently a still
stronger emotion seemed to sweep over the usually
calm and unmoved spirit ; he sank back against the
tree-trunk, as though some strain had been upon him,
and a physical reaction had set in.

He was so pale that Annie sprang up in alarm and
asked if he were ill. But he answered " no," and rose
from the place where he had sat.

" I will tell you more some other time, child." And
he passed through the orchard and out of her sight.
She never forgot that picture. It seemed to the girl's
excited fancy like the vanishing of a high, calm angel
into the obscurity of another sphere.

"I know !" she cried breathlessly, clasping her
hands over her heart to press it into silence ; " I know !
He was a clergyman of the church he loves so well !
The glimpse I had of him was a revelation. Some
dark calamity has befallen him—oh, great and good
man ! " *   *   *   *   *   *   *   *   *   *

The next morning, Annie sat at work in the pleasant little sewing-room. The orchard door swung

ajar, and a nutty, leafy perfume mingled with that of ripening fruit stole persuasively in. The parlor garden was fragrant with the spices of cedar tree and box ; while the tall lilies bowed, stately, in the breeze, above beds of petunias and stock-gillies, and all manner of sweet old-fashioned flowers.

In the kitchen-garden, tricking out the gay rows of beans and neat patches of homely vegetables, there were crimson hollyhocks ; and the golden disk of sunflowers looked over the box-hedge. Earlier in the season there had been a company of lilac bushes in one corner, and in another the rosy luxuriance of the wygelia ; while from the low-eaved porch had hung masses of the grape-like wisteria. Now, the late-blooming honeysuckle, and the summer-long sweetness of climbing roses made the quaint garden a bower, and entered very largely into the calculations of birds and bees and all sorts of harmless, honey-loving things.

When Mr. Wallace joined the family, as he still did towards the hour when Annie had been used to bring him her book, there was a certain constraint upon her manner ; for she felt guiltily that she had perceived more than had been meant for her eye and ear.

The studies that had drawn her so near to her beloved friend, had given place to work with him among the poor—in itself a new bond between them. For, whatever creed was the letter of this man's religion, the spirit of it was to do good.

A universal compassion for his kind is the rarest of all qualities in the heart of man. He may feel sorry for a sick horse, a hungry dog, any wounded creature ; but for him to give fully of unasked sympathy to the mass of his fellow-beings, is uncommon enough to be regarded as phenomenal.

To feel a passing pang of compassion for one in acute, visible affliction, is one thing : to be permeated with an unfailing readiness of commiseration for those mortal ills which are invisible, is another and far less frequent thing. The latter mission was Mr Wallace's. He went about to save the bodies of men as his master had gone about to save their souls.   And he was not rejected ; for he came to the poor, and the poor knew him.

As they sat together and talked, on this pleasant August day, the girl gathered his words into her heart for an endless recollection of him—one of those sweet and solemn reminiscences which, years after, she would linger over tenderly. She was glad that he had made plain to her the power and beauty of his knowl-edge of Christ.   Reverently she always folded down this purest page in the history of him who wished to leave but the simple record—that he lived and died.

" I am going to build a chapel in Rest-Hampton, Annie," he said presently.

" I am *so* glad," she replied earnestly ; " for of course you will be the clergyman "—Annie stopped suddenly.

" In the Church of England," said John Wallace, looking steadily at her, " a man cannot even read the service without orders.   I shall probably go down to the Bishop of the Island and seek the appointment of lay reader, that I may conduct the service.   I shall never preach. I fancy the Rev. B—H—will recommend me," he added musingly.

That was all. More, Annie never knew. It seemed so natural presently, that she tried to put from her mind the strange and sudden apparition of the white-robed figure swaying the kneeling masses of people. It had been one of her halucinations, she concluded.

But the talk of this summer afternoon was more an expression of Mr. Wallace's faith than his creed. So strong and beautiful was the light which shone from this faith that it might have dazzled a more worldly listener than Annie Castlewood.

" Oh Mr. Wallace ! " she cried in her eager way ; " how you *do* believe ! "

" I do indeed, child. I must. My faith is all that is left me out of a shipwreck."

" Do you believe *everything* in the Bible ?—Just as it is written ? "

" Every jot and tittle, Annie. If this is changed, and that is excepted to, and the other is omitted, and half of it is said to be merely typical, what is there for the believer to stand upon ? Uncertainties, vague half-beliefs, lead to denials. There are men who preach from what they call *Christian* pulpits, that ' the Atonement is a monstrous and bloody fable ; ' that Christ's life alone has significance in the work of Redemption :—that Judaism was fatal to God's plan of salvation. With mad distortions of the truth like that, what is left to be the foundation of faith ? The cleft Rock is taken away ; the pierced Side is forgotten.

" Thee reminds me, John Wallace," said Martha

Castlewood, who had entered the room a moment before and paused to gather the thread of the discourse,
"of the old woman who was so wedded to the letter
of the Bible, that when she was asked if she believed
the whale had swallowed Jonah, replied promptly that
she would believe Jonah had swallowed the whale if
the Bible said so."

For Martha liked new doctrines much better than
old ones, and was disposed to take pride in her reason
rather than in her faith.

It was the first time she had ever used sarcasm
towards her guest, and doubtless she repented it, for
she presently left the room, having received only a
quiet smile for her pains.   *   *   *   *   *   *

From here and from there I have gathered words
and opinions which fell from the guarded lips of this
man, of whom it is said by those who knew him:
"*He was tolerant to all. He knew in Whom he believed, and yet he had a reverence for all men's faith.
He had pity, and not anger, even for those doctrines of
negation or denial which say "I reject" in place of
every "I believe" in orthodox creeds.*" Even the unrelenting antagonism of the Puritans could find no
fault in his religion, although the little chapel was to
them a bitter stumbling block.

When it was finished, and stood fronting the wide,
grassy, Rest-Hampton street, John Wallace's heart
went up in grateful thanksgiving. He had something
near him, at last, which was an expression of his own
innermost thought.

" I do not wish any man, woman, or child to leave
his own church and worship with me," he said when

ever the subject of the new congregation was referred
to.

"I have found a handful of people, here and there,
some of them many miles away, who crave what is
called here the Protestant Episcopal form of worship.
The church is for them—and for me.   I sincerely
hope that the sound of its bell will disturb no other
community of Christians who have a house of God and
a clergyman of their own."

But Martha Castlewood was the first to enter its
doors, leading in as usual, her " men folks," by her influence.

There were a few among the sturdy villagers who
never forgave Mr. Wallace the existence of that chapel.
That the rich squire and his family should uphold
the hands of a new priest was a forever unappeased
grievance.   Perhaps the man who carried this affront
farthest was deacon Potts, whose stern Pilgrim spirit,
together with a very decided hankering after the
squire's daughter, led him a crusade against the gentle
scholar.

"It is a question of my religion against John
Wallace's religion," he was given to saying pugna-
ciously.

In his mistaken zeal, he vented some of his antagonism upon the Castlewoods, about whom had crept
that unconscious reserve which surrounds one whose
identity is something unsolved.   The deacon resented
hotly this withdrawal of the best family and the nicest
girl in the village.   Moreover, a thing had come to
pass which demanded righteous intervention :—a
" Romanish Cathedral " had been built under the

very eaves of the church which had held absolute sway over Rest-Hampton ever since the settlement was !

Obadiah Potts was the sheep-dog of the fold. He was one of those fierce disciples who forgot that their dogma is not their gospel. While Mr. Wallace loved his own form of worship, being strong in preference but without prejudice, Obadiah hated all forms of worship excepting his own. He made himself exceedingly disagreeable to his adversary when they met, and even took it upon himself to waylay him in his walks, offering ill-timed remarks in the heat of his wrath.—

"What I want to know is, why one church isn't enough in our place, and why," he added gruffly, "a stranger should come along and fool our people with a strange church, Mr. Wallace."

"It is my seed-sowing," replied Mr. Wallace mildly, fixing the soft radiance of his eyes upon the deacon's hard and florid face : "Is not your community wide enough for me to do my little alms in my own way, Mr. Potts ? "

"Not if your way is to trample down *our* way, sir. This is our town, and not yours ; and you hadn't ought to meddle with the religion of our folks."

In his indignation, Obadiah fell into the vernacular. John Wallace still looked at the man. It was a wholly polite gaze ; for his good taste was too fastidious to permit a stare. But Mr. Potts chafed and fumed under it, as though it had been a sneer.

"My dear Sir,"— Mr. Wallace addressed all men as though they were his equals—" how can I convince you that I wish to meddle with no man's religion. Yonder little church is only my way of saying ' I believe ! ' Perhaps you will not understand me when I say that if this community had been actually suffering for a Presbyterian church or a Methodist church, I should have built that."

" No, I *don't* understand ; " cried Mr. Potts, " and what's more, I think that sort of talk is all cant.   I'm not a talking man, myself, but I can see through pretended piety when I have to." (Potts had red hair and a somewhat fiery disposition.)

Mr. Wallace's pale face took a faint tinge of color. There was an aristocratic hauteur in it which sometimes threatened to overcome the habitual expression of spirituality that it had come—through what tribulations?—to wear. "I cannot see, Mr. Potts, what you expect to accomplish by personal abuse.   It seems to me an ignoble weapon, and an utterly useless one. If I can say or do anything to prove to you that I have no malice in my heart against your congregation and it's prosperity, I will gladly do so."

(He did not add that there were few who gave more to that very congregation than himself.)

" Then I want you shouldn't get Squire Castlewood and his whole family up to your new church."

" I have spoken to them and endeavored to dissuade them," Mr. Wallace replied simply ; " but I rather think it has become a matter of real preference with Mrs. Castlewood and her daughter."

"Oh—no doubt ;" cried the other, his ire rising higher ; " The old lady is half cracked after new things anyway, I am told.   As for the girl, of course you can play at love-making with her, and carry her with you into perdition if you like."

Again Mr. Wallace looked at the enemy who so determinedly antagonized himself in so vulgar a way, This time Obadiah Potts was thoroughly taken aback at the keenness of the gaze. For even though a man may be a saint—nay, it sometimes happens so!—there are still demoniac forces native within him which may rise up and threaten to undo the gentler virtues of a lifetime.

The scathing moment passed however. This man's self-control was almost omnipotent. Mr. Potts hastened to conciliate, in his clumsy way : "You see I know Nancy Castlewood. She's a good girl, but easily led, where her fancy is tickled. I don't blame you for that. Nearly all young women are silly. But still I can't make out the good of two churches to split up a neighborhood."

" I think that there is good—else I should not have built the chapel,—in two churches. There are then many ways of calling human creatures to Christ. If one way fails, with special souls, the other may succeed. Are they not all one, Mr. Potts—your creed and mine ? Do we not both preach Christ and the atonement ? It is our duty to uphold each other, that we may uplift men. "

This was a hard doctrine to Mr. Potts, who had never thought about more than one straight and narrow sectarianism. He did not like it ; but he could not help seeing its charity.

" In these times of strange creeds, " began John Wallace, as if to himself, " of wild theories, of many gospels—the gospel of science, the gospel of philosophy, the gospel of unbelief, and the thousand other gospels of men's making that have no revelation for the saving of men's souls,—in these times of following things new, and despising things old, let us be careful upon what we build. "

" Yes—that is just it, " cried the deacon, only half grasping the other's meaning : " that is why I don't want to see our people led away and unsettled."

" No—no ; " answered the other earnestly: " It is against a too close conformation, a too strict dogma, I would warn you. Tell your people not to build upon their doctrines, but upon Christ. That is the spirit of religion without which the letter is an empty sham."

" And I would tell *you*, " cried Mr. Potts inspirationally, " to beware of priestly teachings, and mummeries that take possession of the imagination and leave the heart unsatisfied."

" You are right, Mr. Potts. The soul does not need a creed or a ritual. The story of Christ and His atonement is so simple and plain in the Bible that it needs no comments of man, no human theories hung upon its divine sufficiency. It is the world not the Bible that makes religion many-sided. Every one has an ' own way ' of looking at things. He calls that the right way. And so it is—for him. His *soul* does not heed it, but his *body* does. His senses, his imagination, his daily life, demand a creed. I have lifted up my creed in this little town, not because it is better than your creed, but because it is told in different words. Do not let us, in serving God, antagonize each other, but qualify and mitigate each other."

Mr. Potts was puzzled, and not at all certain that he liked this compromising doctrine any more than he had liked the other. There seemed, however, nothing more to say in direct and personal opposition, to Mr. Wallace himself. The only thing that remained was to see the Castlewood's themselves, and lay before them their unmistakable duty in upholding the church which all Mr. Wallace's eloquence could not prevent him from believing to be the only safe fold. Moreover, these lost sheep of the true faith were well-to-do wanderers, who could not be spared.

CHAPTER XIII.

A STORM AND ITS REVELATIONS.

" What lacks then of perfection fit for God
But just the instance which this tale supplies
Of love without a limit?   So is strength,
So is intelligence :   Then love is so,
Unlimited in its self-sacrifice :
Then is the tale true and God shows complete. "

THE RING AND THE BOOK.

TOM was gradually—very gradually—rising in the world. Some of the busy merchants among whom he was thrown, recognizing his honesty, made capital of it. His " setting up for himself " had languished ; and when the outside manager of a large shipping firm offered him a salary of eight or nine hundred dollars, he was thankful. It seemed to him magnificent. To Annie, also, ignorant as most women blessedly are of the actual cost of living, it appeared munificent. Her lover had been two years in the unknown city; and now that he began to talk of coming back to fetch her, she found herself looking forward to a new life of untried promises, with something like expectation.

Tom had turned out to be the " fine fellow " her father had predicted, and was indeed more of a success than even that sanguine gentleman had actually expected. Still, the question of a speedy marriage pended in uncertainty—to the outspoken amazement of the village maidens who avowed they would never keep so prosperous and handsome a fellow dangling in uncertainty upon their whims. But when Tom arrived, Annie was completely won over by his manly looks and his ardent devotion. She forgot all those puzzling analytics in which she had been for so long steeped. She forgot her comparisons between Tom's unsentimental attitudes towards her pet subjects, and Mr. Wallace's fastidious appreciation of the spiritual side to every question. She even began to admire the younger man's wholesome love of life and of the world ; and to prefer it, critically, she thought, to Mr. Wallace's unworldly and somewhat impractical renunciations. After all, it would be pleasant to live with Tom, and participate in his fresh experiences and his youthful impressions. Annie was on the rebound from a somewhat over-done exclusiveness of preference. She had had, for the time being, enough of the psychological side of life ; and the natural aspect of things, as apparent to young Hatherton, was a relief. Then she fancied herself in love with her robust lover, and was content to be married.

Tom certainly was handsome, and had, moreover, a fascination of his own, that was the result of good spirits and good digestion, rather than of any actual charm or palpable virtue. He was one of those lucky individuals whom everybody likes, men as well as women ; and yet I doubt if any reason could have been given except to praise his frankness, his young good-looks, and his easy good-tempered way of meeting people and circumstances.

And so, one day, the engagement was formally announced. The village congratulated Annie ; but her mother was silent.

A few nights after, there came to Rest-Hampton, one of those frightful storms of which the whole annals of the coast town had scored but a half-dozen. Whenever one had come, it had left its mark in the little burying grounds, where they laid the bodies of wretched creatures who had perished near the shore.

The earth and sky were enveloped in a dense pall of blackness, shredded each instant by terrifying shafts of fatal lightning. The sea thundered back to the thunder of the heavens ; and the bellowing winds swept the sounds together in one hideous roar.

" God help the seamen to-night," sighed Mr. Wallace, as they sat together over the great glowing logs, too appalled for conversation, and yet shrinking instinctively from scattering for the night. There was some comfort in companionship ; for the blasts of wind that wailed incessantly about the old house rose ever and anon into a wild hurricane, and shook every casement as with frenzied hands of fear.

Annie Castlewood's face was white with a strange dread, and she cowered over the fire listening to each mad rush of the tempest, that seemed more furious than the last. She was sick at heart and in body.

Tom, who had been spending the evening, and was house-bound by the storm, made a few unsuccessful attempts at banter ; but, failing to rally any of the party, relapsed finally into silence. Even the boys were quiet, as they hung about the windows as if alert for some unknown development.

All at once, a sound reached the pleasant room through a lull in the tempest, which made them start to their feet and look, terrified, into each other's faces.

Squire Castlewood, who had heard that signal of despair before, rushed for his great-coat and cap, followed by the boys who upon certain occasions broke from their mother's authority.

"Joshua," cried Martha Castlewood—"thee is not going out—thee will not take the boys out—on such a night as this!"

"I must go, Martha! be quiet—let the boys go—there is no danger—on land."

He spoke in a low hurried way; and then turned and kissed his wife and Annie, who stood white and still as a ghost. John Wallace rose, his clear eyes penetrating through the purpose of the good Squire. At first, he had not realized the meaning of the now repeated sound.

"Can it be a ship, Mr. Castlewood?" he asked quickly.

"Yes—Good God! a ship to go down in such a sea!"

"I will go with you to the shore."

He spoke quietly, but Annie's strained ears detected something in his voice which boded a sudden determination. With that strange intuition which is akin to fore-knowledge, and which is given alone to women, she knew that if there was danger to be risked, John Wallace meant to brave it. She looked at him wildly, and as he turned to leave the room, from her over-strained nerves burst a stifled cry :

" Oh—Mr. Wallace, *pray* don't ! Oh Tom ! go with Mr. Wallace ! Don't let him get in the boat "—and then she fell to sobbing with uncontrollable violence.

The three men looked at her, and exchanged mute glances. Then the Squire spoke out,—

" Yes, Tom, come along. Mr. Wallace is not used to wild scenes like that yonder : and—and—it's a rough night for a town-bred man, Mr. Wallace, a rough night, sir."

Andrews was muffling his master in his heaviest wrappings. Presently the latter said gently,—

" I think, Annie, that Mr. Hatherton had better stay with your mother and yourself. Andrews will take care of us."

But Annie's panic burst out again.

" Don't go—pray don't go," she cried hysterically, breaking from her chair, and seizing Mr. Wallace's arm—" Take me—if you go—"

" Annie, I think that thee has forgotten thyself." Her mother led her firmly back to her chair. In spite of her enforced calm, she, too, was painfully excited.

Tom who had not spoken or moved, excepting to start up at Annie's first appeal, stood and looked, his brow darkening every instant. Suddenly Annie rushed from the room and upstairs. In her own chamber, she dropped panting upon the floor.

" What *have* I done ! what *have* I done ? " she cried over and over, staring with wide, wild eyes into vacancy. " What have I done ? what does it all mean ?

I was out of my senses! Oh, what shall I do? what *will* become of me?"

Over and over the same vacant sentences repeated themselves in a wild monody of desolation.

Presently she heard the men depart. Were there three—or four? Had Tom gone? Perhaps he would never come back. She cared nothing. It was that other. Would any harm come to *him*? He would go to the life-saving station. The men would let him in the boat. Every one let Mr. Wallace do what he wished. They would push the boat into the breakers. The waves would go over it. It would be swamped—again the frenzy seized Annie. She fled downstairs and out of the house like a distracted thing. The blackness was so intense, and the tumult of the elements so overpowering, that she was blown along she knew not whither. The rain drove in blinding sheets through the darkness. The lightning rent the sky, revealing in instantaneous gleams, the wind-swept and drenched and desolate road. She stumbled upon fences and houses; she fell against trees. She saw, in the sharp and terrifying blazes of the lightning, that there were here and there hurrying groups of people stumbling like herself in the darkness. No one else was alone. She tried to run. Suddenly, in a wider blaze of lightning, she saw the figure of John Wallace, struggling through the storm, with bent head and firm steps. She did not know she spoke; but she shrieked again and again:

"Don't go—Mr. Wallace!"

The figure paused, turned: the group who struggled beside him stumbled on. In another glare of green light, Annie saw that he was coming towards her. The next instant she fell panting in his arms.

"Come back," she whispered through her chattering teeth—"Don't get into the boat."

"Annie," he said, speaking very distinctly and calmly, "you are beside yourself with nervousness and fright. Come home at once."

She shook her head, the power of speech having deserted her. She was shaking as with an ague, and Mr. Wallace placed his arm about her almost carrying her back through the storm.

It would not have been possible for any touch to be more impersonal than that with which he supported her backward flight. She felt the coldness of his disapproval even through the reelings of her own overwrought condition, but he had too much discrimination to upbraid her in her unreasonable state. He bore her silently and swiftly over the road where she had stumbled along in her blind frenzy. Perhaps his heart throbbed compassionately in response to this lamentable outbreak from the terrified girl, which had said so palpably—"I love you. I have never known it, but I love you. Pity me!"

John Wallace's self-control was not of the sort to fail in any emergency. He did not press with even a hint of tenderness to his side, the young creature who clung so piteously to him, but held her sternly aloof from his heart. She was none of his. If he yearned to have her so, who shall tell? When they reached the house, Tom Hatherton was standing at the door, gloomy and silent. In the last half-hour, he had taken a new estimate of Annie's probable conduct

during the two years of his absence. There was
nothing in Mr. Wallace's bringing her back to him
without a word, to cause him to alter his opinion.
He had thought the girl upstairs: that she had
actually followed the other was worse proof of her
perfidy than all.

He silently moved aside, without looking at Annie,
to let her pass. She crept into the house, tearless
and miserable, but temporarily restored to her sanity
by the calm control of a master spirit. .

"Hatherton," said Mr. Wallace, looking him calmly
and clearly in the eyes, with his steady gaze:
"You will have to be very careful with that child,
I fear that she is on the verge of a brain-fever."

"Thank you," answered Tom curtly! "you had
better look after her yourself. She is nothing to me,"
and he strode away into the storm.

Mr. Wallace stood irresolute for a second. His pity
yearned over the poor young creature who had given
way so madly to an unsuspected emotion,

"I should only make matters worse if I tried to mend
them," he thought, "God forbid that she should come
to harm or sorrow, through me."

Then he too turned and hurried out into the furious night, carrying a leaden heart in his blameless
bosom.

Annie stole upstairs feeling more like a culprit than
she had ever done in her life, Tom's gloomy and unrelenting face, which had turned from her when she
glanced at him, smote her with intermittent regrets.
But the keen, the poignant, the incessant remorse,
was from a sense that she had dragged from his mas-

terful height, the man who had never stooped to say
to her silly heart, "do you love me, Annie?"

The mother, busy about preparing blankets and
restoratives for possible demand, had not missed her.
Moreover, Martha Castlewood wished to think out, before she met her daughter's eyes, the possible tending
of that painful scene. The older woman was, by nature,
something of a schemer, and even now, busied about
the melancholy details of such a preparation, she could
not repress a certain exhilaration of hope. Surely,
John Wallace would "speak," after that.

Annie was spared the misery of listening to this
sentiment. She crawled into bed without undressing,
and covered her head with the bed-clothes, that she
might not hear the raging of the elements and the
booming of the fatal signal of distress. The cold had
struck to her very marrow. The night wore on woe-
fully. She did not hear her mother's authoritative
knock, or if she heard, it echoed past her concious-
ness in the rush and roar of that awful night.

The panorama along the beach swam continually before her dizzy brain : but most of all there stood out
the face of John Wallace, too gentle to be angry with
her, too just not to be indignant at her folly. She
fancied him stepping bravely into the life boat, and
the frail craft plunging under the huge breakers. She
saw his steady gaze fixed upon some distant object !
She watched a yawning wave rise up and envelope
the boat and its crew. She saw the water dash over
an uplifted head and wash across a serene white face.
Then the face seemed to disappear. The night and
the tempest had swallowed it.

Annie screamed as only a wild thing screams. John Wallace was right. It was brain-fever, the sudden development of which had caused the poor girl's unaccountable excitement, no doubt rather than been produced by it.

But how was Tom Hatherton to know that? For the next morning, proud and disconsolate, wounded to the quick, but unrelenting, Annie's lover with a farewell to no one took the early stage to Sag Harbor, whence the little steamer carried him back to New York, alone, and with a great bitterness in his honest heart.

What of the storm? and the fated ship wrecked upon that desolate coast in the night? Ask the little village burying-ground. It will tell of glad young lives, and gray weather-beaten lives, and weary time-worn lives, that were blown out like sparks in the fury of that blast.

There was a tempest in the brain of the squire's little daughter which matched the terror of the tempest without. But who shall know what late misery, what new ship-wreck, had come to the once storm-swept bosom of John Wallace! Is there not something sinister which guides the blind drivings of a fated life, which casts it ever and anon upon unknown reefs of misfortune? Surely, only the unerring and pitiless eye of an evil genius can so surely, so relentlessly hurl the hapless human soul upon the rocks and quicksands!

John Wallace had sought the shelter of a quiet haven where he believed that the furies could not pursue him. But the storm that drove the sinking vessel upon the Island shore, cast once more at his fated feet the spectre of his life. Meanwhile the melancholy gun boomed fitfully.

There were noble efforts made by the sturdy men of the life-saving service. There were brave fisher-men, too who persisted in launching a boat of their own into the boiling surf. There were half a hundred villagers, full of courage, and ready to lend any aid they might to the futile efforts. But all inexperience was rejected as worse than useless. Only John Wallace prevailed.

"I have spent many a night at sea," he said with his masterful calm. "A storm like this is not un-known to me. In God's name let me go to those perishing creatures."

At first they refused him. So their orders compelled them to do. But when he heard that it was a Scotch bark, he went to the Captain of the life-saving crew :

"I will give you five hundred dollars in aid of your coast service if you will take me to yonder ship."

The man looked at him, incredulously.

"Come sir," he said almost roughly, "this is no time for trifling, Stand aside and let me give my orders, will you?"

John Wallace went over to where Squire Castlewood stood shivering in the rain and cold :

"Mr. Castlewood, I want you here, if you please," "you will see that I mean what I say, Captain Murphy. Look—I hand Squire Castlewood these five hundred dollar notes for you. Will you take me?"

The signals from the ship had ceased. Doubtless she was sinking. There was no time to be lost, now.

The Captain touched his dripping cap ·

"All right, sir: at your own risk. Mind, Squire Castlewood, that's not a bribe for me, but a present to the life-saving service. You will look out for it if we never come back?"

"But my dear sir," cried the dazed Squire to Mr. Wallace, "You surely are not going into that toy boat on this sea! Do pray consider the danger—consider—us all!"

He was thinking of Annie, for whom his perplexed heart bled. John Wallace was thinking of her too.

"It would be best," he said to himself, "if I never went back: if she never saw me again."

Then he grasped Squire Castlewood's cold wet hand and said in his clear penetrating voice.—

"If I never come back, Joshua Castlewood, remember that I shall be grateful to the storm and to God."

And he sprang among the handful of sea-faring men. It took much shouting and many endeavors to launch the boat. Andrews clung to Mr. Wallace, to the gunwale of the boat, to anything he could seize upon, crying like a child, and begging to be taken in with his master. They pushed him roughly away, but not until he had felt the kind pressure of a firm and masterful hand he knew. He sobbed aloud. The next moment the boat was hurtling into the black abyss of waves.

After that it disappeared, and a great cry went up from the watchers on the beach. It was at that instant that Annie Castlewood, shuddering in her bed, a mile away, shrieked. Her spirit, it may be, watched from the shore. For who knows whereabouts is the spirit of a sleeper, or of one bereft of reason? Poor

Squire Castlewood spent the remainder of the night on the wild coast, battling in the darkness with mingled emotions of alarm and perplexity. Andrews, half mad with grief and anxiety, rushed about in frantic misery, hurling copious anathemas at the storm, at the sea, and at the Squire who had let his master go. Tom Hatherton went back and forth the long wild tramp from the coast to the village, where a shadow as of death seemed brooding.

Martha watched terrified, by the bedside of her daughter, who was plainly " wandering."

With dawn, came the abating of the storm, and the return of the hardy little boat. John Wallace had not gone down into the deep. He had come back to his alien life. The wreckers, brave fellows, but superstitious as are all sea-men, used to tell afterwards over many a pot of ale, and with many a mysterious shake of the head, a story which grew greatly in the telling.

There was something supernatural, they declared, the night that the Scotch brig went down. Their boat was in the direst jeopardy and would have been swamped every time, but for some strange power that made her ride the waves. There was some one in the company, they affirmed, who could not sink.

" It was so black you couldn't see your hand before your eyes," a hardy fellow swore, " and yet there was a queer sort o' white light, like a halo, which made one man's face as plain as daylight. That man, was Mr. Wallace, sir," and he always finished with—" I tell you, *I see it myself.*"

" T'was too late, though," grumbled the sailors and wreckers : " The old hulk 'd gawn to pieces afore we reached her. It took us nigh onto an hour to come up to the place. There wasn't but three live men an' one woman afloat. (We picked up the next few days, a good dozen or more dead men about the coast.) T'was poor enough luck. There weren't no cargo worth speaking of that came ashore. Couldn't ha' been worth much, that ship."

"And yet it must have been Mr. Wallace's ship." supplemented the landsmen. For it was observed that, after that day, John Wallace never again walked to the old harbor.

CHAPTER XIV.

ANNIE'S MARRIAGE.

" Why comes temptation but for man to meet
And master and make crouch beneath his feet,
And so be pedestalled in triumph ?   Pray
' Lead us into no such temptation, Lord !'
Yea, but, O Thou whose servants are the bold,
Lead such temptations by the head and hair,
Reluctant dragons, up to who dare fight,
That so he may do battle and have praise.

THE RING AND THE BOOK.

ANNIE'S feeling when she thought of Tom's departure and his probable disappointment, was one of bitterness.   What could he know, she mused, of such acute wretchedness as hers?   Only a being like Mr. Wallace could comprehend so subtle a misery.   Indeed, contemplating the complex nature of her own grief produced a certain hardness towards her lover's commonplace grievance, and she assured herself over and over again that she should never regret him ;— in truth, that she could experience only a sense of relief at being rid of a devotion quite incapable of appreciating her finer moods.

"I had rather worship my hero afar off, all the empty days of my life, than marry any other man upon earth !" she cried passionately in her tempestuous heart. "And I shall be content to live alone in the shadow of this secret love. It is nobler than to bask in the every-day light of a half-hearted affection."

Poor Annie!—poor innocent child! little did she know of the nature of the terrible temptation she was hugging to her breast, when she tried to cast aside the pure love of an outspoken, true soul, and to gather to her wounded heart instead the nameless and irresistible fascinations of a secret and unsought passion !

Who knows what guilt, what degradation, might not have followed in the train of such an abandonment of soul ? At least she did not realize; nor did John Wallace suspect. Only her evil genius knew.

For a while, pride had triumphed. Then Tom, in his unselfishness and unconsciousness prepared for that pride a downfall. He had no thought of posing as magnanimous, or of heaping coals of fire. Nevertheless, the coals fell upon Annie's head and humbled it to the dust. Out of the humiliation of that dust she was saved. . .

Tom had gone back to New York, in a pardonably wrathful frame of mind. He was such an honest fellow, that the bare idea of duplicity on Annie's part was intolerable to him. He thought that he meant to throw over the engagement without another word. But it was unnatural for any thing to rankle in his generous heart, and by the time a week had elapsed, he had shifted his point of view, and made up his mind to overlook her strange behavior as a part of the girl's illness. At least he would give Annie the

opportunity to do so.   It was more chivalrous, any
way, to let the girl break the engagement, if it had to
be broken.

That she had hurt him to the quick he neither
asserted nor denied.   He simply put it aside as something which, God willing, should be forgotten.

And here Tom Hatherton—he that was simple of
thought and ordinary of action, and unpoetic of soul
—rose to that height which is rarely attained among
mortal men : the height of self-renunciation from
which he could look down and say not only " I forgive," but " I forget."

Such forgiveness is divine, not human.   Our fellow man says grudgingly, " I forgive you ;—but the
memory of our offense is never wholly obliterated.
We feel it in the touch of his hand : we see it in the
coldness of his eye.   God says, " As far as the east
is from the west, so far have I removed their trans-
gressions from them : " and, " I will no more remember their sin."

And so it happened, that one day, during Annie's
first convalescence.   Squire Castlewood had put this
little note into his daughter's weak hand : and, after
reading it, she had flung herself sobbing upon his
bosom.

"Dear Annie ; I thought may be I had better go
off for a while, as I'm afraid perhaps you are not quite
sure of yourself.   I only heard yesterday, that you
have had a fever.   It changes the look of some things.
I am sorry you have been ill.   Don't worry about
me.   I love you the same as ever, but I don't want

to force you into marrying me. We can wait awhile longer before saying anything more about it, if you like.

Yours devotedly,

Thos. Hatherton.

" O father !" sobbed the girl, with her arms around his neck : "read what Tom says. Oh, he is too noble for me ! I am not good enough for him."

" Yes you 'are, lass : and he will find it out someday. It was all a mistake. You were ill, that night, you can explain it——"

" No," cried Annie, shivering, " I could never explain that night. It is irrevocable. I never want to speak of it."

" Well—well; perhaps it is just as well, Nancy. But Tom has done the handsome thing. I always, said he was a fine fellow. By and by, when you are better, you can write him a letter, a nice letter you know."

" I must write now. Dear noble Tom ! Oh, father ! I *do* love Tom ! I must have been mad not to have known it always. Prop me up, with pillows please, and fetch me my desk.—Oh father, Tom is too generous, too unselfish for me ! I am not worthy of him. I have been self-absorbed, and hypocritical, fancied my self above him. Oh, how he has humbled me !" and Annie wept bitterly, clinging to her father's arm.

" There—there, Nancy," he cried patting her on the back, as though she had a fit of choking rather than of weeping : " It will all be right, soon. Only get well fast, you can soon make it up to Tom. Won't it tire you too much to write? What would mother say?"

"I *must* write," she cried nervously; with a bright fever spot on each cheek; "don't hinder me, dear father. I must tell Tom—oh! what *shall* I tell him?"

It was a difficult task, for Annie was pitifully weak, her hand trembled so she could scarcely grasp the pen.

Surely the storm had wrought good, but not that which Martha Castlewood desired. Hitherto, Annie had only said to herself: "I may as well marry Tom. Why should I wait? If I wait a hundred years what else will there be—but Tom!"

Now, her whole heart went out to him. Good, honest, kind-hearted Tom! How little had she deserved his devoted faithfulness! How little had she given him credit for such delicacy of feeling, such nobility of nature. She was overwhelmed, almost as much by his magnanimity as she had been by her own folly and selfishness.

Penitence is a good stepping-stone to affection. At that moment, Annie Castlewood loved her boyish lover with a genuine impulse of devotion.

If only she could keep her ideal from troubling her life! If only she could forget!

This was her letter:

"Dear Tom." I wonder sometimes that you who know me so well—the worst side of the ' me,' that is capricious and exacting,—can wish to make me your wife.

" Are you not afraid to think of one day possessing

a creature so unreasonable and difficult to satisfy ?
Perhaps it is because we have grown up together
and known all each other's failings that you are ready
to forgive me all my wild fancies and unaccountable
whims.   I shall have fewer fancies and whims, Tom,
when I am safe in the atmosphere of your unstimulat-
ing good-sense.   Indeed, I am tired of them now.   I
have a great disgust upon me for many things in my
past life.   When I look back, I think that your warning, two years ago, was a needful one, and that I have
been chasing shadows

" Something seems to have fallen from my eyes,—
a veil, a mist, and I see my mistakes.   I see you more
clearly, too, as I see myself more clearly.   You seem
noble and good and true—far, far better than I, with
all of my self-satisfaction and disapproval of the things
around me—and—I *think* I love you, Tom.

" Do not come for me now.   I am too sick to think
of marrying for a long while.   And besides, I ought
to expiate my folly, and atone for my last freak which
cost you the journey back without me.   Wait a year,
and when you come—if you are satisfied with your
bad bargain—I shall be ready.

Annie."

Of course Tom did not wait the year.   How in
human nature could he ?

When he read that letter, so tremblingly penned,
with the pathos of penitence added to the pathos of
illness, a few manly tears fell upon the irregular and
blotted writing, then he folded Annie, figuratively, to
his warm heart, and felt that, for the first time, he
possessed her.   What he wrote—the wonderful man-

ner in which his confidence in himself and in her blossomed out in the sudden sunshine of her shy affection—can be imagined better than quoted.

By grace of his ready tact, Mr. Wallace spoke and acted with a heaven-directed freedom from constraint. Perhaps, after all, the events of that stormy night had made but little impression upon the solid Scotch nature which underlay his sensitive temperament like the solid rock beneath the twining beauty of moss and vine.

Annie, finding nothing for a morbid state to feed upon, felt comfort in this reflection. By degrees the distance between them narrowed, and was finally bridged over by the exquisite good taste of silence.

The reactionary mood which had dawned upon her before that memorable episode, returned with redoubled persistency. Annie's own individuality,— the Self that had so insistently made itself felt all her life—was in abeyance. She was beginning to dwell upon a healthier plane ; and this state of mind was tacitly recognized at the Homestead.

The mother wondered in silence ; for the fact of a reconciliation between Tom and herself was a secret which Annie and her father kept between them.

" Don't tell mother—just yet," she had pleaded ; " I think, somehow, that she may be disappointed."

For Annie's keen intuition had long ago led her to penetrate her mother's satisfaction in the turn affairs had taken ; and she was not slow to perceive that Mr. Wallace's conduct towards herself was watched with a stealthy eagerness which betrayed a certain unspoken desire.

In his own mind, Mr. Wallace had misgivings about the condition of her love-affair. As once, he had wished to deter her from the hasty engagement with Tom Hatherton, he now perceived that it was possibly the only future which would be offered to the girl. Moreover, he had honestly liked Tom, on his last visit ; and the thought that his own personality had probably created a separation between the two, caused him acute wretchedness. While Annie was concluding that he had forgotten all about the storm and its unpleasant revelations, he was pointedly recollecting the fact that Tom had walked away without a word, and probably never meant to return.

His fine fastidiousness shrank from speaking to Mrs. Castlewood about so personal a matter ; he feared that it might distress the good Squire, whom he had learned to love tenderly. There was no one but Annie herself.

It came out as if quite unpremeditated, one Sabbath morning as they walked together down the green lane to the little church, through the twitter of birds and the sea-blown air :

"Why is it, Nancy, that I never hear you speak of your marriage ? Am I too old to be your confidant ? "

He smiled upon her ; but Annie felt,—with a sudden flash of her old intuitive perception of this man's meaning,—the trouble, the pain, of his thought.

Her soft eyes searched his face : then she answered simply :

"Perhaps because it seems a long way off. And yet it *may* happen at any time, Mr. Wallace."

(Tom's last letter having threatened an immediate appearance.)

A sudden pure joy shone out upon John Wallace's countenance, like the light from behind a cloud which was so placid you did not recognize it for a cloud.

"I am very glad for you child. I am very thankful."

"You approve of it, then ?"

"With all my heart. I ought to apologize that some time ago, my solicitude forbade my reading your fortune aright. Tom is a noble man, Annie. He will make you happy."

Somehow—she did not know why—the tears were running down her cheeks.

"He *is* noble," she said earnestly. "Of his own free will, he offered me forgiveness for—many things. I trust I may make *him* happy."

"What a sweet, young story it is, after all," said the other musingly. "The world is so old, Annie, and yet your life and his are still a fresh and untold tale. It is like the birds in the nest—the flowers in the meadow—young—young, each year. May you be blest, child, with an ever young heart.

"Dear Mr. Wallace," cried the girl lifting her sweet tear-weighted eyes to his face ; "*all* happiness is not for youth. Surely you are happy in your beautiful, and perfected life !"

"Yes—I am happy. Always think of me as happy Annie."

Oh, great and self-sacrificing soul ! Oh, true and tender heart ! In that moment of Annie's confessed joy, thou couldst not bear, for very compassion and an almost heavenly sympathy, to let the mournfulness of thy lot cast a shade upon the brightness of her path.

He smiled so brightly that Annie was genuinely deceived, and kneeled down in her place in the little chapel, crying in her heart :

" Dear Lord ! I thank thee that he is glad, and that his life is serene ; that he does not need me."

For, unbeknown to herself, Annie's roots were wound about the feet of this man still. Still, she worshipped him. If he had stretched out 'his hand to her and said : " I am sad, stay and comfort me. When you are gone I shall have nothing ; " all the new impulse towards Tom, and the upspringing of instinctive longings for the woman's goal of wifehood, would have fled as light mists fly before the strong sunlight. She would have fallen before him and cried—" I will never leave thee nor forsake thee."

John Wallace understood. Gently he put away the possibility. It could not even tempt him. His life was a broken arc. Annie's might possibly be a shining circle. At least, it was not for him to take it, and there-with piece out the shattered round of his own existence.

As he stood at the lectern that morning, Annie watched his uplifted face and said to herself :

" I used to think that radiant look was *all* heavenly. Now—I know that he is happy on this earth."

And Annie, too, was radiant. She thought that the lingering sense she had felt, of some hidden force slumbering in her being, had been a feeling that Mr. Wallace disapproved of her marriage.

"Now," thought she, "all will be as placid as the surface of the lake."

So it was—on the surface. But even the lake has unfelt possibilities for storm and terror hidden in its placid bosom.

Of course Tom did not wait a year. How in human nature could he? And Tom was decidedly human.

In six months from the night on which Annie Castlewood had pitched through the darkness crying for Mr. Wallace to come back, Tom Hatherton stood up triumphantly by her side in the little chapel, and Mr. Wallace was in the chancel while a clergyman who came at his request, married them. She had begged so, that he could not refuse her. Only a month before she had told her mother that Tom was coming for her ; that she was to marry him all the same.

At first Mrs. Castlewood was incredulous.

"Thomas Hatherton is going to marry thee—after all that has happened ? After what he could see with his own eyes ?"

"What could he see, mother ?"

Annie's countenance was pale, and she stood looking directly into her mother's face. The latter flinched, somewhat, but she made one last bold play for her lost game.

"He could see that thee has never felt one atom of love for him ; he could see that thy heart will never be his ; he could see that thee has but one thought —John Wallace."

The two women stood looking at each other, one with accusing eyes, the other with defiant ones.

Presently Annie spoke slowly, determined to say nothing which might bring her regrets.

"Whatever he saw, or thought he saw, he was magnanimous enough to forget. I hope that my mother will do the same."

It was so gentle a rebuke, so like the soft answer which turneth away wrath, that Martha Castlewood was touched and frankly begged her daughter's forgiveness for referring to what she said was, after all, but a blunder of delirium.

"Only I have thought, all this while, that it *might* have been "——

She looked steadily at Annie.

"No," said the girl turning away, while the delicate color came and went in her cheeks—"it could *never* have been."

Suddenly Mrs. Castlewood took a step forward and folded her daughter in her arms, with that dry sob in her throat which comes to people who have outlived the period of easy tears. It had rushed over her convincingly that John Wallace had never "spoken;" that Annie was marrying, not where she would, but where she might.

"Never mind all that, mother, dear," said Annie softly, stroking the elder woman's lightly silvered hair. "Don't fret about me, or think that I am not content. Indeed, I believe that I shall be happier with Tom than I could have been with—any other person."

The dignity of her reserve was so nicely balanced, that Annie could give a filial confidence to her parents without ever naming the name of any hope she may have secretly treasured—if, indeed, she knew that she treasured it.

"You know, little mother," she went on half playfully, "that Tom is not introspective or analytic, and that is just what I need. I have thought too much about my thoughts, and felt too much about my feelings, and got into a morbid state of self-contemplation —you know what I mean, don't you?"

"Yes," with another dry sob, "I comprehend thee, daughter ; but I have been helpless to avert this condition. It is my own wayward and discontented self of long ago that has reappeared in thee, causing thee nameless longings and undefined aspirations. I have never been able to come near thee, barred out of thy heart by a too close similitude of texture. There must be some contrasts before there is true affinity."

"I know that, mother : that is why I say Tom will be good for me. He has never been troubled with heart searchings or soul strivings. It is just such a practical affinity that my unpractical nature requires."

"It is not that I have not understood thee," Martha went on plaintively, taking no heed of Tom's reappearance in the conversation, but that I have understood thee too well to meddle with thy complex nature which I knew must work out its own contentment or misery. But I have suffered, Annie, in being thus left upon the outside of thy life"——

"Dear mother," cried Annie kissing her tenderly— "how sorry I am that you have wanted my confidence, while I egotistically fancied myself misunderstood. How strange it is that one heart born of another heart, does not nestle to that other as to a home, but is ever wandering in search of rest outside."

"That thought has often haunted me, daughter. I have felt that it is in this subtle manner wherein the sins of the parents are visited upon the children. I was wilful, Annie, before thee was born; I did not want thee ; I rebelled against thee as a burden. And I have borne my punishment ever since, in having thy restless nature,—so fatally like my own,—elude and stand apart from me as though it said "I know thee not."

Annie sat and pondered a moment. This then was truly the secret, not only of her want of perfect affiliation with her mother, but also of her own incomprehensible variances with herself. She had suspected it always, but, now her mother's words confirmed it. Again, she felt glad that Tom's look upon life was outward, and not inward.

"I have seen the friend who has been so long with us monopolize thee, Annie, and penetrate thy innermost consciousness, and leave his impression upon every fibre of thy being, while I knew that I—thy mother—had no part in thy spiritual vitality."

Martha Castlewood's voice sounded like a wail. Annie sat, conscience smitten, only stroking her hair with cool light fingers.

"And now," she mourned on, "when I had adjusted myself to that monopoly, and believed that at least I should have my ambition for thee satisfied,—if not my love for thee,—thy whole career veers about, and thee is going off on a new tack where I cannot follow thee, even afar off."

"Yes you can, mother," Annie cried eagerly ; "you

will see that this marriage will restore me to you, as
I was when a little child, before I fell into the mazes
of fanciful dreams.   You will come and stay with me,
and we will live together upon a delightful new plane,
forgetting the unsatisfaction of the past."

"Is thee sure that thee does not love John Wallace,
Annie?"

The mother lifted her head and looked appealingly
into the girl's eyes.   They were clear and steady.   In
the reaction from her long dreamy mood, Annie
thought that she spoke the truth when she said:—

"*Quite* sure, mother.   I revere him unspeakably.
It is Tom who has won my love." * * * * * *

And so Annie was married.   The village gossips—
who are in no wise different from other gossips, dear
reader,   only that the term   gives the impression of a
distinctive class—had to adjust their spectacles to a
new view of the case.   Tom Hatherton had not jilted
Nancy Castlewood   after all ;   and they began to see
what a very good match it really was.

They had counted largely on being dumbfounded
at the splendor of Mr. Wallace's munificence in the
form of a wedding-gift.

"It was a lucky day up to Joshuay Castlewood's
when that rich man hap'd upon them," said one.

"They've held onto him ever since, and given nobody else a chance," grumbled another, retrospect-
ively.

And now they waited for their crowning envy in
what the Squire's Nancy might reap from the chance.

But they were doomed to eternal disappointment,
since the substantial box which came up from New

York, on the day before the wedding, was unopened in public. Indeed the story ran that, " whatever it was, Mr. Wallace must ha' been ashamed of it, as he had bid Nancy not to open it for folks to see!"

What was in the box touched Annie to the heart's core :—a complete set of silver (everything that could be made in silver, the Castlewoods thought)—of an exceedingly plain design, as unwrought and simple as the little old tea-spoons which Martha Castlewood cherished as having belonged to her great-aunt. Each spoon and fork and pitcher and pot had this only for ornament in the most legible script : "Annie Castlewood." It was backed by a substantial check for Tom, which, Mr. Wallace said, would help them line their nest.

It not only served to line the nest, but to secure a very modest little one in a neighborhood distinctly apart from the fashionable centres of the busy city.

Perhaps it did not occur even to Annie herself, after the quiet ceremony was over, and the tearful good-byes were said, that "the wedding"—the greatest of all events in the life of most girls,—was to her a much less marked occasion than the different periods she had marked in her vivid acquaintance with John Wallace. Each one of these stood out as a distinct episode in her existence.

There was the day on which he had first stood in the doorway, tall and stately and benign ; there was the morning when he had offered to teach her French and German ; there were several occasions during the two following years, in which she had felt a thrill from his magnetism, not easily forgotten. There was the day on which she had told him of her engagement, and he had said in that low mesmeric voice of his :— *" Child, are you not happy as you are ? "*

Then there was the evening when she had beheld him,—with that peculiar inner vision which he himself seemed to have imparted to her,—rise before her in priest's robes, with uplifted hands of benediction, and a great light in his face. That was the most vivid impression of all, unless it was the next one, when she saw—something saw it !—the waves go over his white face in the midst of a great storm at sea. Truly, her mother had spoken aright, when she said that John Wallace had marked her with his personality ! That had been an absorbing friendship.

Her love for Tom was not at all absorbing. It was her allotted portion. The other was a beatific gift.

And still Annie realized that Tom's love was more wholesome. She fancied it would prove more satisfying. She was still drifting with an under-current : but she did not know it ; for, as yet, her head was above water.

In this sudden reaction against the influence of the man she had idolized,—or was it only idealized ? —Annie had begun to fancy the whole friendship unnatural and therefore undesirable. The recoil was born of that night when she had flung herself upon him in a frenzy of incoherent emotions, and he had held her aloof with so cool and measured an impersonality.

Her pride had suffered a shock which had roused her, and put her upon her mettle. In the first mortification of recollection she had said bitterly :

" He has been a curse to me rather than a blessing. He has nearly spoiled my life instead of helping it. I have grown morbid, and my actual surrounding are unreal to me, while he has fostered in me only the imaginary and the unsatisfying. "

Then had come a great wave of repentance that she should accuse this good man, who had not thought at all to make or mar her insignificant fortunes, but had merely stretched to her the helping hand he stretched to all.

After that, the two ideas settled themselves quiescently, and when John Wallace asked her about her marriage, the whole subject rolled from her mind. They stood, she thought, upon the old footing, outwardly; while for herself, she was upon a secure plane of honest purpose and sound good sense. Mr. Wallace's influence had been stretched to the uttermost. She had let slip her end. Henceforth, she was to be untramelled by any vestige of it.

CHAPTER XV.

A LONELY MAN.

" I am on earth as good as out of it :
A relegated priest : when exile ends
I mean to do my duty and live long.
She and I are mere strangers now ; but priests
Should study passion ; how else cure mankind
Who come for help in passionate extremes ! "

THE RING AND THE BOOK.

ANNIE had gone. If the shadows deepened around John Wallace's life, he did not betray it. A part of the dicipline of his lot had been "to sit aloof," as Emerson hath it. Doubtless, through the self-denials which made up his every-days, his character had come to take its majestic proportions ; for the soul grows by prunings not by indulgence.

His modesty, like his simplicity, was grand ; but little by little he had impressed the Island township with a sense of his force. True to the prophecy of the poet, because he asserted himself, the world learned to come and lean upon him. And still, he felt in his heart a great want that was sometimes a bitter need. Annie, looking towards him from her new surroundings, with wistful eyes, comforted herself with the thought that he had renounced too much from his life to be troubled by the disappearance of a single girlish figure that had flitted across it's long perspective.

"You must write me everything concerning Mr. Wallace, mother,—everything ; " she had said.

And Martha Hatherton, being no less glib of pen than of tongue, wrote faithfully.

There was not much to impart, except that he kept as usual his daily routine of walking ; of teaching the poor ; of giving to all who asked, and of spending long unseen hours over his books and papers.

At one time Martha wrote tenderly of the close and ever-increasing friendship between her husband and their guest.

"There are days," she said, "in which he follows Joshua about like his shadow. I fear he is a lonely man at best. Sometimes I am persuaded," she added with that droll touch of worldliness that was in her, "that he will make a will leaving to us his fortune. Not that I desire to become possessed of greater worldly goods, excepting as it would prove a means of enlarging our narrow sphere, and enabling us to take a wider view of such temporal things as are seemly."

Later, she communicated to Annie a rumor that he had commenced to preach to the sailors and fisher-men at Sag Harbor.

"It is without church, or prayer-book, or gown," she afterwards explained ; "and is in truth only long and earnest talks with that rough but impressionable class."

Twenty-five years later, among the papers in his portfolio, side by side with the sermons he had never uttered, and the Latin hymns he had translated, and the scientifie work he had done, and the literary treatises he had written, were found a few verses which doubtless grew out of this period.   John Wallace's Scotch ruggedness and strength were much more apparent in his writing than in his refined appearance or fastidious manners.   What he said with the lip was guarded and smoothed,—for hearing.   What he wrote was spontaneous and bold—for himself.   For he rarely published any of his work, and then only anonymously in some Scotch Review.

The rough lines, which cannot fail to touch the heart, even though they may not please the ear, were headed :

CHRIST'S FISHERMEN.

" O Fishermen, beside my mighty sea
Know ye not that to men such as ye be
    I came with my first call
    And in the midst of all
Your toil, I toiled out my humanity ?
How can ye spend your hard-earned lives upon
Such periled paths, and not remember One
Who, loving men, walked once a stormy sea
To save them in their faithless jeopardy ? "

*   *   *   *   *   *   *   *

" When seas are calm, and dangers out of sight,
    And all the nets are full ;
Or when wild terrors crowd the blackest night
    And you can only pull
The helpless oars and hold your shuddering breath——
Across the waves, Jesus of Nazareth
May come, as He came over Gallilee.
Ye know not when He cometh.   It may be
At eve, or midnight, or at dim cock-crow
Or in the morning :—when the tide runs low,

Or when the breakers roar
Far up the beaten shore ;
When winds are wild, or when the breezes blow,
At any hour, and over any sea
The Lord may come and ask thy soul of thee.

" Perhaps, some fierce night, in a driving squall
When your frail fishing-yawl
Is plunging through the black and yawning graves
Between the thudding waves,
Still beaten back from the far home-lit shore
You say within your soul, ' Perchance to-night
The Lord will come ; and day shall find me white
And stiff in the white foam.'
But when the sharp, cold morning light has come,
You shall scud chilly home
Forgetful even to be thankful for
The life you hold as careless as before.

" And then, perhaps, some morn when all is fair,
And scarcely with a care
You rock your thoughtless craft from the bright beach,
A sudden gale may catch your sail's spread wing,
Or in your boards a fatal leak may spring,—
Lo ; ere your strength can reach
The smiling shore, you go down fierce and stark,
Bewildered that it grows so ghastly dark
All in the midst of sunshine, while your hand
Is nerved to pull, and with the flashing sand
Not half a league away !
Oh, Fishermen ! I say
When the Lord calls, you cannot bluff your way
To a near safety ; while yet He calls not,
The maddest gust can never cast your lot
At the sad bottom of the restless sea.
And still He tells you, ' Watch and wait for me !
If so be it I come
And find you ready—then be sure your home
Upon the distant shining heavenly shore
Is waiting stormless—safe—forever more.' "

*   *   *   *   *   *   *   *

The gentle scholar's loneliness in the coming days

was made more poignant from the fact that Destiny came and banished his faithful valet from him.

About four years after Annie's marriage, there smote upon Mr. Wallace's ear the story that Andrews —the long-tried and trusty—was falling into bad habits at the little inn, where Ben Adams and his crowd held mild orgies.

What a blow this was to the solitary man, only those who have endured exile can know.

One evening, he gathered all his forces together to meet the certainty, went to the place of carousal, and stood like Fate upon the doorway.

A hush fell upon the clownish fellows who were half joking, half quarreling over their grog, but not before Andrews, semi-intoxicated, had bawled out with a great swagger and hiccough :

" So you think my master's a h'ordinary—gentleman —do you ? well—if you could see a grand place of his —Yes, sirs, a palace—over in—"

Andrews never finished that sentence. He halted suddenly, magnetized by the keen and angry eyes of the figure in the doorway. Never had Rest-Hampton beheld those eyes look so wrathful, so sorrowful, so pitiful ! It made Uncle Seth, who was prosing near by, think dimly of the Face that " turned and looked on Peter." And never was man more instantly sobered than the luckless valet. He picked up his hat with what shame-facedness may well be imagined, and slunk out by another door, not moving his fascinated gaze from his master's stern face, until he was himself out of sight.

Then Mr. Wallace with a brief bow to the subdued

company, turned and walked home, the sternness unre-
laxed and mixed with a pain difficult to realize save by
one who has learned to love a dog or some other humble
and faithful creature that, after years of devotion, turns
and rends him.

The next day, Andrews disappeared—heart-broken
and penitent, but acquiescent. That he had got
drunk and begun to blurt Mr. Wallace's affairs was a
sufficient cause for his humiliation and his dismissal.
Indeed, it seemed, in the poor fellow's eyes, a capital
offense,—that no punishment could expiate.

That they two, so long thrown upon each other's
companionship, did not part in anger, was Andrews'
one consolation to which he passionately clung.

Perhaps Mr. Wallace felt an attachment for the
man greater than he felt for any creature in the village ; but—it was inevitable.

For a long while it was the village opinion that the
valet had gone back to England, and he was greatly
missed by the boon companions of his fallen ways.
But, after awhile, Uncle Seth triumphantly announced
that the man had been sent West. It may be that
John Wallace, looking from the extreme edge of middle
life down the long declivity of old age, could not endure to be left alone upon the, to him, homeless side
of the melancholy sea. It may be that Andrews had
positively refused to so leave his beloved master. Certain it is, every six months, old Seth handled a large
envelope addressed to " Henry Andrews, Loon-Creek,
Colorado."—the then remote wild west.

The old post-man and his cronies had much difficulty in surmising the purport of these letters ; but it

was satisfactorily decided, during the next five years that the valet was pensioned: and much controversy was held over the fabulous sum which could thus pay off the devoted servant. The latter, Mr. Wallace replaced by a youth from The Harbor: the faithful friend, he never replaced, since the new waiting man knew no more of his master's affairs than did Uncle Seth himself.

The occurrence seemed to have a singular effect upon him. How much Andrews had talked, what revelations he had suggested, he never knew, but the fact of his having talked at all seemed to arouse in Mr. Wallace a long dormant uneasiness and suspicion.

There was that in his demeanor which startled Mrs. Castlewood, who had taken upon herself gradually a deep and lasting interest in her guest. Presently it grew apparent to all in the household, spreading stealthily (as all such things which we would cover do spread) to the neighborhood.

John Wallace had become possessed of a hallucination that he was concealing a secret, and that he was watched. He fancied that there was something to hide, which was growing to be a terrible nightmare to him, making him nervous and fearful, even under the friendly roof of the farmhouse.

He was filled with inarticulate apprehensions—always inarticulate ; always by starts and sudden changes of the face, never betraying its cause by words. He held himself by a perceptible grip of self-control that was painful as it was unaccountable. Withal, it was so intangible that no one could approach him on the subject. For he never said, even in secret:

" I am in terror of some disclosure." Only his face and his altered manner proclaimed it on the housetop.

The good squire took refuge in his usual method of being helplessly puzzled : his wife went deeper and was alarmed.

" It is a symptom of insanity," she said to herself ; and she saw with consternation that John Wallace was rousing nameless suspicions, where he had, in all the former years of his abiding, only awakened curiosity.

"There's something behind it all," announced the wise oracles of the town : "depend upon it, he isn't afraid to look folks in the face for nothing. He's wronged somebody, most like."

But Martha shielded him, as a lioness shields her young. Every now and then some coarse-bred man or woman spoke out openly and demanded the secret of her hands. And she—having no secret, and therefore beaten about by questions of her own—was defiantly impervious to their demands or their hints. She would never, by a look or a word, betray that she, too, doubted John Wallace. If she watched him, however delicately, for his own protection, he became mistrustful of her.

" It is only a nervous condition," she boldly averred, "which I have encountered before——in Rhode Island," she hastened to add ; for Rest-Hampton knew there had never been a like case of " nerves," within its precincts.

" There is nothing nerves won't do when they are unstrung. All that Mr. Wallace needs is a journey somewhere for his health."

But to this proposition, Mr. Wallace gave such a

startled and uneasy.protest, that no more was said about it. They could only wait.

Annie, in her new home, heard of the change and waited with a sort of fascinated terror for the denouément. In a few months as though it had indeed been but a mood, the change passed, and John Wallace's powerful intellect and noble tranquility of nature again asserted themselves over whatever delusion had had his imagination in brief thrall. He was so plainly himself, after that, that the Castlewoods drew a long breath of relief, and Rest-Hampton subsided upon the theory of the nervous condition.· *And indeed, what else could it have been?*

This was the way of the climax. During that unhappy and disordered time, when the soundest of brains seemed in unaccountable chaos, Mr. Wallace and Mr. Castlewood were sitting together one evening, in a somewhat uncomfortable silence into which they had fallen after many ineffectual attempts at conversation on the Squire's part. (It was a feature of the former's peculiar malady, that he dreaded being alone, and shunned the pleasant solitude of his study as he might have shunned a haunted chamber. So he sat, like an incubus, with the family.) All at once he leaned forward in his chair, and gazed gloomily at his companion's abstracted face. Some powerful impulse seemed to sweep over him, and he rose hurriedly and began pacing the room. Then he stopped directly in front of the Squire, trembling with some suppressed emotion.

" Sorrow—banishment—suspicion," he wailed in a

strained and unnatural voice that startled the other from his revery.

He stretched out his hand as if to reach that friendly clasp:—" I can bear it no longer," he cried: " Friend, I would tell you "——

He stood with his palm outstretched, like a man transfixed by some sudden and horrible apparition: as though he had slowly hardened into ice—into stone.

Then he turned, his face, dreadful to behold in its ashen unnaturalness, and spoke no other word.

" My dear sir," cried the agitated Squire, to whom the other seemed like a spectre—or a dead man, with his passionate confession frozen, like curdled blood, upon his lips—" Why won't you speak out and say what troubles you ? Surely—surely you know you have my sympathy—my reticence——"

John Wallace—or the speechless spectre of John Wallace—shook his head, and sank back into his chair. Presently his arms fell heavily to his side. His head was erect ; his eyes were wide open and fixed, but they saw nothing. By the time a doctor could be procured, he had recovered from the slight stroke which had passed over his system. After that, the suspiciousness seemed to vanish. The irritability, the watchfulness, the unrest, slowly disappeared. He had once more mastered himself : but his health began to wane from that day.

The strain had been too great even for his wiry constitution. Nature says to the floods and tempests of the human heart: " Thus far and no farther."

By the time that John Wallace was fully restored to his natural condition of mind, and apparently of body, another calamity had fallen upon the rambling old farmhouse under the chestnuts. It was mid-winter. The once grassy village street, as well as the meadows and old apple-orchards, were covered with a deep and unbroken snow. White heaps were piled high upon the carefully trimmed garden-box, upon the twisted boughs, upon the gaunt and silent arms of the wind-mills, upon every available ledge, in fact, not forgetting the village burying-grounds, whose mounds were all levelled to the smooth slope of the hill-side. Only the tops of head-stones jagged the even surface, and gave a fantastic appearance to the new winding-sheet.

Indoors, too, there was a mid-winter sadness and gloom; for the dear old squire, whose hearty voice and pleasant cheer had used to break the silences, were gone. It had been very sudden. Dr. Josiah Clump halted between apoplexy and heart-disease. It was the custom of his patients to live to such a time of life that they departed their accustomed ways by the slow and gradual process called dying of old age: which means—if we, in the rapid and soon-over rush of city-life, have not forgotten its meaning—dropping the faculties one by one, in so gentle a manner as to do no violence to preconceived notions of soundness. They frequently dispensed with any need of aught but encouragement from the village doctor.

But Squire Castlewood had not only cheated old age of a victim: he had also given the physician an unfair chance at diagnosis.

His earthly career stopped short at seventy, which was a departure from Rest-Hampton ways, and a blur upon their traditional longevity.

"Lord!" cried Uncle Seth, (who had been for five or six years known us an octogenarian), "I always said the Squire 'd die young. I always knew he'd kill himself, some day, with his rash way, of rushin' into new things, oncalculated and onprepared. I hope," he added fervently, "that they'll lay him out in his father's military suit as he wore to fight the British in. Now, wouldn't he make a fine colonial corpse? It would be worth dying young for. Lord! I hope, when they come to lay me out they won't forget my great-uncle's buff waistcoat, that's in the seventh drawer from the top, in the old chest of drawers. I've made a will on purpose to write it down. Why really, though," finished the wise old fossil, mournfully shaking his head, "I couldn't be happy, walking about with Peter and Paul, if I hadn't that waistcoat and my grandfather's snuff-box!"

The Squire's last moments had been peaceful. Mr. Wallace sat beside him like one stunned. His eyes were fixed sorrowfully upon the helpless figure of his friend, the last pressure of whose hand was for him.

"John Wallace" whispered the dying man earnestly, "you have taught me without a word, how a man was meant to live. You have taught me faith—charity."

"My dear and faithful friend," said the other bending down and returning the fluttering hand-pressure earnestly; "This is a great blow to me. I had thought to die beneath the kindly shelter of your noble friendship. I had thought that no one but you would be near me when I came to the last. I have trusted you; I have been thankful that I might trust you. I should have died trusting you, if—in the last weak hours of the flesh—it had been forced from me to utter things which I had meant never to speak. I could have trusted you with them."

No other words could have penetrated with such satisfaction the Squire's dulling comprehension. A smile of unutterable content broke over his face, and in the glory of that smile, Joshua Castlewood entered the valley. His only grief had been at not seeingh is daughter; for Annie was ill and could not travel.

CHAPTER XVI.

ANNIE'S SPECTRE.

> " *Could we by a wish*
> *Have what we will, and get the future now*
> *Would we wish aught done undone in the past?*
> *So let him wait God's instant men call years,"*
> *Meantime hold hard by truth and his great soul?"*—

THE RING AND THE BOOK.

AND how have these four years of wedded life gone with Annie? Variably, as wedded life goes with most people. Now and then, we see a beautiful marriage, in which all is an even flow of more than fulfilment. To some happy women, thank God, it is given to realize their ideals.

But we have seen that Annie consciously relinquished hers at the brink of her marriage, and endeavored to take up with a new set of principles. The mental habits of years, however, cannot be overturned in a moment. The birth and death, even of opinions, are attended with both suffering and patient enduring.

Annie had planned that her actual existence must run, henceforth, in some ordered channel, while her ideal life, if it could not be altogether dried up, might flow in another.   Her future had begun to look fair to her, because she had, in justice, forfeited it, and through mercy recovered it.

Then came the test.   Could she succeed in banishing all the dreams, the chimeras, of her lifetime, and not find herself stranded upon a blank monotony of weary commonplaces ?

Time would show.

At first, the young housekeeper had work to do, and was glad to keep her hands busy.   It would be an untruth to represent the Hathertons as absolutely poor in their new beginning.   Poverty is a many-sided word, sometimes with a flippant meaning, bandied about by the avarice of those who live in wide houses, and, having plenty, still grumble for more.   The other name for this sort of Poverty is Discontent.

It is ashamed of the sweet sacrifices which love is glad to make for love.   It looks upon those simple self-denials which are so good for youth and happiness, as hard and niggardly stintings.   It stands, like the skeleton at the feast, at many a modest family board that would seem lavishly abundant in the eyes of actual poverty.

This was not Annie's spectre.   She was not afraid to look her next-door-neighbor in the eyes, and say:

" We are young beginners : we only aspire to be comfortable."

No—Tom and Annie Hatherton were not poor.

They lived economically, but well enough for comfort : Tom was kind and cheery and busy ; Annie was bright and gentle and full of pretty domestic concerns. He thought her a very model of sweetnees, and goodness, and all housewifely industry ; she thought him the best and cheeriestof husbands, and was content.

If it were not that John Wallace alone stands for the hero of this history—and of the mystery which shall presently be shown,—nothing could be more pleasant than to follow the young couple into their checkered career, and to find out from Annie's own lips whether living in an obscure part of New York, as Tom Hatherton's wife, was the experience in the great world for which she had hungered.

Of the vagaries of her girlhood, of the many moods of mind which had developed under the influence of Mr. Wallace, we have seen that she took nothing with her. Only her loyal heart, her loving nature, her large sympathies, her natural deftness went with her from the Island village, where she had, in dreams, planned, and wished, and foregone so much.

She was happy and contented ; and for a while lived above these buried fancies and went singing blithely through her small pretty rooms as though—at the turning point between childhood and womanhood —she had never encountered a riddle.

Tom worked early and late, adding little by little to Annie's home comforts, but leaving her necessarily with but seldom companionship outside of her own thoughts. This was the disaster which told against her good resolutions, in the long run.

If it be thought that this story, like Annie Castlewood's girlhood, is too introspective, and over much given to perplexing problems, let it be remembered that it is in purport. not a novel with a tragedy, nor a story with a moral, but simply a philosophic study of character—such an one perchance as a modern writer sarcastically terms a " psychological romance."

* 　 * 　 * 　 * 　 * 　 * 　 * 　 *

About the time that Andrews suffered banishment, and his master suffered the last alienation of his life, Annie fell into ill health. She had been more than four years married, and as yet there were no children to puzzle Tom with the vexing problem of multiplication, in reference to what they should eat and wherewithal they should be clothed.

But this summer, Annie was ill and depressed She was given to nervous starts and sudden alarms Her mental condition deteriorated with incredible rapidity, relapsing into a strange and secretive moodiness, which had about it the air of mystery or of suspicion. Her state of mind was like a reflection of Mr. Wallace's mood. She greeted Tom with silent tears or with perplexing accusations ; or she held herself aloof from him in apprehensive unrest. Tom was more tender and considerate than ever. He thought he comprehended a reason for her unreasonable state, and his gentleness and patience never failed. It is upon such emergencies that the uses of a sunny nature and a somewhat unreflective texture of mind become most apparent. Tom was able, through his good nature and his absence of imaginativeness, to manage bravely. As for Annie, she struggled against the terrible, and, even to herself, unaccountable cloud, as she had never struggled in her life. It was dreadful to her ; but yet it overwhelmed her. Her struggling was of no avail.

All this while, her mind ran steadily upon John Wallace. She saw him sitting, moody and depressed before the fire ; she pictured him pacing the floor with irritable unrest ; she fancied him starting up and turning an alarmed face to every one who entered the room. Her mother had written her elaborately of his unaccountable mental condition ; but these pictures were all Annie's own, and they haunted her with a ghostly persistency that was incredible to her. More-over, their absolute truth of aspect, and precision of detail made them terrifying.

"If he would only come here," she muttered over and over ; "I might help him : If I could only *see* him " ——

And one evening, he came.

Looking up suddenly from a book she had been try-ing to read while she waited for Tom's return from business, she beheld standing tall and erect in the doorway, the form of John Wallace. He seemed to tremble with some painful emotion, and the beautiful serious light which had made his face divine was blurred and gone. His hand was outstretched as though in utmost appeal from an overwhelming calam-ity ; and in a voice that seemed to come from the depths of some remote despair, he cried to her :

"Sorrow—banishment—suspicion ! I can bear it no longer. Friend, I would tell you——"

The voice died away, as the wind dies away after a sudden gust.

"O my God ! What is it ? what has happened to you ? " burst from Annie's lips. She sprang forward

and seized his outstretched hand in both her own.
There was nothing there.

When Tom came in, half an hour later, Annie was
lying upon the floor, face downward, in a dead faint.
He was much alarmed and rushed for a near doctor.
after placing her upon her back, and trying the ineffi-
cacy of cold water and sal volatile.

. When the white lids finally unclosed from the soft
eyes, there was a certain blankness in Annie's vision
which suggested blindness, or an absence of consciousness that would have terrified a more imagina-
tive person than Tom. They kept turning obstinately to the door, and had a sort of dazed astonishment in them for which the doctor could in no way
account.

"Talk to her, Mr. Hatherton," he said, as Annie
sat up and stared at the door : "I want to see if she
is quite conscious."

"Yes—I am quite conscious," she answered quietly,
her eyes still fixed upon vacancy.

"Then why don't you look at me, Nancy, dear?"
cried Tom, the perspiration standing upon his honest
forehead : "What ailed you, darling ; tell me."

But Annie shook her head, and answered "nothing."

"Could anything have frightened her," queried the
doctor who had good perceptions, and meant to know,
if he could, the reason of his patient's singular look.

"Did any one come in and startle you, Nancy?"

Tom asked the question unhesitatingly. He was
sure there had been no one there.

"No—no! not any one! There was no one there.

Why do you ask such foolish questions, Tom?"
Annie still looked terrified.

The physician watched her critically.

"If anything occurred, Mrs. Hatherton, to alarm you," he said coldly, "you had much better tell me. I could then know what to do for you."

Annie sprang up angrily.

"Who asked you to do anything for me?" she cried. "I am very well, only a little nervous. You have seen women faint before, I suppose?"

The doctor rose with dignity. He quietly asked Tom to call and see him later, if his wife were able to be left, then made his adieus, leaving some simple prescription, which he thoughtfully came back to say he would have put up, rightly supposing that they had no one to send.

When he had gone, Annie turned fiercely upon her husband.

"Never refer to this absurd swooning again. I do not wish to hear about it, or to see that stupid doctor. It was only a passing dizziness." And her restless eyes sought the door once more.

The doctor was not "stupid." Nevertheless, when Tom surreptitiously called upon him and explained Annie's condition and her nervous alarms of the past two or three months, he shook his head affirmatively and told Tom that it was only physical, and that time would soon cure it.

That was the evening on which Mr. Wallace had the slight paralytic stroke. About a week afterwards, came a voluminous letter from Martha Castlewood, telling of the climax to his singular symptoms, and that she no longer feared insanity. " He seems to have found relief in some mysterious fashion, and is now quite like himself," she finished.

But Annie brooded continually, this wise:

" If it were possible that during the crisis of his passing mental aberration, the spirit of John Wallace had come to me, does it not argue upon my own part a terrifying mental susceptibility? and why during those brief clairvoyant moods (she was becoming dimly acquiescent to what her mother would have called ' spiritual visitations') did I only see the man as he was, never as he *had been.* If I must endure the misery of a secret divination, a clandestine spirit-meeting—I know not what to call it !—why could I not penetrate the mystery which broods over his past ? " (She had never before acknowledged or realized how she had desired to lift that veil.)

" Only once," she continued in her perplexity, " was it given me to see him in that other sphere from which he came. He was less a phantom to me then than he must seem to himself in the shadow-life he leads in his exile. O great and good man ! again I ask what calamity has befallen him ! "

Still she grew less nervous, by slow degrees and finally the clammy horror, that had fastened, snake-like, upon her brain, seemed to have glided away.

Mr. Wallace, too, had recovered his usual mental vigor which never again deserted him. And Annie never had another " visitation " as she scornfully called it to herself. The result of that one, however, was startling.

In the autumn, when the birds were flying south,

and a thin vapor was clouding the sparkle of the mornings and the glow of the evenings, a son was born to Tom and Annie

During the illness incident to that event, another revelation was given to the kind and devoted husband, which was a far keener blow than that which had fallen upon his wooing. John Wallace, it appeared, had dogged their married life, very much as he had tracked Annie's maiden affections, with what strange power of infatuation he could not divine.

Annie was delirious: and in her ravings she called only upon one name. This dominating master spirit took every attitude towards her—teacher, friend, priest, guide, phantom : never, Tom acknowledged, as lover. He believed the truth ; that the man was pure, and had never sought to win the girl's heart. She had cast it at John Wallace's feet unsought, from first to last. And she was his wife.

The mystery of the swooning had betrayed itself. Annie was continually starting forward and crying in a voice of anguish. " O Mr. Wallace! what is it ? what has happened to you ? "   .

And then she would fall back nerveless relaxed, with the blank terror in her eyes, that pierced Tom to the very soul. At first he was disposed to think that Mr. Wallace (whom, he pathetically explained to the physician and the nurse, was an old gentleman, his wife's teacher, of whom she was very fond) had actually been there. But Dr. Walton at once disabused his mind saying that it was no uncommon thing for women in Annie's depressed nervous condition to see and hear many things which had no substance.   After awhile the delirium passed, and Tom sent for Mrs. Castlewood ; but, with an instinct of silence which delicacy taught even him, to her he imparted nothing.   Whatever suffering the tender-hearted fellow endured, whatever disappointment stung his generous soul, he meant to bear it alone.   After all, like that other time, it might have been only the derangement of coming illness. For he would not suffer himself to doubt his wife. She had been good and true to him, and until the last spring, light-hearted and loving.   No—Annie had thought no wrong.   She had been terribly nervous, and then terribly ill.   He meant to forget it.   Above all, Annie should never be reminded of it ; she, too, should forget,

Only, when he came upon the little tea-table spread with John Wallace's silver, the night that these painful thoughts were first thrust upon him, he broke down.   It was more than he could bear.   He sat down with folded arms and his boyish head bent upon them, in a stupor of hopeless dejection.   Then he swept all the silver together and put it, with the remainder, in the strong box in which it had come, which stood confidingly, Rest-Hampton fashion, in the little dining-room.   The next day, he had it sent to a bank where they promised to take care of it ; then he bought, ill though he could afford it, a few necessary pieces— only spoons and forks, and a sugarbowl and cream-pitcher, but of the best silver.   On them he had engraved ; "Annie Hatherton."   It would serve as a reminder of her married state, to negate the "Annie Castlewood" on Mr. Wallace's silver.

When Annie was able to eat a little, they came up on the tray. "It is a birthday-present, Nancy," he said, kissing her gently.

Tom was not of a jealous nature ; but he had had his dark hour ; and he bore it nobly, unflinchingly, without the sentimental solace of adjusting cause and effect, which enables many people to console themselves with placing their troubles in a picturesque light.

To Tom, it was a hard, dry fact ; and he endured it. What varnishing he did, was not to ameliorate his own suffering, but to shield and excuse his wife.

If we have despised young Hatherton in the past dear reader, let us now forever remember him as capable of that rarest quality—unconscious heroism.

The little boy throve finely. Annie, too, was grown well and strong, without a shade upon her of those previous months of mental wretchedness. If she recalled the details of that time, or any of her painful hallucinations, she never referred to them. They sank back into the recesses of her mind, with a power of reserve which resembled Mr. Wallace's own. Martha Castlewood never suspected, and was content. Tom and Annie seemed so happy together—indeed they were, in a sweet and chastened way—that she was ready to say in the language of her people, " My daughter was led to choose according to the Spirit."

From this time, Annie clung to her husband with a devotion which sometimes brought tears to the mother's eyes. It was as though she had some atonement to make to him, some debt of love to pay, which was greater than she could bear. Because it was mute, it was none the less consoling to Tom's sore heart, who now believed that—however inexplicable some things had been, and Tom never attempted to unravel the mysterious—his wife loved him.

That she loved him, had ceased to be a sentiment or an assertion with Annie. It had become, from the hour that she looked into her baby's face, the actual, unquestionable and soul-satisfying certainty of her existence, against which she felt that other sway, which she had so long struggled with, could never again prevail. To be sure, it was the fifth year of their marriage, when Tom and Annie Hatherton entered finally into their haven of rest—an unalloyed and mutual devotion, at which stories may as well finish, for there are thereafter no questions, or uncertainties, or changes possible. And unbroken peace of mind does not make a good background to a romance.

The baby was a marvel to them, as is always the case when one turns up, unexpectedly, after several childless years. It is therefore a great step towards insuring a welcome, for the first-born to delay its appearance. Moreover, when two people have come, through many misunderstandings, to love each other restfully, there is an added peace of mind in "the baby."

One day, bending over its crib, the proud and happy father looked trustfully into his wife's face :

"Nancy, suppose we call the boy John Wallace ?"

Annie burst into tears—the first she had shed in the two happy months since the child's birth.

"Oh Tom !" she cried, clinging to his neck, "why are you so good and true and generous ! You would break my heart if—I did not *love* you !"

For, through that silent divination given her by nature, Annie was aware that Tom " knew."

" But you do love me, my darling, and that is why I want to call the boy ' John Wallace.' "

" ' Tom ' isn't a pretty name," Annie said, smiling through her tears, with her head nestled happily upon his shoulder, and his strong arm pressing her to his thankful heart, " Neither is ' Joshua.' Only think of giving such an old name to such a young creature. I think John Wallace Hatherton *would* be nice."

And so it came about with no scene, or especial significance. " Mr. Wallace helped me once when I was in great need of help," Tom had told Annie more than once.

Now he added :

" We must try to persuade him to come and see us. I'll wager he abominates babies ; but may be he will like this one, he's such a splendid boy."

The splendid boy here rebelling against the personal conversation in such close proximity to his dreams opening his big eyes, lifted up his voice, and wept.

Tom picked him up and held him proudly to view.

" Can't you guess how resigned Mr. Wallace would look, if he heard those howls ! "

And they laughed merrily. They had come at that moment for the first time to speak naturally and easily of the man whose shadow had at last gone from between their hearts.

John Wallace could not be persuaded to visit the happy couple in New York ; but Tom and Annie went up to Rest-Hampton for a holiday, carrying the boy with them. Whereupon there was a christening in the chapel, and the neighbors remarked :

"Now the Squire's Nancy's got an heir for all Mr. Wallace's money."

The next time that Annie and her boy paid a visit to the village of peace,—for traveling was not so glib a thing thirty years ago, as now,—the little "John Wallace" as the child was quaintly called, was five or six years old ; and, to the amazement of every one, resembled neither father nor mother, but the man for whom he was named. For nearly five years before his birth, Annie Hatherton had not beheld the face of her "master" ; but the child who then came to her had in miniature those self-same lineaments.

It had puzzled the good understanding of honest Tom. The neighbors commented, and speculated, and finally raked up the old theory that " Mr. Wallace must be, unbeknown, some kin to Martha Castlewood." There were no aspiringly philosophic minds among them, else they might have discoursed sagely upon pre-natal influence.

Annie and her mother discussed the resemblance once or twice with some awe, and then dropped it as inexplicable. Of the spectre in the doorway, no one ever spoke.

But to Mr. Wallace the resemblance was a singular happiness :

" I see myself when I was a little laddie," he said tenderly ; " He is a bonnie bairn, Nancy, and good favored." (As the man grew older, he occasionally resumed some of the Scotchisms of his youth, but only in speaking to his god-son or about him.)

"I was innocent looking like that, myself," he resumed thoughtfully : "Life is an ever-mindful teacher. She never lets go of us. She begins to alter our looks while we are wee bairnies. The longer we stay in this world, the more unlike we grow to our first selves. The boy will look as time-worn as I do, some day."

Annie looked up at him with all the admiration of her girlhood in her bird-like eyes :

"It is my greatest happiness that he should favor you, dear Mr. Wallace. I hope the resemblance will increase continually, not only physically, but mentally —morally—spiritually—"

"No, no, child," interrupted John Wallace gravely ; "wish him like no man. Let him shape his own identity."

*   *   *   *   *   *   *   *

It was in the early summer that Annie had come to the Old Homestead. She wandered about in her old haunts, and her boy's glad young voice woke pleasant echoes in the quiet rooms. The solitary man and the child became fast friends, and the patter of small feet that followed his measured footsteps was music that delighted his soul.

But Annie's heart was divided. She thought of Tom—dear unselfish Tom, who never thought what might make himself happy, but only what would give her pleasure—brave Tom, working by himself at nights over his accounts, in their little sitting-room. How lonely the place must feel! how dreary his solitary breakfasts! Annie's wife-heart yearned over the picture, so she brought her visit to a close—alas! not too soon.

The last evening had come, and a strange presentiment of sadness seemed to possess her imagination, and fill her with forboding. Twilight had settled upon the wide village street. The trees swung their great arms about as if beckoning among their forsaken shades for the ghosts of departed sunbeam and song and cheer. From far away, the murmur of the sea came plaintively, as though it, too, were grieving for some sweetness that had gone with the daylight.

Annie sought the solitude of the South-End Cemetery, to take a wistful farewell of her father's grave. Kneeling upon the soft grass beside the mound, she pressed her cheek upon the new head-stone.

Here Mr. Wallace found her, later, and came to remind her that the dampness was unsafe. He stood looking down upon her in his calm way, and presently spoke :

"You are kneeling on my grave, Annie."

She started violently, and a shiver went through her heart.

"What a dreadful idea," she said, rising hurriedly.

"Your dear father promised that a bit of ground on one side of his resting-place should be mine. If I should never see you again, you will remember, Annie ? "

She nodded her head, speechless.

"Your mother will lie there, one day," pointing thoughtfully to the vacant place on the other side : "and you will come here, with your husband and the lad, to look at us."

"Who knows which one of us shall lie here next," Annie broke in hastily. "It might be the youngest: it might be our boy."

"The graves are mostly for the old," John Wallace said, and paused. Then his twilight voice went on dreamily, as though it were a part of the evening gloom :

"It is a strange lot to crave, that one should be buried in a foreign land among those who are strangers to his people and to his past. And yet, I am content : I desire it."

"Do you never care to see them again—your people ?" Annie questioned, awe-struck.

"If I did, it would be of no avail. There is a mist—a veil—between their faces and mine. But come, child," (to him she never ceased to be a child) "the night-air is growing very chilly."

He led her gently from the hallowed spot, and they walked home in silence.

CHAPTER XVII.

—————" *Thinking how my life*
Had shaken under me,—broke short indeed
And showed the gap 'twixt what is, what should be,
And into what abysm the soul may slip,
Leave aspiration here, achievement there,
Lacking omnipotence to connect extremes—————"

THE RING AND THE BOOK.

THE period of Annie's day-dreaming had passed. Her whole thought was given, now, loyally and lovingly, to her husband and her child. They were her compensation for lost ideals.

Hers was a healthy nature :—one of those sweet and vigorous souls which are forever young, and to whose enthusiasm the perpetual jars and hard judgments and mock-sympathies, of the world bring no chill. And the content which had come, after the first years of her married life, was none the less profound that it had been denied to her in the days of her wooing and her wedding.

She had come upon a plane whose joys and hopes had no fear of disillusion.

While we are young and thoughtless, we look with impatience and some contempt upon the melancholy strain of the old, who insist upon telling us, whether we will or no, that joy soon grows desolate, and our brightest hopes must inevitably become mere ashes of roses. We secretly think them morbid—hypochondriacs—until, presently, mid-way up the slope of young life, we stand face to face with the Eternal verities— Death and Sorrow.   After that, it is easier to believe the croakings of the old.   By and by, we too shall croak.

Tom Hatherton was among those forever happy and unsubdued souls who are not left upon the life-road long enough to learn the sombre lessons of its downhill days.   But Annie's feet came suddenly upon— the Verities.

It is in a darkened room where we find the brave fellow stricken down by one of those fatal, mid-summer plagues which sweep over great cities.

He is in the first vigor of his young manhood.   He has never in his lusty life known the meaning of sickness or bodily pain.   But there he tosses, hot and restless, the purple fever-flush contrasting painfully with his wife's white and anxious face.

The boy is playing unheeded in the room.   Some flowers Annie had purchased at the street-corner because they were country-flowers and might please poor Tom, are lying wilting, where she threw them, when she found her husband palpably worse.   The doctor whom she hastily summoned has come and gone, leaving only the terrible message that there is nothing more to be done.

The wife knows that her husband has but a few hours to live : and yet he is ignorant of his condition. She cannot tell him.   Death is taking him unawares.

In the intervals, between the spells of delirium, he
talks perpetually about the annoyance of losing time
from his business, and how he will make it all up; of
his intentions for the boy's future ; of his plans to give
her happiness ; of the better house they will have next
year. And all the while, Annie hears beneath his
talking—as one hears the ticking of a clock beneath
the noises of a household : " He is dying : one hour !
He is dying: two hours! He is dying: three
hours—"

The thought of death had never presented itself to
this cheerful and wholesome nature. Tom felt the icy
hand upon his brow and smiled, thinking it was
Annie's touch.

"What makes you look sad, Nancy ? has anything
happened ? There was no one in the doorway that
time, was there ? It was only a fainting fit. Some-
one said it was Mr. Wallace : but I knew better. If
he had come you would have told me. Anyway, I
got the silver."

After a pause he went on almost incoherently :

" I seem to be dreaming,—seeing things. Funny
for me, isn't it ? I've always been such an unsentimental fellow. Too unsentimental for you, maybe.
But we've been very happy, haven't we——Look
there ! In the corner ? It is Mr. Wallace ! He
has cut his throat——"

Tom sprang up with a shriek, in the very frenzy
of fever, his eyes rolling like a maniac and the
purple flush deepening every instant. Great God!
was he to die like that ? Annie shuddered. The
child ran terrified to his mother and clung to her

sobbing. She soothed him with his head in her lap, that he might not see his father's face.

"Dear Love," cried Annie to him, beseechingly, winding her arm about his neck, and laying him gently back upon the pillow; "Do not think. Try to lie still and look at me. Try to remember how I love you—*how I love you*, Tom."

Her voice broke into a dreary sob. She drew his burning head upon her breast and tried to bear the coming blow quietly—for his sake.

"He must not know," she thought. "It will be easier for him, if he does not know It will all be over—soon—and he will not have to suffer the pain of parting."

Annie did not realize it; but it was John Wallace's life of self abnegation which had made that courage possible to her

After a while, this delirium having passed, Tom spoke naturally again, although still wandering.

"Poor little girl! Poor Nancy," he whispered with his head upon her breast; "how sick you have been. But the boy is such a fine little fellow—you will be so proud of him, when you are able,"—his strength ebbed, but presently flowed back, and he went on cheerfully:

"As soon as you are well enough, Nancy, you shall have a change. We will go somewhere, you and baby and I: you always wanted to see the world, didn't you? Have you been disappointed, Darling?"

He raised his head slightly to look at her; Annie saw with terror that the fever fire had burnt out suddenly leaving his face gray, like ashes.

"No—no, Tom! I have been so happy, so contented, She broke down in an agony of weeping.

"Don't cry Nancy, " he said gently," you are tired out. What a sorry fellow I am to give you so much trouble. But you needn't sit up with me to-night, you know—I'm such a heap better, I feel quite comfortable now."

"Yes, Love," was all she could articulate, as she bathed his forehead and wet his lips.

"Let us have the boy," he went on, catching sight of the curly head buried in Annie's lap.

She lifted the little fellow up, and after pressing his rosy cheek to the wan and death-struck face, she coaxed the child to lie down in her arms to go to sleep.

"He's a pretty boy, Nancy. It's curious, that look he has of Mr. Wallace. He takes after you though: you know I used to tell you that you favored Mr. Wallace."

Annie smiled in response. She was singing the boy to sleep in a heartbroken voice,

> "*Jesus, lover of my soul,*
>   *Let me to thy bosom fly,*"—

but the words were for Tom. She wanted them to take hold upon his consciousness.

He seemed to be listening; but presently his thoughts came back to earth: life was such a strong good thing to him:

"Last night I dreamed I was at Rest-Hampton, Nancy, wasn't it queer? There was a storm—and confusion: you were out in the rain. I couldn't find you—I ran all about in the dark. At last Mr, Wallace found you and brought you back. But you hurried

away from him and came to me. We were in the
South-End Cemetery. And you preferred me."

He smiled so trimphantly, that Annie tried hard to
force a smile in return. The boy had fallen asleep, and
she laid him in his crib in the adjoining room first
holding him out mutely for Tom to kiss.

Then she sat down and took her husband's hands in
hers. Even in that instant of absence "the change" had
deepened. "Tom," she whispered in a choking voice?
"I love you so dearly ; do you hear me, Love?"

His bonny blue eyes were filmy, and his hand groped
piteously when he tried to pass it over her face. But
he did not suspect. Still, Annie could not tell him.
She seized the groping hand and kissed it passionately,
over, and over, which brought a faint puzzled look to
the glazing eyes.

"Yes," he articulated more and more brokenly, the
pauses growing longer between the words that came
in gasps : "We will go together—on a journey, where
—shall—we—go—Nancy? Perhaps—your father will
go—with us—the snow—is not—over him—now. It
is—summer time. He could—go—we—will all—go—
on—a—journey,"——

Poor Tom's hand relaxed. The last glimmer of
light and life left his sunny eyes. He had gone—on
a journey.

Annie wept, and could not be comforted * * * *

When her mother and Mr. Wallace arrived, in a few
hours, they were too late to save her that first utter
desolation of loneliness.

It seemed so unnatural that Tom, the strongest
gayest, busiest of them all!—should have died : Tom

who was always young and happy! Tom, who had never thought of death however remotely, as coming to himself ; who had a long fair future before him, and a son who would need his manly encouragement.

At her father's grave, Annie had gathered peace. He had fought his good fight ; he had finished his course. But Tom had just begun his battle in the world—for her sake.

" Oh, if I had only known, long ago! If I had only never pined to come away from that peaceful place ; The fever would not have found him there! It is cruel —cruel ! "

And so she moaned on with incessant upbraidings and self reproaches.

"My child," aaid John Wallace gravely, "you do wrong to grieve in that hard bitter way—as one without hope; never let sorrow make you bitter, Annie. Pray to be delivered from unsanctified affliction."

"But he was so young—so full of life and courage!" she sobbed, still rebelling. " And it was so long—so long, before I loved him ! "

The other did not notice her last wail.

" Yes—he was young ; but that is good, Annie—to die young. To be spared the long struggle and downfall of life. To live to grow old ; to lose the freshness of hope, the firmness of courage—*that* is the hard thing. Tell me, child, which is better, to be lying there with his soul at home in the bosom of God ; or to be standing here—as I stand—a stranger in a strange land, with my soul pent—hindered——"

He broke off in emotion, looking at the silent figure, as one who coveted its repose.

"Oh Mr. Wallace!" cried the bereaved wife: "Do you think it is best—for Tom? will *he* be satisfied with—his brief life?"

"*When I shall awake in His likeness, I shall be satisfied.* Do you think any earthly content can compare with that, Annie? Be sure that your husband's life is perfected. After a while, it might have been marred."

"But he died," poor Annie spoke brokenly—"with his mind full of this world. I tried to tell him, but—it was all over so soon!"

"He died as he lived; a pure and innocent boy in spite of his four-and-thirty years. There was upon his soul no stain of having wronged or injured a single human being. Come here, laddie,"—to the boy, who had come into the room, rosy and happy from a visit to some kind neighbor's house. "Once your mother said she wanted you to be like me. She was wrong there. You must be what your father was ; kind, sunny, tender to all."

"Uncle John," said the child with the artlessness of six years : "I love Papa very much, and I'm sorry he's going to be put in the ground—Benny Ball says so. But I'm to be like you when I'm a man. Papa said so, and Mamma, too." . . . .

And so had closed the sixteenth year of John Wallace's sojourn at Rest-Hampton.

Wherever he went there was comfort and healing in his words ; but he himself was not comforted, not healed ; else would have closed that long exile.

When the little nest which he had "lined" for the young couple had been despoiled and made desolate

for the departure, Annie returned to her native village, almost as much a stranger to her towns-people
as Mr. Wallace had been. They hung aloof from her
sombre mourning gowns and her pale, sad face, not
because " buryins " were unpleasant episodes to
them ; but because she who had never quite assimi-
lated with them, now seemed to go less than ever in
their way of thinking. She escaped from their expressions of sympathy like one who can endure, but
who cannot yet say, " I endure." When the Squire
had died a half year before, the "chorus" questioned
ironically :

" Hadn't Mr. Wallace ought to marry the widow ? "
But now, although he had well nigh reached his three-
score-and-ten, they said in good faith :

"I reckon he will take the *young* widow now."

But the two bereaved women lived quietly on with
their pretty lad, among the large cool rooms and the
orchard bloom and fruitage of the Homestead. And
John Wallace was never nearer to either of them than
an angel in the house.

The boys came home on visits ; but they had struck
root elsewhere. Martha grew old rapidly, and found
true rest for her chafing spirit in " John Wallace's
religion."

Annie's face looked deplorably youthful in her
widow's cap. She was but thirty-two, and might well
have been just beginning with happiness.

"Mamma," said the little boy to his mother, one
day : " They say, down in the village that you are to
marry uncle John. Is it true ? "

" No, my son," answered the widow gravely ; " the

people who say such things are very foolish, and do
not know your uncle John. Marrying and giving in
marriage "—she continued dreamily to herself, "are
as far from him as from the saints in heaven."

"But they say," persisted the child, "that you
loved him very much, and were going to marry him,
only papa came and took you away. Is'nt that true
either?"

"It is true that I have always loved him—just as
you love him, my son—ask him if I have not," she
added smiling, as Mr. Wallace came into the room.
To be with Annie and the boy was his greatest pleasure.

"It is well that I am old, and that time is therefore
not very precious to me, Nancy," he said; "for I waste
it all upon the laddie, here."

"Uncle John," cried the little fellow, still bent
upon the pursuit of his question; for children are per-
sistent creatures; "why didn't you marry my mamma?
she says she loved you when she was a little boy like
me."

Mr. Wallace and Annie both laughed at the child's
oddity; but the latter hastened to add that he had
picked up some remarks in the village about which he
was very curious.

"They *was'nt* remarks," said the boy, offended.
"Phœbe Milford said so."

Mr. Wallace laughed again, and lifted his little
namesake upon his knee.

"What did Phœbe Milford say, laddie?"

"Suppose," Annie broke in quickly, "that Uncle
John tells little boys they must not repeat everything

they hear.   People are so very injudicious, Mr. Wallace.   I sometimes think that the class of mischief-makers is larger than any other—unless it is news-mongers."

Annie's "old fire" still broke out at times, in spite of the nun's face in the widow's cap.

"Well, if you marry my mamma, you must marry me, too," cried the boy, not perceiving quite the drift of his mother's reproof.

The scholar's arms were about the child, whose pretty curly head nestled against his lonely bosom. He looked across its restless gold, long and earnestly into the sweet face of the mother, whose eyes were steadily bent upon her work, and whose color came and went as it had been wont at sixteen.

"Annie," he said; and his voice had all the penetrating power which marked its mellow cadence.

"Mamma," cried the child, when the pause had seemed to him long enough; "Don't you hear?— Uncle John wants you."

At last she lifted her eyes and confronted his, gravely and wisely, and withal, questioningly.

What she read was a long beseeching, yearning passion, that was somehow mastered—guarded—conquered, while it yet spoke.

"Uncle John does *not* want me, my son," she answered, firmly and clearly.

"He called you," said the child, perplexed.

"I spoke your mother's name, laddie," said John Wallace, with slow effort, "because it is very dear to me."

"Then you are going to marry her ! and it's true

after all?" The little fellow jumped up and down upon the arm of the chair. Marrying was but a vague term to him, that had somehow caught his fancy.

Suddenly John Wallace rose and put the boy from him. He walked unsteadily over to where Annie sat, white and crimson by turns.

"Child"—how low and altered was his voice!— "Do you know how I have longed"——

He stopped, gazing into her trembling face with a look of anguish ; then he turned and went away.

For some reason, taught him by the irony of Fate, Annie Hatherton's gentleness and tenderness were as unattainable to him as Annie Castlewood'e youth and beauty had been. If she had not known it before, she realized it fully then, that she was doomed to be but an episode in the life of a many-sided man. It was inevitable.

CHAPTER XVIII.

THE END.

" I have done with being judged,
I stand here guiltless in thought, word and deed,
To the point that I apprise you,—in contempt
For all misapprehending ignorance
O' the human heart, much more the mind of Christ."

THE RING AND THE BOOK.

WE pass mutely over a space of nearly fifteen years. What was there in all that passive existence of John Wallace at Rest-Hampton to record? That he ate and slept; that he thought and dreamed, that he walked and wrote; that he served the poor; that he amused himself sometimes but was more often serious; that he was always reticent. And now has come the last of the thirty years during which he dwelt in the village of Peace.

The little Quaker woman, who had tacitly welcomed him upon her threshold as belonging to a wider world about which her stunted fancy lingered; who had later recognized the lofty soul of the man himself— had long since been bowed with infirmities, and passed away, having received from him, during her last illness, much consolation from a far better world than the one for which she had so long hungered. "The boys" had married and made homes for themselves elsewhere; thence, every now and then, there was an inundation of young life let loose for a summer holiday in the sweet and silent rooms of the old Homestead, where the widow and her son did loving homage to the failing years of the gentle scholar.

To keep the young man with them, Mr. Wallace, to the consternation of prudent Rest-Hampton, had hired a tutor, and he was about ready for college. After that, he was to go to attend the Divinity school of a famous university; for the boy had looked earnestly upon the life of his benefactor, who was giving him so liberal an education, and said, knowing that it would please him so well: "I shall be a clergyman. I shall preach to men the firm and beautiful faith I have learned from Uncle John."

In his gentle decline, this purpose of the young man who bore his name, was the greatest interest Mr. Wallace possessed.

He had grown to be an old man; and yet to Annie, his looks seemed the same that had greeted her as a merry child singing through the great hall on that far-away, misty April evening. She perceived the dimness of age gathering in her hero's wonderful eyes, with the whiteness of Time upon his head; but to her, he seemed still to bear himself with the same uplifted aspect, as though the mutability of life could not touch him. She could make out—as she made out the approach of her own wrinkles and gray hairs —that at eighty he had not the unbowed figure, full of elegance and grace, and symmetry, which she had

admired at fifty ; but the spirit—that which looks
from the windows of the intellect—was unaltered.

And indeed he was comely yet. His snow-white
hair lent a placidness to his still keen and clear-cut
features ; and the intensity of his gaze was subdued,
not quenched. But there was a mortal change at work.
It was not an apparent decay in the health : his
habits seemed unimpaired ; but little by little, it became evident that John Wallace had eked out his
peaceful days at Rest-Hampton. At last, he betook
himself to his bed, and without a murmur, prepared to
yield up his long and silent life.

One day, he called Annie to him and said gently :

" You have been so good to me, Annie—so good.
Almost it has seemed as if you knew all—and forgave."

He paused dreamily. Perhaps it was in his mind
that he wished Annie to know why he could not have
loved her, and to forgive it. Then, after a silence
which the widow respected, he went on :

" I wish that I could leave a fortune to your boy.
He is the only thing in the world that has this name
of mine—this wandering name,—that is but a waif.
Your boy, and the little church, yonder ! I should
like to make them both rich. But Annie—now that
I come to die, I have nothing ; my wealth is not mine
to bequeath "—she turned her head away that she
might not see the struggle in his face :—" With my
death—my claim ceases. I have apprised my solicitor. No more money will come. It will go—to those
who have ceased to know me. . . . . I am no more
than a beggar who has abundant alms while he lives,
and then dies—and is forgotten."

His voice, clear to the last, and firm with that strange grip of consciousness, faltered for a moment, and then rang out with a sort of self-scorn.

At times his mind wandered, but never beyond his control, never into the regions of the past. Whatever was untold in his life, he meant to guard it to the end.

Once he said :

" I want to be buried in the South-End Cemetery, child, close to your father and mother ; and close to the church. Let it seem as if the little spire rose from my grave, reaching up to God. . . . . . Put nothing on my tombstone, but that I was born and died—give me a pencil, Annie."

She brought him what he asked, weeping. That John Wallace was to die seemed to her like the end of the world.

As he took the pencil in his hand, she noticed that it trembled and had lost its power.

He wrote :

"John Wallace,
Born in Edinburg, Scotland, Dec. 31, 1789.
Died " ————————————————

" You will fill out the rest for me—in a few days," he remarked, smiling. . . . .

On the eve of his death, he fell into a child-like sleep. Annie wandered restlessly about the house. Since her mother had died, seven years before, she had not looked upon death. But now that John Wallace was passing from life—" dying of old age," as Rest-Hampton said, it seemed to her that all the death·

beds she had known—her father's sudden and easy one ; Tom's strangely unconscious one ; her mother's prolonged and peaceful one—culminated and acted themselves over and over before her eyes. Only now she felt an unspeakable awe, knowing that death was to come this time in a new form ; that John Wallace's last battle with the flesh would be something more triumphant, more near to the uncalculated possibilities of human supremacy, than anything she had yet known.

She had sent for her brothers, who were tenderly attached to the household friend, and who were in the house ready to give what assistance they could to the sick man.

The next day, the last of John Wallace's life, he began again about the boy, showing how near he was to his heart.

" I wish to tell you, Annie, that—since I could not leave a fortune to your son,—my money has been mine by tolerance, not to will away—I have saved something for him from my income. I hope that it will keep him—in his studies—to bring him to a high place in the church."

He reached out and drew slowly a small box from the drawer of a little secretary beside him.

Taking from the box several papers, he handed them to Annie.

" There are the bonds and securities : it is only a few thousands ; but it will help him to start in his career."

But the widow, for weeping, or some other reason, hesitated.

" Will you not have them, Annie—as a token of
our long friendship?—almost your life-long ? "

Still she held back.   How could they live and
possess something of Mr. Wallace, with himself—
gone ?

" Our boy will be here, presently," she said at last ;
" they have gone to the Harbor to fetch him.   He
came up on the boat last night."

And at this moment the young man entered.   He
had grown to be a tall and manly youth with the open
smile of his father, and the sensitive mouth of his
mother.   Over all was still that firm look and singular
magnetism which gave him the likeness to John Wallace.   As they looked up, it startled them both.

" My son "—Mr. Wallace spoke with tremulous
tenderness, and stretched out his hand which the
young man took lovingly—" I am glad you are here.
It does me good to look upon your face once more.   I
am proud that you have my name and somewhat of my
look.   Surely God was merciful to one who had
nought to call his own."

His voice faltered : then he went on steadily :
" Your mother has been a true friend to me.   Your
people have been my people, and their God, my God.
It is because of the love of this household that I have
not been a homeless man "——

It seemed to Annie, then, that her heart broke.
Harry Castlewood, who was in the room, sobbed a
sob from his very soul.

The young John Wallace stood white and grief-
stricken, but mastered his emotion as his namesake
himself might have done.

After a while, the clear penetrating voice went on :

" I have saved a little money for you, John Wallace. Will you take it from an old man, as his parting remembrance ? "

The physician entering here, the sick man endeavored to prop himself up on his elbow, and spoke with distinct emphasis :

" Dr. Clump, will you witness that I now give this lad—who is called for me—these bonds and securities. There are reasons which prevent my making a will. This money I have saved from the income of past years. There are only a few thousand dollars—I owe these friends much more "— he sank back exhausted upon his pillow, while the young man turned away, the tears rolling unheeded down his cheeks.

After that Mr. Wallace sank rapidly. There was nothing more to be accomplished : he was entering into rest.

In the afternoon, the mail brought him a number of letters ; but he was too far gone to open them.

" Shall I read them to you, Mr. Wallace ? " Annie asked, bending close to his ear.

He started, and a strange dart of suspicion crossed his face.

" Read them ?—no, child—what are you thinking of ? Take off the outer envelopes and give them to me."

She brought them and laid them on the coverlet by his hand. He lifted one and scanned the large, bold writing : then handing it to her, said feebly,—

" Burn it."

As it disappeared to ashes in the glow of the open wood-fire, he watched it musing,—

"Why should I care now? Of what avail is their friendship, or enmity. To-morrow, I shall see all, know all. Some day, they, too, will know."

He raised another, and studied the address: it was in a crabbed and difficult hand enough. He smiled in a faint sort of scorn and signalled to her to burn that also.

The third envelope was directed in small, delicate writing.

"Ah!" he murmured to himself, a quick flush passing over his calm face—"from her. She will not believe, then, that I am dying. When I wrote last I warned her to write nothing more—If she should betray me!"

He half started up, and laid his hand upon Annie's arm.

"This is what you must do—burn them—if any letters should come. But most of all, burn hers!—no eyes must see even the envelopes of—my lady correspondent."

"I will do just as you wish," Annie said soothingly, taking the letter he held towards her, writing downwards. She reverently laid it upon the fire. Perhaps some woman had written it who would have given her life for John Wallace's love.

Just as the flames touched it, he made a gesture as though he would recall it; but when Annie moved as if to do his last bidding, he waved her back, and the delicate paper, flashing up for a brief second, fell to ashes.

He lay for a long while as if asleep.   Once, rousing himself, he turned to the sad watcher beside him, and stretching out his gentle hand laid it upon hers.

" You must not let this grieve you, Annie.   Think only that I am thankful—that the last day of my life is the happiest day.   I have lost all consciousness of grief, all memory of regret.   Is not that a triumph? And yet————

> ' One cannot judge
> Of what has been the ill or well of life
> The day that one is dying—sorrows change
> Into not altogether sorrow-like ;
> I do see strangeness but scarce misery,
> Now it is over and no danger more.' "

The last words were uttered with a sort of lingering loving chant, as though they were precious to the spirit of him who quoted them.   So he had been used to quote from his well-stored memory, in his long talks with the girl who had loved him.   That he should fall into this fond old habit, on this day, was a sweet and bitter drop in the widow's cup of grief.

It was a frigid day, that thirtieth of December and the eve of John Wallace's birthday.   Towards evening a wild wind arose.   On just such a night, Mr. Wallace had gone down upon the icy beach and into the stinging fury of the black sea—for the love of unknown souls in peril.

But on this night, it was his own soul that must venture forth into the deepening darkness of coming dissolution—and there was no boat that would breast the bitter waters to carry human protection or solace to him.

He was not afraid. He knew his haven : the Lord Christ was walking upon the sea of death.

"*I know my God. I know that my Redeemer liveth,*" he had cried exultantly, only a few hours before.

But now, the mortal shuddered in its utter lonesomeness, hurled upon the desolation of that parting which severs the spirit from the body it has so long known. He moved uneasily, and watched the figures of friends and neighbors as they came and went, with ever increasing disquietude. At last his struggling utterance broke forth :

" Annie—send them away—all of them. I want to die alone—"

" Some one must remain", said the doctor authoritatively.

" May *I* not stay with you ? " Annie entreated.

" Yes—you. I would die alone—with you ! " he cried with feeble frenzy.

The widow quietly compelled them all, the loving, the anxious, the curious, to withdraw ; which they did with some reluctance—those good people who, like unlovely birds, always flock to prey upon the sanctity of death.

" Promise me," he gasped clinging to her hand in the darkness that was deepening about him, " That if I should falter—if I should lose myself,—if I should say aught that is strange—you will not remember it —you will not hear it."

" Dear Mr. Wallace ! " Annie cried, kneeling by his bedside, and clasping her arms around his trembling frame. " Trust me as you would have trusted my father. Do you not know how sacred you are to me? How, more than my life, I guard your wishes and would guard your words if they were such as you say? Do not—*do* not fear me! Think of me only as a soothing presence that would go with you to the brink of eternity, and never carry back to the world the faintest glimpse of what is there."

She strained her senses for some response, some word or look that might show whether or not he heard and was comforted.

If that revered and beloved one had had aught upon his mind which he would have left upon the hither side of immortality, she would have taken it upon herself and borne it silently to her grave—if so his spirit might bound upward relieved by a confidence, or a confession.

But it was not to be. After that one outbreak, John Wallace possessed his soul to the last, never relaxing for an instant the stern composure which had, through so many years, been his check and his power-

Those who had gathered for the solemn occasion, hung about the door, complaining bitterly among themselves that they were thrust outside. At last the most of them went grumbling away.

The wind rose wilder and wilder. Annie gazed upon the broad, thinking brow which betokened the conscious power of a calm intellect, and marvelled at its peace.

The servants at the Homestead and the few neigh- bors who remained, paced restlessly outside the room of the dying man, whispering that it was an awful thing to leave Nancy alone at such a time, and in such a storm. But whenever any one unfastened the door, ever so stealthily, Annie would raise her hand with a forbidding gesture.

" My mother is not afraid," John Wallace Hatherton said proudly, turning from the hall-window, where he had stood watching the storm. They had seen that ; and also that the dying man needed nothing.

It was a fit night, the village Pastor said, for John Wallace's self-reliant and indomitable soul, untamable as the elements, to go forth alone and battle with the blustering forces in space.

The Parson did not mean that literally ; but his eloquence rose to the occasion.

"He's not having a struggle," remarked the more practical doctor. " He seems to be sleeping, and will most likely go off without word or sign."

But John Wallace was not sleeping.

Ever and anon when the riot without was fitfully vehement, he would say a few wandering words which Annie could not catch. Once, it was something about " the ship," and "the poor fellows who were going out into the Great Perhaps without a God or a human hand." Once he said :

" *The days of the years of my pilgrimage are a hundred and thirty years : few and evil have the days of the years of my life been.*"

And, still later, when the fury of the storm had died away into a low moaning sound, he looked peacefully into Annie's eyes and smiled—his rare, exquisite smile, that seemed to bring before her a thought of the angels of God:—the smile that she would soon never see again, though she lived to be ninety.

" Annie," the smile was in his eyes still ; " Read to

me. Read the cummunion service. I would partake of the Last Supper—in spirit."

Annie drew the little inlaid book, with its gorgeous illuminations and its mysterious devices, from under his pillow. As she found the place, he said, gathering his powers for a last effort:

" Put it—in my hands—afterwards."

Annie kissed the dear hands that had done no man harm : and the two knew that it was understood .

Then she began to read, finding strength not from her own breaking heart, but from the calm, brave heart beating its last pulsations beside her.

" *For in the night in which he was betrayed, he took Bread, and when he had given thanks he brake, and gave it to his disciples, saying ' Take, eat, this is my body which is given for you : Do this in remembrance of me.'* "

Oh, the comfort of the sacrament ! sole supporter that can bear up in everlasting arms the departing soul !

The face was lit up now with a luminousness from heaven, which made Annie, upon the earth, tremble. But she read on steadily, bending over and putting her lips so close to the dying man's ear that the words were breathings rather than utterances. Her son and the two Castlewoods, had entered quietly and were kneeling near the bed.

" *The body of our Lord Jesus Christ—which was given for thee—preserve thy body and soul unto everlasting life.*"

He still smiled, and his voice came back from the other world to finish those significant words :

" *Feed on him—in thy heart—by faith—with thanksgiving,*" he uttered distinctly.

"*The blood of our Lord Jesus Christ which was shed for thee, preserve thy body and soul unto everlasting life.*" read Annie, with unutterable solemnity, and paused, to look again at the radiant face.

There was no sign or token left. John Wallace had fallen asleep.

If he finished that solemn sentence, it was heard by the Sons of God.

INTERLUDE.

PART I.

Comprising the Subsequent Meditations and Determinations of Leslie Bracebridge, Poet.

IN the course of this narrative, has just come and passed a chapter which we called perforce *The End*, because therein was written the end of John Wallace's life; or rather, the end of that portion of his life which was in itself but the finale of something not yet made apparent. * * * * * ·

It is the Summer of 1879. Close upon the heels of the Tile Club, there came among the first summer guests to Rest-Hampton, an artist. He was an artist in the widest sense of the word, which does not imply a Painter, or a Musician, or an artisan among the fanciful things of fashion.

It may mean often only a Thinker. We shall call him this time a Poet. And surely this young man was not a Painter : he did not " do " the windmills in black--and--white ; nor make " a harmony in gray " of the graveyard. On the contrary, the two burying-grounds appeared to him particularly bright and sunny places, and entirely free from those lugubrious associations usually attached to cemeteries. Even at twilight, when the painters who preceded him had sat in rows upon the flat tombs "laying in" sombre effects of gloom and grayness, our Poet would stroll about in one or the other of those hallowed acres, in company with a few inquisitive sheep, that seemed to live contentedly enough among the daisies and the dead.

He thought that the mild light of evening hovered longest among the still warm stones that had been bathed all day in the rich summer sunshine. And if the sea-fog, too, seemed to creep in soonest there, why that was only natural in so sequestered a spot.

But then—he was not a Painter ; he could not take a truly impressionable view of things. He was only an artist at soul. Moreover, he wrote letters to journals—those great hungry, fact-devouring organs, which demanded a constant supply of things more substantial than impressions. He had just despatched the letter which, somewhat flippantly, opens this story. Something in the old, South-End burying ground had taken hold of his fancy ; but he had not yet been able to utilize it very definitely.

It was a white slab, not yet greatly mellowed by the disintegrating effects of sea-air, which any visitor to Rest-Hampton may see, upon which is carved beneath a simple design of cross and crown : *John Wallace, Born In Edinburgh, Scotland, Dec.* 31, 1789 : *Died In* (here there is a mossy blur———)*Hampton Dec.* 30 1879."

He cogitated a good deal upon the simplicity which distinguished it from the elaborate eulogies on every side.

" Perhaps," he ruminated, "the man was lost in some wreck upon the coast, and they never could find out anything about him."

At length he began to be curious : somehow, the unknown man took the proportions of a hero to his idle imagination.

It is a marvelous thing upon what the human mind can seize hold to create an ideal. A tombstone is enough to hang a history upon; a name may be magnified into the substance out of which to make a mystery, For there is hero-worship, more or less dormant, in each of us ; and it needs only an illusion to set at work all of the intricate mental and spiritual machinery necessary to the making of a hero.

Our Poet began to look up the material out of which his phantom hero had been made. Very likely it would turn out to be but poor clay, after all, he thought cynically, But looking over an old file of the local newspaper to see if any mention of a ship-wreck tallied with the date on the tombstone, he came across this notice :

JOHN WALLACE.

The death of John Wallace is an event which will be long remembered in Rest-Hampton. It has deprived that community of a highly valued citizen and a venerated and beloved friend. Although a foreigner by birth, a native of a land whose inhabitants are noted for the strength and persistance of their national prejudices, Mr. Wallace was a dear lover of his adopted country, and that, too, tho' he had attained the mature age of fifty-four, when he reached our shores.

*   *   *   *   *   *   *   *

Mr Wallace was a gentleman of polished and refined manners, of extensive information, of cultivated taste and possessed of a very keen sense of the humorous. He was an incessant reader and in his reading kept pace with the progress of the busy, active age in which we live.

Although nearly eighty five years old at the time of his death, he never had thought himself " too old to learn," and the writer has often been struck by observations of his indicating his readiness to receive and acknowledge newly discovered truths from whatever source they might be made known.

A firm maintainer of the old fashioned High Church principles in which he had been educated, he was too large-hearted as well as too wide-minded to be capable of bigotry or exclusiveness ; of cant, whether religious or political he was a hearty hater, if any one so kind and gentle could experience such an emotion.

Concerning his deep unaffected, simple, childlike piety, we will not undertake to speak. But such a man has little need of newspaper eulogy. His Christian life and peaceful end are his best testimonials.

We have but a few more words to say. He came to Rest-Hampton a stranger, He died among affectionate friends who will ever cherish his memory."—

But he had already gathered facts which suggested a lovely life. The man, then, had really lived in Rest-Hampton, and to some purpose,it seemed.

He began to make inquires about " this John Wallace " among the villagers, and learned, what other idlers have learned since of the simple old town, the plain story of a man who lived peaceably in the place and conferred the benefits of great wealth upon its inhabitants. His name is a well beloved one in the hamlet, and those who speak of him do it with reverence and honor.

"A good man," they say, "and a gentleman ; but strange, strange ; " with significant head shakings.

" *What* was strange ? " asked the Poet curiously.

And then he would receive in a mysterious undertone, with perchance a solemn forefinger tapped upon the forehead, or other rustic pantomime, some such vague response :

" Well now, stranger, that's just what nobody knows," or, " Well, you see, he lived here for thirty years, and nobody ever saw or heard of any kin," or, " Indeed, sir, but *that* is the mystery."

" But what did John Wallace do that was odd ? " persists the inquisitor, aware of some injustice in such vagaries.

" Nothing; leastways except to build a church ; and to give all of his money to the poor."

Then the villager brightens up and a happy inspiration strikes him : ·

" P'raps you never see the new window we put up to him in his church yonder, no ?—Then come along with me. . . . . . . Now, jest look at that ! Its a beautiful window, and cost a heap of money ; leastways for the folks here to pay."

The memorial window, like the tomb-stone, however, bore no hieroglyphics out of which could be deciphered the old, old truth of the man's finished story.

At last, rummaging again over the musty, eight-years-old newspapers, he came upon one more clew to the buried life.

THE MYSTERY (?) OF THIRTY YEARS, EXPLAINED.

Why talk of mystery, and seek to throw
Around the grave of that old man
A cloud of wonder, and of blind surmise ?
Of mystery forsooth, in him who knew

* *For the use of these verses, and the preceding fragment of obituary, I have kind permission of the writer.*

No artfulness, or cunning craft of men,—
Whose heart was open as the day itself,
And whose pure life (as pure as man's could be,)
Forbade suspicion, or a thought of wrong——

*   *   *   *   *   *   *   *   *   *

To us he brought a simple, loving heart,
A mind stored richly with scholastic love,
An open hand to all the lowly poor—
He spake but little of the distant land,
Of home and friends, few were the words he said,
Because he chose to live from all apart——
(*It is not true* that never from his lips
The names of loved ones were allowed to fall,
For he who writes hath sometimes heard the name
Of Father, Mother, Sister, and of all,)
T'was only that he did not deem it wise
To publish all his history abroad;
And tell to all who e'er might seek to know,
Affairs *that only to himself belonged.*
No further mystery than that was there;
No other than to every heart belongs;
No other Mystery about his life
Than unto many, who shall read, doth cling.
        ——His life
To God, and acts of Charity was given,
(Yet not in penance for some former deed)
But simply and alone because his heart
Was full of Sympathy and Christlike love——

*   *   *   *   *   *   *

Then speak no more of Mystery to them
Who knew and loved him for those thirty years.

*   *   *   *   *   *   *   *   *

So Lived! so Died he! with a heart all free
From sordid baseness or corroding sin,
The only Mystery about him thrown,
The Mystery of Godliness alone.

                New York, Feb. 17th 1871.   A. H.

" That was evidently written by some one who
knew the man well, and who nevertheless indignantly

repudiated the idea of a vulgar mystery," mused the Poet.

And he went back to the graveyard to look again at the tombstone, and to question the possibility of getting light upon the subject. Had he been a lawyer, dear reader, he would doubtless have devised a direct method of attaining a surer result. But as we have said, he was only an artistic soul ; and he was dazzled with the possibilities of the case. He liked this story of John Wallace, which seemed to have no beginning, only a faultless ending. He thought he perceived through its transparent form, a moving source, such as is the essence of light in the diamond ; and he wondered if this clear gem of human-kind had not known a dark imprisonment of trial in some remote, deep place. How else could it have caught a sparkle which was pure and serene, and yet was fashioned of the dull carbon of experience.

For this much the young man had learned of the ways of mankind ; that there is nothing which savors of expiation, nothing which comes to be a self-purifi-cation, which has not behind it the thing for which it atones.

He wandered about here and there ; he asked much and learned little, always returning to the graveyard, as if, by any means the silent marble could testify of the diamond which is akin to it.

All that he gathered was this : that John Wallace who had lived and died in the little sea-side town, had had a previous history—a mystery, most likely. Think-ing further, he added this on his own part : "*and some woman must have been in it.*"

It is a dangerous thing to add to a detective procli-
vity a preconceived belief.   Searching about for this
inevitable woman—and missing her—the Poet came,
naturally enough, upon the widow Hatherton.

Is it a blunder to fall upon sweet Annie Castlewood, old, faded, wrinkled, perhaps (since she was now
past fifty-five years of age), and force her to give up
the tender and secret sentiments of her dreamy youth ?

It is the sad blunder from which we shall all suffer,
one day, unless we stumble first, without the premo-
nition of old age, upon that other blunder—death.

Let those at least, who are women, protest that they
love the fading widow's whitening hair more than the
flickering sunshine of the girlish head.   For so they
would like the world to do unto them.

Still, I hear the world say that it will not be entertained, life-fashion, with the spectre of a woman who
has outlived her romance.   Why should it, when
there are fresh hearts and unwritten stories perpetually
crowding to the front, and trampling into oblivion the
finished destinies and silvered locks of the last generation.

It is true that the widow Hatherton was long past
fifty-five, and had outlived her dreams—or at least the
possibility of their realization.   But if Annie Castlewood at sixteen was pretty and winning, Annie
Hatherton at fifty-six was majestic.

She had the rich color in her cheeks which Rest-
Hampton salt air preserves for its matrons ; and the
lustre of her lovely eyes was in no way dimmed by
tears, but seemed rather to be heightened by the con-
trasted luxuriance of her silver hair.

" Nancy Hatherton's *that* handsome," ejaculated the younger women about her, somewhat enviously ; " It's a wonder her looks never fetched her another husband—together with John Wallace's money ; " which the village persisted in believing he had sown broad-cast over the goodly acres of the Homestead.

Perhaps Deacon Potts, still a morose and uncompromising bachelor, might have enlightened them somewhat upon the handsome widow's opportunities.

She had continued to spend her summers peacefully with her son at the old farmhouse, their winters having been passed for some years in the neighborhood of his university.

But Wallace Hatherton had a charge now, and the long pleasant summers were cut down to a month or six weeks during each year. It was in the midst of one of these uneventful seasons that the Poet came upon them unawares.

PART II.

Containing the Observations and the Reservations of the Widow Hatherton.

"THERE is nothing to do but to hunt up this Mrs Hatherton," the young man had concluded to himself, with a magnificent indifference to the person and qualities of the lady. This youthful scorn for the individual was rather surprised from its poise when, in answer to his card whereon he wrote confidently "Leslie Bracebridge," there came into the room a tall and stately woman, whose white hair above her brilliant eyes and fresh cheeks, gave him a startling sensation of contrast and possible force.

He had sought her out with his anticipation in full swing, as a self-appointed spectator of a long finished drama, which she was to rehearse for his sole benefit. It experienced something of a back-set, when in reply to his eager and confused demands upon her knowledge of the person whose identity he sought, the widow answered coldly.

" I scarcely comprehend *what* you wish to ask me, Mr. Bracebridge." (Annie still accentuated sometimes.)

" I want," he cried excitedly, " to find out this mystery, this romance, which has been buried here."

" I think you will scarcely find any materials out of which to weave a romance," she said, gravely. " Mr Wallace's life with us had always been among common places, and I see no reason to suppose that there is anything enigmatical in his having lived here."

Mr. Bracebridge stared. In rushing headlong towards what had taken hold upon his fancy, it had not occurred to him that he was to come plumb against a wall of unresponsiveness, just where he had reason to look for the gate of inspiration.

" Do you mean to say that it never occurred to you to suspect the man of masquerading ? "

" I never for a moment suspected Mr. Wallace of doing,—or of having done—*anything* that he could not explain, if he had cared to."

The widow's handsome face held a certain defiance that baffled the young man, while it piqued his further interest.

" There has been a wheel within a wheel here," he mused somewhat sententiously : " doubtless this Mr. Wallace was not altogether guiltless of a love-affair, even in his mysterious retirement."

" Can you describe the gentleman to me, Mrs. Hatherton ? "

She paused. The man she had known and loved so well stood before her as in the flesh ; but how was she to describe those lineaments ?

Presently she said :

" I fancy no one has ever yet seen a portrait through the eyes and lips of another, Mr. Bracebridge. If I tell you that Mr. Wallace was tall and muscular ; that he was pale and classic : that he was grave and

majestic ; would it convey to you any notion of an individual ? "

She smiled.   The Poet thought he had never seen
so lovely a smile, and began to wonder if—even in
this out-of-the-way corner of earth—there might not
be more than one individual worth studying.   Moreover, where had she picked up such English ? Surely
not upon Eastern Long Island.

" Can you think of nothing a—a little more distinctive, in manner or appearance ? " he asked, smiling
back.

" There was," said Annie Hatherton slowly, " a peculiar luminousness in his look.   I have never seen a
face that could at times so radiate the spirit.   Also,
he was a man who possessed *great personal magnetism.*
Wherever he went, he was master, in a quiet and
unobtrusive way of his own."

" Thank you, Mrs. Hatherton.   The personality of
your friend begins to dawn upon me.   You have
given me a substance to grasp.   But where," he added,
puzzled, " did a man who was a Scotchman born and
bred, get a pale complexion and classic features ? "

" I think we never were impressed with the fact of
his being Scotch—until the last.   He had probably
spent most of his previous life in London, since his
speech and ways were English."

" Did he profess to be an Englishman ? " asked the
other, eagerly.

" He made no professions of any sort," answered the
widow, coloring.

" Nevertheless," said Leslie Bracebridge after a
pause, speaking meditatively, " his nationality asserted

itself in the stolid strength of his resolution, and in an astounding ability to keep his own counsel. Nobody but a Scotchman could have persisted in so determined a disguise."

" May I ask what reason you have for adopting the supposition of a disguise?"

" Your towns-people have told me many things which point both to exile and to disguise."

" My towns-people talk a great deal, for want of better occupation," Annie said, scornfully. " Mr. Wallace did not choose to discuss his family history with them—why should he?—and they retaliate in slander."

" No," cried the young man earnestly, not wishing to quarrel with his only chance of enlightenment; " I have heard only good of Mr. Wallace. It is on this account that my interest is enlisted. Pray, Mrs. Hatherton, do not think I would unravel the enigma to find out a crime. Mysteries are not necessarily evil."

Annie looked searchingly into his face :

" I do not know you, Mr. Bracebridge, but I take it for granted you will agree with me that if a man who is pure and good and true, has behind him *years of which he never speaks*, there is some reason which every gentleman should respect why they should not be raked over, and discussed and published. This man lived and died without revealing any extraordinary thing which may have been in his experience. I think it was *his motive* so to live and die. I, for one, shall never lift the veil to pry into a reserve which went unbroken to the grave."

The Poet was a sensitive creature enough, and he winced under the mild rebuke of this woman, who by right of her seniority, could thus address him. He sat twirling in his hand a small gold pencil which he had ingenuously taken from his pocket with the intention of making notes of the conversation.

" Pshaw !" he cried to himself, rallying with an effort, " I did not come to this out-of-the-way place, and stumble upon an interesting secret, to be baffled by the scruples of a fastidious old woman who knows nothing but proprieties."

Then he returned to his former tone of humble politeness, rather ashamed of his secret anger :

" Perhaps you would not mind giving me a few corrected statements about this Mr. Wallace."

" What are the statements you wish me to correct ? "

" At least the woman is no fool," meditated Mr. Bracebridge ; and spoke cautiously :

" I have gathered—perhaps unjustly—from what I have heard, that John Wallace was supposed by many to be a semi-lunatic—or a monomaniac."

" A sounder mind, a clearer judgment, a better balanced character never was ! " cried the widow indignantly. " He was *absolutely without eccentricity.* They are poor fools who told you that ! Having no better mystery to feed upon, they have invented a groundless lie."

" Was there not some supposition that he came over to America in company with a gentleman who was connected with lunatic asylums ? "

" I never heard any such supposition, Mr. Bracebridge," Annie Hatherton's eyes were still flashing. Who was this young upstart, that he should come and lay before her—who was John Wallace's friend— all sorts of silly stories in reference to a man whose only peculiarity had been that he loved his fellow man, and that he dealt justly with all?

" Well," said the visitor, apologetically, reading some thing of her thoughts," I see that I have allowed my imagination to be ridiculously worked upon. I wish," he added appealingly, after a pause, "that I could right myself and my motive in your eyes, and that you would allow me to ask you a few questions which do not presuppose any information on my part."

The widow relented and let one of her own smiles— Annie Castlewood's smiles—break over her face After all, why should she blame this young man who had only believed what he was told?

"If you are unprejudiced, and really interested in Mr. Wallace, *as I knew him*, I shall be glad to answer you."

" May I propound questions like a Yankee? "

"Oh yes! I am used to that. It is the way, here."

"Well then," brightening up, "the valet—the person who came over with Mr. Wallace—has nothing been heard of him since his master's death? "

" I myself wrote to Andrews—to an address in Colorado which Mr. Wallace had used, thinking perhaps there were those with whom he might communicate. There never was any reply."

"And yet," suggested the Poet, " he is the only person from whom one might get absolute certainties."

" I fancy he has left the place in Colorado where

we supposed him to be. There is much drifting about in the far west."

Leslie Bracebridge glanced surreptitiously at a list of notes and queries he had sketched out for use upon this occasion. He wished to forget nothing in this—his opportunity. These notes and suggestions were not in good legal form, but jotted down piece-meal, as he would have noted the wandering ideas for a yet unthought-out poem ; or—had he been a painter —as he might have made the color-notes for a picture not yet matured in composition. It suggested simply that the material for an artistic study had fallen into his hands, and he meant to secure what outlines he could.

"Do you think," he commenced again very modestly, "that his name was in reality John Wallace ?"

"I certainly shall never think otherwise. You ask me singular questions, Mr. Bracebridge. They are somewhat offensive, since they savor of accusations."

The thought of an assumed name, a false position, was like a living lie to the half-Puritan, half-Quaker and wholly conscientious and upright soul of Mrs. Hatherton. She revolted from the thought in con-nexion with a being at once so high-toned and so simple-minded as the hero of her girlhood, the friend. of her womanhood.

"I beg your pardon," said the young man hastily, "I meant no accusation. I only repeat the things I have heard. Was there no mark upon Mr. Wallace's clothing, or in his books ?"

"There was only his name upon his clothing;" the widow looked defiantly at her interlocutor :

" His books had no mark upon them; you can see for yourself if you wish ; will you come with me into the study he occupied? "

Mr. Bracebridge was delighted. He was now approaching his facts—his outlines.

" What I want is Facts, not sentiments," he mused. " I can supply the color and the harmony for myself.'

When they were seated in the old room, where to Annie's sensitive mind the spirit of John Wallace still brooded, the young man took a rapid survey of the quiet but elegant appointments, the well-filled book cases, until a portfolio caught his quick eye, and he asked leave to glance at its contents.

The widow hesitated :

" I doubt if he would have wished them disturbed, since he showed them to no one in his lifetime. I have kept them all these years, untouched ; for as he destroyed his other papers, doubtless he intended also to destroy these."

" But if I could only have one, Mrs. Hatherton ! as a loan—a souvenir ! I have so fallen in love with this man, that I should like to posess something which he had done."

He looked so eager, so pleading, that Annie reluctantly drew from the portfolio a sheet of thin yellow paper, on which was transcribed in a fine, literary hand, the translation of a Latin hymn ;—Francis Xavier's.

It seemed to the widow that the shadow of John Wallace, which had followed her nearly her whole life, stretched out a misty hand as she gave up the paper.

" A thousand thanks, madam, you are very good.

But what is this cypher ? " The Poet's eyes sparkled.

" I presume that the letter Z is the signature it pleased Mr. Wallace to use in writing."

Leslie Bracebridge dared no further upon that ground.   He felt it quake beneath him.

" And may I ask—pardon me, it often has to be be done in case of sudden death—were there no letters which came afterwards ?—which required to be opened ?—which demanded attention ? "

The widow looked at him coldly.

" Mr. Wallace's death was not sudden.   He was fully prepared for it, as doubtless were his friends. *There was nothing which came after his death.*

The Poet sat and thought.   Presently he looked up.

" Have you never written—has no one ever written —to his friends ?   Of course you knew their names and addresses from the letters he sent."

" Mr. Wallace sent all of his letters to one person —his banker, or solicitor, I do not know which,—in London."

Bracebridge fell back, it being upon his lips to exclaim,—

" And you do not call *that* a mystery ! "   But he read a certain fine warning in the widow's eye, and held his tongue.

" I believe it is the custom," she said calmly, " for Americans travelling in Europe to have their letters forwarded through a banker.   Undoubtedly Mr. Wallace supposed that strangers here do the same."

" Yes—of course," murmured the other, abashed by the ready wit of the reply, " only travellers do not—

of course you perceive the difference—address the envelopes to their banker, merely in his care."

" That is immaterial. There are many ways of conducting business."

The widow spoke grandly. Bracebridge hurried on to the next point, fearful of another blunder. This fiery woman affected him somewhat as the threatenings of an earthquake in his vicinity. He wished to accomplish his purpose and get away.

"Can you recall the name of that gentleman, Mrs. Hatherton ? "

" Certainly. Mr. Roderic Clarkson, Lothbury, London, E.C."

It was modestly noted with the gold pencil, which was then consigned to the pocket of Mr. Arthur Bracebridge, who remarked that, as he was not a reporter, he need not take notes.

" Did it never occur to you to write to this gentleman and inform him of Mr. Wallace's death ? "

" I did so," the widow replied, "and received a courteous reply. His client had warned him that his days were numbered, and that he had left ample provision for his burial. Mr. Clarkson did not invite my confidence, I assure you."

Here Mrs. Hatherton rose and crossing the room returned with a volume in her hand which she handed to her visitor, having first found and hastily turned a page.

" I take the liberty, Mr. Bracebridge, of giving you this book, which belonged to Mr. Wallace, and of which he was very fond the last year of his life. Perhaps you will be able to take some hints from it—especially from the paragraph I have marked—that will suggest to you the fallibility of human judgment, the unworthiness of unjust suspicion."

It was *The Ring and the Book.* The Poet's eyes fell upon the page, and as he read, the color mounted high into his cheeks :

> " So are we made, such difference in minds,
>   Such difference too in eyes that see the minds !
>   That man, you misinterpret and misprize—
>   The glory of his nature, I had thought,
>   Shot itself out in white light, blazed the truth
>   Through every atom. * * * * * *
>   Yes, my last breath shall wholly spend itself
>   In one attempt more to dispose the stain,
>   The mist from other breath foul mouths have made
>   About a lustrous and pellucid soul ;
>   So that, when I am gone, but sorrow stays,
>   And people need assurance in their doubt,
>   If God have yet a servant, man a friend,
>   The weak a savior and the vile a foe,
>   *Let him be present by the name invoked.*"

" You will accept a warning—or call it a rebuke if you choose—from an old woman, Mr. Bracebridge ? "

Annie smiled gravely, and the young man seized her hand.

" I thank you, madam," he said : " you have opened my eyes to the truth of this man's character. I shall look now, not for a mystery, but a heroism."

And still these two were destined not to part without one more misunderstanding—so different were their outlooks.

" Did Mr. Wallace never speak of any correspondent—by name ? "

There was a pause. The figure of the dying man,

—so weak in the failing flesh—so strong in the triumphing spirit,—rose before Annie's eyes. She saw herself kneeling by the bedside, and burning those unread letters which had come too late.

" If there are any more—and I am not here—you will burn them like that, Annie ? "

And she had promised, sobbing.

A sob rose now, and checked her utterance. In a few moments, during which her visitor had thought her busy searching her memory, she said gently,—

" Never by name. Once, he spoke of a lady correspondent."

" If one could find her ! " half articulated Mr. Brace-bridge. He had not acquired much courage as yet, since he had found the widow somewhat difficult to deal with. Moreover, his purpose had not yet matured. It gathered as he went on.

" I wrote a letter," volunteered Mrs. Hatherton, interested in spite of herself, " after Mr. Wallace's death, giving the details of his sickness, and offering to attend to the removing of his—remains, if his friends wished it. There must be some one, I thought, who would wish it. I sent the letter to *The Lady Correspondent of John Wallace;* in care of the London solicitor."

" In due time there came a letter in response—a most finished and refined letter, with a certain literary flavor about it, thanking us for all our kindness, of which the writer said Mr. Wallace had spoken much. She thanked me, also, for the details I had given her, which she said were most comforting to many people. As for his body, they would not disturb it. Doubtless he would prefer to rest in the seclusion of that spot, and that good name, which he had chosen for himself."

"'That good name!'" echoed the Poet. "My dear Mrs. Hatherton do you not perceive that the name was not his own?"

"I do *not* perceive it," she replied flushing with the suddenness of the thought: "I suppose the words to refer merely to the lovely reputation he had won among us, of which I wrote."

The Poet thought differently, but was too eager now in the pursuit of a possible clew to dispute the fact?

"And what was the signature?" he demanded naturally enough.

"It was signed," Annie spoke in a low voice, looking away from her interrogator in some embarrassment, "'*The Lady Correspondent of John Wallace.*'"

Leslie Bracebridge sat staring at his companion in unmitigated astonishment, and presently her fine eyes turned courageously upon his own :

"There was no reason," remarked she distinctly, "why the lady should *not* sign her letter precisely as I addressed it. I did not ask any disclosure in return."

Her companion did not seem to hear her defence of the dead man's position. He muttered, half to himself.

"Wonderful, wonderful! Do you not think so, Mrs. Hatherton?—that this man's singular reserve should communicate itself to all with whom he came in contact. The valet—the Solicitor—the Lady Correspondent—('yourself,' he mentally added;) It seemed like a scheme of silence, a many-sided plot to mystify "————he stopped suddenly :

" I believe I was to confine myself to interrogations. Pardon me if I was led into a comment."

" I think we had better deal with the facts only," Annie said calmly.

" Facts ? oh yes ! But I should so like to see that letter—if it were not for troubling you," his sentence trailed off apologetically.

" It is not the *trouble,*" Annie said, with her old emphasis ; "it is that I have no right to make the letter public."

" I am not a very large public," murmured the Poet, meaningly ; but the other let the matter quietly rest, and Bracebridge had to glance at his notes for a new suggestion.

" Was there no seal—no crest anywhere ? "

The widow winced, as though the question pierced her self-command with a sting of disclosure :

" Yes : Mr. Wallace wore a ring with a crest, or cypher, upon it."

" May I see that ?—as a matter of interest, you know."

It was never taken from his finger, Mr. Bracebridge."

" Oh true !—of course ! but was there no duplicate ? "

" There was a duplicate; but I think that neither of them was the family crest. It was a sort of mitre and cross design—I have fancied it might be a Bishop's crest————"

Annie stopt abruptly. Why should she cast her secret and sacred imaginations before this stranger.

He was intent on the crest. " You say there was a duplicate of the cypher on the ring ; "

" Yes, answered the widow in a still voice ; for it pained her to touch thus openly the thing which had gone from her life : "It was cut upon the ivory cover of a little prayer-book."

" And you have that ?——"

" No, I have not. I wished to keep it ; but Mr. Bracebridge, can you not comprehend that I felt I had no claim upon anything which belonged to Mr. Wallace's past—to what you are pleased to call his mystery? He loved that little book, and always carried it in his breast pocket. I left it with him."

In her vivid imagination, the woman who had been his friend saw him as he had lain at peace, his hands folded restfully over the little book that might have told his secret, and his grand face looking more than kingly in its statuesque repose. The tears she had repressed gathered in her eyes at last.

Bracebridge bowed his head in silence. He could not but acknowledge that there was a certain grandeur of renunciation in this woman's having put away from her all possibility of solving a question which he could perceive had lain somewhere near her heart.

" In this narrow community, and among these narrow people," he mused philosophically, " such a relinquishment could only have been reflected from the man's own life of abjuration."

" Then you have nothing at all—as a souvenir ? "

" Nothing,—excepting these few papers and books," with a wave of her hand.

" And they do not appear to refer backward in the least."

The young man felt his energies flag, but presently he roused them to ask :

" Could you make that crest ?—trace it, you know, or something like it."

" No," said Annie firmly ; " I do not recollect it with sufficient distinctness. It was, as I have said, a cypher, rather than a crest."

Leslie Bracebridge sighed restlessly. " This wo man," he thought, " is trying to baffle me." And having no further suggestions upon his list, and no further excuse for remaining, he arose as if to go. Suddenly he turned and asked :

" Did you never, Mrs. Hatherton, form any sur- mise as to Mr. Wallace's former position or occupa- tion ? "

It was a direct question, and Annie answered sim- ply, with her old candor of speech :

" I have not been without curiosity, Mr. Brace- bridge. Sometimes I find myself putting together little items to make a situation. In the letter which I received from Edinburgh, I gathered that the posi- tion which Mr. Wallace had held was a high one, judicial or clerical. It has occured to me, personally—" Annie paused, the haunting figure in the white robe rising once more before her—" that he might have been a clergyman—a dignitary of some sort, in the church of England."

" A Scotchman and yet a churchman. It is odd." The Poet hesitated : " If you were asked, Mrs. Hatherton—you who surely must have known him well in his—thirty was it not ?—years residence with your family,—what would you say were his leading traits ? his chief characteristics ?"

The widow thought a while before she answered slowly :

" I should say that the thing which entered most largely into his composition was self-denial, self-renunciation. For the rest,"—her eyes filled with tears : it was nearly ten years since she had seen John Wallace laid away, and yet she sorrowed silently for him whose life had been to her both uplifting and satisfying ; " For the rest, he was *a cultivated, refined, benevolent, Christian Gentleman in all the associations and actions of his life.* We always ridiculed the occasionally suggested idea that there was any mystery in his previous life.   If you are going to follow this matter, I entreat you not to make use of my name or my words in any way.   I could not rest if I thought that he whom I revered as John Wallace were about to be paraded before the world as a questionable person."

" Certainly, certainly," responded the other warmly. " Be sure that your wish shall be respected, even if I should endeavor to follow so dubious a trail.   But have you not just betrayed to me that you yourself question the identity of the man ? "

" I tell you I have never had the ghost of a reason to suspect his identity," she said almost angrily : and the visitor, bowing, withdrew.   As he left the shadow of the vine-covered stoop, the widow's voice detained him.

" Mr. Bracebridge," she said coming out and standing proudly beside him, yet with a certain feminine yielding in her face and gesture :

" I am a woman and therefore contradictory. Although I do not wish my name used in this matter which you may follow out, if—sometime, you should chance to pick up the thread of Mr. Wallace's life, I should like to see how it unravels." .   .   .   .   .   .

The twilight of Annie Hatherton's life closed again about her, to be no more disturbed by word from the living or voice from the dead.

How much of tender fiction she nursed in her heart for reality, how much of questioning incredulity she banished from it as a whim, who shall know ? Only those who have likewise journeyed in their experience after the never-to-be-explained *ignis-fatuus* of some illusion, some haunting soul-myth that is not their own. It was John Wallace's shadow she had pursued.

Poor human creatures ! The half of our lavish natures we waste in twining about an object, an ambition, an idol ; the other half we spend in unwinding their poor clingings. . .   .   .

" My life," she mused, standing wistfully that same evening in the melancholy mist which crept over John Wallace's grave, " is like a broken shaft, without meaning or finish ; while his is perfected in form, polished in outline, complete in expression. He died having achieved his silent purpose of some unknown vicarious suffering, not spelled upon his tomb. I live : and having aimed at many poor ends, have achieved nothing."

And the Poet, as he strode away from the wistaria,

and jessamine, and honeysuckle-ladened doorway that had known for so many years the coming and going shadow of John Wallace, he, too, mused this wise :—

" Force and gentleness ; justice and self-renunciation ; these then seem to have been the chief components of the creature I am to handle. Rather lofty traits, and delicate to manage,—Hum—hum ! Let me see,—

"'*The Ring and the Book !*' It must have been a new book when the Great Unknown was fond of it. A metaphysical, ruminating, analytical sort of man, no doubt. Well, well! I shall read the volume for his sake as well as for Robert Browning's, bearing in mind what that widow with fine eyes had the courage to say to me. Then I shall go forth and find the man himself."

BOOK II.

THE SHADOW.

" Well now ; there's nothing in nor out o' the world
Good except truth ; yet this, the something else,
What's this then, which proves good yet seems untrue ?
This that I mixed with truth, motions of mine
That quickened, made the inertness malleolable
O' the gold was not mine,—what's your name for this ?
Are means to the end, themselves in part the end ?
Is fiction which makes fact alive, fact too ?
The somehow may be this how."

THE RING AND THE BOOK.

CHAPTER XIX.

A LONDON SOLICITOR.

*" God who sent me to judge thee meted out
So much of judging faculty, no more.
Ask Him if I was slack in 'use thereof."*

THE RING AND THE BOOK.

A SELF-APPOINTED task has often all the glamour of
a mission about it. We are frequently so possessed
with the intensity of our own imaginations, that to
fulfil them becomes a sacred duty. Perhaps there is
a truth in this fancy. The Fates may hold us respon-
sible for our inspirations.

Leslie Bracebridge had a few hundred dollars and
the remainder of the summer at his disposal. Moreover, he had always meant to hunt up his Scotch relatives and introduce himself to them.

" My mother was a Leslie," he said. " She used to
hear from cousins in the south of Scotland. Here is
an opportunity to find my own kin––and to stumble
upon John Wallace's romance."

For he was aware that the thread upon which he
had strung his odd fancy for finding the story of an
unknown man was but a slender one.

He made a few hasty arrangements, and in a weeks'

time found himself aboard one of the ships of an inexpensive line, bound for London.

"I shall call upon Mr. Roderic Clarkson first. After that, I start for Edinburgh with very likely a handful of addresses. I may make my fortune in two ways. First socially; that is not to be despised. I shall fall among John Wallace's relations, and be entertained and introduced by them into the aristocracy. Secondly, I shall obtain facts—why not?—for which the American public will pay handsomely. Our people are greedy for any undiscovered thing. They shall have a new romance. I will call it ' *The Lady Correspondent of John Wallace.*' Why!" he cried stamping furiously about the deck, "the very name has a thrill about it! A publisher would pay for that without reading the MS. It is unique."

Still, the young man was not distinctly mercenary. His determination to follow up the story he had happened upon may very justly be ascribed to one of those relentless infatuations which seize upon the artistic temperament, and, taking possession of it, lead many a man into unaccountable ways.   *   *   *

Who that has crossed the sea under the pressure of some haste, does not know the feverish anxiety with which the voyage is beset? Especially those few last days on shipboard when the profound risks of the deep are passed, and you sail along the desired shore with the haven still ahead.

All this was over for Leslie Bracebridge, however, and he leaped ashore into the bustle and crowd of the Great City, with a bounding sense in his blood of something to be achieved without delay.

But there was delay, after all. There were lodgings to secure, and the "square meal" on terra firma to partake of, by which time it was towards dusk. The exclusive looking buildings which displayed Mr. Roderic Clarkson's name, as Solicitor in Chancery, among other equally aristocratic and imposing ones, were closed. Round about and in and out, among the barrister's offices and the banks, wandered the poet in a maze of curiosity and appreciative enjoyment ; he was feasting in anticipation upon the charm of a discovery.

The next day, he was on the spot betimes, eager to grasp his pet dilemma by the horns. The offices were not yet open to the public ; and small boys, assisted by cuffs and commands from very young and very pompous clerks, were sweeping out and generally putting to rights for the day. Our poet thought he had never known places of business to open so late, and to wear such a distant air of reserve. It was very uninviting ; and depressingly unlike the familiar courtesy of the American professional man's den. His ardor of the night before cooled a little, and he began to experience twinges of that uncomfortable quality called nervousness ; and to wonder if he were not about to perpetrate a very rash thing.

It was too late for qualms of conscience, however. He had already presented his card to the least supercilious-looking of the dozen supercilious clerks, and informed him that he would return at midday. The clerk stared at him, politely but coldly ; which gave him an impression that the solicitor was something of a Personage, and was accustomed to serving other Personages of unquestionable position. That he felt himself to be merely an atom in the great nameless mass of nobodies, did not add to his ebbing courage. He was sure the clerks knew he had come on doubtful business, and were despising him for his humility. At last, there was nothing to do but to face the interview. He felt himself shrink and dwindle incredibly as he was ushered through a suite of preliminary apartments, after an interminable waiting time spent in a gradually filling ante-room.

He heard his consciously unknown name pronounced from room to room by dignified and middle-aged and majestic gentlemen, each of whom he momentarily fancied to be the great solicitor himself. To his sensitive ear, there was a tone of scorn in the several utterances of his name, as who should say— *"What does this young man want? Who is this obscure individual called Bracebridge?"* Then he came into the presence of an elderly man, who was physically, and to all appearances mentally a giant. Now the poet was modest in his inches, and he felt himself acutely to be a pigmy by the side of this the awful Personage.

The Personage was by rights Sir Roderic Clarkson; but he kept the dignity of his baronetcy for social life, preferring for his professional renown, that greater dignity which is of personal power and ability. He scrutinized through his single-barreled glass the timorous intruder, as a sceptical biologist might scrutinize, through his miscroscope, a new specimen of animalculæ. Still there was nothing affronting in his manner. Without doubt, Sir Roderic was near sighted

"Good-morning, Mr. Leslie Bracebridge," he said stiffly, English fashion.

If ever that young gentleman devoutly wished to back out from an inevitable situation, it was then and there. All his glib speeches forsook him and fled.

"I am from America—from the States," he began feebly. He felt a wild desire to blurt out :

"I am supernaturally commissioned from John Wallace's ghost."

Actually, he could think of nothing else to say—a chaotic state which wiser minds than his often fall into, in an emergency.

Mr. Roderic Clarkson moved his neatly gaitered feet with a slightly ominous suggestion of impatience.

"What can I do for you, Mr. Bracebridge?" he asked politely.

"I have come to you" (it was the only modification of the absurd speech which the poet could think of) "from the friends of John Wallace."

"Yes?" The monosyllable was distinctly interrogative. Clearly the great man's composure was not stirred. He did not propose to help his victim out.

"John Wallace means nothing to him! Doubtless he is used to mysterious correspondents," thought poor Bracebridge, wondering what on earth he had planned to say next. He thought of the ease with which he had plied the widow with questions, and smiled bitterly at his own temerity.

"I am very anxious—they are very anxious—to learn something of Mr. Wallace's past life," he said desperately. He could read in the solicitor's coldly penetrating eye, that he had anticipated some such indirect and poverty-stricken announcement.

"I believe I had some correspondence with the people whom you refer to. Some years ago. At the time of Mr. Wallace's death. That was sufficiently satisfactory, I presume."

The solicitor spoke in distinct periods with a majestic sort of measure.

"No—not quite," stammered the young man blushing furiously; "There are those who were bound to Mr. Wallace by ties "—what *was* he saying in his desperation?

"Ah, indeed! Perhaps I do not comprehend. What do you mean by ties?" said the other measuredly.

"Ties of friendship—and all that!" cried the poet, a cold sweat breaking out upon his forehead; "there is a young man who is called for him—to whom he left considerable money "——

"No doubt." Sir Roderic spoke stiffly: "there may be a whole village named for him. But what have I to do with all this? The young man received the money, I suppose?"

"He did; but you have, sir, information which would be of great service to those people—and to me."

"Excuse me : who are you, Mr. Bracebridge? The young man himself possibly?"

"No," cried Bracebridge, wishing devoutly that he was; "I am a writer, sir. I have become possessed of this idea; to follow backward through what clew I may find, the life of John Wallace to its source."

He was becoming more tranquil and confident.

"Ah—yes. A reporter. I have heard of such

methods. In America. And you wish me to help you. In your laudable enterprise?" with an ironical smile.

"I should be greatly indebted to you, Mr. Clarkson, for a few addresses—merely that."

"That, Mr. Bracebridge, I cannot do. It is needless to remind you, I fancy, that the affairs of my client, are not mine to dispose of."

"Then you are bound to secrecy? And there *is* a mystery?" ejaculated the young man, unguardedly.

"I did not say so. A lawyer never discusses his clients' matters, I merely declined giving you the addresses of Mr. Wallace's relatives. Is there anything more you wish to ask?"

The Personage moved his gaitered feet again; young Bracebridge started forward in consternation.

"I beg you, sir, to give me some inkling—some hint to direct me; I have crossed the ocean to follow this trail. It will go very hard with me if I have to give it up. I am pledged—as it were,"——he did not finish.

The solicitor looked sharply at him. There must have been some charm about his boyish face, which, having won upon the widow Hatherton's heart, now appeared to touch the stone which lay in the great man's breast.

"Perhaps you have some claim of relationship," he said gently.

"No I have not. But I've got this thing on my mind to that extent, that I cannot rest day or night, until I see through it."

"May I ask what you have to gain?"

" Literally nothing," cried the Poet, his notion of a warm reception among John Wallace's people having vanished into space.

" I have taken it up as a sort of mission—a hobby, if you will.   It could do no harm, and—and I am willing to pay for my information."

Sir Roderic Clarkson waved his hand, with a gesture of dismissal :

" I cannot countenance any liberty. With my clients, Even after their decease.   I am sorry, Mr. Bracebridge.   But it is impossible to assist you."

He laid his hand upon a bell.   This air of finality gave his visitor a sudden courage.

" Only tell me this, Mr. Clarkson—and I will not trouble you further.   Was his name in reality John Wallace ? "

" It was not : "   Sir Roderic rang the bell.

" Was Edinburgh—or London, the scene of his life, up to his leaving for America ? "

" Both.—Thomson ! "(to the brass-buttoned boy who entered,) " I am ready to see Sir Harvey—"

" Just give me this grain of satisfaction," entreated the baffled Poet, clasping his hat fervently to his heart ; " was there a crime of any sort ? was he banished ? "———

" I beg your pardon, Mr. Bracebridge.   I have said I could not help you in the matter."

" But if I find him !—if I identify him !—you will at least tell me ? "

The young man's persistence seemed to please the older nature which had doubtless known its eagernesses also, else it would not have found success :

" If you find him—yes. But don't come to me, with all sorts of people. I warn you that I am not patient."

" Thank you—and good-day," murmured Leslie Bracebridge, humbly, backing towards the door by which brass buttons was admitting another anxious visitor.

" I couldn't well have got less out of him," he muttered : "And yet—it is something—that promise ! For *I shall find the man who called himself John Wallace.*"

*　　*　　*　　*　　*　　*

It was the height of the season in London ; but the festivites of shop and theater, of street and park, could not detain young Bracebridge. He had an object before him ; and that was Edinburgh. * * * *

A quaint old city, built eccentrically up and down an abrupt declivity of rocks. Steep and narrow streets, queer shops ; a crowd—a jumble of roofs ; a great mass of rock-like castle overhanging all : that is Edinburgh. That is where our Poet found himself, blown about, without thread of direction, to his purpose. Drifting about without a sail upon this unknown current had the excitement of hazard, however. Suppose his intention drove on to wreck ! At least he would have passed a summer of novelty.

He began to consider the feasibility of searching the city directories and birth records, until he reflected that he had no clew, no name to look for. Perhaps if he presented himself to the American Consul——Pshaw ! Very likely that individual had never heard of John Wallace ;—how should he ? Bracebridge smiled cynically. He thought of the Bishop of Edinburgh, remembering that the man he sought for was a churchman. But what should he say? The absurd sentence that had presented itself about John Wallace's ghost occurred to him again. This time Bracebridge laughed aloud; clearly, he must look among circumstances for some extraordinary event which he could fit upon his man. It was the motive he must seek, not the man. "It is like constructing an antediluvian creature from a single bone," he thought: "I shall not hunt for my bone; I must happen on that."

And so it was that, wandering about the intricacies of the rare old Capital, he came upon the dark and dreadful shadow of the Edinburgh Prison.

One of those queer sensations called presentiments swept across the Poet's brain, and he found himself haunting the prison with a persistency which he could not account for, since his mind was not set upon the fact that John Wallace's mystery had been a crime. And still the place fascinated him. He wandered about its precincts, using every opportunity allowed to visitors to enter; and questioning every one with whom he came in contact.

But prison officials are a surly set; and it was not until he heard of the existence of an old minister of the Scottish Kirk, who had taken charge of the chapel services in jail and prison for thirty years previous to the last decade, that he got any insight into Penitentiary affairs.

This old man had become superannuated and was retired from office and pensioned; all of which fed his garrulity to an incredible degree. Indeed auld Parson

McCairn lived upon his prolonged versions and reminiscences of past labors and experiences, with a
tenacity of which only the Scotch composition is capable.

What pangs of penance the young man was bringing upon himself in his voluntary seeking of the old
parson, he little knew. Nor is it probable that he
would have shrunk from the ordeal, since it held for
him a faint and shadowy hope that somewhere, in the
misty mazes of the old man's memory there might
linger a motive for his Mystery, which began to assume the look of a Martyrdom.

CHAPTER XX.

THE STORY OF A PRISON.

—————*" The act, over and ended, falls and fades ;*
What once was seen grows what is now described,
Then talked of, told about, a tinge the less
In every fresh transmission, 'till it melts,
Trickles in silent orange or wan grey
Across our memory, dies and leaves all dark,
And presently we find the stars again."

THE RING AND THE BOOK.

LESLIE BRACEBRIDGE cultivated this old creature, with a nice homage that delighted the ex-parson's soul. It was difficult to keep him to prison stories ; for he had had more than one flock in his life-time ; and his reminiscences wandered over an immense field—mostly among the poorer classes.

At last, however, it was impressed upon his somewhat thickening wits that his new friend was particularly interested in the prison-work he had so faithfully done. Then he preached over again the long dry sermons he had thundered at the convicts. He spun tedious yarns of refractory criminals whose punishments he sighed to relate. He harped upon mysterious criminals about whom nobody ever discovered anything ; and pious criminals who tried to convert the jailor and the turnkeys; and slippery criminals who had a genius for escaping and a corresponding fatality for being recaptured.

These prolonged recitals, the Poet endured, partly as a means of studying a, to him, unknown side of human nature, but mostly because of the growing impression lurking in his bosom, that John Wallace had somehow—at some time—chosen to cast his lot in that dismal place. Moreover, the old Parson had a decided way of his own, and was not to be stopped, or deviated from the course of any narrative upon which his garrulousness set out.

Unconsciously, Bracebridge was looking for his "bone." And moreover—that lurking impression! If, in the course of events a presentiment seems to fulfil itself, how powerful, how wonderful, does not the recollection of it grow? But how about the myriads of presentiments which, in spite of nourishing and cherishing, come to nought. They are forgotten.

Finally, however, the Poet got hold of the prison record, and studying it carefully came upon this entry :

"*Jan.* 10, 1840. *John Wallace Monteith, gentleman, sentenced for twenty years imprisonment for forgery of will of Sir Randolph Monteith Bart. under circumstance of trust.*"

Written below was :

"*Escaped, March* 21*st* 1840. *Left country. Never been heard of since.*"

Over this slim record, Leslie Bracebridge pondered and thought. Then he armed himself with a bottle of fine old Port, a pouch of excellent tobacco, a fresh reinforcement of patience, and went to see auld Parson

McCairn. The old man was sunning himself in the
soft drowsy August shine that brought into full relief
the myriad wrinkles of his more than four score years.
His rough and weatherbeaten face belied what was in
reality a kindly nature; and this contrast came out in
a certain mildness of speech-form which was pleasant
enough to hear. He belonged to that class of Scotch
people who have sluffed off their brogue, through a
certain sort of education ; but not being either of the
fashionable, or literary, or business world, have retained the quaintness of expression so eminently Scottish.

"John Monteith, is it ?" he began in his old-fashioned way, which was at once rambling and precise : " It's
a troublous story, I doubt not, and I scarce mind
whether or no I can do the telling. It may come to
me betimes, however, seeing that I can mostly recall
what came to pass in those forty-five years of prison-
teaching, when the Lord was gude eneuch to abide
my puir efforts. Na—I cannot call to mind the man
all at once :—a gentlemen, you say he is written down ?
There's nought bye-ordinary in that. I mind well
many a gentleman that's come to abide in Edinbro'
Prison. It's no always the low and hard-working class
that fills such-like places. There's been a power o'
book learned men, and high tradesmen, with a
sprinkling of better folks—men and women—that's
come upon yon dark place in my time. But John
Monteith! I mind not anything past the common
that chanced with him."

"He escaped—in a few months," suggested Bracebridge, warily.

"Escaped ? Truly I have gotten into years that it

should sliy me when any came loose from their bonds."

He sat and puffed meditatively at his pipe, until presentlp a gleam of recollection lit up his little shrewd eyes.

"Aye—Aye! John Monteith. I mind him well, now. He abode in the prison but a brief season, though he were a long whiles in the jail; for the reason that the trial was uncommon slow of action. I mind how quiet he would bide at the service of a Sabbath; and how great a liking for him the wardens and jailors had betimes. Doubtless they helped him out of his captivity; for there was none of them that did not secretly name John Monteith innocent. And truly he had the air of one that knew the Lord. Likewise, I was oft-times mindful that he had about him the look and the ways of one who suffers for the sake of shielding another.

"Weel, weel! It a' comes back to me now. There was a bonny bit lass that used to come day after day, and tarry with him in the jail :—a ward of his, or his father's I mind not which—a gold haired creature, wi' big dancing blue een that had a soft, scared look. She was aye there of a Sabbath when I went ben; and her een looked mirthful like, in spite of the tears fallin' silent all the whiles."

The old man paused as though he could, even at that late day, conjure up the sweet picture: then he went on musingly;

"She was the lassie that John Monteith was to marry upon; but the folk of the bonny leddy were stiffnecked and unrighteous, she being an heiress, in

her ain right, and John Monteith being a poor second
son, without a penny to call his ain.

" For albeit the elder brother was imbecile, and no
fit to inherit a fine property, it was feared by them
that the auld baronet, who was testy eneuch for any
thing, would make him his sole devisee and legatee.

"Now the inheritance of Sir Randolph Monteith's
properties by the imbecile son would have been so
grievous a calamity, that John Monteith and his friends
persuaded the people of the lass that it could not come
to pass, and it came to be hoped that the will would
be made upon the second son, who was aye good and
well-beloved by the kin and by the community. Sure
eneuch, at lang last the auld baronet died ; and when
the will came to be opened there was the name of
John Monteith and none other. But the lawyers, who
it was apparent thought to make much of the job,
stirred up a great to-do, crying that there had been a
wrong done, and the will was a forgery.

"I mind not if it were so or no ; but if it were, the
Lord who knows his ain made it clear to me and to
many, that John Monteith was nae the man to do sic
a deed.

"Ye see Mister Bracebridge," continued the auld
parson, after meditatively replenishing his pipe," the
young leddy was a ward of the Monteiths and lived wi'
them, though she had kin of her ain. They were
given to seeking the things of this warld and were set
upon giving her to another ; and seek it to aye hinder
her marrying upon John Monteith, who was puir in
this warld's goods, to their thinking.

" Weel—there was a power o' testimony, and more

witnesses than is common, mostly among'st the people of the bairn ; for John Monteith never raised his voice nor his hand to rightly defend himself. But I mind there was a sight of plain evidence that went for nought when the prisoner were pronounced guilty. It is no common for great folk hereabouts to attend the trials ; howsomever, the court was full to overflowing, seeing the best people in the land knew John Monteith and liked him well——and for the matter o' that, sae did the lowly. But as I was saying, there were more evidence in his favor than against him : only that the lawyers and such have aye a way o' turning things to some body's weel or woe."

" Did John Monteith have no lawyers ? " questioned Bracebridge eagerly.

" Na, na ; leastways, I mind not any of account. He was a sort of lawyer himself, and made as though he would conduct his ain case. I call to mind the uproar there was in court the day the sentence fell ; for indeed it was made apparent to all that the deed was putten upon a harmless creature. But he sat there— John Monteith—I see him now, as it all comes back upon me,—how grand and still and stately he lookit ; and how serene he bore it a', refusin' to defend himself by so much as a word. His silence was like that of a man who, being guilty, has naething to say ; but his look was like that o' a man who, being innocent, yet is desirous to suffer. He carried ever that look, in jail, in the prison, at the service, at his wark—like as of some superior being who endured for anither body. I mind weel the Lord marked that look and kent it a'."

Here the old man fell a-dreaming ; and when the Poet roused him, his thoughts had rambled away from the story, and it was not without effort that his mind was brought back.   At last he fell again into the train of recital.

" There was one thing which I aye marvelled at, and that was, though her folk had prevented the lass from marrying upon John Montcith when he was an unblamed man, and stood high in the eyes of the world, yet when he fell under the condemnation of a great crime, and was disgraced, with the prison walls closing about him, they let the lass visit him in jail. (Later, when he had escaped, the lass, I am told, had gone likewise.)   It aye came over me that her kin knew mair nor they would let be proven o' that will. Howsomever, I have heard that the bonny bairn came back heart-broken and alane."

" But who was accused of the forgery besides John Monteith ? " burst in Leslie Bracebridge, his imagination having failed to supply a direct course to the rambling narrative.

" Woe's me ! " cried Parson McCairn ; " Did I not tell ye that ; of a truth, that is the marvel of the whole thing.   Nae body was what you may say, accused.   The ither story was suppressed,—kept back,— covered over : ye ken a way there is in court o' doing that, when the rich and great are threatened.   But it was as plain as day to them that harkened at the trial to the much speaking of the lawyers and judges—that the lass hersel,—Jennie Stewart she was ca'd—had done the foul thing.   Aye, ye may weel stare.   You see, in spite of the ill will of the connexions who wanted the lass to marry upon a wealthy laird—she lent no unwilling ear to John Monteith and was liken to elope with him, when the brother came and brought about a quarrel. After that came the old baronet's death, and the will in John Monteith's favor, and the accusations made by the kin."

" Did John Monteith never deny the charges against him ? " A swift undercurrent—a sudden theory of John Wallace had sprung up in the listener's mind.

" Na, I tell ye, mon. He neither affirmed nor denied. He sat there with his bonny head aye raised proud and calm, and his clear een fastened upon the young thing that had brought all the misery upon him. If he had but once lifted his voice, he could have turned the world in his favor."

" And what did she do ? How did she behave ? "

" That is the curious part,—'though I am no one to blame the courts,—but after the first few days, when she began crying upon the judge to bear her witness that the prisoner was an innocent man, and saying daft-like things, they carried her out of court and gave it out after that, how she had lost her wits, and had no more the right use of her senses. I was in a manner taken by surprise the first Sabbath after the prisoner John Monteith was brought into confinement, to see the bairn in her ain senses. I was at no hand adapted to read out plain the meaning o' tangled things ; but it was clear to my een that the lass knew mair o' that will than any ither boddy, save John Monteith ; and that she had threatened her kin wi' the telling, if they did not leave her to gang her ain gate and go ben with her lover in the jail.

"Later, when it was a' over, the trial and the sentence; and he came to abide in the prison, the prisoner carried with him that air of innocence which made it easy for him to win out again.   I had aye my ain thoughts that the lass was in a manner privy to his escape, and mayhap had helpen it on wi' siller— though I was never one to blame the wardens with deceitfulness."

"And what became of John Monteith ?"

"Aye—what?"   Parson McCairn puffed vigorously at his pipe.   "There was wark enough made about it; but I doubt not every boddy was glad to give him the slippit.   It's all been lang syne, an' naeboddy has heard tell o' the prisoner, John Monteith since."

"But the girl; did she disappear finally ?"

"That now I canna' call to mind, being no hand for curiosity myself,—no that its an ill quality in the main—but I was about the Lord's work in the jails and prisons, and couldna' follow the misguided out into the world itself.   I mind that she went and came back, however, though it's a' lang syne."

"Do you think I could find her, Parson ?"

"Wae's me, mon!   What for will you find her? Belike she's an auld body now, and has nae wish to upturn the darksome place of her bit youth."

"But I think," began Bracebridge cautiously, "that I know something of John Monteith, after he left here.   I think that I have found his footprints in America."

"Aye—aye.   Verra like.   America's an awfu' place, and is ever gettin the ill o' ither countries.   I'm told they send over paupers, and convicts, and the like, to build up their society. It'll be a sad world, there."

"Where did these people, these Stewarts, live?" queried the Poet, modestly, declining to enter into a defense of his native place.

'"Deed an' I canna' tell you that. The whole o' Scotland reeks wi' Stewarts, I mind nothing more o' the people than the lass' bit story."

The old parson had grown testy, and was plainly proof against further questioning. He had told out his tale, to his own thinking.

It was a frail thread for the youth to fasten upon for his clew; but he continued to haunt the prison precincts, asking fruitless questions about John Monteith, the Stewarts, whom he could in no way extricate from the mass of their name. He became more and more convinced that the man who could grandly sacrifice himself in the face of evidence so easy to turn in his favor, was like to that other man, who, unknown and untracked, bore himself with the self-same mien, across the sea.

To listen to the half-forgotten fragments of a once thrilling story, mumbled over by a prosy and dull-souled narrator, was but a poor substitute, to his ardent nature, for a full knowledge of the thing he sought. For he knew that such dull and stale repetitions can rob of their pathos the darkest tragedies. Pondering it over, he followed out the trail suggested by Parson McCairn, and came to believe:

1st. That John Monteith, (or John Wallace) had not committed the crime:

2nd. That Jenny Stewart was the guilty person:

3rd. That the just and pure soul of the man had recoiled from the creature who could do a dark deed and then be forced to permit another—one whom she loved—to suffer the penalty; and that in escaping, he had refused to take her and her guilty secret with him.

"It all falls in with John Wallace's solitary life—his lack of interest in the women about him—that majestic widow, for instance, who," Bracebridge reflected, "must have been young and pretty—thirty, or forty years ago."

Yes: it was altogether a likely story. In fact, during several weeks, in which he had come and gone and waited and watched and pried and questioned, and found nothing that bore any resemblance to the dead scholar, the probability grew strong upon him and he determined to pay Mr. Roderic Clarkson a visit.

Nevertheless, when he found himself once more beneath the searching eyes of that august person, the probabilty began to tremble in the balance.

"Well?" queried the Solicitor in Chancery, who recognized himself and his business, lawyer-fashion, at once: "I presume you stumbled upon John Wallace. Immediately, Mr. Bracebridge."

"Not immediately; nevertheless, I think that I have found him Mr. Clarkson."

"Ah?" with his cynical, superior smile.

"Yes; I have found a great and good and generous man who took upon himself voluntarily the sin of another."

The Solicitor's face changed slightly ; a look of surprise reddened with a flush of annoyance crossing it.

" Go on," he said briefly.

" He was a man who could sacrifice himself; for he renounced everything rather than let the shadow of a crime fall upon one he loved. Am I right so far, Mr. Clarkson ? "

" Go on," impatience mingling with the brevity.

The man of letters regarded the man of law with a suddenly waxing triumph. The probable John Wallace was assuming magnificent proportions, and already's young Bracebridge's heart was thumping audibly.

" He never lifted his voice to defend himself from base imputation, because it would have been so acasy to prove who had done the deed."

" May I now interrupt your eloquence to inquire, Mr. Bracebridge, *Where* you discovered this individual. Who showed such a vast capacity. For self abnega tion ? "

The solicitor's irony roused the other's spirit, and he answered firmly :

" I found him,—or the trace of him,—in the Edinburgh Prison."

Mr Roderic Clarkson's face brightened perceptibly : " Well ? "

" I found him," continued his antagonist still confidently, " in the person of John Wallace Monteith, who was sentenced-unjustly I am persuaded, for twenty years imprisonment for the forgery of a will ; but who escaped to America in 1840——"

The old lawyer rose with genuine dignity :

"Mr. Leslie Bracebridge, you have been at great pains, I do not doubt, to discover—the wrong man."

"Can it be possible?" cried the other excitedly.

"And I may as well tell you this," pursued the solicitor, "That you will never find John Wallace. Among convicts or felons."

The poet was crushed, and proceeded to bow himself hastily out of the presence of that cynical smile, which had returned as soon as its owner heard the mention of the Edinburgh Prison.

"Perhaps it will not make your search any too easy," the great man added, relenting as he had done before towards the youth and enthusiasm of his visitor, "to suggest that if you look here. In London. You will come nearer to the history you are seeking."

Again the young man cried "Thank you," and made his dazed way into the street.

"Here—in London!" he echoed: "Great heavens! And London is twenty times the size of Edinburgh! I shall never find a clue!"

And he walked disconsolately about the never silent streets, until the mists of evening had aided the smoke of the day to obliterate the Great City

CHAPTER XXI.

THE STORY OF A MADHOUSE.

" So did this old woe fade from memory
Till after, in the fullness of the days,
I needs must find an ember yet unquenched,
And, breathing, blow the spark to flame. It lives
If precious be the soul of man to man."

THE RING AND THE BOOK.

DOES not every one know what it is to wake, some
dreary morning and find—through loss, or disappointment, or absence of that vital interest in things outside of ourselves which we call happiness,—that life
has turned a blank side towards us? That we no
longer realize the acuteness of either joy or pain ; but
go monotonously about our humdrum duties with a
benumbed sense of spiritual remoteness which makes
the world seem hollow enough, and even our own
selves unreal.

There was a touch of this bitterness of disappointment which mingled with Leslie Bracebridge's uncertain experiences during the next week or two of un-
directed wanderings.

He went among scenes of squalor, as though they
knew any secret but their own wretchedness. He
plunged into places of vice, as if they could tell of

aught but their own ruin.   Here and there, Shadows
mocked at him, saying. " We are what you seek. We
are the lost who are found."

For what had at first been but a freak of fancy had
now grown to be a mania with the poet, who relapsed
by rapid mental stages into that one-idead state which
is but little removed from insanity.   Possibly it was
this melancholy condition of the mind which drew
him sympathetically to a great Asylum for the Insane
which shall here be nameless, since the tragedies once
told there are best forgotten.   Moreover, he remembered the idle Rest-Hampton tale ; that Mr. Wallace
had " come over " with the physician of an Insane
Asylum.   Unfortunately, Bracebridge was not a profound student of the psychological.   He noted more
the obvious actions of men and women than the drift
of their unfulfilled intentions.   Of this he was conscious.

" If I succeed in evolving John Wallace's ghost
from the secrets of a myriad of lives, it will be by
grace rather than by natural acuteness," he mused
thankful that his search was a hallucination and not
a mission.   And still the ghost tempted him on.

·The London world was enveloped in a cloud of per-
sistent rain when he first made his acquaintance with
the doomed House of Misery, where the immured,
who are but unfortunates are treated as criminals.
The chief supervisor displayed the annals of the madhouse with pride, as a hotel keeper might gloat over a
full and flourishing establishment.   Often he chanced
upon a name or a suggestion which struck him as
tempting an investigation. He was therefore at pains to

gather up much worthless information, and several dire tragedies of which his pen took secret cognizance. But none of all these spectres of the past answered John Wallace to the roll-call of his spiritual perception. Then he went to other scenes. At last, when he had searched London over in an aimless fashion, and was about giving up the effort in sheer disgust at his failures, it occurred to him that he had made no notes of the women's department in the great asylum he had first looked into. Undoubtedly the women had stories which would add palpably to the article he meant to prepare for tickling the public palate. And so it happened that he gravitated back to the gray walls of the House of Suffering.

About midway through the female wards, Leslie Bracebridge and his guide came upon a hideous old woman of seventy or over, who had wildly disordered white hair, and fierce tiger eyes. She was the solitary inmate of one of those little cage-like rooms without windows, and with iron-grated doors, where are thrust those hapless wretches who are deemed "violent," and doomed like murderers, to solitary confinement. She was talking and gesticulating wildly ; and when she caught sight of Bracebridge, stretched out a claw-like and skinny hand crying : " You, there, whoever you are ! I tell you it was I that did it !— they won't believe me, but it was ! "

" What does she mean ? " queried the young man gazing compassionately upon the miserable wreck of womanhood.

" H'it don't mean nothing, really sir. She's h'always going on like that," said the attendant who was "showing him through," it being visiting day at the Institution.

" I should like to talk to her," said Bracebridge, beginning to take out his note-book. Doubtless this hag would fit admirably into his " *Tragedies of a Madhouse.*"

The guide then unlocked the grated door, remarking that Meg was " 'armless, but troublesome. " The half furious creature was out of her cell at a bound.

" She is horribly active—for so old a person," remarked Bracebridge drawing back in acute distaste of her sudden proximity.

" Oh ! she's h'active h'enough," said the keeper. " We h'only keep 'er shut h'up for fear she'll do 'erself some 'arm. She'd like to kill 'erself—she would, eh, Meg ? "

" You'll never believe me, so where's the use of answering," said the mad woman, sulkily : "I killed some one, once. That's enough, I don't want to kill myself. I've expiated ever since. He told me to repent—repent—repent ! what good has it done ? I shall be mad all the same, always ! I *know* I'm mad. Those yonder "—pointing scornfully to a couple of hideous creatures in straight-jackets, with short hair, who laughed and sang ribald songs—" *They* don't know they are mad. I am mad ; but not as mad as they think. They don't believe my story and call it mad talk. If I weren't mad, I shouldn't tell it ; but it's true.

" Why, this old creature talks rationally enough," said Bracebridge : "and moreover, she talks well. She is a good specimen." And the note-book was

opened. The young man did not mean to be heart-
less; but youth and good luck are always callous towards age and misfortune. It is an inevitable law of
unregenerate human nature.

"H'oh!" laughed the attendant; "you're not
much h'used to lunatics, sir, h'if you take their talk
for rational. The worst of them makes h'it sound quite
sane like mostly—h'at least the visitors thinks so,"
she added with a chuckle.

"At any rate, I should like to hear this story of
hers:" and Bracebridge motioned to the old creature
to sit on one of the iron benches in the corridor
while he cautiously took the next.

"No," she muttered sulkily; 'why should I sit
down? 1 don't get my liberty often; I had rather walk
about. Besides, you'll not believe me. Nobody does."

"What do you want me to believe?"

"That I killed him."

"Whom?"

"My husband."

"Great heavens!" muttered the Poet nervously;
" what a singular avowal."

"There!" cried the jade: "I knew you'd not believe me." She had been watching him furtively.

"Perhaps I shall believe when I hear."

"No, you won't. But I'll tell you. It was too
long ago to prove. They won't take it up in court.
I write to the judge whenever they'll give me a scrap
of paper. I've written stacks of evidence. But they
never send it. Do you think I'm fool enough to believe it's sent?" She laughed harshly; and then
went on: "If they would let me out, I'd go before a

judge and accuse myself, and take an oath upon the
Book that I killed Alan Forbes."

"How did you kill him?"

"Take me before a judge and let me be sworn—"
she cried, her eyes and cheeks beginning to burn
more fiercely: "Then, if I confess, he may come
back."

"Who?—Alan Forbes?"

The woman laughed, her eyes rolling and glaring. "As if I wanted *him* back! and how could
he, when I killed him? They'll lock *you* up for mad,
if you talk like that. Oh!" she cried, with a sudden pathetic change of tone and look, "I've confessed and confessed to everyone that comes; and
none will believe me! Go find Judge Keith for
me!" She burst out with a wild and terrible anguish—"Go out into the world—across the sea—anywhere—and find him. Go bring him back and tell
him that I have expiated."

She was sobbing in a frenzied way, and wringing
her wretched hands. Bracebridge felt his compassion stirred to the quick, but his curiosity was still
unappeased.

"Who is Judge Keith?"

"He is my lover," she cried, in a stealthy whisper;
her sudden anguish changed in a flash into fierce
and cunning secrecy: "*He saw me do it*, and he
could not live in the same world with me, and not
accuse me—for he was the soul of justice—and
honor—" She broke off, glaring with dreadful ani-
mosity at the keeper who here returned and paused,
grinning at the pair.

" She's got that far 'as she ? There's a lot yet. I
' ope you h'aint tired, sir. She's got herself somehow
mixed h'up with Judge Keith, who, I'm told, really did
disappear years ago."—

" Hold your tongue—devil ! " cried the mad woman
with a menace in her voice. " Don't you speak his
name ! Send her away," she cried, appealingly to the
stranger whose ear she had got. " She is a fool. She
thinks she knows. *I alone know why Robert Keith left
his home, his friends, his fortune, his position, his good
name,"—*

Her words died off in a wail ; but there was a
majesty of truth about the wretched creature's whole
mien that transformed her in the Poet's eyes. The
attendant laughed coarsely and passed on. Meg
watched her with hatred in her eyes.

" They are all fools," she whispered contemptuously
in one of those swift startling changes only possible
to the deranged. " They call my talk mad. Hear me
—you. *Will you or will you not believe me ?* " Her
tone was so menacing, she looked so threatening that
Bracebridge hastened to assure her of his entire cred-
ulity.

" Are you a lawyer ? "

" No, but I can fetch you one," he said soothingly.

" Pshaw ! I know what *that* is worth ! nobody keeps
a promise—to a lunatic. Get out your book, there,
you shall at least take my testimony."

" I will take it, and publish it," said Bracebridge
earnestly.

" Yes," she cried in sudden excitement. " Publish it far and wide. Send it across the sea, that

it may reach Robert Keith. He doesn't call himself that. He has some other name—I forget. Write."

Her tone was so commanding, and her bearing at
odd moments so majestic, that the young man was
puzzled what manner of woman this lost being had
been. He began to write nervously. Then she spoke
calmly, distinctly, and with a singular elegance of
intonations :

"My name is Margaret Blair. That is my maid-
en name—the one Robert Keith knew me by. I
was but sixteen when Alan Forbes married me.
He was a drunkard and a devil. Here, in the presence
of witnesses and the open court, I swear that he was
a fiend incarnate."

(Then followed some terrible denunciations which
the Poet omitted.)

"I left him after three years and came to London,
and lived quietly under my maiden name, I was not
afraid of Alan Forbes following me, for he was never
sober, and was moreover afraid of the Penitentiary.

"I had money of my own, and I took a pretty place
out of town, where I lived with only my old governess
for protection. I had but few relatives, and I made
out to them that I had gone to India with a cousin
who received and forwarded all my letters.—Tell me,
does this sound like mad talk?"

"No—oh, no!" cried Bracebridge, amazed and subdued.

"Write :—Judge Keith had the next place. If
an angel ever trod the earth, it was Robert Keith.
Only he was an angel of justice as well as of love.
He was forty-five years old when I first met him,

and had a grand face—like the angel Gabriel. He
had never looked upon a woman to love her : but he
loved me. I could not have had wickedness in my
heart, or that god-like man would not have loved me.
But he *did* love me! for five years. We were to be
married and *I never told him about Alan Forbes!* I
could not. It seemed too terrible to have been true.
I could not believe that I had ever been scorched by
such fires. Then,"—she sat down suddenly and
clutched Bracebridge's hand in her claw-like fingers.
He could feel the sharp nails upon his flesh :

" *Then—that—devil—came to light—and—found
me out.*" She gasped the words slowly, and sat panting for a few seconds. In the house there was a bustle
somewhere down the corridor, and two keepers carried
off a rebellious wretch, shrieking. It brought her
back to her recital with terrified haste.

"Go on. Write. They will come for me next—
and then my mind goes ! oh, write !—He came more
drunken, more bestial then ever. I concealed his
existence from the great and good man that loved me
and meant to marry me. I knew he would never forgive my deception—how could he ? I grew anxious
and ill. He questioned me tenderly. I lied to him.—
Say, do you believe me ? "

" I do indeed. What you say bears the evidence of
truth. I have put it all down."

" You are good," cried the poor creature piteously.
" No one else has let me get so far—that wicked,
coarse woman is always near. Go on ! Write it down
—that I have confessed, and that I repent," she cried
wildly.

"You must first tell me what you did, and how Robert Keith found you out," said Bracebridge soothingly.

"Yes, he found me out. The fiend who had been the curse of my youth hung about, debauched, sly, degraded, malicious. He suspected something, I think. A dozen times his vile presence barely escaped detection. But *I loved Robert Keith and was determined to marry him*—in spite of that other. You think it absurd, perhaps, for a hideous creature like me to talk of love and marriage. I was not hideous then. Robert Keith said that I was beautiful. Now I can't see myself, but I see the others. I look like *that*"— she pointed to a miserable and filthy creature with disheveled gray hair, and then went on, almost incoherently, the words stumbling hotly one upon another, in her haste to tell her woe:

"Twice I paid him to keep away, but he always came back. One day, after a week's respite, when I had all my belongings packed to go away to the hills—professedly for my health—he stumbled into my morning room, intoxicated, brutal, and in a raging fever. Before I could have him removed, he had fallen into a sort of fit—a convulsion—something of the sort. I was forced to send for a physician, who pronounced it the worst form of delirium tremens, and said that the man must die.

"'When?' I questioned feverishly; for I was half mad with the thought that Robert Keith might discover him. 'Soon,' he said: 'In a week—any time: another fit will kill him.'

"I covered my face in terror. If he should live—a

week! How could I keep it all from Robert! I wanted to tell the physician not to help him, but I dared not. *I was not mad then.*

"That night the convulsion came back. 'Now he will die!' I thought, and trembled for joy. But he grew better. The night wore on. By mid-day the next day, after the doctor had come, and given me hope—hope?—It was the anguish of despair!—and gone, I could not bear it. He *must* die. I ran and fetched a phial of laudanum and forced it between his teeth. I said to myself: 'It will put him to sleep!' But all the while that I was pouring the liquid down his throat, I knew that I meant to kill him.—Are you writing every word?"

"Every syllable," said the other, showing his short-hand notes.

The woman sprang at him like a wild beast:

"You have been trifling with me," she hissed in his ear. "That is nothing—mere scratches. You too have deceived me!"

"On my word of honor it is genuine," cried Brace-bridge, retreating hastily: "It is a new method of writing. I can read every word:" and he read several sentences at random.

"It is very curious," she said slowly; "but I will believe you. Write: Suddenly, as I stood with the empty phial in my hand, I looked up. There was Robert Keith with a terrible look in his grand and luminous face.

"I was paralyzed with terror, and a sudden horror of what I had done. He held out his hand for the phial. I can see him now," she moaned shivering, "as he stood there, tall and firm and terrible—like an accusing angel—holding out his hand.

" 'Who is that man you have murdered ?' he asked.

" 'My husband !' I cried passionately and in desperation ; but I was afraid of the dreadful look in his face. 'Have mercy upon me !' I begged ; but all the same I knew that he would not have mercy, but justice." The ill-starred creature fell back, panting.

"And did he betray you ?"

"Betray me !—He !" a fiery glance of intense scorn darted from her blood-shot eyes. "If he only had—I might have died in the prison—or on the gallows—what matter, so it was not here and after years and years of torture. He would have been spared the fate he took upon himself, and I should have escaped this hell-house. Do you think death is worse than this—do you ?"

She laughed frightfully. A chill went through the Poet's sensitive frame, but he mastered himself and went on steadily :

"But you have not told me what happened—afterwards—after he had discovered what you had done. I cannot write your testimony if you leave that out."

"Afterwards !" she cried wildly. "How can I tell ? I never saw him again—I never saw his face after that look, when he stood like the avenging angel—or wait ; I did see him—once ; in another country,—America or India,—but I forget. It pains my head to talk of that. When I came to myself; after weeks of fever, he had gone—no one knew where. That was his way of administering justice. Some one must expiate. Jesus of Nazareth suffered that way."

" Did no one else, suspect ? "

" No—no one. When the doctor came, he found Alan Forbes dead, and I was lying on the floor in a swoon. He thought it was grief. Afterwards, he told me I had done well to rub the patient with spirits, to pour some down his throat ; but that nothing could have saved him. Then I knew that Robert Keith had tried to resuscitate the man ; or tried to cover up my guilt."

The poor wretch sat gazing into the ink-pool of her lot, relapsing fast into her usual stupor or incoherence.

At last Bracebridge succeeded in rousing her once more."

" I sought him all over England. Then I went to Scotland and searched for his people ; for I knew he was of Scotch birth,"—

Here the Poet started up, and then sat down again without speaking.

" At last I found them and heard from them that he had left the country—given up his position on the bench, his fortune—everything—and gone, no one knew where, or why. They thought that his mind had suddenly become deranged, and that if he recovered he would return. But they had not been able to discover any trace of his whereabouts. They were not very near of kin : his parents were dead and he had neither brother nor sister. That was why they did not discover him. But I discovered him. I left no stone unturned, no method untried. But it was such a great way off—oh ! " cried the poor creature

—" my head—my head!" and she pressed her hands to her forehead as if in bodily pain.

Bracebridge looked at her compassionately; but he had another story to fathom besides the tragedy of her wretchedness.

" And you followed him?" he asked distinctly.

" Yes!—oh, yes! but he sent me back. Don't ask me of that; you are not assembled in the court-room to ask me of that, before these witnesses. They are here to listen when I accuse my own hand of the murder of Alan Forbes. They are not here to listen when I accuse Robert Keith of cruelty and injustice —he who was a very God of justice? I tell you, I will not answer one question more. No man shall ask me of my secret: it is my crime that is your business, my Lord and gentlemen of the Jury—not my humiliation."

" But where was he, when you followed him?" persisted the other, reaching with such eagerness for the broken threads, that he could not for the moment accept the sudden cloud of lunacy that had returned over the wretched woman's hitherto direct narrative.

" How dare you seek to follow me on that journey?" cried she, springing up with a threatening gesture, but at once fell back with her hands upon her head, rocking and moaning.

" How shall I find him—you want me to find him," persisted the baffled Poet, regarding her with a deepening sense of despair.

" Go and find him—as I found him. Seek for him over the world—as I sought. Find him—a man en-

tombed among the graves of his hopes. There was a
mist about him : and he was carried up in it, like an
angel. There was a storm at sea, and he walked upon the waters, like a Christ. Oh ! you will know him,
if you find him. There is no other creature upon this
earth with that awful, God-like look in his face—oh !
my head, my head ! "

The woman seemed to swoon away, and in his
fright Bracebridge beckoned to the attendant who
hovered near, suspicious of the climax.

" She h'always gits a spell when she's h'excited
with talk," remarked that female gruffly, and she
pushed the half insensible creature into her cell : " I
can't see why folks wants lunatics to talk. Old your
tongue, Meg, or h' I'll sleeve you."

" I wonder if she was crazy when she followed that
man to America—or India—or wherever it was,"
mused Bracebridge aloud.

The attendant paused in locking the heavy grated
door to stare at him :

" La, sir. You don't mean to say you believe a
word of that story ! "

" I do indeed ; and I think I know Robert Keith."

" H'as to Judge Keith—'e's well h'enough. H'I've
'eard there were such a person ; but that Meg should
mix 'erself h'up with 'im—that's the joke. Like
enough, she's h'always been crazy."

The frenzied creature, who had partly roused up on
being thus rudely thrust into her cell, here flashed
out with a final effort of departing reason and strength.
—But why follow to its hideous climax that revolting
tragedy. Let us draw a veil rather upon the awful

spectacle which can be presented by one who is—in spite of all—a human being.

"Great Heavens! what a dispensation!" cried the Poet, as he stood outside the gloomy gates of that Inferno, and seemed to read over its grated entrance the old, old sentence of woe :

"*Lasciate ogni speranza voi ch' entrate.*"

Could it be that while he was planning to entertain the public with other and lesser misfortunes, the mystery of John Wallace had risen up and confronted him in so hideous a guise, thrusting its cruel secret upon his flippant intention ?

The young man tried to imagine a conscience so acute that it "could not breath the same air" with one whom it felt called upon by the sacredness of the highest judicial position to condemn, and by the tenderness of personal feeling to acquit. So this poor criminal herself had viewed the matter.

He recalled the conscious look upon Mr. Roderic Clarkson's stone mask, when he had spoken of John Wallace as a man who had suffered for the sin of another. The perplexity was such that Bracebridge determined to see the great solicitor at once.

All the way to Lothbury, in the quick darting little hansom, which sent the crowds of London skimming by like the figures upon a magic-lantern slide, the young man wrestled with his problem. It almost seemed as though the questions were not—"*Is this John Wallace?*" but "*In doing this thing was he right, or wrong?*" And he came upon the large brass plate, "Mr. Roderic Clarkson, Solicitor in

Chancery," before he had made up his mind about the calamitous tale.

It was more than a month since he had been there last ; for time had not stood still while he dragged the great city for the dregs of its miseries.

Mr. Clarkson, he was informed, was ill, and had gone to Brighton. He might not return before late in the Autumn ; if quite recovered he might possibly be back in a fortnight or two.

All this in the monotonous tone of oft-repetition which is unmoved by the anxieties it aggravates, and the chagrins it crushes. It was a fiat.

When Bracebridge returned to the asylum, he was informed that no one would be allowed to see Meg Blair, in future, as the excitement of speech had been proved most injurious to her. In vain he pleaded that he had reasons which were of importance for seeing her once more. It was impossible. The laws and restrictions of an insane asylum are absolute. The mad woman, and her possible revelations, were gone from him forever, but there remained with him an assurance that his search was ended. This belief filled him with a restless impatience to wring from Sir Roderic Clarkson's reluctance the affirmation he desired. He lingered in London until it became evident that the solicitor's visit to Brighton was likely to prolong itself through the Autumn, and then the stir of the huge metropolis became unbearable. Moreover, he was haunted by the spectre of Margaret Blair's misery, which he felt somehow was owing to his encouragement of her passionate recital.

Very likely the poor wretch would henceforth be consigned to perpetual incarceration in the loneliness of her cell ; or at best would be debarred from ever again finding the relief of telling her wild story.

CHAPTER XXII.

THE STORY OF A RUIN.

" ' This grey place was famous once,' said he—
And he began that legend of the place,
As if in answer to the unspoken fears,
And told me all about a brave man dead;
Which lifted me and let my soul go on. "

THE RING AND THE BOOK.

THE restlessness which had come upon Leslie
Bracebridge since his failure to see the London solicitor, had driven him forth to take a journey among
the seldom explored wastes of border country.

There are miles of moorland which it seems truly
a desecration for steam to traverse ; and running in a
low and distant line are the Cheviot Hills.

Ah ! Jean Gordon ! It must be that thy mighty
shade, which once inspired a Meg Merrilies, haunts
this region yet ; for the Poet presently came upon a
scene that carried his fancy back to the border gypsies of a hundred years ago.

The farther from London he felt himself transported the more there came over him a spirit of peace
which enabled him to "bide a wee," as the Scotch

folks say.   What haste was there to set the seal of certainty upon the denouement he had found, and thereby to end the purpose of his summer's quest? Now that the time had well-nigh come when he was to hold in his hand the lost links of the dead man's career, he suddenly came to a regretful pause upon the brink of the *finale.*

Some of the staunch Scotch closeness gathered about his interest in the "old woe," and he wondered, at last, by what right he had made it his.

He spent days in wandering among the unvisited regions that he had chosen unawares.   The loveliness of the moors, the serenity of the hills, the mournfulness of the brackens, all spoke to him of silence; and he became a veritable dreamer among the wastes.
* * * * * *   It was a mellow evening, and he found himself creeping about in the gloaming as though the spirits he had sought to disturb were beckoning towards a vast and remote solitude.   Just beyond lay a decayed and poverty-stricken little village, which was half concealed beyond a group of hills in a desolate region he had not yet traversed.   He was tempted onward until he found himself among the sickening sights and odors of squalor, filth, and pestilence, quite unusual in thrifty Scotland.

The people whom he saw dawdling about in the filthy yards and lanes had a look of gypsies or vagrants; and the Poet soon found himself in a state of wonderment as to how they managed to subsist, since he saw nothing that suggested industry of any sort, or even tilling of the fields which were wide wastes of bog or heather.

Yet it was plain to be seen that the ruinous habitations had been by no means built to be the hovels of the poor. They were of a large and stately appearance, which, in spite of their filthy and dilapidated condition, still bespoke past grandeur.

Vice and wretchedness stared from every shattered window and gaping door-way, crawled over every broken sill, and ran riot about the neglected gardens.

Half-starved pigs and sickly children swarmed in unlovely picturesqueness over the whole festering village; while the men and women glowered at the new-comer with the surly looks of those who regard a stranger as an intruder.

" What is the name of your village ? " Bracebridge asked politely of a surly looking fellow who lounged against a bit of broken wall, pieced out by a long since overgrown hedge.

" Deed an' I dinna ken that," growled the man.

" Don't you live here, my friend ? "

" We bide in't. whiles."

" Has it got no name ? " persisted the visitor, who it may be seen was not without determination.

" Na—its got nae name, the day."

" May I ask, what did it used to be called ? "

The man muttered an oath and blurted out:

" It were ca'wd Cammerden Manor," and shuffling around presented the broad of his tattered back to any further conversation.

Bracebridge laughed quietly to himself, but went on, quite sure that he would encounter yet the Scotch garrulity which is fairly interspersed with its gruffer characteristics.

A brawny, red-haired woman called out to the man in a harsh voice like the scream of a pea-fowl:

"Yer muckle daft, Tam Binnie! Did ye nae mind the braw claes an' gentle havins o' him as speered at ye? Canna ye open yer mouth for siller?"

The man repeated his sullen oath in reply, and the visitor passed on, unmolested, through the stench of the long straggling village street.

The next day he was drawn thither again by what magnetism he knew not. This time he held converse with one or two creatures of more likely appearance than the man first addressed. As well as he could decipher from the broad Scotch speech, (which was perchance eased to his ears somewhat, as he had been used in his childhood to the dialect of a Scotch nurse) he made out that the Manor had been, fifty years ago, a settlement of great and wealthy people, who came down from Edinburgh, and some from London, for half the year to live at their ease upon the fine hunting and fishing lands, where they had built "shooting boxes" and country mansions that were rival palaces in their beauty and completeness.

The Earl of Earnshope had owned the village and the country round about, and a great castle not far away, across the moor.

There were Melton Brae, and Ellerslie, and Bryn Gowen, and many more fine places that had belonged to the gentry, but were long ago gone to ruin.

Bracebridge was filled with curiosity about the pasing from the soil of its land-owners in so few years, knowing that not to be the way of the old world. But all the information he could get was that the region was haunted ; and that the great folks had been scared away by a curse which had fallen upon them. Even the present occupants seemed to hold some superstition about dwelling there, affirming that they did but " bide in't."

" What became of the fine houses ? he asked of the dirty crowd that his shillings had drawn about him. A slipshod woman replied promptly :

" Deed an' they say it was the deil's fire."

" What became of the former inhabitants of the village ? "

She shook her head : " There might be some as kent ; but maistly we be puir ignorant boddies that hae com' frae ilka parts an' squatted upo' the lan'."

" Is there nobody left of all the former inhabitants ? " Bracebridge demanded in amazement.

" Na—naebody at a'."

And forthwith, he began to frequent the place, sure of finding something poetic back of this ignorance and squalor, and desertion.

One afternoon in the afterglow of the wide sunset, he wandered deep into a little wood, and came suddenly upon the wild beauty of a noble ruin. It was the remains of a small but majestic structure which had once been a Gothic church, one could see, by the fragments of majestic windows, and the shattered portion of a tall belfry that was still standing.

Enchanted with his luck in stumbling upon so rare a bit of sequestered loveliness, he tramped about in artistic content among the ivy-mantled turrets and into the long desolated sanctum of the chancel, where the stone pavement was weather-stained and displaced.

The altar stairs were broken by the harshness of the elements, and mended again by many colored mosses and all manner of creeping things, that nature sends to repair the ravages of her stormier moods. The pulpit, the railing, the pews, every fragment of wood about the edifice, had been burned away, or carried off by the wild villagers of whom Bracebridge had had a glimpse.

The Poet felt himself transported into a region of speculation and wonderment that caused him to take no note of time. And the gloaming had crept stealthily upon him : the bats and owlets and such like denizens of solitary and melancholy places, were stirring before he could tear himself away. When he did, it was to meditate resting for the night among the doubtful shades of the village, hoping that he might thereby chance upon some one who could tell him the tale of Cammerden Manor and its downfall.

Making his way through the growing darkness, towards a light that gleamed faintly from a patched window upon the edge of the settlement, beyond which was the wild moor, he presently knocked at a hinge-less and broken door.

" Whist ye—what's wanted ? " cried a piping voice like that of a very old man.

" It's a stranger that is benighted and wants shelter," cried Leslie Bracebridge in return.

" Eh, but its puir shelter I've got the nicht. Ye'd best gang up the town to Jeems Leckits. He'll hae ye a heartsomer welcome than a lane body like me."

" But it rains, and I want shelter very much. It matters not what sort."

Here the visitor ventured to push the door a little, and squeezed himself through the crevice into a low and miserable room where an old man lay upon a pallet of straw, such as the Scotch people call a "shakedown."

"Come ben if yer maun," piped the poor old creature; "There's nought but the cobble for ye to gang ower."

"The cobbles are far better than the morass I should fall into, unless you will let me in from the night and the storm," answered Bracebridge pleasantly. "But are you sick, friend?"

"Aye, aye," muttered the other; "Its an ill place en' no ticht frae the winds and rains, an' my puir auld body's unco fu' o pain. I doubt but I'll be in the deed-thraw erewhiles."

"Are you alone?"

"Aye, sir, lane syne the morn. The leelang day there's nor wife nor bairn to threep at me. I'm maistly driven to gang clean daft wi' the lonesomeness o't."

"I am glad I came in, then," said the young man, in genuine compassion. "You will let me wait on you I hope."

"Na—na," cried the other fretfully: "There's but a wheen mair to bide gen the bairn comes ben. She wad mak the bit parritch."

Leslie Bracebridge sat silent upon the broken chair, and looked around the wretched place. It was utterly barren of comforts, stript of necessities.

"After what are ye speerin i' the place, mister,' said the Scot suspiciously, turning his disheveled head and staying for a moment the roving of his restless eyes ; " Be ye a tax man come to luke after the goods folks ha' na' getten ? "

" Indeed no," said the Poet reassuringly : " I have come to look for the story of Cammerden Manor ? "

" Eh ?—what ? " cries the other, starting up on his emaciated elbow, which presently gave out and let him down heavily upon the straw, from which his foxy eyes gleamed fiercely :

" Who towd ye o' Cammerden Manor ? "

" A woman down the street, but she did not know much more than the name."

" Na," snarled the old man. " She did na ken muckle, truly. Yon puir sackless boddies o' squatters hae got naething to do wi' Cammerden Manor."

" Somebody must know something about it," began the visitor, feeling his way gingerly along : " Perhaps you can tell me, my friend, more than the people yonder."

" Na, na, I tell ye I dinna threep at Cammerden Manor. Waes me, but my heart is sair to hear telt o' that name ! "

Bracebridge produced a handful of small coin from his pocket, and deposited it upon the table, which, with two broken chairs was all that the hovel contained.

" That is to pay for my lodging," he remarked ; " and my supper if you will give me some. And now if you will tell me your name, we can have a cosy talk."

The old creature stared hungrily at the money. Death was indeed upon him ; the cold sweat stood already upon his forehead ; but the greed of the mortal was still unquenched.

"Aweel, aweel," he muttered;" I'm unco fu' o' years ; an' its been mony a day syne I hae seen the like o' sae muckle siller. But wae's me: It winna' heal my greetin for the likes o' Cammerden Manor. An it canna keepit the deed-thraw awa."

"Are you one of those who lived there, then ? "

"Aind," he cried : "Is it *ain* ye ca't? I'm the lane, mister. The ithers hae a' been flitted this twa score year."

"Then you can tell me what I want to know."

Bracebridge leaned forward and looked eagerly at the restless eyes that gleamed so keenly at him.

"I want to know about yonder church that has fallen to decay."

"Yon kirk!" He sat up now, and beat about the wretched bed with his bony hands : "Gude Lord—gude Lord! Is't the tale o' the kirk ye maun be gotten for siller?——Na, then, mister, tak' it awa'! I warrant I winna tell that the noe, as nane kens but my ain single sel. I hae not telt that these thirty year an' mair."

"I do not wish to buy your confidence," said Leslie Bracebridge quickly, seeing that the old man was angry, and fearing he would spend his still remaining strength ; "But you will tell me your name?"

"Auld Sandy, they ca' me," he answered, briefly.

"And who is the bairn that will soon come home ? "

"It's my bit grand-dauchter Bel." His thin face brightened ; "She makes odd shillins' nae an' then at wark amang ither folks as is no fit to latchet her shoon."

The face fell again.

Soon there was a patter of small quick feet on the door-sill, and presently a tidy little lass of twelve, or thereabouts, came quickly into the room, her tattered shawl and hood dripping with rain, and a pretty smile on her rather wan face.

"That child has never had enough to eat in her life," was the visitor's inward comment.

The old man reached towards her feverishly.

"Eh, Bel, puir bairn, here's a gentle as is come to bide the nicht, an' has getten a' that siller for ye, no to be owin' naething the whiles."

The meager little face flushed quickly.

"Grandfather," she said, "We hae na got a place to putten folks in as pays siller for their keep."

"Never mind, Bel," interrupted the young man, stifling a queer choking sensation in his throat. "I like your grandfather, and would rather be here than at the best house in the village."

"Eh," she said, quaintly tossing her pretty head, "There's nae ither house sae muckle better redd than ours. Howsoever, sir, I doubt if ye wad like to eaten the parritch an' oat-cake which is all a' we hae the nicht. Happen I had better tak' your siller to the shop an' fetch ye sommat ither."

Bracebridge assured her that he was most fond of porridge ; and while she was busy putting the two or three cups and platters upon the rickety table, and stirring the mess over a heap of smouldering moss she was coaxing to burn, the grandfather watched her with pride, muttering as if to himself.

"She were aye douce an' deftlike. Her mither

deed when she were a wee bit lassie o' twa year. Puir, wee, bonny Bel !"

The little thing turned her eyes affectionately upon the old man. Even in that poor hovel, love was not unknown.

" Hang me if I wouldn't like to go out and buy them a supper of meats and other viands that very likely they've never even seen," muttered Bracebridge, " But I doubt if there is a shop where anything decent can be got in the neighborhood."

After they had eaten the frugal meal, the old man with a tolerably good relish, the child with a womanly sparingness which again brought a lump to the visitor's throat, the dip candle spluttered in its socket, and he began to fear there would be no story that night, even if his singular host could be induced to part with his choice secret. Presently when the child had set things to rights, she said simply :

" If tha pleases, sir, its but a puir bed I hae getten to offer ye, savin its tidy."

And so it was tidy—the child's own straw heap which she had spread with a clean linen.

She crept away into a hole in the wall, which had served as a " next room" in better times ; and soon her fresh young voice was heard singing softly to herself, while the old man dozed fitfully, and the visitor still sat watching the carefully smothered moss fire :

" *I am far frae my hame, an' I'm weary often whiles*
For the langed-for hame-coming, an' my Father's welcome
  smiles,

I'll ne'er be fu' contented until mine een do see
The King in his beauty in my ain countrie.
The earth is flecked wi' flowers mony tinted bright and gay ;
The birdies warble blithely for my father made them sae ;
But these sights an' these sounds will as naething be to me
When I hear the ransomed singing in my ain countrie."

The old man joined in the next verse without seeming to rouse up.   The words of the quaint sweet hymn
fell upon the Poet's ear with a pathos he had never
known in the whole course of his life ; while the tune
had all of that Scotch plaintiveness in it which makes
their songs so dear to those serious people.

" Iv'e his gude word of promise that some gladsome day the
*   King*
To his ain royal palace, his banished bairn will bring ;
Wi' eyes an' wi' heart rinning ower we shall see
The King in his beauty in his ain countrie.
My sins hae been mony an' my sorrows hae been sair,
But there they'll never vex me, nor be remembered there ;
For his bluid hath made me white, an' his hands shall dry
*   mine ee,*
When he brings me hame at last to my ain countrie."

"It is their evening hymn," thought Bracebridge ;
"They sing it together from habit, out of all this
poverty and misery."

Presently the old man started from his doze, and
struggled to prop himself upon the straw pillow.   He
gazed wildly around upon the flickering light of the
candle, and the dying ebb of the fire, and then seemed
to listen, his cracked voice silent this time :

" Like a bairn to its mither, a wee birdie to its nest
I fain wad be ganging noo unto my Saviour's breast
For he gathers in his bosom witless lambs like me
An' carries them himsel' to his ain' countrie.
He's faithfu' that has promised an' he'll surely come again
To keep his tryst wi' me, at what hour I dinna ken,
But he bids me still to wait an' ready aye to be
To gang at ony moment to my ain countrie."

" Puir Bel," he muttered ; " puir, witless lamb. Aye but it's gude that he's faithfu' as has promised."

Then his glance fell upon the young man who sat with bowed head and something like a sob in his throat. It seemed to turn the current of his thoughts.

"Whist ye," he whispered. " Has the bairn gone the noo ?—eh, Bel ? "

He elevated his feeble voice to a shrill call, and the child came instantly from her den, having thrown her ragged coverlet about the single garment she wore. Her bare feet were clean-washed and rosy on the cobble floor.

" Hand me a dip, Bel. The maister and me will be liken to speer a bit,"

The little one hesitated. Very likely she had but one poor candle left, and her thrifty wisdom rebelled against such unseemly extravagance.

" Aye—aye ! I ken it wilfu' waste an' woefu' want. We've plenty o' the last, an nae muckle chance at the ither. But the gentle boddy's siller behooves to pay for a dip—aye, an' for the story likewise. I mind not he bides in our bit hut for the likes o' the parritch. It'll no be mony licht that I burn mair," he added to himself.

Bracebridge plucked up courage, and when the little maiden had fetched a fresh candle, he waited patiently for the dying man to speak.

The rain fell heavily, the wind moaned drearily. The elements seemed to saturate the wretched hut with their woe. Even the darkness of the night seemed to gather and thicken with nameless terrors within the room. The Poet watched the feeble light with a chilly fascination; he feared every instant that it might be obliterated by the palpable gloom settling heavier and heavier upon everything. Outside, upon the wild and solitary moor, he could not have felt more alone.

A sickly hue of death had crept over the old man's features. The place was full of the signs of coming dissolution. It seemed to the appalled watcher that the very atmosphere reeked with death.

At last the poor soul came back to consciousness. "Well noe," he began presently; "It's lang syne word or breath o' auld acquaintance passed my lips. But what wad ye hear about, mister—mister—"

"Bracebridge," finished the other, then added:

"I should like to learn how the rich and aristocratic Cammerden Manor came to be transformed into this mean and squalid settlement without a name?"

"Hist, Mister Bracebridge, an' what for d'ye want a name for a parcel o' squatters as kens naebody an nabody winna be liken to ken. They're an ill-favored set, the scum o' the country side, belike. We're no in that lot, Bel an' me, praise God."

"You have no friends here then?"

"Nane, I tell ye—'though mebbe that'll be waur

for the bairn when I'm gane hame"—he clutched the fragments of coverlet with his pitiful hands, and went on with an effort:

"After the dire calamities that befell Cammerden Manor mair than forty year agone, I was left alain here upo' the moors—savin' the deserted houses, an' the smoking ruins o' Ellerslie, an' Bryngowen, an' Melton Brae, an' waur' nor a'—the bonny kirk. After that, they cam from ilka side, yon fuil boddies as tuck free holt o' the empty neuks deserted by the bonny birds that had flitted."

"But what happened?" cried the listener, observing in alarm the filming eyes of the old man, and his wandering manner.

"Its a lang story—maist like an auld wife's tale. I doubt me ye'll think the threepin' worth the measure o' your siller. But I maun mak it up to ye in some gate. Weel—weel! Cammerden Manor were rightly a weel-to-do place and unco fair to look upon. The earl war a fine gentle an' lived like ony prince wi' his great leddy an' their sons an' dochters. .

"Ane son Lord Percy—I mind not if he were the second or third, for I was but a lad mysel' sixty year agone—he had tuck to the Church—no the Scottish Kirk but that they call the Anglican. For they had na bided muckle in Scotland, but had their learnin' in Lunnon which I am persuaded is a place fu' o' a' evil.

"When he—Lord Percy that I speak of—came back, a weel-learnt mon, an' sae religious, naething wad do but the Earl maun build him a kirk:—no that they ca'd it a kirk, but I canna bide to name strange names the noo—nigh upo' the Castle. The Castle's gone the noo, nae stane left upo' the ither; aye an' sae is maist o' the kirk. "

The old man heaved a sob. Outside, the wind and rain made melancholy moan. Then he went on, not without physical effort:

" The rich an great families that dwelt round about, they made unco rejoicings ower the new kirk ; an' likewise the peasantry that lived upo' the Earl's lands made plain to want Lord Percy for their pastor. —I mind the gude Lord winna hae his people fall into priestly ways, an' may-happen it were that deed that brought the calamities upo' the place. Nevertheless, aside frae this doubty teachin', Lord Percy were a godly man, an' sae also were the Earl. I gotten a'. this frae my father, who fell himsel' into the snare o' the new thing, an war chosen to be clerk o' the bonny, braw kirk. I had my upbringin' in these ways ; but when confusion came upo' the place, I saw that it war a judgment against them. My father were calt Sandy Meer, like mysel' ; an' he were a gude honest man wha' ne'er telt a lee, Mister Bracebridge, nor take't a bit siller frae ony mon i' charity."

He halted for breath, and his listener nodded gravely in acceptance of the introduction. He knew that the innate Scotch pride rankled even here to receive an unearned penny.

" Was Cammerden Manor an old place?" he asked puzzled to trace its apparently recent origin.

" Na, na. It were a new settlement, putten up like a toy-village to please the fancy o' the Earl an' his friends. They dwelt maist o' the year in Lunnon, or

Em'bro, an' came to the manor for their pleasuring.—wae's me! I canna bide to ca' it a' back. It's sair—sair! An' bonny Bel—she's no my ain.—But Lord, Lord! I canna tell that!"

The old man seemed to relapse into a wandering mood from which he fell into a stupor. His face was so ashen, and his fallen jaw so ghastly, that Leslie Bracebridge felt for his flask of brandy and hastened to force some down the gurgling throat.

He revived a little and began to talk in a rambling fashion about the Earl and bonny Bel. At last he seemed to collect his wandering wits, and fastening his fading faculties upon his guest for an instant, tried to rally his forces:

"I were not done wi' the tellin', maister, but I fear me death hae grippit me hard. Ye maun getten the rest frae anither than me—how that the bairn is no my grand-dauchter at a'—"

"What other—who is there, Sandy?"

The Poet felt the egotism of his position: that with a something in the room he dared not name, he should cling to his base curiosity, and trouble the worn-out spirit for its last vestige of mortal memory.

"He were a gude mon—Lord Percy—an' prechit mony a year, wi' a luke i' his een like his maister. But the deil cam an' sowed tares in his bonny field. It war waur for him—it war waur for his leddy—it war waur for a'! But he's gang—he's gang—lang syne."—The voice trailed feebly off into incoherent mutterings.

"Is Lord Percy dead?"

"Deed?—na, na. That war better if he had deed.

He's wráng, they say, in his head. He's tarryin', they say, ower the sea—wae's me ! "

The old man flung his gaunt arms about, and presently lay gasping in what seemed indeed the "deedthraw." Bracebridge made a desperate effort to revive him, calling meanwhile for little Bel, who ran sobbing out into the rain and the darkness to fetch help.

He came to for a moment and asked for the bairn.

"She will come presently—with help. "

Auld Sandy fixed his glazing eyes on the strange face above him, and said with his struggling breath :

"It's too late the noo—for help. Ye maun speer at the Earl—he that was the auld Earl's son. He knows a,' belike."

"Where shall I find him, Sandy ?—Who is he ?"

For in the chaos of the old man's story, the Poet had beheld an apparition ! and the face mocked him with a smile that said : "I am the wraith you would discover !—Follow me. "

There was a sickening rattle in the dying man's throat : at last he articulated :

"I' the auld Buke o' the kirk—Bel maun fetch it— puir, wee Bel—" and he spoke no more.

All that night and the next day he lay in a stupor. Death fought hard for the hulk of Auld Sandy ; and the Scotch tenacity of life made the struggle a terrible one.

Bracebridge made every effort to find aid among the wretched villagers ; but they hung back and said he was "nane o' theirs."

"There's nae docther, nae preacher, nae siller for

a buryin', " sobbed poor little Bel, her womanly courage forsaking her.

Once the laboring soul came back to the hither
edge of that " sad, obscure, sequestered state " upon
which it was emerging, and sighed brokenly :

" Dinna greet, bairn. There'll be summon to tak'
thee by the hond. "

A sudden impulse overcame Leslie Bracebridge's
ordinary self, and spoke for him like an inspiration :

" Don't fret for Bel, Sandy. I will take her and
care for her. She shall not be left here."

It was wrung from him by the old man's death
agony. A sudden light flickered over the ghastly
face.

" May happen the Earl's better nor I thoucht.
May happen he'll be just. God guide thee, Bel—gang
wi' the gentle to Em'bro ; gang to the Earl, an· tell
him "——

But death hindered the rest.

Some queer spell was surely upon the young man,
that he could not have let auld Sandy die with a heart-
ache for his helpless little charge. Unconsciously
and without a moment's warning, he realized that he
had brought upon himself an incalculable responsibility.
What was he to do with it ? In the midst of his romantic vagaries, his seeking after misty and inexplicable things, he had suddenly come face to face with a
fact that he might find difficulty in ridding himself of.
Perhaps he had a semi-heroic fancy that he was making
mute atonement for his forced desertion of the woman,
Margaret Blair, whom he had left to eke out her misery
in unmitigated neglect.

True it is that our lives are like circles, forever touching, crossing, interlaced with other lives. We cannot handle one misery without a consciousness of the terrible magnetism which draws other miseries to it. Leslie Bracebridge had hardened his heart and walked away from the mad-woman's degradation. He reassured himself that he had come to seek the mysterious, and not to save the lost. And lo! in his path, like the " witless lamb " straying at dark upon the brink of an abyss, he had stumbled upon little Bel. What could he do but snatch her in his arms away from the gaunt wolf standing in the doorway, and from that other beast which goeth about like a roaring lion to prey upon helplessness and innocence.

What he meant to do with the child, he did not know. All that he realized was this ; she had fallen upon his mercy, and he accepted her meekly from Providence as one of those inexplicable dispensations which do not seem to follow any particular misdeed of our own, but evolve themselves from the circumstances about us, very much as our irresponsible birth is evolved from the chances of our day and generation.

CHAPTER XXIII.

THE SECRETARY'S STORY.

" Undoubtedly it is the end ;
Yet thence comes such confusion of what was
With what will be,—that late seems long ago,
And what years should bring round, already come,
'Till even he withdraws into a dream
As the rest do."

THE RING AND THE BOOK.

"Should you like me to take you to the Earl, Bel ? "

She looked up with that hopeless air so pathetic in a child, and said with a half sob:

"Ony place. I hae got na hame, the noo."

For in the old prayer-book, containing the Church Service, which little Bel had found for Leslie Brace-bridge, he had deciphered these words : " *Sandy Meer, Clerk of the Church. Of the household of the Earl of Earnshope,* ——*shire, Scotland."*

In another hand beneath, and in fresher ink was scrawled : " 16 *Tweed Court, Dumfries Street : Edinboro, Old Town."*

As unaware as Bel herself what this last address might lead to, the Poet took the homeless bairn by the hand and brought her to Edinburgh. If no shelter was offered the child, he meant to find a safe home for her in some asylum.

When they reached the quaint city, the lights were twinkling up and down the steep streets and dirty lanes of the Old Town. It was a rainy night, and the rock-like castle was obliterated from the murky sky.

Bracebridge left his little charge, whom he had fitted into decent clothing at the first town where they had stopped, in care of a motherly looking landlady, the proprietress of a genteel inn he had struck upon the borders of the ancient quarter he sought.

" It will be best for the child if I can find her kin at once," he thought, never doubting that the address would unearth somebody willing to take the waif from his hands. After some difficulty he found the place in Dumfries Street—an obscure and filthy tavern, where two or three burly fellows were making merry over their grog. He was glad he had not brought Bel along.

The tavern-keeper was a great brawny Scotchman, whose speech the poet could not understand, and who failed likewise to comprehend him, being somwhat addled with whiskey. At last some faint inkling of the stranger's meaning dawned upon him.

He " knew nawt o' auld San'ny," and roared in Bracebridge's face, when he persisted in mentioning the homeless child, that, he had " weans enouch o' his ain."

At last, in desperation, the young man fell back upon the name of the Earl of Earnshope, saying he had been commissioned by the dying man to bring the little girl to his lordship. The man stared:

" Weel noe—what for dinna ye hae that ower, mon ? The Earl, is't? Gude be wi' us ! Ye maunna tell it's Sandy Meer as is deed ! An' the Earl's grandson as were spirited awa' is come to licht after a'. Bring the bairn here, the nicht. Ther'll be siller to getten for her find.—Puir Sandy ! he were a brither o' my ain mither. May hap the auld body 'll kent sommat as'll thraw licht upo' the matter o' yer claverin."

But the old woman, when she was fetched, could only shake her palsied head as she hobbled about on her staff, and mumble :

" Na—na: I winna tell't—I winna tell't—San'ny wad grupple me deed ! It were an awesome secret. An' he hae kepit the secret an the child a' these years. He were unco fuil, I tell't him, an' daft like to hae a finger in sic a foul thing. An' noe—he's deed a' together. But ye maunna bring the wean here We'll be putten i' the jail if we getten the wean"— But the man interrupted her harshly, berating her in unintelligible Scotch for her stupidity in not seeing that they could make a fortune out of the matter.

" In coorse it's nae the lad hissel " Mister, for that were a matter o' forty year ago ; but its a wean o' the Earl's grandson as auld Sandy hid awa', I'll wager me wits on't. Sandy Meer's been in hiding these forty year wi' that guilty secret, an' ye've been diggin' him out the day ! Fetch the wean here, an' we'll look to her— Na, howld yer tongue there, will ye ? " and he menaced the old crone into inarticulate mumblings : for she had broken out afresh, warning him not to lay a finger upon the bairn.

Leslie Bracebridge listened and reflected. One

thing was clear: these people should never see the
child: another—that the man must not know of his resolve; a third—the whereabouts of the Earl's family
must be ascertained.   It was not into the hands of a
superstitious old crone and a brutal lubber that he
meant to trust the strange destiny cast upon his
care.

"Very likely the child is asleep by this time," he
said cautiously: "I cannot bring her to you to-night.
To-morrow morning, look for me.

"But I should like to see the Earl's place," he added,
paying lavishly for the grog he had not touched: "is
it hereabouts? I might pass it, to-night."

"Na—na. Its nae i' the old town, mon. Its
ower by all that's rich an' great. It's a canny place,
baith gude an' gran; but I'm tel't there's nae chick
nor childer to keep it i' the family. Gude Lard!"
he cried, starting up and over-turning a chair noisily
—"ef the wean thee threeps on were a lad—Gude
Lard! but its a wench tha says?"

"Yes—a girl; but I fancy she will not turn out to
be the Earl's great-granddaughter after all. You've
got no proof, you know."

Bracebridge spoke carelessly, and sought to withdraw without more parley. What he wished was to
escape these people. The Scotchman, now throughly
sobered, detained him by the button-hole and gave
him a shrewd wink.

"Eh, mon! When I'm getten the siller, I'll be after
droppin' thee a bit," and he winked again, chuckling
inwardly. "I've got proofs eneouch, never fear."

Bracebridge assented.   He must feign to accept

the man's cunning as he accepted his sudden thee-and-thou familiarity.

" I must hurry back now," he explained, " so as to have the child ready early to-morrow. What time are you open here ?"

The man laughed a coarse laugh and added, with a coarser oath, that he would be up betimes. After some more suggestions and arrangements, the Poet broke away, mentally thanking his lucky stars that he had so easily eluded the grip of the crafty Scotchman. In his own mind, he doubted the fragmentary testimony in reference to little Bel's origin. It was probably a coarse wile, suddenly hit upon by the low cunning of a rascal in whose memory there lingered some foundation for his fabrication.

" I must throw him off the track. He must not go to the Earl until I have settled the question one way or the other," thought the young man, conscious that his limited capacity for artifice might fare badly if matched against the probable trickiness of the other.

" I never could be diplomatic," he sighed, realizing that here might be a necessity for astuteness.

" It's ower against the new town. They'll tak' you the way ony gate, " the man had said, and the next morning found Bracebridge and the child driving under a huge stone gateway that led to a massive and somewhat forbidding pile of granite architecture that had many towers and turrets, with small windows and high battlements.

Carved in stone upon the gateway, and also over the massive *porte-cochère* where the coach stopped, was a coat-of-arms of which the writer took careful note. It was the original of which a rough scrawl had been made in the prayer-book he carried in his pocket.

Before leaving the Inn he had despatched a messenger to No. 16, Tweed Court, saying that the child seemed ill, and he had carried her into the country hoping to restore her health before bringing her to Dumfries street. He had then taken the one cab that the neighborhood boasted, and driven to the railroad depot; from which, after ostentatiously purchasing two tickets, and passing with a handful of passengers into the back of the station, he had wheeled around and jumped into a coach which drove them out by the way of the rear entrance.

Priding himself greatly upon having thus circumvented for a time a shrewder creature than himself, he awaited complacently the next emergency. The affair was beginning to smack of a romance, and he was quite pleased to have given rein to a rash impulse in adopting the misfortunes of an unknown child.

When the great door swung back upon its hinges he bethought himself to ask for the Earl's private secretary, making a bold move towards the appearance of business. He had left the child in the gatekeeper's lodge, with orders that she was upon no account to quit the place, and was himself shown into a small but richly fitted-up office on the left of the great hall. He had barely time in crossing this bit of the hall to notice that it was magnificently adorned with pieces of sculpture, figures in bronze, and suits of rare old armor, when upon the threshold of the small apartment he was met by a florid, middle-aged man with the conventional sandy hair of Scotland, who bowed awkwardly, and after seating his guest, waited with national imperturbableness to learn his business.

"I wish to make some inquiries," began Brace-bridge, triumphing over the secretary's awkwardness, "in reference to the old estate, which belonged to the father of the present Earl of Earnshope, and was called Cammerden Manor."

The secretary stared as well he might:

"And what may be your business with my lord's possessions?"

"My business is chiefly with *his family*," replied the Poet with significant emphasis. He was determined to carry out this matter with a high hand, and not suffer the abasement he had endured at the hands of Sir Roderic Clarkson.

The secretary stared on.

"I have come from the death-bed of an old man,— one Sandy Meer—who was a retainer of the late Earl's, in his youth; whose father was clerk of the Church built by my Lord of Earnshope for his son, Lord Percy Cammerden."

"Well?"

The interrogation was barely removed in pronunciation, and not at all in intonation, from the broad Scotch "weel," but it had a particularly insolent sound to the young man's acute ears. He reflected that there was nothing which could aid him but sheer boldness, and the utmost stretch of the imagination upon points hinted at by the inhabitants of No. 16, Tweed Court.

"It is from what I gathered from this old man,

362 THE SHADOW OF JOHN WALLACE.

—and others,—that I have been able to trace out a singular clew to a half-forgotten mystery in the Earl's family."

" Well. "

" Are you aware of any such mystery ? "

A pig-headed look came into the secretary's face :

"Those are matters we never speak of in the household of the present Earl. "

Leslie Bracebridge's heart gave a bound. The stupidity of the other was making admissions that could never have been wrung from his obstinacy.

" Do you mean to say that you have never heard reference made to a grandson of my lord of Earnshope—the late Earl—who was living in exile—in obscurity ? "

" I said nothing about it. It's not my business, " answered the man stolidly.

Bracebridge made a still wilder dash at the coveted discovery.

" I am possessed of facts which would be of great interest to the present Earl of Earnshope. I have discovered traces of a child who is probably the only heir to this great name. "

" What do you want for them ? " asked the other with a grim sneer.

" I want——justice—restitution !

The Poet brought his hand down heavily upon the mahogany desk at which the other sat ; and the two men contemplated each other in a certain cat-on-the-roof fashion.

" Where's the child ? "

" Safe."

" What do you know about him."

" I know the child to be the direct descendant of Lord Percy Cammerden."

" Prove it."

The secretary's color had risen ; and he himself rose and confronted his visitor menacingly.

" I will ;—provided you verify certain statements which I shall proceed to make in reference to Cammerden Manor.

" Well."

" After Lord Percy, second son of the then Earl of Earnshope, took orders in the Anglican church, his father built him a church and gave him a living upon certain estates of his which were in the border country, and which went by the name of Cammerden Manor."

" Well."

" You are to affirm or deny my statements, if you please."

" Na—I'll do nought o' the kind," cried the other dropping into the Scotch as his ire rose; "you've not proved that you are a man with a right to make a claim like that."

"Oh—very well," said Bracebridge, feigning to rise :

" There are others who will not mind profiting by the information I was willing to give you gratis. I shall see a solicitor in town."

And he made a movement as if to depart. He had studied human nature to some effect, lately.

The Scotchman wrestled with his devil a moment, and the latter prevailed :

" If it's no offense to my Lord or my Lady," he began cautiously, "there'll be no harm I fancy in my giving the yea or nay to your story. But it's little I know of Cammerden Manor. I've not heard the name, only remotely, this many a year."

" Cammerden Manor was destroyed—principally by fire—forty years ago," said the Poet impressively. He knew so little, (if he may be said to have known anything absolutely) that he had to make the most of each point. Presently, when he had secured the stealthy interest of the secretary, he meant to make him finish the story.

At this moment, Leslie Bracebridge had entirely lost sight of John Wallace. The man and his "old woe" had faded before the present perplexity which enveloped the "witless lamb" he had found upon the waste.

" Yes—it was destroyed—principally by fire," assented the Scotchman cautiously.

" But there was another misfortune which befell the family,"—— Bracebridge was feeling his dangerous way——" about the same time."

" Well," relapsing into something of the former stolidity.

" It was the disgrace which came upon Lord Percy, and caused his disappearance from Scotland."

Here the visitor's ground grew unsafe. The next step might betray his ignorance. He paused ; but the Scotchman showed no signs of taking up the thread of the narrative. At last he leaned forward and laying his hand upon the elder man's arm, whispered with slow emphasis :

" What——became—of—the—child ? "

The secretary started, for the portentous manner of the other was not lost upon him. The present Earl, he knew was the youngest son by many years. The Lord Percy who had disappeared was the second son, and the rightful successor, when the oldest son died childless, to the title and estates of Earnshope. His disappearance had for so long a period been accepted as final, that the present Earl had come through a succession of deaths, to his possessions without a question.

The two men regarded each other fixedly—the one with a startled endeavor to learn how much his opponent knew—the other with a keen resolve to abstract something more.

" Of course," hazarded the Poet, " you know that this child was a boy ? "

The secretary nodded.

" And that he was consigned to—oblivion, and kept in ignorance of his birth and ancestry ?"

The secretary nodded again.

(" Lord, I thank thee that I am not as stupid as this clown," mentally apostrophized Leslie Bracebridge, figuratively casting up his eyes. The man had committed himself. The ground grew safer.)

" Can you explain to me any just reason why that child should have been disinherited, robbed of his name and position, defrauded "——

" Hold, man ! " cried the secretary, in a hoarse whisper : " I will tell you why that child had no claim upon the estates of Earnshope, and why he was best kept in ignorance of his antecedents. *He was not the son of Lord Percy Cammerden.*"

The Poet's eyes sparkled.   He leaned back in his chair breathing a devout "at last!" in the depths of his soul.   After all his floundering, something had floated to the surface of the murky waters he had dragged, and he grasped it.

All that the secretary perceived was that his visitor assumed a confident, almost aggressive bearing, and that he said defiantly :

"I beg your pardon ; that fact was never proved."

"Proved—proved !" cried the other excitedly "was it not proved to Lord Percy's misery that his wife was faithless, that she was no better than an adultress— and him on the verge of being raised to the Episcopacy ? Do you suppose it was not proved to him before he threw up everything and disappeared——"

"To America."

Bracebridge spoke in a suppressed tone.   The discoveries that were pouring upon him had an overwhelming effect ; but he preserved his acuteness.

"To America ?—Yes, and no. How should I know ? A man who wishes to be dead to all the world doesn't usually leave his address behind him."

"The man *is* dead."

The Scotchman jumped up and began pacing the little office.   Then he paused in front of his guest whe sat calm and unmoved, waiting for further developments.

"How in the name of——did you get hold of all this information ?"

"Partly through your imbecility," replied the Poet within :

"From several sources," answered the Poet without·

" Of course, of course," said the secretary impatiently, somewhat recovering himself : " Lord Percy must
have long since died.   He was not a young man when
it all happened."

" He was fifty years of age when he went to the
States.   He lived to be upwards of eighty," remarked
Bracebridge oracularly.

" And—you are an American, I fancy ? "

Bracebridge assented.

" And you know that this illigitimate son is living ? "

" He is not living.   He died in obscurity and
poverty.   But please recollect that I do not endorse
the illegitimacy."

" What are you going to do about it,—after all
these years—when everybody concerned is gone to
dust ? "   The secretary spoke with a sneer.

"Everybody is not gone to dust.   The son, who
was robbed of his heritage has left a child—who is to
be righted."

" Good God," cried the Scotchman, a pallor forcing
itself over his ribicund complexion : " Is't a boy ? "

But Bracebridge had no idea of weakening the effect
of his revelations by admitting the sex of his protegé.

" The child," he answered with dignity, " is here—in
Edinburgh—in my custody.   The old man who succeeded his father in concealing the child—as the father
had concealed Lord Percy's son,—is dead.   He died
leaving the child to me.   I have come here to confront the family with this wronged creature."

Something very like a shiver went through the
Scotchman's frame :

" My Lord will never recognize him ; my Lord will

be able to prove it all a fraud," he began feebly.   Then he broke off, and sat drumming upon the table with nervous fingers.   Presently he recommenced, speaking hurriedly, with a furtive glance at the door :

" You had better leave this matter to me. You had best not anger my Lord with thrusting an ugly possibility upon him, when it is too late to do anything to rectify any mistakes——"

" Pardon me.   There was no mistake.   It was a terrible wrong.   Lord Percy went into voluntary exile because he felt himself to be a disgraced man.   That did not disinherit his son."

Bracebridge actually began to assume the role of a philanthropist who only desires disinterestedly to right the evils within his reach.

" But—but—" stammered the bewildered secretary, "don't you see that if it had been Lord Percy's son that was to be born, he wouldn't have been disgraced, he wouldn't have left his wife—he wouldn't have given up the honors offered him—he——"

" Allow me to interrupt you," the Poet said calmly, " what honors do you refer to ?"

" Why the honors offered by the Anglican church, man ! They would have made a Lord Bishop of him the very day he disappeared.   It nearly broke the old Earl's heart.   He had had a fine ring made, with the Bishop's seal upon it, and was proud enough when he gave it to Lord Percy that very week.   I'm told that the ring was the only article of value the unhappy man took with him."

Leslie Bracebridge drew a quick breath or two. He saw John Wallace rise once more before him.

He remembered the seal ring, and the widow's hesitating remark that the design resembled a cipher of some sort rather than a coat-of-arms.

"What became of Lord Percy's wife?"

"Gude God, man! As if I knew! All I have gathered is that he married when he was about forty a young girl of seventeen, and that they had no children. My Lady was not a daughter of one of the noble families, not even a lady of the aristocracy, but was from some unknown parts, and had, I've heard the old servants say, a wild and headstrong look. They even chatter," here the Scotchman's voice fell still lower—"about gipsy blood, and say that my Lord got her from the border country: that he was bewitched, in fact; but that's only the talk o' the ignorant."

"That has nothing to do with the point. The lady was Lord Percy's wedded wife, and the son when he came, was their lawful child."

"Wait," cried the other feverishly. "Let me prove the contrary to you. For God's sake don't go to the Earl with that old story. Let me tell you how it all came about. After they had been married some years there came to Cammerden Manor, which I have heard was a wonderful place for learning and intellect, and had the finest society in all Scotland—and yet was a frivolous place, new and showy, and full of gay doings without knowledge of the stern virtue of the kirk"— (The secretary evidently disapproved of rank Anglicans) "but," he added, "tempered by the pure goodness and kind works of Lord Percy himself, who was a God-fearing man, there came to Cammerden Manor a young man who said he had a new gospel of some sort ; a new revelation, he called it, abounding in strange sounding phrases, and marvelously deep explanations of very simple Bible truths."

The Scotchman paused for breath.   His taciturnity had died hard, and he was palpably not given to talking in paragraphs.

"Well," he went on reluctantly, as his visitor still preserved the demeanor of one unconvinced ; " Well, Lord Percy's young wife was dazzled.   I've heard it said that she had a fine mind and was much pleased to hear the profound and difficult meanings that were put upon the gospel truth—you know the rest ? "

"I know what is alleged, but I contend that Lord Percy was deceived—duped by those who wished to rid themselves of him."

It was a daring assertion, intended to tempt a longer recital.

The other jumped up, and began fuming about the room in desperation.

"Deceived—Duped ! Good God ! Lord Percy had not an enemy in the world.   His family worshipped him ; his people made an idol of him, it broke the old Earl's heart when he went away. It broke his brother's heart, who was feeble and set a great store by him ; it broke up the community, the rich people left the place ; the church, they said was haunted and fell to ruin ; the people who lived there upon his bounty, scattered and fled, and some, they say, went mad and set fire to the town——"

" Stop," commanded the Poet, " There was one thing they failed to do. *Why did they not find Lord Percy ?* "

" Find Lord Percy," echoed the brow-beaten man—
" find him ?   Do you suppose they didn't ransack
England, and Scotland, and Ireland, and the Conti-
nent, too, for the matter o' that?   Do you suppose
they didn't send to India, and to your America ? But
what could they do ?—he was gone.   I believe, for
my part, that he jumped into the sea.   I will not believe that he lived to be upwards of eighty."

" That is neither here nor there," said Bracebridge
with a gesture of disdain.   " Go on and prove to me
that the child was illegitimate."

" *My lady told it herself,*" cried the other, warming
to his subject.   " She was led away more and more
by the young preacher, who presently began to say to
her that her husband was not enlightened as to the
new revelations which had been given to the world ;
that he was old in his way of thinking, and narrow in
his way of preaching ; that he could not comprehend
the things of the spirit ; but that somehow, they—My
Lady and the young adventurer—could form a mysterious sort of union which made two people one in
spite of their earthly estate—in a spiritual fashion—
you understand, only I do not recollect all the argu-
ments which were used.

" My Lady it seems, had never rightly loved her
husband, who nevertheless adored her with his whole
strength.   She was weak, and easily persuaded that
she owed it to some new light within her to leave Lord
Percy and join herself to the other man.   It made a
great scandal, but Lord Percy would not believe it.
He declared that she was partly deranged, and brought
her back, and treated her like a little child who has

wished to do wrong, but whom he loved too well to punish. And as no man in the country stood higher than Lord Percy, or was more beloved, the world made out to believe as he believed.

" It went on for a matter of three years, after which she seemed to be reconciled to her husband, and finally to have forgotten all about the tempter whom the Earl caused to be removed from Cammerden Manor. During this time they were preparing to make Lord Percy the Bishop of Edinburgh : for he was known throughout all Scotland and England, too, for his great wisdom and piety. But he had refused, saying there could be no questions such as had disturbed his fireside brought into the family of a Vicar of the Church. When, however, my Lady seemed changed, he—who could think ill of no creature, least of all the wife he loved, never dreaming that she was deceiving him and undermining him—he accepted, and the day for the consecration was fixed."

The Poet was watching the speaker intently, and as he paused for breath, made a slight movement with his hand to bid him continue.

" It may be that her conscience smote her so sorely that she could no longer deceive so good and noble a man. At any rate, when the time drew near my Lady had fled from Cammerden Manor—with the wicked creature who had tempted her to her ruin. She left a confession, saying that the child about to be born was not the child of Lord Percy, and that she could no longer conceal from him that she had been visited often and secretly by the young man—whose name I forget—and that she could not endure to give birth under her husband's roof to a child not his own. She was wild, she wrote, with grief and remorse ; but it was irrevocable.

" From the hour she left, Lord Percy never lifted his head. He had borne her infatuation like a hero —like a martyr ; only seeking gently to open her eyes to her wanderings, not believing, pure and innocent man, where they would lead her. But when he knew all, when he realized the perfidy of his wife, it seemed that his world had come to an end. They could not rouse him ; he went about with his eyes to the ground, taking a last farewell of everything and making what arrangements he could for the good of his parish and the poor of his flock. Then he disappeared—to India, the old Earl always believed ; but it was to America, you say ? "

" Yes—to America," answered the Poet, from a strong inward conviction that he had laid his hand, unwittingly, upon the substance whose Shadow he had so long and vainly chased. For the moment, all the researches of the past looked like vain imaginations. John Wallace stood confessed, with bent head and eyes to the ground. This time ths apparition had a personality that was like veritable flesh and blood. He was clothed in the vestments of the Church ; upon his finger was the ring Annie Hatherton had known ; his hand held thoughtfully a little ivory-covered prayer-book. Leslie Bracebridge wondered in swift contempt how the misty figure of Robert Keith, in his judicial robe and wig, could have allured him : and still more, what there had been in the bare outline of John Wallace Monteith, beyond the name, to tempt his foolish fancy.

A sentence of the widow Hatherton, about " a high dignitary in the Church," came back to him, as forgotten things will, in an emergency. Across the gulf of time and well-nigh oblivion, the phantom suddenly became a luminous presence, not unlike the glorified vision once manifested to Annie Castlewood.

CHAPTER XXIV.

LOW LIFE AND HIGH LIFE.

" All's a clear rede and no more riddle now.
Truth nowhere lies yet everywhere in these—
Not absolutely in a portion, yet
Evolvable from the whole: evolved at last
Painfully, held tenaciously by me.
Therefore there is not any doubt to clear
When I shall write the brief word presently. "

THE RING AND THE BOOK.

THE Poet rose and paced the floor meditatively.
He was exalted, exuberant, but most of all, he was
overwhelmed. Now that he had found the man he
sought, he feared him. He feared too, the entangle-
ment into which he had walked blindly.

"I suppose you are convinced now that the child
was illegitimate," sneered the secretary, eyeing him
nervously.

"What became of Lord Percy's wife—ultimately?"
queried Bracebridge for response.

"She came back after a year or two I believe,
penitent, wretched,—more like a wild woman than a
sane lady. When she learned his fate, she went mad
for a spell; then—for they bore with her for Lord
Percy's sake—she went away, declaring that she

would seek him over the earth until she found him
and got his forgiveness. Poor wretch! She had
that all along; but my lord was dazed, like, and many
thought he had lost his senses : to go away and hide
his shame like any common man."

"And what did she do with the child?"

"The preacher's brat?—What matters it? Could
a bastard be anything to the Earl of Earnshope?"

"The child was never proved a bastard," insisted
the Poet obstinately : "The woman was very likely
out of her head when she made that declaration."

"Mad or not, they say she turned witch, and
haunts the neighborhood of Cammerden Manor. None
of the Earl's family has ever gone back to look at the
place. All the rich and great people fled from it
as from a plague. They say——"

"I know—I know," interrupted Bracebridge impatiently ; he could now take up the thread of the story,
and hastened to do so. "It is a haunt for beggars
and thieves. Some one ought to reclaim the property.
It belongs—as everything else does—to the child who
has been defrauded and degraded."

"You still adhere to that fiction?" The secretary's
face was flushed and angry. He had soared above
his usual plane to tell the narrative and had done it
well.

"I shall do so until I get more convincing proofs
to the contrary than any you have given me."

"What right have you—what interest?" cried the
wretched man.

"The interest of humanity." The Poet actually
believed himself. The secretary leaned forward and

touched his arm, with a furtive glance to right and left :

"Let me beg you not to anger my lord by interfering as a stranger in his affairs. Leave me to hint a thing or two to him, and then—then—if there's money to pay for silence,—and all that,—why I'll see that you get your share. "

Bracebridge recoiled. The low greed of the tavern-keeper in Tweed Court had seemed a natural outgrowth of his breeding and surroundings. But that this middle-aged and respectable man, the trusted instrument of a probably high-toned and noble master, should make to him a proposition so utterly devoid of ingenuousness and good-faith, staggered him.

He had contemplated the cause in the light of a discovery, and undertaken to follow it up experimentally, as one might follow out the plot of an unwritten story. Mercenary motives had never occurred to him ; still less had he considered that he might be involving himself in a matter more delicate than straight-forward. Even his note-book was forgotten.

" It serves me right for my double-faced way of assuming to know what I subsequently wrung from this unwise steward, " he muttered.

Clearly the man was not to be trusted.

" I will throw him off, as I threw off Tweed Court. Whatever comes of it I will take the child to the Earl myself, and then wash my hands of the whole business. They may right her or wrong her as they choose. Certainly they will not ill-treat her : But first—first—I must ascertain if this banished lord be indeed the melancholy ghost who sat aloof from the

stir of actual life in a far, alien town, beholding and
not participating in the ways of men. "

Then he offered the secretary his hand in parting.

"I am glad we have come to an understanding,
Mr.—Mr.—"

" Hotchkiss, " supplied the other eagerly, produc-
ing a card ; "and by the way, sir, you have not mentioned your name."

" So I have not—allow me. " and the visitor wrote
' Henry Smith ' glibly upon the card, appending the
address of the modest Inn where he had put up with
the child, on his arrival at Edinburgh.

"If you will call at this place to-morrow morning,
Mr. Hotchkiss, we can talk over the matter more
fully. "

"I must get him out of the way when I come here,
to-morrow, " Bracebridge had concluded rapidly.

"Thank you ; at what hour shall I come ? "

" Early : at eleven o'clock. "

And after more thanks and adieus, the two parted,
the secretary politely escorting his guest to the door
and handing him a card upon which he had written a
line which he said would admit him without words.

Leslie Bracebridge trod on air.

" It is John Wallace himself," he cried in breathless
exultation : and yet the story of Robert Keith came
surging back upon him while he said it " I will go
at once to Mr. Roderic Clarkson. I will follow him
to Brighton," he mentally vowed. In the meanwhile,
the present side-issue must be settled. When they
had driven away from the narrow and noisy streets
of the Old Town, Bracebridge had felt that he was

escaping from the designs of Tweed Court. Now, his sensation was of hastening from the entanglements of Earnshope : and he drove towards the open country. "I must take lodgings in the suburbs for to-night. And by the way!"—

He brought his hands together with a sounding clap that startled little Bel and made her lift her blue eyes questioningly to his face. "I'll play both rascals a trick at once. They deserve it. Let them fight it out between them."

He burst out laughing, and Bel smiled up at him confidently.

"Little one," he said sententiously, "do you know that great issues hang upon your identity?"

"Yes, sir," answered the child obediently, and smiled again. Bel's smile was wonderful.

He looked upon her, presently, with a feeling akin to awe. The miserable waif, who but for him might have been starving upon a desolate heath, had she indeed the blood of that high and pure man in her veins? That she might have been born of John Wallace's race, seemed to swallow up the other probability of her noble antecedents. As Leslie Bracebridge had come to dwell upon his hero's character, there was no dignity, no honor, which all the peers of the realm could add unto him. The man's own nobility of soul and beautiful life were the grandest inheritance of which he could conceive, although he could not possibly tell whence he got this belief. He was sure the widow had not meant to give him the impression of anything remarkable about the person she had simply vindicated from false charges.

Whence, then, could the Being have arisen, whose giant-like proportions overshadowed everything he had formerly considered lofty ? It was a mystery. The man's own spirit must have hovered still about his mortal dust, and assumed by degrees an immortal shape in the highest form of human power and dignity.

When the new lodgings were found, after Mr. Henry Smith had taken precautions to dismiss the cab at a small park, and walk about for a half-hour, the first thing he did was to despatch a note by mail to Tweed Court.   Then he set himself to amuse the child : and at last the day of waiting wore itself out.

*   *   *   *   *   *   *   *

The next morning, a stout florid man walked punctually up to the little Inn and inquired of the motherly-looking landlady for Mr. Henry Smith.

The woman didn't know any such name.   She had "only three lodgers at that time, an elderly gentleman who was called Robson, and two commercial travelers by the names of Scragget and Forbes.   The elderly gentleman had been with her for some months, and was a sufferer from gout.   The young men had but just arrived, and "—

Here the portly gentleman cut her short.   He didn't care anything about Scragget and Forbes.   What he wanted was to see a Mr. Smith—a gentleman with a little boy, who was stopping there.

"A little boy, sir ?" echoed the landlady, puzzled.

"Yes, yes, woman," fumed the other ; for he was impatient to find his game.   "He hasn't gone, I suppose."

"Why, sir," said the good woman apologetically, "he 'asn't what you might say, gone, for he 'asn't never come. But there's another person here as is looking for the gentleman likewise. Only it's a little girl."

The secretary eyed her doubtfully. She had so mixed her personages that he was at a loss to comprehend her.

" Blow the stupidity of these English," he muttered.

"'Ow very h'irritable Scotchmen be," was the inward comment of Mrs. Bowles.

Of course the person she referred to was none other than Mr. Henry Smith, thought Mr. Hotchkiss.

" Well, show me to him, if you please," he managed to say courteously.

She led the way into a stuffy little parlor, where stamping about in undisguised wrath was an irascible and groggy individual, who was none other than the representative of No 16 Tweed Court.

He looked up hastily, but failing to recognize the intruder, stuffed his hands into his waistcoat, and went on with his stamping.

" Is your name Henry Smith ?" demanded Mr. Hotchkiss unable to control his impatience.

" Na—is't yours ? " retorted the other, roughly.

The secretary did not deign a reply. He picked up a seedy annual of some twenty years back, and tried to content himself, pulling out his watch from its fob every few moments and consulting it with smothered denunciations upon the delay.

At last, Tweed Court could no longer endure the situation. He rang the bell lustily which brought the landlady hurriedly to the room.

" Ye telt that the gentleman wi' the child has na been here sen yester'morn ? "

" He drove away from 'ere in a cab, the first thing after breakfast yesterday."

" An' ye ha' na getten his whereabouts ? "

" Ow could I h'ask a gentleman where 'e's goin' to when e's paid 'is bill ? " asked the injured Mrs. Bowles.

The other inmate had been listening intently, as a terrier listens when some-one says—" Rats!".

" Where did he get the cab ? " he demanded quickly and without preface.

The tavern keeper turned and glared at him :

" What is't to you ?   What be ye spyin' afther, ony, way ?   What's Mr. Henry Smith to ye, the day ? "

Mr. Hotchkiss rose with dignity :

" I am here by appointment, to meet him. Pray have *you* any business with him ? "

" D——n it," cried the other—" he's letten it out ! It'll be all up wi' us if the fuil 's letten it out. . Be you a lawyer, sir ? " he added with crest-fallen anxiety.

" I am—to all intents and purposes," replied the secretary, angry also that there should be any other participant in the secret which had tempted him. Doubtless, however, this clown was a necessary evil brought from Cammerden Manor, as the only individual who could swear to the child's identity.

He sat drumming upon the table for a few moments, and then said with magnificent condescension :

" Perhaps,—ah—if you could find the cab that Mr. Smith drove away in, we could make something out of this mistake."

He still believed that the Mr. Henry Smith of his yesterday's acquaintance meant to deal fairly by him ; and he wished the other party safe out of the way.

" Na," snarled the burly Scotchman," I'll no be putten out o' what's my ain business, mister. It's nae lawyer I'm wantin' i' the matter. Ye maun better be lookin' afther the cab yoursel'."

The atmosphere of the stuffy little parlor grew hot with suppressed contention. The landlady came and went anxiously, at one time trying the effect of diverting conversation, at another offering the persuasion of a mild semi-temperance concoction of which the secretary partook stiffly; but Tweed Court (who seemed to have some acute reason for concealing his name) growled out that he " had nae muckle taste for mither's milk, but wad hae a good grog or naething."

As the lumbering old clock in the corner hitched itself towards one o'clock, Mr. Hotchkiss rose and rang the bell with dignity :

" Mrs. Bowles," he said impressively, " I cannot be detained any longer waiting for Mr. Smith. There has doubtless been some just cause for this delay. When he arrives, will you say to him that I will look for him to bring the boy to "——

" The what ? " cried the tavern keeper bounding in between Mrs. Bowles and the secretary : " A b'y d'ye ca't ? an' he telt me it were a lass. Gude Lord, gude Lord ! That wad be better 'n a' ! An' it's given me the slippit he's done afther a' ! "

" So this fellow is *not* a necessary evil, and knows nothing definite. He is merely an interloper," thought the secretary.

"Girl or boy, it's nothing to you, my man, and if you don't get away from this place pretty soon, you and I will have a settlement."

Mr. Hotchkiss did not actually mean fight. He merely thought to intimidate a man who was doubtless a swaggering coward. But Tweed Court was keen to scent battle; it was his native air.

"Come on, then," he whooped; and before the secretary could face about, had him by the nape of his neck.

Mrs. Bowles screamed, and rushing from the room used a womanly precaution towards self preservation: She double-locked the door upon the combatants.

The two men by this time, had rolled upon the floor in fierce embrace. When the constable, wisely summoned by the same cautious female, arrived, Tweed Court sat victorious upon his fallen foe, whose face was ignominiously flattened in a pool of blood that came, however, from no more serious a wound than a bloody nose.

The victor, against whom Mrs. Bowles readily testified that he had made the attack was marched off to the lock-up; while the injured secretary, having paid heavily in good shillings for his release, limped sadly into the identical cab which had borne Bracebridge and little Bel away from their pursuers. * *

And what befell Leslie Bracebridge meanwile in his difficult undertaking? He had played sharp with two sharpers; and now it behooved him to show himself a gentleman.

The secretary's card had passed him easily by the

lodge, but was carried suspiciously up the broad pol-
ished-oak stairway by a magnificent lackey.

"It is the Earl himself that I wish to see," he had
said, grandly, and with the card had sent his own, on
which he wrote confidently :

" *Upon hurried and private business which it would
be against the Earl's interest to confide to his secretary.*"

Presently the magnificent lackey returned :

"My Lord was not in, but my Lady would speak
with the gentleman."

The man spoke grudgingly, Bracebridge thought.
Very likely he despised the hired coach which stood
at the door, with a small and wistful face looking from
its dingy window.

The Poet followed his discontented guide up the
grand sweep of the stairway, and was bowed into
a tiny reception room,—a jewel of a room, set in the
rich casket of the castle.

"Received by the aristocracy at last!" he cried
mentally ; "but I am not sure that I owe it to John
Wallace's ghost, after all!" For his reverence was
somewhat threadbare, and he could even joke, at times,
over his quest.

Then the door opened, and with a stately sweep of
draperies, there confronted Leslie Bracebridge a creature of so grand a mien and so lofty a countenance,
that he was overwhelmed with admiration.

She held herself with cold pride, as if she questioned the stranger's privilege to gaze upon her lovely
face. But something he saw there spoke of a noble
nature and a true soul.

"You have business with his Lordship which cannot wait, I believe?" she said, with that low musical utterance which is not of any country nor clime, but belongs only to those who have reigned in the sphere called "high life." Unquestionably, this woman was a queen there.

"I think that I have, Lady Earnshope," answered Bracebridge gently: "I have stumbled unawares upon some singular facts which I will give your Ladyship, with your permission. You may, or may not, find them serviceable."

She motioned him to a chair at some distance from the one upon which she seated herself, and from which he could see, in an adjoining room, an aged and beautiful woman who reclined upon a divan, with the air of an invalid.

"Perhaps I had best be brief, and your Ladyship will pardon me if I seem abrupt?"

Lady Earnshope bowed her stately head, and the young man began:

"Some little time ago, in travelling through the Border Country, I came upon the remains of Camerden Manor, which I believe belonged to the Earls of Earnshope?" (No response.)

"I found there, an old man, who called himself Sandy Meer, and who was dying of old age—and starvation, I presume."

The lady was listening carefully. She had been toying with the long, silky ears of a Scotch-terrier that had followed her into the room and curled himself upon her lap when she seated herself. But now she ceased, and sat quite still.

"The old man was in such a dire strait, that I could

not conscientiously leave him; for there was no one who came near him excepting a little girl who was too young to know what to do in the emergency. It appeared to me that for some reason this old creature was cut off—isolated—from all about him. There seemed to be some fear or superstition concerning him."

Bracebridge watched the proud face closely, and he thought he saw it's expression waver.

"Does your Ladyship know of such an old man, and such a child, hiding in secret among the forsaken ruins of Camerden Manor?"

"I know nothing of what you speak," she answered coldly and calmly, and began stroking again the silky cars.

"Perhaps then, I have made a mistake, and that there is nothing, after all, to tell your Ladyship."

"You may continue your story, if you wish. I know nothing to object to in the old man."

"From what he said, though inarticulately I confess, I gathered that the child who was with him was the daughter of a man whose existence your Ladyship has very likely forgotten. I refer to the son of the present Earl's older brother, Lord Percy Cammerden."

Distinctly, this time, Leslie Bracebridge saw the beautiful countenance change. A sound, too, was heard in the adjoining room, and the white haired invalid had sat up on her divan, leaning forward like one who is startled.

"I am not aware that Lord Percy Cammerden left a son."

"I understand that the fact is a disputed one.

Believe me, Lady Earnshope, I have no wish to pry into affairs which do not concern any one but the Earl of Earnshope. Only, I have taken the liberty of bringing the child to his notice, that he may decide the question for himself."

" You are exceedingly courteous," said the Lady of Earnshope, brushing the dog from her lap with the wave of her white hand that seemed to carry dismissal to the young man also : " Undoubtedly the Earl will look into the matter. Will you be kind enough to leave the child's address with my husband's secretary."

" Lady Earnshope," said Leslie Bracebridge rising with a flush of color on his brow, " the child has no address, because she has no home. If I had left her in the wretched hovel where I found her, she would have starved to death also. She is waiting your decision, in a cab below."

The Lady of Earnshope rose also. She seemed to tower above her visitor, in the cold dignity of her scorn :

" You have taken an uncalled-for liberty, Mr. Bracebridge. I must request you either to take the child away with you and not trouble the Earl further about the matter, or to leave her at the Lodge until he shall conclude whether there is anything in your statement. In the latter case, I must beg that you will consider you have sufficiently done your duty, and leave the affair once for all to his Lordship's option."

Leslie Bracebridge bowed low :

" Certainly, Lady Earnshope. The child is nothing

to me but an object of humane consideration. I can conscientiously consign her to your hands."

"And whatever compensation you wish for your trouble you will be kind enough to mention to Mr. Hotchkiss who is doubtless in his office," continued the Lady of Earnshope, loftily.

"Pardon me," said the Poet proudly, "I desire no compensation whatever for doing my duty : but "—

Here the desperateness of his determination to strike one more blow for his main chance nearly overcame him, in the presence of so proud and beautiful a creature.

"What do you desire, if not compensation?" asked my Lady distinctly.

"I desire to know if I am not speaking with one who can give me some clew to—*The Lady Correspondent of John Wallace.*"

The beautiful eyes looked full into his with an expression of amazement not unmixed with alarm :

"If I have not questioned your sanity hitherto, Mr. Bracebridge, I cannot help doing so at so remarkable a digression"——

Here, as she stretched out her faultless hand to touch a silken bell-rope, they both caught sight of an apparition in the doorway. It was the pale invalid, who had noiselessly crossed the adjoining room, and stood with white face and unearthly eyes fixed upon the disconcerted young man. She seemed to pant for breath, and clutched the door-frame for support.

Lady Earnshope stepped forward, but not until she had pulled the crimson cord.

"Madam," she said with gentle firmness, "you are

too ill to rise alone. You should not have crossed the room without Lettice."

" What did he say ? " muttered the other between shaking lips : " What is he talking about ? I could not hear distinctly ? "

" He is saying some exceedingly foolish things," retorted my Lady, leading the older woman with gentle compulsion to a chair.

" But what about the Lady Correspondent "—

" Really, Madam," interrupted the calm, musical voice, " I could not comprehend this gentleman's vagaries. Falconer, " to the lackey who appeared " you will show this gentleman to his carriage. And Falconer "—looking grandly over her shoulder as the humbled Poet withdrew behind the liveried coat— " Send word to the Lodge, that his business at the Castle is concluded."

The liveried back which Bracebridge meekly followed seemed to expand with triumph.

" Rejected by the aristocracy," he muttered, all the exultation faded from his face : " And really " he added with a hopelessly puzzled air, " I don't know yet whether I owe it to John Wallace—or not."

At this precise moment the tavern keeper was being marched off by the constable, while the belabored secretary limped away. Perhaps of the three, the Poet was the most crestfallen.

CHAPTER XXV.

"UNDOUBTEDLY IT IS THE END."

" One poor pleading more and I have done
But shall I ply my papers, play my proofs,
Parade my studies, fifty in a row,
As though the court were yet in pupilage,
And not the artist's ultimate appeal?

THE RING AND THE BOOK.

" I AM going to leave you here, Bel," remarked the young man, as he descended from the cab at the door of the Lodge. A servant was following on foot to verify this statement to the inmates of the Lodge.

The blue eyes opened wide with a deprecating surprise.

" You are to go and live at the Castle, little one. They will be very kind to you," he continued, seeing the startled look.

" I dinna want to le' ye, sir," broke from the child who clung to his hand; " I wad reyther go ben to your hame." And she burst into tears.

" But I have no home—nor any wife nor children, Bel, and I live on the other side of a great sea," the Poet answered somewhat staggered at this new consideration. He had no idea that his little protege had attached herself to him in her quaint, demure fashion.

"It is a fine place there, and you will be very happy," he hazarded, smothering an honest doubt.

"But they winna luve me, sir," she sobbed." An' Grandfather telt the folks as lives i' gran' places is hard and cauld as stane. O please dinna' sen' me there ! Le' me stay here."

Leslie Bracebridge had a soft heart. He was a poet, remember, and somewhat out of his element as detective and newspaper reporter. "Wait, Bel," he said, lifting her from the cab, and kissing her gently on the forehead.

Then he went into the Lodge, and began to talk with the woman,' who eyed them wistfully from the door. She had lost her only child not long before, and little Bel's bonny face had won upon her heart the previous day.

"She is an orphan, and is thrown upon the Earl's charity," he explained. " Perhaps his lordship would be glad if you would keep her. He would of course pay you——"

" O Sir," cried the woman, her eyes brimming over " It's not the pay I'd be wantin'. It's the bonnie lass. She's that like my ain lost Bessie, as it breaks me hairt wi' luve to see her. Couldn'a ye manage to leave the bairn wi' me a' togither ? "

"I fear I can do nothing definite about it," Bracebridge said, perplexed. In his effort to do the best for the little creature he had, it seemed, overstepped what would have been a safer and simpler plan. Going to the cab where he had left the sobbing child, he led her tenderly to the woman.

" Would you like to live here, little one, and have a mother of your own ? "

For answer, wee Bel lifted her head to the kind face above her. Then, without a word, she ran to the arms outstretched to her. The woman folded her to her heart, sobbing.

" O Sir," she said, " my gude mon wi' be unco happy the day. He said, yester'e'en, that the lass was so like our ain, he couldn'a bear to luik at her. But if she could belong to us, he wad luve her the same."

" I am sure that the Earl will make no objections to your keeping this child : " and Bracebridge wrote hastily upon a card to the effect that as his suspicions were very likely unfounded, he hoped the child might find a home with the kind people who wanted her.

This he addressed to Mr. Hotchkiss. ."The fellow will never dare intimate that he had any secret under-standing with me," he concluded. Then he bethought himself of the tavern keeper.

" If a man should come here, and talk about one Sandy Meer ; or want to meddle with the child in any way, do not admit him : He is a worthless rascal," he said to the woman, who promised readily.

Then he turned, and lifting the little Scotch maiden in his arms, kissed her for the last time.

" God bless thee Little Bel. Thou art sheltered, poor wee lamb."

" Tha's been sae gude to me, Sir," murmured the child, shyly, looking with sweet confidence into his eyes, and smiling through her tears.

" Thank heaven I've accomplished some good,—in-cidentally,—in all this business," the Poet thought as he drove at last to a hotel, somewhat relieved, it must be confessed, to be no longer encumbered with the friendless child.

When he had lunched and consulted the railway time-table, he found that he had barely time to make the express train for London.

Once on board, he had leisure to think. The apparition of the invalid woman's pale and scared face in the doorway of Lady Earnshope's boudoir, impressed him more and more. There was something in that terrified look which the younger woman had comprehended, and desired to cover.

"What if that white and stricken creature were *The Lady Correspondent of John Wallace*—and "— here the blood gave a tingling leap through the young man's veins—"*his wife !* "

*   *   *   *   *   *   *   *   *   *

When Leslie Bracebridge came upon the now familiar offices in Lothbury, and read the impressive name—"Roderic Clarkson, Solicitor in Chancery " for the last time, he was nearly as agitated as upon his first visit. But this time it was hope which stirred his bosom—triumph, rather than trepidation.

He had made bold strokes, and played what seemed now to have been a marvelous game.

"I'm a lucky dog, after all," he thought, " to have things turn up in my path as they have done. It isn't every fellow who picks up a denouement for the hunting."

Then he began to map out the pending interview.

He had, on consideration, decided to march up to

Mr. Roderic Clarkson and say, not timorously, but boldly and with authority :

"I am undecided, Mr. Clarkson, whether to name your client, whose history I have been tracing back to its mystery, Robert Keith, formerly Judge on the bench in this city, or—more probably—Lord Percy Cammerden, second son of the Earl of Earnshope."

He went over this speech many times, familiarizing himself with its conciseness, and with the expression of the solicitor's face when coldness should give way to unavoidable amazement and interest.

He even felt the grip of the august hand, and received serenely the congratulations sure to reward his extraordinary success. Perhaps Mr. Clarkson might go so far as to hint that he would find a young man of his caution and discretion valuable in such matters of extreme delicacy as frequently fall to the care of solicitors who have the affairs of great families in their control. He might, peradventure, make an offer.

"Such an office would have its uses, its fascinations—for a while. On the whole, I might be induced to accept—should the terms be generous. It would give me a certain prestige "——

When Bracebridge's cogitations had reached this point, he was standing in the outer vestibule of the sombre rooms which seemed from some cause to have attained an accession of dignity and gloom.

There was no smile or other recognition upon the face of the person who opened the door to usher him into the writing-room, although he had several times performed that office, and the Poet distinctly identified his countenance.

Bracebridge received his duty-bow quite airily, and remarked, taking a confident step forwards :

"I wish to see Mr. Roderic Clarkson. Is he returned from Brighton ?"

The fellow looked at him, he thought, supercilliously.

" Sir," he said in an incomprehensible tone.

Bracebridge repeated his demand with great force of dignity.

" Mr. Roderic Clarkson—Sir?" echoed the other with what seemed like insolence.

"Yes," cried Bracebridge impatiently ; "can't you tell me if he has returned?"

" I beg your pardon—" said the clerk, not offering to let the visitor pass—" Sir Roderic Clarkson is dead."

" Dead!" gasped the Poet, and for an instant was ready to fall down; this had in no way occurred to his remotest calculations : " Dead! when—how—where ? "

" A fortnight since. Of overwork. At Brighton," responded the clerk monotonously.

" Who carries on his affairs ? "

" The gentlemen of the Firm."

" And who are they ? "

" Mr. Giles Wilberforce and Mr. Henry Morton."

" I wish to see one or the other of them."

" I beg your pardon. Which gentleman did you say ? "

" Mr. Morton," cried the excited visitor, hap-hazard. The name sounded less awful.

" He is at present in court."

" Mr. Wilberforce, then," (impatiently.) "Now I've got to begin at the beginning again." (despairingly, *sotto voce.*)

After the usual routine of ceremonious delay, which now seemed absurdly irksome to the young man who had achieved so much, and felt therefore that he had a right to despatch, he was ushered into the presence of a wiry little man with mutton chop whiskers, the precise complement of the courtly Sir Roderic. The well-laid scheme of commencement; the speedy triumph; the final hand-shake and congratulations had all faded.

Leslie Bracebridge's mood was scarcely equal to the unexpected effort before him. The sudden fall from exultation had thrown him into chaos.

"My business has been with Mr. Clarkson." he began half apologetically, despising himself for his humility.

The new senior barely lifted his eyebrows in token of assent.

" He is a typical Englishman," thought the Poet, shivering as though an ice-bath had descended upon him. " More impatient and less polite than his predecessor."

" I regret extremely his decease "———

(The eyebrows were again stirred.)

"But I do not doubt that you can conclude the matter for me."

He bowed, and the Poet proceeded nervously:

" My business was in reference to John Wallace "
—(a pause: no sign of recognition in the icy face)—

"who was a former client of Mr. Clarkson's;"
—(another pause: still no show of interest)—"who
lived for many years in exile in the United States "—
(third pause)—"and who died some ten years since "
—(final pause).

Bracebridge had come to the end of his recital, and
had elicited no sign of response from the owner of the
mutton-chop whiskers.

He cleared his throat and commenced again, with
very much the helpless feeling of battering his head
against a stone wall :

"Possibly you know of the affairs of this gentleman—or can ascertain for me ? "

"What is the precise business you were transacting
with Sir Roderic ? What had he undertaken to accomplish ? "

The young man winced.

"I had undertaken to accomplish the business for
myself. Sir Roderic merely promised to confirm my
efforts."

"Then I am to understand that he was not engaged
in making any investigation for you, Mr. Bracebridge."

"N—no."

"Was there any estate in trust ? "

"I think not,—since Mr. Wallace's death."

"Nor any heirs who were minors ? "

"None that were acknowledged as such."

"What, then, was the business you were transacting ? "

"With the identity of the man himself," answered
Bracebridge recovering his wits : "I was empowered

by Mr. Clarkson to discover his former client's actual position—his name."

" Do you mean that you were employed by my late partner for that purpose ? "

" Not precisely ; the search was my own.   But he lent me his interest—his sanction—"

" Then this was *not* a business matter, Mr. Bracebridge ? " with cold inquiry.

" To Mr. Clarkson it was not."

" But merely some personal affair of your own, which Sir Roderic was pleased to amuse himself with."

" I presume that is how you would regard it."

" And had nothing whatever to do with any case or present client of his ? "

" None that I am positive about."

Mr. Giles Wilberforce was a good inquisitor, and had reduced all the Poet's resources to atoms.

" Then, sir, all I can say is that no such personal interests were left in the hands of the present firm at the late Sir Roderic Clarkson's demise."

" But, Mr. Wilberforce, this is a very serious matter to me—and to others.   It may possibly affect the Earl of Earnshope. Do you not know of this affair— this man who called himself John Wallace ? "

" I am sorry to be obliged to reply that I do not. We have each retained exclusively our own clients. Only such were transferred to me, or my partner, personally, during the late Sir Roderic's last illness, as signified their desire to be so transferred.   I believe that I have never heard of the name of John Wallace."

" Could not you look up some papers—anything— which would throw light upon the subject ? "

" If there were such papers, you would have to prove your right to ask questions in regard to them."

" My right is the permission of Sir Roderic Clarkson," cried Bracebridge eagerly—" and the possible interests of the Earl of Earnshope."

" We have the honor of representing the Cammerden family in London," remarked Mr. Wilberforce quietly.

" Then cannot you glance at the—the affairs of the late Earl, say some forty years back, and see if that name occurs. It would be a great favor."

The cold stare vouchsafed in reply put the Poet's courage to final flight. Evidently it was an unheard-of offense to ask a solicitor to glance at anything which did not belong to the present issue and to the person making the demand. Moreover, the law shows no . favors. Mr. Wilberforce waited for some explanation to be offered as a guaranty of his interlocutor's right in the matter. None coming, he answered abruptly :

" I cannot possibly do anything of the sort."

" I have already seen Lady Earnshope and discussed this thing with her," hazarded Bracebridge, not intending, however, to quote that conversation in detail.

This last was not without effect. Mr. Giles Wilberforce rang a bell.

" I will at least make inquiries," he said.

A clerk appeared, to whom the solicitor stated briefly that the papers of a certain client called John Wallace, who had died ten years before, were required.

The clerk disappeared, and the owner of the frigid

visage resumed his writing as though no one were present.

After what seemed an intolerable delay, the clerk re-appeared, saying that the papers had all been destroyed, among those of many other deceased clients, at Mr. Clarkson's written order, a week previous to his death.

This Mr. Wilberforce communicated formally to the Poet, as though he had not heard every word of the statement, which sank like lead in his bosom.

He could not take it all in at first.

"What does it all mean?" he stammered.

"It means that we can give you no information whatever in reference to the person about whom you have made inquiries."

"But the other partner—Mr. Morton."

"Mr. Henry Morton is the junior partner of our firm. He attends to an entirely different line of practice. I may affirm, without hesitation, that the matters of trust are mine."

"You don't—you can't mean," cried the baffled man, "that this is the end?"

"Undoubtedly it is the end," replied the chilly solicitor, unconsciously quoting from *The Ring and the Book*, whose forever unsolved problem had run, like a perplexing thread, all through Bracebridge's tangled endeavor; "unless you have interests or claims of sufficient weight to warrant your engaging in serious litigation."

"O dear no! I am sure of nothing! I am baffled —beaten."

Bracebridge rose with a dazed and weary air. The

fruit of all his effort crumbled away, like an apple of Sodom, in his hand.

As the lawyer touched the bell that summoned the next client, he turned to stammer something about the " value of services "—always an appalling problem to the uninitiated. But Mr. Wilberforce replied curtly that he had found no memoranda of his affairs ; doubtless Sir Roderic had been humoring himself with an entirely personal fancy.

The Poet stumbled out, muttering over and over to himself, " *Undoubtedly it is the end.*"

He wandered back to his lodging-house, where he was for some days prostrated with a bad fever, not so much from physical derangement as from disappointment and the reaction after severe mental excitement.   So said the apothecary.

When he first recovered from the stupor of his fever, it was to hear the landlady say to this gentleman :

" He's a gay young fellow, and of good blood, for all his plain looks.   He's done nothing but chatter about Lord Percy Cammerden, whoever he be, an' the Earl of Earnshope.   He has fine friends, happen."

And so an exorbitant bill from the honest woman, as well as a considerable one from the apothecary, was added to Bracebridge's mortification and misery.

His pocket-book was hopelessly reduced ; he had met none of the enchanting people or agreeable episodes that were to welcome him.   On the contrary, he felt that he had been abused by many indifferent and disagreeable persons, and all that he could say of certainty was this : " Undoubtedly, it is the end."

FINALE.

COMPRISING LESLIE BRACEBRIDGE'S FINAL MYSTIFICA-
TION AND MORTIFICATION.

> *" O why, why was it not ordained just so?*
> *Why fell not things out so nor otherwise?*
> *Ask that particular devil whose task it is*
> *To trip the all-but-at-perfection,—slur*
> *The line o' the painter just where paint leaves off*
> *And life begins,—puts ice into the ode*
> *O' the poet while he cries " next stanza—fire!"*
> *Inscribes all human effort with one word,*
> *Artistry's haunting curse the incomplete!*
> *Being incomplete, the act escaped success * * * * **
> *What was there wanting to a master-piece*
> *Except the luck that lies beyond a man?*

THE RING AND THE BOOK.

THE Play is played out. The puppets that have
moved upon the village stage; the later, would-be
actors that have crossed and re-crossed wider and
less clearly defined boards, are all swept away, while
the veil of obscurity descends, like a curtain, upon
the whole. But is the Drama complete? Somewhere, the *mise-en-scène* was at fault.

During many acts, the hero has not been visible
before the uncertain foot-lights, or among the shifting
side-scenes, though his spectre has perpetually haunt-

ed the shadowed background.   Even the magnificent
Prologue which the Poet was preparing, failed of utterance.   He has in his hands, all written out the action of his tragedy ; but the *dramatis personæ* have
eluded him.

He comes back to the little village of peace, and
sits down thoughtfully before the white slab that bears
this still unsolved mystery,

" John Wallace."

But nearly two years have elapsed, since he came
disconsolately to the end of his endeavor.   The Autumn was then so far advanced that he made up his
mind to finish the year in Scotland, " among his kin,"
he modestly decided.

After some delay, he found a near branch of the
Leslies living in great comfort in Edinburgh ; and
these hospitable people made him so warmly welcome
that the winter stole away, and spring followed it before he could tear himself from the pleasant associations.

His uncle, a physician of some standing, took a
great fancy to the rather impractical young man ;
who in return, attached himself warmly to his cousin
Grace.

At first his heart was so sore about his disappoint-
ments, that the occasion of his visit to Scotland was
never referred to.   By little and little however,
through the softening influence of his cousin's sympathy, the whole story came out, and was, strange to
say, tolerated by the good doctor, much to the surprise and delight of Grace Leslie.   She was not without romance ; and the unsolved riddle caused her

endless surmises and wonderment. One day, she was
sure that Robert Keith was the missing man ; the
next, she felt assured that Lord Percy Cammerden
and none other was the spectre who had posed as
John Wallace. They went together to the Lodge of
Earnshope, and always found little Bel safe and content.

"His Lordship has na' troubled us aboon the
bairn," the woman said. "It's Mr. Hotchkiss as wad
speer at me ower muckle. But I telt him the lass
were my ain niece, an' he ha' letten it go, I ween."

"Has not anybody from outside come to question?"
Bracebridge asked.

"Na—savin' once, when a great sweerin' gomeral
cam' an wad hae a blink o' the bairn, ony gate.
I telt him that I had na' seen chick nor childer
save my ain i' the place this twelve-month. He was
unco wroth, an' my gudemon was liken to pouther
his pow wi' a watering can."

Bracebridge was content. Things seemed to have
come to a joyous end for wee Bel.

"Are you happy, little one," he asked the child,
who already began to take on the fresh sweet roses
of childhood.

"Aye! I'm that happy Mister Bracebridge. It's
unco lang syne Iv'e wanted bit or broth. If only—"
and tears glistened in her pretty eyes—"grandfather
were na' lyin' where the cauld blasts o' the winter
wind will blaw ower his head, when the summer's
done. Grandfather feared the snaw," she added with
a sob.

"The wind and snow cannot hurt him now, Bel,"

said Grace Leslie, gently : " It is always spring-time in the country where he has gone."

" She's a gude bairnie," interrupted the foster-mother apologetically, " an' makes ilka things look braw aboon the bit house. But she will greet for the grandfather, whiles. Eh, mister," she added in a whisper, " It's a wonder the Earl does na' covet her gowden head glinting i' the sunlicht. I'm afeared mony a time when I see him take note o' the bonnie lassie. Waes me! I winna grudge my Leddy her braws, nor a' her gear, savin' she leaves me the bairn."

Bracebridge bethought himself, and was able to re-assure the woman that the child was safe.

Doctor Leslie, having heard the whole many-sided story, made what inquiries he could upon the out-skirts of the Earl's family history ; but John Wallace still sat in the Great Dark, like some remote being inscrutable to the curiosity of the common herd. Or, shall we say, rather, in the Great Light, lived

" The snow-white soul that angels fear to take untenderly."

And beside him was the shadow of little Bel.

At last the parting came. The Poet's disappoint-ments had settled into a quiet forgetfulness, and he felt that his winter of satisfaction had more than com-pensated for the summer of chagrin. But another year had passed before he had courage to seek the primitive shades of Rest-Hampton.

It was the middle of July, 1882, when he reached the familiar precincts of the little village that John Wallace had named Peace.

Here he found a change. Could it be ?   *   *

Witness his testimony given in a letter published by the same journal which had printed that other letter from what he was pleased to name " Artist-haven," which made up the preliminary chapter of this book. *   *   *

" Yes, there is a change. Something has happened to Artist-haven, since the Tile Club came down upon it and disturbed its sequestered content.

" It is seen in the new buildings rising jauntily here and there, crowding out the shingle cottages and great trees that once made such a picturesque vista of the long, green street. It is felt in the alterations that are beginning to crop out upon the meek faces of the old houses themselves. It is heard in the bustle and stir about the new railroad that is soon to desecrate the sweet silence of the hamlet, whose broad and daisied highway may be ripped up with a gash of iron tracks before these sheets are dry from press.

" Let us see where comes the difference.

" It is not so much in the outward aspect of the town itself, as in the altered appearance of the beach. Once, the sea beat in lonely majesty upon the long stretch of sands, heaving now and then into those great breakers that roared up and down the coast like the storm waves upon far northern rocks.

" Now, it is transformed into the sporting ground of a noisy and merry crowd whose voices drown the chanting of the surf, and fill the wanderer's soul with loathing. They have spread a fancy-bazaar effect of gay-colored tents abroad upon the peaceful sands, where they dart in and out as much at home as a flock of pigeons upon a painted dove-cote.

" Nor do they desport themselves only upon the beach. All about the low-pitched farmhouses ; over the broad expanse of green still traversed by meandering roadways ; by way of the disjointed old stage-coaches which once carried the semi-occasional visitor, or the almost as episodical mail ; even among the mouldering graves of their progenitors, the villagers have at last welcomed that nomad of fashion—the summer boarder.

" What their great-grandfathers beneath the sod— what, indeed, the fathers themselves only a few innocent years back—would have said to such an invasion, remains an awful mystery to be meditated upon in the bosom of each family.

" Not the ravages of the Indians themselves among the homes of those early settlers could have carried greater dismay to their Puritan bosoms than this oncome of the world and the flesh—accompanied, in their eyes at least, by that other power of evil called ' the devil.'

" Their prayers and their prowess might deliver them from the terror of the savage ; but who could deliver them from the insidious snares of the wicked one ?

" However it happened, who first began it, can never be told. But all at once—as if one of those great breakers had reared up and overwhelmed the land beyond the dunes—a current of modern innovations has swept over these out-of-the-world farmers and the well-to-do gentry, who had hitherto led equally secluded lives. Now they find themselves the beholders of, and in one sense the participants in, all the fascinations and some of the follies of fashionable life.

"They are precipitated for a few months of each year into the bewilderments of 'a resort,' the unaccustomednesses of which serve them as food for comment during the remainder of the twelve months. Their dearest customs are knocked from under them ; their oldest prejudices are shocked out of them ; but the never-to-be-resisted passion for penny turning has seized upon them. The traditions of peaceful and untempted generations of the past are forgotten ; they retire to their kitchens and garrets, while the heretofore unviolated parlors and chambers of their ancestors are given over to the enemy.

"And such parlors ! and such chambers ! who that has not seen them can be initiated through unsympathetic print into the mysteries of those great old chimney-places, the prim unconsciousness of tall mantel-shelves, and the unaffected simplicity of old mahogany, that does not know it as a priceless boon !

"Look at that stately old house, yonder, with its wainscoted walls, its aristocratic "stoop" and quaint stairway ! Peer into some secret corner if you can, you 'Summer Boarder,' and see if your heart—for even you must have a heart—does not stir and leap with a thrill of more than curiosity at the relics which lie crumbling away piece-meal, leaving, of all their shredded histories, only the must and dust of forgetfulness.

"Here is an old gold and ivory cane, its head inlaid with gems ; who brought that costly bit from over the sea? and what long-buried aristocrat leaned his lace-frilled hand upon it through a proud and stately old age?

"And there is a porcelain jar with its handful of ages-ago-dried rose leaves :—Austin Dobson might have written a rare *pot-pourri* upon such as that.

"Yonder are fragments of rich India china bespeaking forgotten wealth ; bits of obsolete English ware, telling of the ancestors who "came over" from the green hills and rich homes of the Mother-land. But there are only occasional surprises. The plainest of Puritans are suggested by the austerity of these "salt-box cottages" that make up the bulk of old Artist-haven, betokening more the rigors of self-denial, than the luxuries of wealth in those early settlers who bought their land from the Montauk Indians in sixteen-hundred-and-I-forget.

"But the fragments of those difficult days, whether of Puritan plainness or of patrician condescension, are alike dear to the simple-minded inhabitant.

"Ah! blessed Angel of the Resurrection! what canst thou do with the broken hopes and forgotten dreams of which came these shattered facts?

"The Summer Boarder cannot answer that.

"As for the change, they like the new life right well. these semi-sophisticated people, who seem, to us of the busy world, to have lingered out of another time. Their horizon has widened until they, too, have glimpses of a society to them as vague, hitherto, as were traditions of the courts of the Bourbons to their great-great-grandfathers.

"Their field of interests has suddenly become so enlarged, that they no longer must needs confine their familiar gossip to the limited and prosaic recitals of neighborhood births and christenings, marriages and deaths, with an occasional treat-to-topic of a vessel wrecked upon the beach.

"Their ambitions, too, have expanded out of all proportion with their lowly shingle roofs, and new ideas are beginning to dawn beneath the great horse-chestnut trees. The picturesque farmhouses, for so many generations *en naturel* and guiltless of even whitewash, are here and there beginning to glow with a new adaptation of Pompeian red paint upon their shingled sides; while a settlement of cottages, in the Queen-Anne-gone-mad style of to-day, has sprung up by the sea.

"Probably the villagers of Artist-haven had never considered their proximity to the ocean in any other than a utilitarian light. Surf bathing, *en masse*, was a remotely-conceived-of vulgarism. But now, those who descend to see it, behold their beach transformed each morning into a veritable encampment of Philistines; while town vehicles, and elaborate toilettes, and all the *embarras de richesse*, have put to open shame their rude and cheap ways and means.

"The butterflies that alight upon them through July and August, in their wide quest of novelty and pleasure, leave behind them with every flutter, a whole trail of dazzling perplexities and glittering allurements. Even before the days of the Tile Club, there had come a few of such, who sowed seeds for our story. But now, the flutter is universal—the new notions are far spread. Whether or not the inhabitants are happier for their new gains, and the losses by which they are purchased, who shall say?

" It is but the inexorable law of social progress and change, which sooner or later is coming to fulfil itself in every remote corner of earth. If it is better or worse for them, perhaps even themselves cannot tell, as they begin that struggle after the never-to-be-attained possibilities of society life.

" After all, the question comes which, it may be, the venerable sleepers under the lichens had to settle in their own less worldly way, whether it is wiser for a man to rest contented with whatsoever things he hath ; or whether he may, without detriment to his good conscience, press forward to reach after the worldly things which are continually beyond his grasp.

" Had they found the answer to this human problem, and carved it,—the sons upon the fathers' tomb-stones, —better were those fallen slabs for our study than all the wisdom of Egypt's pyramids."

*   *   *   *   *   *   *   *

So it will be seen that Leslie Bracebridge had received his sorrow's crown of sorrow. As in his first letter to the press he had not referred to John Wallace, so in this last, he left his disappointed quest untold. He wandered about disconsolately before he could make up his mind to hunt up the widow Hatherton. The only thing he had to show for his long effort was the drawing he had made of the Cammerden coat-of-arms, which Mrs. Hatherton might identify as the same that John Wallace had worn upon his ring :—

"Only, if he was Lord Percy, that was a Bishop's crest," he sighed.

Then he wandered back into the South-End burying ground, and sat thinking his own pensive thoughts. Here at least there was no change. The spot was cheerful with summer sunlight, and barren of even the suggestion of a ghost at that prosaic hour of the forenoon, but he recognized all the sweet and sympathetic features which had won him to the spot.

At last he concluded to seek the one creature in the place who had probably not welcomed the summer-boarder with matter-of-fact thrift. Mrs. Hatherton had doubtless withdrawn in scorn from even a contemplation of new departures.

He strolled listlessly up the village street, until he came to—— What? The great chestnuts that had formerly sheltered the home of the Castlewoods, without a doubt. But the Homestead was no longer there. .Or rather, its shell might have been there ; but it was so bedaubed with paint, so bedizened with ornamentation that the Poet stood aghast.

"Who would have believed that such a fine sort of woman could condescend to truckle to fool notions !" he exclaimed angrily, and gave the knocker a sounding rap.

"It's a wonder she hasn't a front door-bell," he remarked contemptuously : "only that would not be aesthetic. To think of such a senseless craze having invaded this out-of-the world "—— Bracebridge paused in the midst of his mental harangue ; for the door was flung open with a flourish by a jaunty colored servant with "New York style" stamped all over his smart livery.

"Beg yo' pardon, sir," he said airily, when the visitor mentioned the widow's name.

"Mrs. Hatherton," repeated Bracebridge tartly.

"No sir; she don't live here, sir. Mrs. Vander-Voort occupies this house for the summer."

And Leslie Bracebridge found himself bewildered upon the sidewalk.

"I have changed the name of my prospective novel," he muttered cynically: "It shall be called 'A Book of Disillusions.' '*The Lady Correspondent of John Wallace*' refused to become my heroine, and even the man's one surety has deserted me. Rest-Hampton itself is a myth."

Here a troop of over-dressed little girls flaunted by with their miniature babies and toy perambulators. They were decked out, like their probable mammas, after the fashion of the demi-monde.

Out in the street a flashy village cart dashed past, driven by a bold girl with black eyes. A pattern lackey sat motionless, face outward, behind, and a great jingle of chains went with the heavily caparisoned horse. There was a shoddy vulgarity in every jingle.

While the Poet stood musing, the familiar figure of a villager came stalking along. It was Obadiah Potts, now grown wrinkled and white, but still upright and severe in his demeanor.

In answer to the young man's polite inquiry respecting the whereabouts of the widow, Mr. Potts answered stiffly:

"She's gone to England, with her son, to live. She

rented the old house last Fall to some fashionable people from New York. They've made a fine place of it already."

"*Et tu Brute,*" thought Bracebridge with a sigh. Even this austere looking native had gone over to the enemy. Clearly, the inhabitants did not echo the wail that had gone up from his poet's pen.

" I wonder how the artists feel," he murmured:

And then it occurred to him that he had as yet had no glimpse of those white umbrellas dotted upon the landscape. Very likely the artists had migrated from the place in a body.

Obadiah Potts was saying something boastful of the popularity " our town " had attained, which Brace-bridge did not catch, until he was roused from his revery by an exclamation of pride and satisfaction :

" Look there now ! *Ain't* that purty ? "

The young man turned and beheld a high drag, drawn tandem, and filled with ladies, coming along at a flying pace.

" I tell you, sir, we didn't used to see such sights, here-abouts. It'll be the making of Rest-Hampton."

The great chestnuts rustled their dark green shadows ; the old elms, just beyond, bent and swayed their long arms in a soft sea-wind that stole across the fields and flats ; while the scent of ripening fruit came coaxingly from the deep-hearted retirement of the ancient orchard. Even a sunflower nodded familiarly over the garden wall, and a tall lily bent its head graciously beneath. In vain nature exerted her sweetest influences. The Poet felt that all was out of harmony, and his heart was unresponsive to the old sweet strain.

"Pshaw," he cried angrily, making his way to the hotel to take the next stage that would carry him from the disenchanted village, "I don't believe that there *is* any mystery : and what is more, I don't believe there ever was such an ideal place as 'Artist-haven.'"

Later, as he sat trifling with the mid-day dinner offered him, he soliloquized this wise :

"I have made a silly attempt to dramatize the life of a man whose heroism was above my comprehension. I had better have taken the advice of that handsome woman, the widow (who, by the way, I absolve from the curse I put upon her when I thought she had spoiled her house.) I had better have acknowledged the proportions of the man to be beyond my scope, than have got up all the paraphernalia for a tragedy,—and then failed to grasp my hero.

"It was like playing with gods and angels ; only the Greek poets could do that,—and classic old Milton. The Titanic outlines of my psychological researches only show up the puny weakness of my results. John Wallace, standing alone in his power and his gentleness, with his motives unknown, and his mystery unsolved, is a grander character than any mock hero I could produce, with all my side-lights and stage properties. I shall now take to writing epics ; or, at least, my coming romance shall not aim to be a metaphysical study."

And taking out "The Ring and the Book," which had borne him the silent company of its comment, he opened it at random and read these words of startling significance .

> " And so an end of all i' the story.   Strain
> Never so much my eyes, I miss the mark.
> ————Learn one lesson hence
> Of many which whatever lives should teach ;
> This lessson, that our human speech is naught,
> Our human testimony false, our fame
> And human estimation, words and wind."

AFTER-CHORD.

" But if you rather be disposed to see
In the result of the long trial here,—
This dealing doom to guilt, and doling praise
To innocency,—any proof that truth
May look for vindication from the world,
Much will you have misread the signs, I say.
God, who seems acquiescent in the main
With those who add ' So will He ever sleep '—
Flutters their foolishness from time to time,
Puts forth His right hand recognizably ;
Even as—to fools who deem He needs must right
Wrong on the instant, as if earth were heaven,
He wakes remonstrance—' Passive, Lord, how long ? ' "

—The Ring and the Book.

www.ingramcontent.com/pod-product-compliance
Lightning Source LLC
Chambersburg PA
CBHW030811110726
47900CB00006B/1591